AFRAID TO FLY

L.A. WITT

RIPTIDE
PUBLISHING

Riptide Publishing
PO Box 1537
Burnsville, NC 28714
www.riptidepublishing.com

Afraid to Fly

Cover art: L.C. Chase, lcchase.com/design.htm
Editors: Delphine Dryden, delphinedryden.com/editing, May Peterson
Layout: L.C. Chase, lcchase.com/design.htm

ISBN: 978-1-62649-500-5

First edition
January, 2017

Also available in ebook:
ISBN: 978-1-62649-499-2

AFRAID TO FLY

ANCHOR POINT

L.A. WITT

TABLE OF CONTENTS

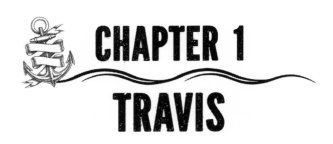

CHAPTER 1

TRAVIS

"**Y**ou know the only reason I come to these things is because you want to go, right?"

Kimber batted her eyes at me and smirked. "Aww, the sacrifices you make for your baby girl."

"As if I haven't made enough already." I parked outside the hotel where the command had rented the ballroom for the evening. I was actually amazed this tiny town had a big enough hotel to host something like this, but wonders never ceased.

The lot was mostly full already, so obviously this year's Navy Ball was a popular one. Great. The more, the merrier, said everyone right up until the cops had to be called.

I stepped out of the car, fussed with my black bow tie, and buttoned my jacket. It was a bit snug; either I needed to spend some more time at the gym, or I'd damn well better get this uniform let out before Kimber strong-armed me into *next* year's ball. For tonight, I just prayed like hell the single button holding it together above the gold cummerbund didn't snap off.

On the other hand, standing up straight and pulling in my midsection did take some of the strain off my back. Not enough to go without my TENS unit—I'd been clinging to that fucker since breakfast—but it helped.

At least I wasn't wearing a back brace this year. That combined with my dinner dress uniform had been downright suffocating. God help me if I had to restick one of the TENS pads or untangle a wire, or if the fucking battery died again, but I'd deal with that if it happened.

I could do this. It was only a few hours.

I stood up straighter, sucked it in, and adjusted my jacket.

A few *long* hours. Joy.

On the sidewalk, Kimber fussed with the strap on her bright-red dress and swore under her breath.

"Stupid . . . fucking . . ." She rolled her shoulders. "Okay. I think I'm ready."

"You sure?"

"Shut up." She laughed. "You have my ID, right?"

I tapped the pocket where I kept my wallet. "Yep."

"Okay. Good. Let's get inside. It's freezing out here."

"Well yeah. It's October." I didn't mention it would be warmer if she *wore* the jacket draped over her arm, mostly because she'd get me back later when I bitched about being too hot in *my* jacket. Never mind that I was required to wear mine whether I liked it or not.

As we headed inside, I tugged at my lapels and my sleeves, and suppressed a groan. The ball was an annual form of torture that was ostensibly to celebrate the Navy's birthday. I was pretty sure it only existed so we'd all have a reason to wear our dinner dress uniforms. Or, more to the point, a reason to clean them, iron them, and spend half an evening cursing at all the medals and insignia that refused to go on properly, all before scrambling to the on-base tailor because *maybe* we'd put on some weight since last year.

But Kimber loved these shindigs, so she came with me as my "date." And even if I thought this fell somewhere between waterboarding and watching *Sex and the City*, I tamped down my distaste as we walked inside.

The ballroom was packed with round tables and decorated to the gills, looking as glorious as any Holiday Inn banquet. The organizers were well aware that there were a lot of people here with varying degrees of PTSD, so they didn't go crazy with strobes or spotlights or anything like that. No disco ball over the dance floor. No funky lights from the deejay's booth. The sunken lights overhead were dim, creating a nice atmosphere, and everything was soft and subtle enough to avoid ruining someone's evening.

With any luck, the food would be decent, but if the last five Navy Balls I'd attended were any indication . . . well . . . I wasn't holding my breath. Just as well. As snug as my uniform was this year, I would *need* to hold my breath if I actually ate very much.

"So." Kimber looked around after we'd checked her coat. "Where should we sit?"

I scanned the room for familiar faces, and found Norris, one of the guys from my office. He and his wife had commandeered a table on the opposite side of the room from the buffet. Wise—the buffet was going to get crowded as hell once the lids came off the chafing dishes. At least it would be reasonably quiet over here.

We joined them and claimed a couple of chairs on the side facing the front of the room. There was a lot of pomp and circumstance at these things, and the people with their backs to the front would have to spend a good hour twisted around to face the right direction. The pain in my back intensified just thinking about it. The tingle from the TENS still helped, but I had to wonder how long that would last. Good thing the control box was the perfect size to fit in the pocket of my trousers where it was inconspicuous and within easy reach if I needed to crank it up. Which, judging by the tightness in the middle of my back, I would.

"I'm going to go get a drink." Kimber nodded toward one of several bars. "You want anything?"

"Yes, please." I took out my wallet and pulled out her ID, which I carried tonight since she didn't have any pockets and hated purses, along with some cash to tip the bartender. "Whatever you're having."

"Unless it's fruity and comes with an umbrella, right?"

I wrinkled my nose. "Obviously."

"Got it. Back in a minute."

Peering the growing lines at each bar, I said, "Good luck with that."

"Eh. I'll be fine." She grinned. "Plenty of eye candy."

"Uh-huh. Go." I playfully shooed her away, and she headed toward the bar. While she was gone, I looked around for more people I knew. Almost everyone from my office was planning to come—*open bar* was the quickest way to persuade officers and Sailors alike to show up, after all.

Sure enough, Captain Rodriguez, our commanding officer, was walking in with her husband. They'd barely taken off their coats before the executive officer, Commander Johnson, was right in their faces, brown-nosing like he always did. I rolled my eyes. Yeah, making captain was a political game—didn't I know it—but Captain Rodriguez didn't like kiss-asses. Well, fine. Let him earn himself some "not a chance, asshole" points. One less commander for me to compete with for that coveted promotion.

I left him to his idiocy and looked around again, and—

My stomach flipped.

Lieutenant Commander Fraser.

The crowded room was suddenly empty. Everyone else faded into the shadows as my brain superimposed a spotlight over him like some sort of cheesy 1980s prom movie special effect.

Holy shit.

I'd been ogling that man since he'd transferred to NAS Adams recently. Tonight he took "oh my God" to a whole new level when he strolled into the Navy Ball in his dinner dress uniform. The short jacket and tailored trousers made even the least attractive man look good, but Fraser . . . Jesus. Something told me he hadn't struggled with getting into his uniform. It all fit like he'd been poured into it. The trousers hugged his slim waist, and the jacket clung comfortably to his shoulders. The button holding everything together in the front didn't look like it was straining at all, and he didn't appear to be sucking in his gut under the cummerbund like the rest of us.

He'd been hot before. Tonight he was going to be the reason I wound up drooling on my not-quite-as-nicely-fitted uniform.

Of course that was *before* I realized he'd come in with a date's hand on his elbow.

And that date was a man.

Come again?

I shook myself, blinked, and stared.

Lieutenant Commander . . . Fraser . . . is . . . gay?

Why the fuck had I not gotten that memo?

I looked around for Kimber, praying like hell she'd made it to the front of the line and acquired something cold and alcoholic for her hopelessly crushing dad. Even if it was fruity and had an umbrella, I needed it. Now.

She was almost to the front. Two guys were ahead of her, one of whom was gathering a handful of drinks. So it wouldn't be long.

I turned back toward Fraser.

From the first moment I'd seen him at work, I'd been tripping over my own feet. Didn't matter if he was in his blue camouflage utilities, or shorts and a T-shirt at the gym, or in civvies when we crossed paths on the base, or . . . or this. He had the kind of sharp, somewhat weathered features that were catnip to me. Smooth and flawless was fine and good, but especially as I got older myself, there was something about the lines by the corners of his eyes and the traces of silver in his sandy-blond hair that tongue-tied me all to hell. And of course he worked right down the hall from me, so it was a wonder I got anything done anymore.

He turned his head, and from across the room, our eyes locked.

I quickly turned away. Probably too quickly—the sudden twinge in my back made my teeth snap together—but better than still staring after I'd already been busted.

C'mon, Kimber. C'mon. Hurry.

Minutes later—while I was sneaking my three hundredth glance at Fraser—my daughter shouldered her way through the thickening crowd and held up a pair of brown bottles. "Two beers."

"Awesome. Thank you." I took mine, and we clinked our bottles together. Then I took a much-needed deep swallow, which of course did nothing to lessen the effect of gay dinner-dress-uniform Lieutenant Commander Fraser *does not compute, does not compute . . . Did he just make eye contact again?*

I really need to let out this uniform before next year. Can't breathe.

"Dad?" Kimber tilted her head. "Why are you blushing?"

"Blushing?" I sputtered. "I am not."

She eyed me as she sipped her own beer. "Let me guess—you're hot because of your uniform."

I glanced down at my jacket. Goddamn. I'd had an alibi right there and didn't even think to use it. "Um . . ."

"Now you're really blushing, Dad."

"Shut up," I muttered, and took a drink.

"I'm just saying."

"Yeah, yeah, yeah." I elbowed her playfully. "You're just saying—"

"Hey, Commander."

Fraser's voice sent my heart into my throat. Good thing I hadn't had a mouthful of beer right then, or it would've wound up all over Kimber. Or Fraser.

Schooling my expression, I turned around. "Hey, good to see you."

"You too, sir."

I shook his hand, smiling despite my pounding heart. "We're technically not at work. Call me Travis."

He gulped, like he wasn't sure what to do with the informality. "Oh. Okay." He glanced down, probably realizing our handshake had lasted a few beats too long, and withdrew his hand. "I guess call me Clint, then."

So Lieutenant Commander Fraser was really Clint, a guy who had a boyfriend and looked incredibly hot in his dress uniform. Yeah, *that* was going to make things easier around the office.

His eyes darted toward Kimber, and to his own date, as if he wasn't sure who should introduce who first.

I cleared my throat. "Well, um . . . This is my daughter, Kimber."

"Your—" His eyebrows jumped a bit, but he quickly extended his hand. "Nice to meet you."

She smiled as they shook hands. "Hi."

"Hi." He let her go and gestured at the guy beside him. "This is Logan. My . . ." he hesitated, "date."

Logan glanced at him, as if he wasn't sure how to respond to the hesitation over the nature of their relationship, then drained his beer bottle.

Clint shifted his weight, avoiding eye contact for a moment. Beside him, Logan rolled his eyes. I couldn't help wondering if Clint's hesitation a moment ago had been because he was second-guessing how out he wanted to be—*that ship has sailed, my friend*—or if there was some underlying issue between him and his "date."

Finally, Logan turned to Clint. "I'm going to get another. You sure you don't want one?"

Clint's lips tightened, and he shook his head as he muttered something that sounded like, "You *know* I don't."

Logan gave a quiet, semidrunken laugh, nudging Clint with his shoulder. "Back in a minute." He didn't wait for a response, and headed for the bar. And despite how early in the evening it was, he was already noticeably unsteady on his feet.

Clint watched him go, and slowly pushed out a breath. "Sorry about . . ." He glanced at Logan's back. Lowered his gaze. Shook his head. "Anyway. Um." He coughed and looked around. "Looks like this command puts on a decent ball."

I nodded, scanning the room again while I willed my pulse to come back down. After a moment, I turned to him. "Don't get your hopes up about the food, though."

"Get my hopes up?" Clint laughed, crinkling the corners of his eyes and sending my heart rate right back up into the stratosphere again. "This isn't my first command. Trust me—my expectations are as realistic as yours."

Chuckling, I brought my beer up to my lips. "Good. Then you won't be disappointed."

He started to say something, but hesitated and shifted his gaze away. If I wasn't mistaken, some color rose in his cheeks.

Beside me, Kimber smothered a laugh.

I glared at her, and she quickly gestured with her beer bottle. "I'm going to go mingle."

"Okay." I fished my wallet out of my trouser pocket. "Here. In case you need a refill." I shoved a five in her hand for tips and shooed her away, and she shot me a mischievous grin and—when Clint still wasn't looking, thank God—a wink. Then she was gone.

And I was suddenly alone with the guy who worked five offices down from mine—not that I'd counted—and had a boyfriend or "date" or something who'd gone off to get a drink he probably didn't need. The silence lingered uncomfortably for a moment, but Clint finally met my gaze and spoke.

"So, how do you think we did on the inspection?"

Normally, I hated shoptalk at functions like this, but sometimes it was a godsend. What better fallback for some socially awkward guys—gay and drooling or not—who couldn't figure out what else to talk about?

So we discussed the inspection, and I focused half my attention on that and half on playing it cool. Not letting him see how much he'd flipped my world on its ass simply by showing up with a man. Except what difference did it make? It didn't matter if he was gay when he was obviously spoken for. Unless there really was some trouble brewing between him and his date.

I tamped that thought down. I was *not* an opportunist who'd swoop in the second someone's relationship ended. It was an absolute certainty that I'd be thinking about him later with a hand on my dick, but it wouldn't go any further than that. Damn what few scruples I had.

As we talked, I sipped my beer, and for once, didn't feel the need to go outside for a cigarette. I only smoked when I drank, and that itch for nicotine was definitely there beneath my skin, but I didn't give in because I didn't want to go outside. I had a moment to talk one-on-one with Clint-not-Lieutenant-Commander-Fraser. The cigarette could wait.

Someone tapped the microphone at the front of the room and announced the cocktail hour was over. Everyone took their seats.

And wasn't it just my luck . . .

Clint and his date sat down at my table.

CHAPTER 2
CLINT

Every Navy Ball went through a series of traditions. The chaplain's invocation. The oldest and youngest Sailors in attendance cutting the cake together. The acknowledgment of the unoccupied table setting to remember the POWs and MIA who weren't with us. After eighteen years, I'd pretty much memorized the routine.

Tonight, it all seemed miles away. Something happening in some other reality while I sat here, surrounded by people and somehow feeling completely isolated as I shifted my gaze from one coworker to the next, wondering if things would be different on Monday.

There wasn't much I could do about it now, but I still wasn't sure if this had been the best way to come out to my new chain of command and coworkers. It had worked for a buddy of mine at my last base. He'd come to the Christmas party with his now-ex-thank-God-boyfriend, and aside from a few double takes, no one had really missed a beat. After that, nothing had changed as far as I'd been able to tell. Aside from quietly making bets on when he'd cut the loud-mouthed, sexist, racist son of a bitch loose—three weeks, it turned out—everyone had treated him the same way.

Hopefully the same would be true for me after tonight. I hadn't come up with any other realistic or more subtle options for letting my coworkers know I had a boyfriend. Work it into a conversation? Put a picture on my desk that made it clear we were a couple? Make some big awkward announcement? I should've just mentioned him in passing and let people do the math.

But no, somehow, showing up with a man and letting it simply be known had been the best idea. No one really seemed to notice or care, so that was good. If anything, they were giving Logan the side-eye, but

I thought it had less to do with him being male and was more about the bottles he'd been damn near deep-throating in rapid succession.

Slow down, idiot. You're shitfaced before anyone else is even buzzed.

One thing was for sure—if my coworkers were taking bets on when I'd kick Logan's drunk ass to the curb, I wanted to know so I could get in on it. I was this close to done with the guy, and dinner hadn't even been served yet.

Which . . . hurt. I was angry with him tonight. We'd talked about this. Just one time, could he take it easy? But no. He'd been drinking since before I'd even picked him up, and we both knew he'd keep drinking until the beer ran dry.

I sighed, heart sinking. I liked the guy. I really did.

The longer I sat here, though, the more it felt like the last straw. I didn't—and *couldn't*—drink, and being around him when he was drunk was a problem. We'd *fucking talked about this*, damn it. He'd promised he'd do better, especially tonight.

And now here we were.

This must've been how my ex-wife had felt on more occasions than I cared to admit. There were only so many times a person could hear *This is the last time—promise!* from someone with booze on his breath before enough was enough.

Naturally, the straw would break the camel's back tonight. At the Navy Ball. As I was introducing him to my coworkers as my boyfriend. First time since my divorce that I was in a relationship. First time in my life I was in a relationship with a man. It had felt good to think about going someplace public together. About saying, *I'm with this person.* It was like I was taking a huge step and moving on with my life. Now, instead of being out of the closet, all I could think was I wanted *out.* Of this room, of this ball, of this goddamned relationship.

I took a long drink, wishing it was alcoholic, and that stopped me in my tracks.

Oh dear God. Yes. If being with Logan made me want to drink, then he needed to go. Like . . . soon.

Sorry, Logan. You fucking blew it.

I felt bad about it, too. He was a nice guy and all—not a borderline skinhead like the asshole my friend had brought last year. The sex hadn't been half bad either. But Jesus fucking Christ, the man could drink.

After tonight, though, now that he'd been slurring his words and wobbling on his feet right there in front of my new coworkers when he'd *sworn* he wouldn't, it was going to have to be addressed one way or another. By the time the cocktail hour ended, he'd been on his third beer, not counting the pre-gaming before I'd picked him up.

A couple of guys at the next table watched him. Then they glanced at me, brows pinched with what looked like sympathy, before turning their attention back to the CO. She'd been speaking for a while now, and for the life of me, I couldn't recall a word she'd said.

Wasn't this night off to a fantastic start?

Now I was out as seeing a man I was five seconds away from dumping. On the bright side, I wouldn't have to sweat over pronouns when I started dating someone with a lower blood alcohol content. Though my coworkers would probably all be confused as hell if I mentioned going out with a woman—I swore nobody at my last several commands had ever heard of bisexuality.

Eh. It was what it was. If they thought my closet had a revolving door, so be it. I just hoped nobody was a dick about me bringing a guy. So far so good, but there were a lot of people here. How they'd treat me in private—say, at the office on Monday—remained to be seen. Every command was different. Some of the guys at NAS Adams were on the conservative side. Some seemed pretty open-minded. The last CO was apparently marrying his boyfriend soon, and I hadn't heard anyone screeching about that, so I was hopeful. But still worried. Because God knew one queer coworker plus one homophobe could equal a seriously hostile environment. I knew too many people who'd learned that the hard way.

"Hey. Clint." Logan nudged me clumsily. "Earth t'Clint."

I shook myself. When had the CO stopped talking? Were all the ceremonies over?

I turned to Logan. "What? Sorry."

He laughed. "Space cadet." Gesturing over his shoulder, he said, "I'm gonna get another drink. You *sure* you don't want anything?"

Gritting my teeth, I said, "No, I'm fine." *And you don't need any more either, especially if you're too drunk to remember why I don't drink.*

He rose unsteadily and stumbled off toward the bar.

Scowling, I reached for my sweaty glass and took a drink.

A few years ago, I probably wouldn't have been quite so annoyed that Logan was getting this drunk. And I probably would've had a couple of drinks with him. On the other hand, a few years ago, it would've been a moot point because I would've been here with my ex-wife. Neither of us would've been drinking heavily anyway because it'd been one of a handful of nights each year that we'd rented a hotel room for some couple time while the kids had stayed with Grandma and Grandpa.

But those days were over, and my ability to drink myself senseless had played no small part in destroying my marriage, and—

I winced at the painful barrage of memories.

Have a drink? No, thank you.

He knew why I didn't drink, though, and he kept asking. Not only would he keep drinking himself stupid, he'd keep egging me on to join him. Aside from the shit inside my own head, Logan was the single biggest threat to my sobriety these days.

And somehow, I'd had to wait until we'd announced our relationship to God and everyone to realize I couldn't spend one more night with him. I couldn't—

"Clint?" That time, it was a voice that didn't raise my hackles.

I turned toward Commander Wil—*Travis. Not at work. Call him Travis.*

He lifted his eyebrows. "You all right?"

"Yeah. Yeah." I waved a hand. "I'm . . . I'm good, yeah."

He watched me, no expression at all to let me know if he was concerned, or thought I was an idiot, or maybe a little of both.

I took a swig of ice water and casually looked around to avoid Travis's blue-eyed scrutiny. If he thought I was an idiot, he was right. I was relieved that I didn't have to worry about whether people knew I was queer—it was the first time I'd ever done anything close to coming out, so that was a shaky plus. But I wasn't so sure I liked being the guy who was dating the cute-but-sloppily-drunk dumbass. Maybe this hadn't been such a good idea.

I twisted around to find him in the crowd. He was at one of the bars, having an animated conversation with someone who looked equally inebriated.

Maybe *it wasn't a good idea?*

Swearing under my breath, I turned back around. This was going to be a long night. Lord help us all when they opened up the dance floor.

Moments after Logan stumbled back to the table, a waiter came by to send us up to the buffet.

"All right!" One of the guys from Travis's department stood, rubbing his hands together. "Chow time."

"About damn time." Travis winced as he rose, and his daughter said something I couldn't hear. He gestured dismissively. With his other hand, he gingerly rubbed the middle of his back. Then he twisted like he was trying to loosen up a crick, and followed her toward the buffet. I hadn't known him long, but I'd never seen him walk without a limp, and it seemed more pronounced tonight. His daughter motioned for him to go ahead of her as they joined the line. As I watched them—surreptitiously of course—I swore she was deliberately positioning herself so anyone squeezing past them would bump her and not him.

It wasn't unusual to see service members with visible pain, especially if they'd been in for any length of time. Being a commander, he'd probably been in at least a couple of years longer than me. Plenty of time to get battered and beaten by the nature of the job. And since he had wings on his uniform, he'd been a pilot at some point in his career. Maybe he'd ejected. God knew every flyboy I'd ever met who'd survived an ejection walked a little uncomfortably at times.

I pulled my gaze away from him so no one would catch me staring. Wasn't that what I needed—bring a guy to the ball, realize we were a huge mistake, and then get caught ogling another man. Yep, this was going to be a great night.

The buffet line moved quickly for once, and we made it to the table lined with chafing dishes. For as drunk as he was, Logan managed to load up his plate and make it back to his seat without incident. I didn't know if that impressed me or annoyed me. Nothing made it harder to tell someone "you've got a drinking problem" like evidence that he could function fine when he was intoxicated. My ex-wife could attest to that one.

As I sat down with my own plate, Travis caught my eye over the rim of his water glass. He glanced at Logan, then back at me, but said nothing.

Jesus.

I had expected to feel conspicuous tonight, but not like this. Being out was fine. Sitting with the drunken idiot I needed to dump, across from the man I'd sell my soul to sleep with? Crap. Clearly it should've been a pre-ball sign when I'd been getting steadily more frustrated with Logan while fantasizing more and more about Travis. Who I had known would be here tonight.

No, I had not thought this through.

Except he had a daughter, so he was probably straight. Except that assumption made zero sense because I had three kids and I was anything but straight. The only things I knew about Commander—about Travis was that he had an adult daughter and wasn't wearing a wedding band. So basically, I knew nothing about him. Aside from the fact that I'd been wanting him since I'd transferred here.

Fuck my life.

Avoiding eye contact with anyone, I picked at my food. It was decent, all things considered—I'd been to some military functions with food that was barely fit for human consumption—but any appetite I'd had was gone. How much longer was I assigned to this command? Would it be pathetic to start prodding for a transfer to someplace where this Navy Ball hadn't happened?

Yeah, it would be. And I wouldn't. Especially since I was probably the only one here who'd care about any of this after tonight. But goddamn, in this moment, it sure felt like the reasonable, rational thing to do.

I reached for my drink and cautiously glanced around the table. Logan was chatting with Wolcott's wife, who was almost as drunk as he was. Everyone else was caught up in their own conversations— in between shooting the two drunks irritated looks—including Travis and his daughter, who were talking about something with Stevenson and her husband.

Discreetly, Travis took something out of his pocket and looked at it under the edge of the table. I thought it was a smartphone, but his phone was next to his drink. And whatever was in his hand had a couple of thin wires coming off it. His daughter glanced at him, concern pulling her eyebrows together, but neither of them said anything.

Then he shifted, grimacing, and put the device back in his pocket. As he did, his eyes met mine, but we both quickly broke eye contact. I thought some color appeared in his cheeks. In this light, though, it was impossible to be sure.

Travis returned to his conversation, and I returned to chasing a piece of . . . beef? Well, it resembled beef, anyway, and I chased it around my plate with my fork.

Logan nudged me. "I'm going to hit up the buffet for more. You want anything?"

"No, I'm good. Thanks."

He got up, wobbled hard enough he had to grab my shoulder for balance, and clumsily made his way toward the buffet. I watched him go, feeling like the world's biggest asshole because I was already rehearsing how I was going to cut him loose at the end of the night.

Yes. Tonight. I didn't need this anymore. Especially if I was going to stick to that promise I'd made to my ex-wife, our attorneys, the judge, and the fucking Navy to stay out of the bottle.

Do you want this guy, or do you want your kids back?

My throat tightened.

Yeah. Tonight—*done.*

Then I realized that, while the ballroom was still noisy with dozens of conversations, my table had fallen silent. When I turned, I realized everyone was watching Logan or me. The last few heads turned, and they were all looking at me.

Heat rushed into my face. I cleared my throat as I reached for my glass.

Oh God. Say something. Say something!

Bailey snickered, tilting his glass toward Logan. "Boy can really hold his liquor, can't he?"

I pleaded with the ground to open up and swallow me right then and there, but managed a quiet chuckle. "Ex-Marine. What can I say?"

To my great relief, everyone at the table laughed.

"That explains it," Stevenson said. "The Marines can *hold* plenty of liquor. Problem is they don't know what to *do* with it."

"Not like Sailors," Bailey said proudly.

Everyone laughed again and raised their glasses. I was still mortified, but joined in. At least they were all taking him in stride.

"You have my sympathy." Travis absently ran his finger around the rim of his drink. "I took a guy like that to a buddy's wedding once."

I blinked. "You . . ."

"Yeah." Travis chuckled, gaze fixed on Logan. "Ex-Marine too, if I remember right. Anyway, he drank like a fish, and it was a fucking disaster."

Kimber groaned. "Oh my God. You're talking about Nate Grayson, aren't you?"

Travis nodded.

Bailey smirked. "Wasn't that the guy who hooked up with the bride's dad?"

"Yep." Travis grimaced. "I'm surprised my friend still spoke to me after that."

The table again erupted in laughter, and suddenly everyone was coming out with disastrous wedding stories. I couldn't have been more relieved, especially as Logan returned to his seat.

But at the same time, my stomach was wound up in a whole new set of knots.

So Travis . . .

Took a guy to a wedding?

He's . . .

No way.

So now I felt like an epic idiot for being nervous about coming out to this crowd. They obviously all either knew Travis was gay, or didn't care. Shit. I really should've just mentioned in passing that I was dating a guy, and that would've been the end of it. Especially since tonight would also be the end of me dating his ass. Pity I hadn't gotten my head together before I'd made myself look like a tool in front of the man I'd been lusting after. The man who, it turned out, was not-straight enough that he openly and casually talked about taking a man as his date to a wedding.

Yep, this night was one for the history books. Best night of my life, or some bullshit like that.

Movement at the other side of the room caught my eye, and when I turned my head, that knot in my stomach turned to pure horror. The deejay and his assistant were settling in behind the booth, probably getting ready to fire up the music.

Which meant dancing.

I slowly turned toward Logan. He was in the middle of animatedly telling some story to Wolcott's wife, unloading half his drink on himself, which he so far hadn't noticed. But he would. Once that music started, he'd be on his feet, tugging me toward the floor, and I would have to fake my own death or go into witness protection rather than risk crossing paths with any of these people ever again.

I touched his shoulder. "Hey."

He faced me. "Hmm?"

"Listen, um . . ." I hesitated. "Maybe we should get going."

Logan's glazed eyes lit up, and he grinned as he slid a hand over my thigh. "Yeah, we should."

I fought the urge to squirm out from under his touch. He was in for a surprise when we got to his place, but if the prospect of going home and getting laid—even after we'd *just* eaten—was enough to get him out of here so I could break this off? Fine. Leading him on for an hour if only to get us away from my coworkers before I dropped the hammer . . .

Well, I'd find a way to sleep at night.

As I pulled into the parking lot below Logan's apartment complex, my stomach lurched. Regardless of how much I hated confrontation and awkward conversations, this one needed to happen.

Being around him when he drank was dangerous, I reminded myself. Unless I wanted my life to fall apart again, I had to stay sober, and that wasn't easy when I was around someone who wasn't, no matter how much I liked the guy. Or the sober version of him, anyway. It hurt, and it would for a while, but I . . . I just couldn't anymore.

So he had to go.

And now that we were here, it was showtime.

I shut off the engine, and Logan stumbled on his way out of the car. Fortunately, it was dark and he was distracted, so he didn't see me rolling my eyes before I came around to help him.

He steadied himself on the door. "Man. I am . . ."

Drunk? You don't say.

I held out my hand. "Keys?"

He fumbled in his pockets before he finally found them, and dropped them into my hand.

Thank God he lived on the first floor. I was not in the mood to help him navigate stairs—the walk up to his door was challenging enough.

"Watch that step," I said, as if he'd never approached his own apartment before.

He looked down, and as hard as he concentrated on taking that step, I wondered if he would've face-planted if I hadn't said something. Jesus.

I unlocked the door, toed it open, and handed back his keys.

Grinning, he tugged at my jacket. "Come on in. Let's tear up your uniform."

I pried his fingers off my clothes. "How about no."

"Huh?" Logan stiffened, and he might've even sobered up some. "What the fuck?"

"I'm gonna go." I straightened my jacket. "And listen, you're a great guy and all, but I think it's time to—"

"Seriously? I went to that boring bullshit and hung out with you and your coworkers, and we're not even going to fuck?"

I folded my arms across my chest, probably making a mess of my medals in the process. "Looks to me like you're too drunk to fuck."

He laughed. "Oh come on. We've fucked when I've been drunker than this." Logan reached for my waist, and I sidestepped the advance.

"Yeah, I know we have." *Why didn't I do this sooner?* "And we're not going to anymore."

"Why the fuck not? You weren't complaining last time—"

"You wouldn't have noticed if I had been," I snapped.

He blinked. Then his eyes narrowed and he stabbed a finger at me. "This is bullshit, Clint. I didn't go sit through all that Navy shit just so we could—"

"You know what?" I put up my hands and took a step back. "We can talk about this again when you're sober, but I'm done. I'm out." I started to leave, but he grabbed my elbow.

Any other time, he might've been able to pull me back toward him. Tonight, though, lunging at me like that was enough to throw him off-balance, and he used my arm for support more than to actually stop me.

I casually pulled away from his grasp, leaving him to slump against the wall. "We'll talk later. But I'm done with this shit."

This time, when I turned to go, he wasn't quick enough to catch up with me. He shouted after me, though—screaming slurred obscenities and suggesting I go fuck myself if I wasn't going to fuck him.

"Thanks for making my decision that much easier," I muttered as I got into my car. The slamming door cut off most of his shouts. The engine coming to life muffled the rest. Without so much as a backwards glance, I pulled out of the parking space and left his apartment complex. Whatever he was shouting at me I couldn't hear, but his neighbors undoubtedly did. Fine. Let them call the cops or the landlord or whatever. I was over it and I was out of here.

Tomorrow, when he was sober, we could hash this out properly. There'd be more shouting and swearing, no doubt, and the finality would hurt, but I was one hundred percent done now. And feeling like an idiot for holding out until tonight just so I could bring a date to the Navy Ball.

A few blocks away from Logan's apartment, I stopped at an intersection. Left would take me to my place. Right would lead back to the hotel.

Tapping my thumbs on the wheel, I looked at the clock on the dash. It was only ten. The ball usually went until one or two at least.

Which meant there was time. I could go back. See if Travis was still there.

And what if he is, Clint? Then what?

My heart sped up and my stomach fluttered.

Yeah. Then what?

Only one way to find out.

So I turned right and floored it.

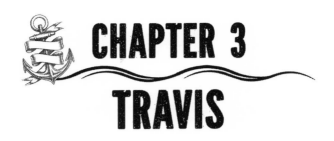

CHAPTER 3
TRAVIS

"**H**ow are you holding up?" Kimber leaned over the back of her chair. "You look like you're in pain."

I'm always in pain, sweetheart. I smiled. "I'll be fine."

"You sure? We can go if—"

"I'm fine. Promise."

Her eyebrow arched. "Dad, you're sweating."

I dabbed at my forehead, and sure enough, my fingers came back slick. As I wiped them on my napkin, I forced another smile. "Listen, it's not going to be any better or worse at home. And these chairs are surprisingly comfortable, so I don't mind staying a while longer."

"Dad, if you're—"

"I'm fine. I might go out and have a cigarette, but otherwise . . ."

She scowled, but shrugged. "All right. You know we can leave anytime."

"I know. Go have fun."

"Okay. Just say so if you want to take off."

"I will. *Go.*"

She headed back out to the dance floor, and I took a deep swallow of ice water.

That cigarette was tempting as hell, especially after I'd been through a couple of beers, but I didn't move yet. I wasn't sure I dared, because the truth was, the pain was getting unbearable. The TENS unit was turned up as high as I could stand it, to the point it was more irritating than helpful. Instead of the electrical pulses feeling like spiders dancing on my skin, it felt like they were *biting* my skin.

I sighed. Well, there was no point in burning up the batteries for nothing, so I turned the unit down.

I'd gone through all the Motrin I'd brought with me. More and more, it looked like the only way I was sleeping tonight was with the help of one of the pain meds I'd been hoarding. Medical was stingy as fuck about anything besides Motrin, and the Navy frowned on using actual painkillers for any length of time. Another one of those things that was technically allowed if Medical deemed it necessary, but was a bullet train ticket to a medical retirement.

So on that rare occasion I got my hands on something stronger, I rationed that shit like they were the last pills on earth. When I did take them, I just prayed that wasn't the week I was called in for a random drug test.

I shifted in my chair, gritting my teeth at the fresh pain exploding along my spine. Good thing I had those strong meds at home, even if the means of acquiring them had been unpleasant. I was probably the only man alive who'd ever been thankful for a kidney stone. That weekend last spring had been hell, but I'd gotten a bottle of Percocet as a consolation prize and still had most of it left, so I actually stood a chance at sleeping tonight.

Now I understand why no one can tell the difference between a chronic pain sufferer and a drug addict.

I wiped a hand over my face and breathed as deeply as my uniform and muscle spasms allowed. Kimber was having a good time, and I didn't want to cut her evening short. These events were rare, and she didn't get many other opportunities to dress up and dance. Maybe someday she'd be ready to go to clubs and parties again on her own, but until that time, she stuck with events like the Navy Ball. And I'd happily go with her and knuckle through the pain until she was damn good and ready to leave.

I flagged down a waiter and grabbed another glass of water. For a minute or two, I wondered if I could talk him into getting me some ice—preferably wrapped in a dish towel, thank you—that I could lean against, but decided against it. Kimber would take one look at me getting an ice pack from a waiter, and drag me out the door.

A cigarette might help. The thought of it made some of the Pavlovian response kick in and relax muscles all over my body. Not the ones that hurt, of course, but maybe if I actually went out and lit up, I'd feel better.

Holding my breath, I rose. Fresh, eye-watering pain shot down my spine, which I'd expected, and I carefully breathed through it as I buttoned my jacket.

Yep, definitely gonna have to get this fucker tailored before next year.

The button held, though. Before I left the table, I checked my pockets for my cigarettes and lighter. Then I looked around, found Kimber, and held up my cigarette pack. She nodded before going back to what looked like a flirty conversation with an enlisted kid.

I worked my way around the edge of the room instead of through the crowd so no one would jostle me.

I made it to the exit and stepped outside into the chill October air. I hadn't even realized how stuffy the room had become until I was breathing fresh, clean, vaguely salt-scented air.

Fresh, clean air that was about to be polluted thanks to the Camel I was about to smoke. I pulled one out of the pack, put it between my lips, and lit it.

That Pavlovian effect intensified. The nicotine wasn't anywhere near my bloodstream yet, but even as I took that first drag, some of the tension in my neck and shoulders eased. I cautiously rolled my shoulders under my tight jacket. The spasm in the center of my back wasn't moving anytime soon, and the TENS wasn't helping much.

Get ready for me, Percocet. I took a deep drag from my cigarette. *We're going to bed together tonight.*

In the parking lot, a car door slammed. The distinct click of dress shoes came closer, and I turned my head.

And almost dropped my cigarette.

Was I already getting loopy on the Percocet I hadn't even taken yet? Or was Clint really back? Strolling up the sidewalk? Coming right toward me? *Alone?*

I blinked a few times. Nope, this was no phantom drug side effect. That was Clint, and he was back, and was . . .

Right here.

I stood straighter, schooling the wince out of my expression. "Hey. I thought you called it a night."

"I did. But then . . ." He shook his head. "Anyway. Can, uh . . ." He gestured toward the door to the ball still going on without us. "Can I buy you a drink?"

"Uh . . ." *I really am having premature hallucinations, aren't I?*

"I . . . Seriously?"

"Yeah. Kind of feel like . . . uh, like I owe you and everybody else for putting up with Logan." As soon as he said it, something in him settled, as if he'd been searching for an explanation and finally found one that satisfied him. He took a deep breath, and shifted slightly, as if he couldn't quite stay still. "Do you want anything?"

Oh, I definitely want—

"A Coke is fine. I've, uh, gotta drive." Which was true. Kimber had had quite a bit to drink tonight, so it was either me or a cab. "Here." I reached for my wallet. "You fly, I'll—"

"I'll get it. Don't worry about it." He flashed a shy smile. "Should I come back out here, or . . .?"

"No. I . . ." I glanced at the cigarette in my hand, then dropped it on the ground and crushed it under my heel, ignoring the twinge that motion sent from my hip to my back. "I was heading back inside."

"Meet you at the table?"

"Sure. Yeah."

We separated, and I headed back to where we'd been sitting earlier. Everyone else had cleared out—they were either dancing, socializing, or waiting for more drinks. Fine by me. I didn't need anyone watching me lower myself into my chair like I was eighty-five instead of forty-five. Or notice me cursing when a spasm knifed across my back and made my eyes water.

I leaned my forearms on the table, lifting my shoulders as much as I could to stretch the aggravated muscles. The spasm started to subside, but it wasn't in any hurry.

"Are you all right?" Damn. Clint's voice.

I nodded, and cautiously released my breath. Lifting my head, I forced a smile. "Old injury." I took out the TENS unit and cranked that fucker back up. "Still likes to come back and haunt me sometimes."

"Those are a bitch, aren't they?" He set a Coke in front of me and sat in the next chair with what might've been a Coke, or maybe Coke and something stronger.

I rolled my stiff shoulders. "Eh, life in the military, am I right?"

"I'll drink to that." He raised his glass. "This life ain't for the faint of heart."

"Amen." I clinked mine against his and took a sip.

"And, um . . ." He lowered his gaze. "By the way, I hope my date wasn't too much of an idiot for—"

"Don't sweat it. You should've seen Wolcott's wife at the Christmas party last year."

He met my eyes. "Really?"

"Oh yeah. And Stevenson's husband got so shitfaced, he tried to pick a fight with the chaplain."

"The chaplain?" Clint sputtered. "Over what?"

"Who knows?" I shrugged. "When you're that drunk, why does anything need to make sense?"

I couldn't be sure, but I thought he winced. Averting his eyes again, he quietly said, "Isn't that the truth."

I studied him, not sure if the wince had been leftover embarrassment from his idiot date, or something deeper. Whatever it was, he probably didn't want to get into it, so I changed the subject.

"So, um." I drummed my fingers nervously. "Are you settling in okay? To the new town and all?"

Clint nodded. "It's nice to be out of the desert."

"The desert?" I paused. "Oh right. You came from Nellis, didn't you?"

"Yep. Man, I did not sign up for the Navy to spend my life in Nevada."

"Could be worse. I know a few people who've landed in Nebraska."

He wrinkled his nose. "Ugh. The Navy does not belong in landlocked states."

"Tell that to the Air Force," I muttered. "They're the ones who need the Navy to operate the complicated, technical shit."

That got a laugh out of him. Nothing like the good-natured rivalry between military branches to lighten up a conversation.

"So, you were a drone pilot, right?" I asked.

His laughter faded a bit, and he sat straighter. "We prefer RAP. But yes."

"RAP?" *Come on, Travis. You haven't even taken the drugs yet.* "Remind me what that is again?"

"Remote aircraft pilot."

"Right. Right. Got it." I took a sip of my drink, and with it, swallowed a few smartass comments about how a fancy name didn't change the fact that if you don't leave the ground, you're not a damn pilot.

Says the man who hasn't left the ground in too many fucking years.

As if for emphasis, one of the spasms in the center of my back tightened, catching my breath. God, if I'd been sitting here with anybody else, I'd have flagged down my daughter, bowed out, and gotten the hell home for my date with Percocet. As it was, I probably wasn't going to last too much longer, but this was the first chance I'd had to sit down with Clint, one-on-one, outside the office, and with the knowledge that he wasn't straight after all. I could breathe through a few muscle spasms if I had to.

"How long were you a drone—RAP?"

Clint fidgeted, wrapping both hands around his drink and staring into the glass. "Little too long."

Okay, so that topic was a minefield too. Maybe the best approach was to let him choose a direction, and I'd follow his lead.

The silence hung there for an uncomfortable minute or so.

Then, finally, he said, "So your date really hooked up with the bride's father?"

A relieved laugh burst out of me. I didn't even care about the pain it sent radiating across the back of my ribs. "He really did. That was . . . awkward."

He chuckled. "I can imagine. Did she at least know her dad was into men?"

"Nope." I shook my head slowly. "Pretty sure it was news to her mother too."

"Oh my God."

"Yeah. Let me tell you, nobody was surprised when the bride's sister eloped the next year, and her brother had a dry wedding a few months later."

"I believe it." He held my gaze, giving me a chance to see how dark his eyes really were. "They didn't blame you, though, did they?"

"No, no. Hell, the bride actually felt really bad for me because she thought we'd had something serious going on. She felt a lot better once I told her we'd only been out on a few dates by that point."

"That's good. I can only imagine what holidays are like in that household now."

I grimaced. "I heard through the grapevine that they were pretty awkward for the first couple of years." I was about to mention the number of antiques and heirlooms that were smashed the next day after the father of the bride's walk of shame, but right then, Kimber appeared beside me.

She looked at Clint. "Oh hey. I didn't know you came back."

Clint shrugged. "Had to drop someone off."

Kimber mouthed a silent *Oh*. She glanced at me and gestured with her beer bottle toward her seat, eyebrows up as if to ask if it was okay to sit down.

I nodded back, so she did.

"Getting tired of dancing already?" I asked.

"Just need a break for a few minutes." She took a swig, then peered into the bottle with a scowl on her face. "What the hell? When did this one get empty?"

Clint and I both laughed.

"They have a way of doing that, don't they?" he said.

"Little bastards," she muttered.

"You want another one?" I asked.

"Hell yeah."

I rolled my eyes. "Drunk."

"Shut up. I am not."

"Uh-huh." I glanced at my soda, and realized it was getting pretty low too. "You know, I could use one myself. I'll go get them this time." I started to stand, and something in my back . . . moved. It wasn't a spasm. It wasn't a twinge. It wasn't even really pain—just that ominous shift of soft tissue that meant things were going to get *bad*.

Kimber gently grasped my arm. "Dad?"

"You okay?" Clint asked.

I swallowed. "I think it might be time to call it a night."

Instantly, Clint was on his feet. "Do you need a lift?"

I closed my eyes and exhaled. As much as it killed me to admit it, I needed someone to drive us home tonight. Swallowing my pride was the best option I had right then, so I turned to him. "You don't mind?"

"No, of course not." His keys were already in his hand.

"I'll go get my coat." Kimber let go of my arm. "Do you have the claim ticket?"

"Yeah." I took out my wallet, fished out the ticket, and passed it to her. "We'll meet you outside."

"Got it." Ticket in hand, she hurried toward the coat check.

I leaned on the chair for a second, cautiously stretching my back to gauge how bad this was going to get and how fast. Pretty bad and pretty fast, if the rapidly spreading tension was anything to go by.

"We should get out to the car," I said, concentrating on not letting my rib cage move more than it absolutely had to while I was talking.

"Good idea." Clint walked ahead, clearing a path for me as he went. As soon as we were outside, he turned around. "Why don't you wait here, and I'll bring the car up?"

Without speaking, I nodded. I could have kissed him right then even if I *hadn't* been fantasizing about it for ages. I wasn't in the mood for anything that didn't involve sleep or pain pills, but he was a saint for being this considerate. Or maybe I'd just spent too much time with people who weren't.

Moments later, Kimber appeared with her coat over her arm, and Clint parked at the end of the walk. Thank God I didn't have to put on a coat. The dinner jacket I was wearing was warm enough anyway, and the motions would have been too painful.

With my daughter's help, I eased myself into the passenger seat of Clint's car. Then she got into the back, and Clint pulled away from the curb so carefully and smoothly, he must've had experience driving with someone who was in a lot of pain. At the stop sign at the end of the road, he stopped just as gently.

"Which gate?" he asked.

"Gate two," Kimber said. Though she'd had quite a few drinks tonight, she was sober enough to direct him back to our house, so I left her to it. Meanwhile, I closed my eyes and concentrated on breathing without snapping my ribs off my spine.

After we'd left the base and were on the highway, she asked, "You have some of the strong stuff at home, right, Dad?"

"Of course." I turned to Clint, half expecting a raised eyebrow over what I meant by *strong stuff*, but when he glanced my way, the only thing that registered in his expression looked like genuine concern.

I closed my eyes again.

And while she continued directing him toward our place, I sent up a prayer of thanks that he'd come back to the Navy Ball tonight.

By the time I walked into my kitchen, every muscle from my shoulders to my hips was cable tight. Taking off my dinner jacket took way more work than it should have, and not just because I needed to lose five or ten pounds before the next time I put it on. Kimber helped, carefully tugging it off my shoulders and down my arms while I held my breath and tried not to collapse from pain. Thank God she lived with me, or I'd have been sleeping in my uniform tonight. Wouldn't have been the first time.

She put the jacket over a chair while I toed off my dress shoes.

"Need me to get the cummerbund too?"

I glanced down. Shit. I'd forgotten about the little bastard and its buckle behind my back.

"Here." She stepped around behind me. "I'll get it." A second later, the cummerbund went slack.

"Thanks," I said.

"Need anything else?"

"Only if you've got some elephant tranquilizers and a handful of morphine."

Kimber laughed quietly. "Sorry. Fresh out."

"Damn it."

Her forehead creased. "You've got your drugs, though, right?"

I nodded, gesturing toward my bedroom. "Yeah. I'm good. Thanks again."

"You're welcome. Let me know if you need anything else. Besides, you know, elephant drugs."

I chuckled as much as the pain would allow, which wasn't much. "Will do."

"Okay. Good night, Dad."

"Good night, kiddo."

She headed down the hall, and I went into the master bathroom to get that coveted Percocet.

I took the top off and looked inside.

Oh fuck. Was I really down to my last four?

I rattled the bottle, jostling the pills inside, and sure enough . . . only four.

Well, that posed a hell of a dilemma. Tough it out and save the pill? Or take it now and hope I could get my hands on some more before I ran out?

Fuck it. I'd figure out how to get more later. After all, when I hoarded pills for a rainy day, this was the kind of rainy day I had in mind. As it was, I'd be sleeping in my tux shirt and trousers because I couldn't maneuver enough to take them off.

Yeah. This was one of those desperate nights.

So I chased the pill with some water, went to bed, and let the Percocet carry me away.

CHAPTER 4

CLINT

All the way home, I worried about Travis. It was a good thing his daughter was with him. Though she'd been drinking tonight, she still had her wits about her, and she'd be there if he needed anything. I wasn't sure I could have left him completely alone.

Not that he would've given me much choice. I barely knew him, but I could already tell he was one of those people who would knuckle through rather than ask for help. Which meant the pain must have been bad tonight. He'd been obviously uncomfortable for most of the evening, especially toward the end, but then there'd been that palpable shift. When he'd tried to stand, but halted, something in his eyes had changed, and he'd gone from *I've got this* to *I'm fucked.*

My blood had immediately gone cold. A million worst-case scenarios had run through my mind, and I'd looked to Kimber to gauge her response. Though she'd been concerned and knew her dad needed to get home, she hadn't panicked. Apparently this was something that had happened before. I was still worried, but took it down a few notches when she didn't freak out.

Now that they were home, he'd hopefully taken something good and strong.

What a crazy night. The whole evening had been a weird mix of emotions. I'd been nervous as fuck about coming out to my command. Relieved that no one had batted an eye. Also relieved in a weird way— if also hurt—when I'd walked away from Logan's apartment. Guilty like I'd led him on and used him to come out, even though I hadn't. Giddy when I'd shown up at the Navy Ball to find that Travis was still there. Off-balance because Travis had causally let it slip that he wasn't as straight as I'd assumed.

I had to wonder now . . . what would have happened if Travis hadn't had to cut the evening short?

I shook my head and pushed that thought away. He'd been there with his daughter, for God's sake. Nothing would have happened.

As I pulled onto my street, I wished I'd at least gotten Kimber's number so I could text her and make sure he was all right. Except she was probably asleep by now. And he'd be fine. It wasn't a big secret that he had some old injuries. Some days, his limp definitely seemed worse than others. He'd walk slower. He'd break a sweat on the short trip to and from the vending machine. He'd glare at the stairs leading up to our offices, but in the couple of months I'd been here, I'd never once seen him break down and use the elevator at the end of the hall. Stubborn fucker.

I also hadn't seen him in this much obvious pain, though. How and why he'd hung on so long at the Navy Ball, I had no idea. All I knew was when I came back from cutting Logan loose, Travis had still been there, and I'd finally had the opportunity to talk to him.

It was a start. There was no telling if I had a snowball's chance in hell with him—for all I knew, he had a boyfriend who hadn't wanted to come to the Navy Ball—but the simple fact that he was interested in men and had given me the time of day was promising enough to leave me grinning.

You're pathetic. You know that, right? And you just *broke up with someone.*

Eh. Whatever.

I parked outside my apartment and headed inside. After this roller coaster of an evening, I was fucking exhausted. Not ten minutes after I walked through my front door, I collapsed in bed.

And for once, I slept.

The next morning, I felt so strange, I had to lie there for a while and figure out what the hell had changed. What was missing.

Oh. No dreams.

I closed my eyes and exhaled. I'd actually made it till morning without waking up in a cold sweat, or shaking, or sick to my stomach.

I'd been so utterly wiped out, even my PTSD-addled brain had completely shut down and let me crash for an entire night.

It wouldn't be a trend. Tonight, the dreams would be back, and it would be another long, rough night like usual. I expected it, especially after my breakup had added some fresh stress to the pile. But damn if I wasn't going to bask in how great it felt to have had a *good* night for a change.

So of course I made the mistake of checking my phone. Six voice messages from Logan. Awesome. There went my pleasant mood.

Without bothering to play them, I tossed my phone on the nightstand and went to take a shower. I didn't need that shit right now. Or ever, but I supposed we still had to tie things up and be done with each other. As content as I was to let last night be the end of it, I owed him more than just walking away while he was too drunk to know what was happening.

After my shower, I sat down to hear what he'd shouted into my phone. As if to prove exactly how hammered he'd been, each message was harder to parse than the one before. He hadn't known me long, but long enough to know there was no point in leaving me a message—most of the time, I didn't open them.

Or maybe that was what he'd hoped. Maybe he'd been drunkenly venting and figured I'd ignore the actual messages and go straight to calling him back. He probably hadn't expected me to play them and actually hear him telling me what an asshole I was, or how he could see why my ex-wife had gotten tired of my tiny dick.

Way to win a guy back, idiot.

Apparently I had made the right decision last night. And dumping someone by text wasn't my style, but after one too many colorful voice mails on my phone—one of which made a slurred reference to my *kids*, for God's sake—I made an exception.

Have a nice life, Logan. I'm out.

I sent the text, and felt . . . nothing. Maybe some relief, but not much. Our brief and messy excuse for a relationship was already cool in the grave as far as I was concerned, and sending him that text was one more shovelful of dirt on top of the casket.

Leaning back on my pillows, I exhaled. It said a lot that I didn't find myself pining over him at all. Maybe I was still numb. Or maybe

I should've done this sooner, and I'd already gone through all the post-breakup emotions before I'd even dropped the hammer. All I knew was, his messages boiled my emotional response down to *if it's gonna be like that—good riddance.*

And there was also . . . Travis.

Quietly crushing on him from down the hall at work was one thing. A little one-on-one while he was looking sexy as fuck in his dress uniform? The same night he'd let it slip he was into men? Some extended eye contact that might or might not have been my imagination? Holy shit.

And now I had to wait until Monday to see him again? *Fuck.*

In an effort to keep myself busy and pass the time until then, and maybe to exorcise my now-ex-boyfriend, I spent the weekend cleaning my apartment from top to bottom. There wasn't an inch of tile grout that didn't get scrubbed, and I even managed to unpack a few more of the boxes still stacked in the second bedroom. Amazing how much could be done to the surfaces in a thousand-square-foot apartment, but it kept me busy until late Saturday night. And as a bonus, I worked myself hard enough to earn another dreamless night.

Sunday, there wasn't a speck of dust left in the apartment, so I tackled my car. Then unpacked a few more boxes. Then ironed my freshly washed uniforms.

And finally, it was Monday morning.

And I was back at the office.

And . . .

There he was.

His back was to me, and he was poring over a report or something with the CO as they headed down the hall toward her office. He was walking much better than when I'd dropped him off on Friday night. He was still limping, but that was normal.

He was in uniform, of course, and even though I'd seen him a million times, I couldn't stop staring. The blue digital camouflage uniforms were not my favorite thing about the Navy. There was something about the uniform that seemed to strip away all semblance of individuality. Which was sort of what uniforms were meant to do, but this one in particular seemed to erase *everything*. Facial features, skin tones, even eyes—they all seemed to turn generic when people wore these uniforms. I'd had coworkers I didn't recognize in their civvies because I'd only seen them in blue camouflage.

Travis, though . . . I couldn't mentally blend him into a crowd if I wanted to. No amount of camouflage dulled a single thing about him. After seeing him in his dress uniform? Jesus.

I pulled my gaze away from him, and realized I'd just checked out in the middle of a conversation with two coworkers.

"Sir?" Petty Officer Vincent cocked his head.

"Um." I hoped my face wasn't as red as it felt. "Could you run that by me again?"

They both glanced past me, then at each other. Vincent smothered a laugh, and Turner didn't even try to hide his amusement as he held up the folder we'd been discussing. Right. New training procedures.

I coughed again. "Make sure I've got copies of that for the next department head meeting. And we're going to need a classroom for next week."

Turner nodded. "Yes, sir. I'll have the copies on your desk before lunch."

"I'll schedule the classroom," Vincent said. "Are you doing two classes or one?"

"Two. And dear God, don't put us in room four in the afternoon again. When the sun reflects off the water, it's blinding."

He laughed. "Yes, sir."

They went off in separate directions, and I glanced around in case Travis had reappeared. He hadn't. Like me, he had work to do, and I guessed he'd gone to the CO's office or a meeting or something. Probably just as well—he was distracting enough without even being in the room.

So, I headed to my own office to take care of the stack of papers growing in my inbox.

Our offices were at opposite ends of the hall. Though we were on the same floor, we were in different departments. Travis supervised a few dozen officers and civilian contractors while I ran the training department. Sometimes I wished I did work for him—at least then I'd have the occasional excuse to stop into his office. On the other hand, I'd probably make a complete ass of myself. Go in to ask a legitimate professional question, get tongue-tied, say something dumb . . .

Yeah. This was for the better.

In my own office, I managed to focus on my tasks. It wasn't the most exciting gig, and I was happy for that. My blood pressure was still through the roof after my previous assignment. Flying remote aircraft from an air-conditioned room and blowing shit up had seemed like a cool job on paper, but it turned out to be dangerously high-stress and ultimately traumatic enough to turn my whole life on its head.

These days, instead of flying aircraft on the other side of the world, my days were spent pushing paperwork, setting up presentations, and teaching classes that bored me more than they did the students. A few years ago, that would've been my idea of hell. Now? It kept me sane and employed. Might never get promoted again thanks to some incidents surrounding my divorce, and a good night's sleep would be rare until I died, but I had a job. For that alone, I happily embraced daily death by PowerPoint.

Didn't hurt that I had a seriously attractive coworker who didn't seem to be far from my mind these days. I squirmed in my chair. What I wouldn't have given just to . . . *touch him*. Lock a door, find a bed, make out until my lips were raw. My brain started sliding into one of the many fantasies I'd had about him, and the funny thing was, I almost never saw us tearing up the sheets. Just thinking about kissing him was enough to—

Someone knocked on my office door, startling me away from the schedule I'd been working on. "Come in."

The door opened, and . . . Oh dear Lord.

"Hey." I smiled, thankful my desk and uniform both camouflaged my hard-on. "How are you doing?"

Travis smiled back. "Good. Good. I, uh, wanted to come by and say thanks again for getting us home after the ball."

"Don't mention it. You look like you're feeling better."

"God, yeah. Much." He tilted his head to one side, then the other, as if to show he had some mobility again. "Like I said, it's one of those injuries that likes to come back to haunt me. Could've picked a better night, though."

I was curious, but didn't press, and anyway, he wasn't done.

"Listen, the reason I came by . . ." He shifted his weight. "Let me buy you lunch or something. I really feel like I owe you for the other night."

I wanted to tell him he didn't owe me a thing, but the prospect of having lunch with him was too good to pass up. "Sounds great."

He smiled. Almost laughed. Like he'd been holding his breath while he waited for me to respond, and was relieved I'd agreed to go along.

Are you kidding? I'd be stupid to say no.

"Okay, well." He gestured over his shoulder. "I should get back to work. I'm having lunch with Captain Rodriguez and some blowhards today, but let's do something tomorrow. Say, eleven?"

Yes, please. "I'll be there."

"Great." He held my gaze for a second. "I'll see you then."

I nodded, trying not to compromise my cool exterior. It was lunch with a coworker. No big deal.

He started to go, but paused. "Oh, by the way, a bunch of us are going out to the O club tonight. You want to come along?"

The offer didn't sound nearly as appealing as he probably thought. I didn't drink—although *God* I wanted to—and I didn't particularly like hanging out with ex-pilots.

Tonight, though, I could handle being the only RAP around a bunch of smart-aleck flyboys. I could handle being around gallons and gallons of booze I couldn't touch. After all, Travis was going.

So I smiled. "Sure. Looking forward to it."

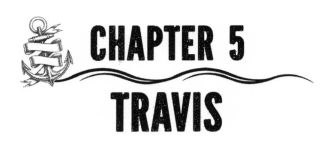

CHAPTER 5
TRAVIS

It still sometimes amused me—and on bad days, depressed me— how much our office resembled a normal, civilian environment instead of a military one. We even had cubicles, a watercooler, and the odd potluck for a birthday. If not for the uniforms and the framed photos of our uppermost chain of command, it would be hard to tell us apart from a corporation.

Exactly what I'd had in mind when I went to the Academy.

But, hey, at least I still had a career. There'd been some talk of medically separating me back when I got hurt, and I sometimes felt like I had the Forced Medical Retirement of Damocles hanging over my head, so I couldn't complain. Even if I'd traded my wings for an office and hadn't worn my flight suit in way too long, I had a paycheck and benefits I couldn't get anywhere else. If that meant working under fluorescents in a boring, pastel office complete with motivational posters on the wall? Fine.

I carefully twisted and stretched, trying to work out some of the tightness in my back. At least it wasn't as bad as the other night. Kimber and I had even discussed me retiring yesterday, but just the thought of it made my skin crawl. The Navy made a lot of postcareer promises on paper, but I knew too many people who'd been screwed in practice. When we stopped being useful to the military, the tumble down the priority list could be quick.

So, even if staying in meant working at a desk and making myself run a mile and a half twice a year, it was a job. It was the closest thing I'd ever have to stability.

Shortly before lunch, I was on my way back to my office after a meeting, and passed through the shared area between the training and admin departments. Clint and three of his people were discussing something beside the whiteboard where they scheduled all of their classes.

A few feet away, some of my guys were hunched over someone's phone.

One laughed. "That's insane!"

"Right?" Lieutenant Bailey grinned. "It looks even better on a tablet, but still—check *this* shit out!"

The group with Clint craned their necks.

"What're you guys watching?" one asked.

"Someone got a video of a terrorist training camp eating shit during an airstrike." Bailey turned his phone toward Clint and the others.

Clint grimaced and turned away a split second before the *thump-boom!* came from the phone.

"Aloha snack bar, motherfuckers!" Bailey said, and the group burst out laughing.

Except for Clint. And the petty officer standing next to him who looked like he was about to break a sweat. Or throw up. Maybe both.

"Lieutenant Bailey," I said. "Don't you have work to do?"

The red-faced lieutenant shoved his phone into his pocket as the others quickly dispersed. "Sorry, sir."

I turned toward Clint. The petty officer was still a bit green, but Clint had a hand on his shoulder and looked him right in the eye.

"You okay?" he asked in a quiet voice.

The poor kid nodded. "I'm good. Just, uh, wasn't expecting . . . um . . ."

"Why don't you go wrap this up?" Clint pushed a folder into the kid's hands. "Use my office if you need to."

The petty officer swallowed hard and nodded again. "Thank you, sir." With that, he hurried toward Clint's office, probably grateful for the escape and a moment to himself.

Clint met my gaze.

I raised my eyebrows. *You okay?*

He nodded subtly.

"All right." I looked around at the rest of the guys, who were watching me uneasily like some kids who'd been busted fucking off at school. "Everybody get back to work. And Lieutenant—could I see you for a minute?"

"Yes, sir," he muttered.

I shut my office door behind us, cutting off the muffled snickering from his coworkers, and faced him. Leaning against my desk, I folded my hands in front of me. "Listen, if you guys want to share that shit with each other on your own time and your own equipment, be my guest. But let's not pass it around here, all right?"

"They asked to see it, sir. I was—"

"Yes, I realize that. I was there. But LC Fraser and Petty Officer Vincent obviously don't enjoy watching or listening to—"

"What?" He laughed and gestured over his shoulder. "Fraser was a *drone* pilot. He used to do that shit, so what's he got to be—"

"It doesn't matter." I hardened my voice, hoping he caught the warning in my tone that I wasn't going to stay civil and calm for much longer. "It might just be that he doesn't enjoy watching footage of people being blown up. I don't care for it myself, and neither do some of the other people in the building."

Bailey scowled.

I resisted the urge to sigh with frustration. Sometimes, it was like trying to keep kids in line. "Listen, you don't object to the policy of not slamming doors in the office, right?" I inclined my head. "Since you know damn well that can fuck with someone who's been to a combat zone?"

Bailey shifted his weight. "We're just having a little—"

"Let me rephrase that, *Lieutenant*." I looked him in the eye. "No more of that shit in my department, and it's not up for discussion. That's an order."

He stiffened a little, and nodded. "Yes, sir. Sorry, sir."

"Dismissed," I said through my teeth.

He gave another nod and left my office. After the door shut, I rolled my eyes and wiped a hand over my face. Sometimes the kinder, gentler Navy tried the hell out of my patience. I didn't mind seeing some of the abusive disciplinary methods go by the wayside, along with a lot of the hazing that happened in the name of tradition, but there were days when the old Navy really appealed. Like when I wanted to drag someone into my office, get in their face, and scream at them until their vocabulary was reduced to *yes, sir* and *sorry, sir* and *won't happen again, sir*. When I didn't want to explain myself or make an attempt to reason with the subordinates who, a decade or so ago, wouldn't have even *thought* about questioning a superior officer.

Cursing under my breath, I went around the desk and eased myself into my chair.

As I downloaded my overstuffed inbox, I glanced at the door the lieutenant had gone through. The military's old model had been effective in its own way, but it *had* been a hot mess too. Screaming in someone's face and finding out a moment too late they were irreparably traumatized by something that had happened on the battlefield six months ago—that didn't do anyone any good. And cultivating a reputation as a leader who screamed in his people's faces and ruled with an iron fist was a good way to intimidate subordinates into being afraid to approach him when they needed to. I'd learned that a few years ago from a close friend who'd lost a lieutenant commander to suicide.

Sighing, I faced my screen again and started working my way through emails. I wasn't crazy about coddling my subordinates, but if it got results and didn't alienate me from my people, then fine.

But just let *me bust you doing it again, Lieutenant* . . .

The workday finally ended, and the video incident had been more or less forgotten. I didn't see Lieutenant Bailey even looking at his phone. I'd passed the petty officer in the halls a few times, and especially toward the end of the day, he'd seemed to be back to normal. I had no doubt Clint was keeping an eye on him, so I didn't approach him about it. And for that matter, Clint had returned to his usual self as well. When we crossed paths, he smiled before continuing on his way.

Good. Most of the people in this building, including some of the civilian contractors, had been to combat at some point, which meant there was plenty of PTSD. It was more obvious in some people than others. Like Lieutenant Commanders Stevenson and Norris, who were the reasons every door was marked *Please Don't Slam*.

Or Chief Radford on the third floor who'd had a violent flashback after a bookshelf in the office adjacent to hers had been shoved too hard into a shared wall. Or the time it had taken several people a good five minutes to catch their breath after a seagull had crashed into a meeting-room window.

The last thing anyone in here needed was some idiots who thought it was fun to watch footage of air strikes and sniper kills. Most of the time, if they were watching anything on their phones or computers, it was cat videos or song parodies. I was willing to let that go as long as work was getting done. One more combat video, and I'd ban electronics from the office so fast all their heads would spin.

But everyone seemed to have gotten the message, and Clint and his guy were all right. Hopefully this would be the end of it.

Now that the day was through, I shut off my computer and headed out to join everyone at the officers' club on the other side of the base. As I walked in, there were a few guys from base security milling around, but they didn't seem to be there in any official capacity. They were fucking off on their phones, talking about a recent football game—they'd probably come here for a late lunch, not to respond to any kind of disturbance. On my way past, they all murmured, "Good afternoon, sir." No one saluted since we were indoors and not wearing our covers, but I responded with a nod and, "Good afternoon."

It was still kind of weird to see enlisted personnel hanging out at the officers' club instead of their own enlisted club, which was across the street. Times had changed, though. Like a lot of bases, the E club and O club here on NAS Adams were open to everyone unless there was a special event, which would be exclusively officer or enlisted. And I couldn't begrudge them for coming here—the food *was* pretty fucking amazing.

When I walked into the lounge, about half the people from my department were there along with several from Clint's—including him—and had taken over a table in the corner. Most had beers, but two or three had nonalcoholic drinks. We did this often enough that I trusted them all to make their own designated-driver arrangements. That, and one of the first things I told a new check-in was, "If I ever get called in front of the CO because you got busted for DUI, you'll regret the day you ever thought to join the Navy." They all seemed to take that warning seriously—in twenty years, I'd only ever had one subordinate nailed for DUI—so while I kept an eye on them when we went out, I didn't worry too much.

I swung by the bar to get a beer for myself, then joined them.

Surprise, surprise—as I sat down, they were in the middle of giving someone a hard time. If I'd learned one thing about people— especially guys—in the military, regardless of rank, it was that they were all constantly on the prowl for a reason to bust someone's balls.

The current lucky winner was, ironically, Lieutenant Bailey.

"Look," Stevenson said with a smirk, "all I'm saying is, if you can park a C-130, you can park an F-150."

Wolcott chuckled behind his beer. "Maybe the difference is he had a copilot back then."

"Hey!" Bailey rolled his eyes. "I told you guys—Chief Hanson's giant fucking SUV was over the line. I had to park over the *other* line so I'd have room." He brought his mostly empty glass up to his lips. "Gimme a break, assholes."

"Uh-huh. Totally makes sense." Norris nodded. Then he held up a finger. "Oh, except for the part where Chief Hanson's been on leave since Tuesday."

Bailey winced, defeated, and everyone burst out laughing. They all clapped his shoulders and sent him up to the bar for more beer. It was a form of the walk of shame among my guys—you hadn't truly conceded until you'd bought the next round. Poor son of a bitch. He'd probably have everything from driver's ed booklets to fake parking tickets under his wiper blades for the next month or two.

Before he'd even come back, they'd shifted their sights to Ensign Lee, ribbing him about all the bumper stickers on his wife's Jeep, which he was driving this week. I was honestly surprised he hadn't rented a car instead. Pricey, but better than letting this group catch him in a vehicle that proclaimed *No, This Is Not My Boyfriend's Jeep* and *Silly Boys, Jeeps Are For Girls*.

As Bailey returned to the table with two pitchers of beer, he joined right in, probably happy to have their focus on someone else. In five minutes, Lee's ride would be forgotten too.

I laughed and rolled my eyes. The group was mostly good-natured about it. If someone was really bothered, they always backed off. At least when I was around.

While they bantered and carried on, I tried to look anywhere but right at Clint. The last thing I needed was for the guys to catch on that I was checking him out. Again. Still. Whatever. It had taken them weeks to let me hear the end of it when I'd been caught taking a long, appreciative look at Admiral Young's ass last year. It would probably be years before I heard someone say "Rear Admiral," and didn't want to crawl under a desk and die. Assholes.

I couldn't help myself, though, and stole a few glances at Clint, and not just to check him out. Every time someone came out with another story to one-up the last, he seemed less comfortable. He shifted. Stared into his glass. Chased ice cubes with his straw.

I bristled whenever someone looked his way. This was his first time hanging out with the group, so maybe they'd go easy on him. They would if they knew what was good for them.

Or maybe not.

"Hey, Fraser." Bailey reached for his beer. "You're a drone pilot, aren't you?"

Clint squirmed, looking about as thrilled as he had over the video earlier. "I was, yeah."

"Was?" Norris said. "So why don't you fly anymore?"

I couldn't decide if the hint of sarcasm on *fly* was real or in my imagination. In the past, I'd joined in with ribbing the drone pilots about all the G-forces they must've sustained in their cushy desk chairs, or how many times they could eject before they were grounded, but only when I was with feisty drone fliers who gave as good as they got.

Clint was on edge already, and the question from Norris was obviously not helping. He tapped his nails on his glass. "Oh. Well, you know how it is." He laughed, and it sounded forced. "Decided I was bored with that game and wanted to play *Call of Duty* instead."

The guys cracked up, and Clint chuckled, but when his eyes darted toward me, his expression said nothing if not *get me out of here*. And I was the one who'd invited him here in the first place.

Way to go, Wilson.

I stood. "All right, you idiots behave. I'm going out for a smoke." I met his eyes, tilted my head toward the door, and raised my eyebrows.

Clint held my gaze, then rose. "Mind if I join you?"

Please do. I smiled. "Sure."

We went outside onto the deserted, tree-shaded patio, which overlooked the gently sloping hill that led down to the golf course between here and the flight line. At the edge of the patio, as far from the door as we could get, I sat on one of the picnic tables and lit up a cigarette.

Clint sat on the other table, forearms resting on his knees and fingers dangling between them. "So did you just take up smoking or something? Because I swear I've never seen you take a cigarette break."

"I only smoke when I drink." I brought the cigarette up to take a drag. "Or when I see a shipmate who obviously needs a break."

His face colored. He quickly looked out at the golf course. "Thanks. I, uh . . . appreciate it."

"Don't worry about it. And listen." I pulled in some smoke and breathed it out. "Sorry about the rest of the guys. They're just hotheads who like shit-talking."

"Yeah, I know." Clint laughed with a touch more feeling this time. "This isn't my first base."

"No, of course not. But after the video, and—"

"It's all right." He smiled. "Honestly. It's all right. I guess I'm not a fan of . . ."

"Sea stories?"

"Air stories." He turned toward to me. "Can't really add much, you know? I flew drones." Something about the self-deprecating comment didn't land quite right. It was like there was an undercurrent, an unspoken plea for me to read between the lines and not push for details.

"I don't blame you." I tapped my cigarette. "When you're off work, the last thing you want to talk about is work, am I right?"

Another laugh, this one sounding like more relief than humor. "Yeah. Exactly. And hey, this morning . . . you didn't read Lieutenant Bailey the riot act or anything, did you?"

I shook my head and blew out some smoke. "Nah. I asked him to keep stuff like that out of the office. He does it again, *then* I'll read him the riot act."

"Thanks." Clint didn't look at me. "I don't think they meant any harm."

"No, of course not." I tapped my cigarette over the ashtray, then took another drag. "He's never been anywhere near combat, though. It's hard to imagine how much a video can affect someone when all you've done is float around the Pacific on an aircraft carrier."

Clint nodded slowly. "True. They're lucky. For their sake"—he shifted his gaze back to me—"I hope they don't ever see combat."

"Agreed. Would be nice if no one did, but . . ."

"Yeah. It'd be nice."

Neither of us spoke while I finished my cigarette. Odds were, I would never see combat again. I would be medically disqualified before the ink was even dry on my orders. Clint . . . it was hard to say. I didn't know his history, why he was no longer a drone pilot when manning was so critically low in that field, or why a video of an airstrike would fuck him up like that. Physically, he seemed okay, and the military was not at all above sending in soldiers who already had combat-related PTSD, so if the Navy started deploying ground troops again . . .

I banished the thought. I didn't want to think about him or anyone else going over there.

We sat in silence for a long moment. I debated smoking another cigarette if only to give as an excuse to stay out here, but he glanced at his watch and sighed. "I should probably head home."

Disappointment tugged at my gut, and I looked at my own watch. "Yeah, I guess it's getting late."

He rose. "Hopefully Keller doesn't mind me prying him away from the crowd."

"What? Why?"

"We drove in together this morning. He lives in my building, so we carpool."

"Oh. Well . . ." I hesitated. "If you want, I can drive you home. After the other night, I think I owe you a ride." The instant the words were out, I cringed. "I mean, I owe you—"

"I know what you meant." Clint chuckled. "Sure. I'm not gonna say no."

I could have gone inside and kissed Ensign Keller for driving in with Clint. I played it cool, though, and stood. "All right. Shall we go in and settle up?"

After we'd taken care of our tabs—all of about four bucks for Clint, since he didn't drink—we let everyone know we were leaving.

"See you guys in the morning." I wagged a finger at the group. "Don't burn the place down or anything, all right?"

"Burn it down?" Bailey laughed, swinging his beer wide enough he almost dumped it down Stevenson's front. "Come on. You know that shit only happens when you're here."

"Which means it's definitely a good time for me to leave." I turned to Clint. "Ready?"

He smiled, not possibly knowing how much that fucked with my blood pressure. "Whenever you are."

"Let's roll."

As we headed out to my car, an unfamiliar fluttery feeling rose in my chest. Glancing at Clint only made it worse. Better? More intense, anyway.

Bizarre. Was I . . .

Giddy?

CHAPTER 6
CLINT

As Travis drove through the gate and off the base, I sent up a prayer of thanks that on the day he'd offered me a ride home, it had been Keller's day to drive. Perfect. Even if I had no idea what to say or what might happen, I wasn't about to say no to some more time alone with Travis, and my lack of a car gave me the perfect excuse.

Pity I couldn't muster up much conversation. It was just as well Travis was driving too. I would've been all over the road, and I hadn't even had a drop to drink. Stone-cold sober and I barely had the brainpower to give him the stupid easy directions to my apartment.

Way to take advantage of having him alone.

With less than a mile to go, I said, "Thanks again for the lift."

"Don't mention it." He smiled. "Like I said, you got me and my kid home the other night, so I owed you one."

Right. Returning a favor. Don't read anything into it.

"Eh, I think we're even after you bailed me out back at the club."

Travis laughed. "Not really. I probably should've warned you about that when I asked you to come tonight."

"It wasn't like it was much of a shock. I do work around them, remember?"

"True. True." He tapped his thumbs on the wheel like he was nervous or something. "Still, I could've at least given you a heads-up that once they get some beer in them, they—"

"It's okay. Really. I've been in the Navy for eighteen years. I know how it all works."

He glanced at me, his forehead creased and eyebrows knitted together, but he relaxed a bit as he faced the road again. We drove in silence for a few blocks. Then he rested a hand on top of the wheel and his other arm on the console and, gaze fixed on the road, he said, "So I'm curious about something."

Please, please *don't ask why I don't fly drones anymore.* "Sure."

"Why did you come back the other night? To the Navy Ball?"

My throat tightened. "Uh . . ."

"I'm just curious. You and your date hightailed it out of there, so I guess I was surprised to see you come back. Especially . . ." he hesitated, "alone."

"Well." I muffled a cough. "I needed to get him home. And leave him there. After that, I guess I . . ." Heat rushed into my cheeks. "I mean, it . . ." I gestured up ahead on the left. "Oh. This is the place."

"Here?"

"Yeah."

He put on his signal and turned into the lot, and I hoped the momentary interruption was enough to make us both forget what we'd been talking about.

"Should I, uh . . ." His eyes flicked toward me. "Should I park, or—"

"Just take one of those." I pointed at the guest spots near the entrance.

Travis turned into one, but left the engine idling. For a moment, neither of us spoke.

"So . . ." I gulped. "Thanks for the ride. The lift."

He chuckled. "Don't mention it. Thanks again for the other night." He winced. "Getting us home, I mean."

"I know what you meant." I went to unbuckle my seat belt, but didn't, as if it were all that was keeping me from jumping out of the car and putting some breathing room between us. "Anyway, I appreciate the— I guess I'll see you at work tomorrow."

"Yeah. I mean . . ." He focused on something in front of the car. "Yeah. Yeah, I'll see you at work." Hesitantly, maybe even a bit cautiously, he turned to me. I wondered if his heart was thumping like mine was. He said nothing, but I swore I could feel the unspoken *you didn't answer my question.*

The humming engine emphasized the silence between us, and my inability to look him in the eye only made his gentle scrutiny that much harder to ignore.

Finally, I couldn't take anymore.

"There's, uh . . ." Whoa, my heart really was going crazy. "Can I confess something?"

Travis inclined his head. "If it's the whereabouts of Captain Rodriguez's tape dispenser, I don't want to lose my plausible deniability."

I laughed for real, which helped me calm down. Sort of. Got me breathing, anyway. "If I knew, I wouldn't tell you."

"Good. So . . ." His eyebrow arched. "What's your confession?"

"Well." I exhaled. "Okay, you know what? I'll just put it out there. The other night, when I left and then came back to the Navy Ball . . ." I stared out the windshield.

Travis watched me. He didn't say a word, and somehow the silence was worse than if he'd prodded me.

Finally, I shook my head. "I'll be honest—I hate those things. It's like prom for adults."

Travis laughed. "Me too. They're awful."

"But you went?"

He shrugged. "My daughter wanted to go." He studied me. "And you went too."

"Yeah." I focused on the building ahead of us again. "Yeah, I . . ." Oh hell. No point in dancing around the topic, was there? "I brought Logan because I wanted to come out. To the command. Put it out there that I have—had a boyfriend." I covered my face with both hands and muttered, "God, it sounds so stupid now."

"But mission accomplished, right?"

"Something like that." I pressed my thumb and forefinger into the bridge of my nose. "And instead of getting it off my chest and being out, I realized our relationship was a disaster." I closed my eyes and sighed. "What I should have— Christ, I was such a fucking idiot. I could've just come out, you know? Mentioned him. Not made such a big deal out of it."

"I don't think you really made a big deal out of it. You showed up with a guy like it was perfectly normal. Since, you know, it *is* perfectly normal."

Said the man who probably hadn't been looking down the barrel of forty the first time he'd had sex with a man. Maybe all this was normal for him. Or even for this command. For me? Not so much.

I lowered my hand. "Well, it's done. I left early with him because we needed to end things and be done with it."

"You did look pretty miserable."

I nodded. "I was. So I cut him loose. I still feel like a dick for that, but the drinking, it . . ." I rubbed a hand over my face. "I couldn't cope with it anymore, you know?"

"But then you came back to the ball." That question. That still-unanswered question.

"I did."

"For a reason."

The question stubbornly hung in the air and wasn't moving. I'd brought up the subject with every intention of telling him exactly why I'd left and then come back, but now that we were knee-deep in the topic, I choked.

Travis turned off the ignition, and the engine shuddered once before falling silent. Now the quiet was *really* uncomfortable. "Clint."

Oh shit. We're still on a first-name basis, aren't we? Would this be different if you were still Commander Wilson?

I turned to him, wondering when my hands had started shaking.

He looked me right in the eye. "Why did you come back?" The question was gentle. Like he was coaxing the answer out of me, not interrogating me.

"I came back . . ." I took a deep breath. "For the same reason I went out with everyone tonight." I swallowed. "Because you were there."

He straightened slightly. "Is that right?"

"Yeah. I guess I wanted to talk to you more. After the conversation over dinner, and . . . I mean, I didn't even realize you were gay until—"

"Bi."

"Huh?"

"Bi." He smiled. "I'm bi. But go on."

"Right. Right. I didn't realize you were, uh, into men until that night. When you said something about taking a guy to a wedding."

Travis took off his seat belt. I jumped when it snapped back against the door. Again when he put his hand on my thigh. With the heat of his palm radiating through my camo pants, I thought I was going to go up in flames right then and there.

What the hell is happening?

"I mentioned that guy on purpose," Travis said softly. "For two reasons."

"Yeah?"

"Mm-hmm." His voice was even quieter now, forcing me to lean in to hear him. "One, so you'd know you weren't the only queer guy at the table. Or in the office, for that matter."

I glanced down at his hand on my leg. When I looked at him again, I swore he was even closer. Or had I moved closer? Whatever the case, there wasn't nearly as much air between us now.

"And—" I nearly choked on my own breath. "And the second reason?"

A grin that seemed equal parts sly and shy spread across his lips. "Because . . . Well, I wasn't going to make a move on a man with a boyfriend, even if you guys didn't seem too thrilled with each other, but I guess I might've been testing the water."

I would've laughed if I still remembered how to breathe. All the "you're kidding" and "seriously?" responses died at the tip of my tongue because the hand on my leg and the nearness of his lips made the answer pretty fucking obvious. And as he came in even closer, and my heart beat faster, and his fingers pressed into my leg, and—

"Wait, I—" He stiffened suddenly.

Damn it!

"What's wrong?" I asked.

"I, uh, had a cigarette earlier."

"I don't care."

"But . . ." He swept his tongue across his lips, which electrified my whole body.

I squirmed in my seat. *I don't care if you smoke. Just kiss me, damn it.*

His eyes flicked from mine to my lips. I wasn't sure if it was my heart pounding that hard, or if I could actually hear his, but somebody's pulse was going wild. And mine kept racing faster and faster as we hovered there, neither of us making a move to close the remaining distance.

To hell with it. I hadn't gotten anywhere in life by quietly waiting for someone else to make things happen, so I ignored my nerves, reached across the console, and kissed him.

Immediately, his arm went around me. I let him take the lead, and God, yes, he took it. His tongue gently parted my lips, and he deepened the kiss as if his nerves and hesitation had simply vanished. He wasn't too aggressive, but he damn sure knew what he wanted, and I let him explore my mouth like I explored his.

Yeah, I could taste the smoke, but it had been too damn long since I'd kissed a man who didn't taste like booze. And really, when *had* I ever kissed a man like this?

Fuck. Holy fuck. All those times when I'd wondered if I was really into men or just curious seemed ridiculous now. Of course I was attracted to men. Kissing Travis, running my hands all over his clothed body, breathing in his aftershave—oh yeah. I was into men. Especially this one.

He slid his hands up into my hair. Though my hair was short, he found enough of a handful to pull my head back.

Oh God. If you kiss my neck, I swear I'll—

Oh. Sweet. Jesus. Yes.

He kissed his way up and down my throat so eagerly, I thought he was going to sink his teeth in. And when he didn't, I was disappointed. What the hell? Fuck it. I loved what he was doing even if he didn't bite me.

"For the record," he said against my neck, "I am *really* glad you came back to the Navy Ball."

"Yeah," I panted. "Me too." I shivered, which made the seat belt dig into my hard-on. "You know, we might be more comfortable if we went inside."

Travis pulled back and looked at me. He swept his tongue across his lips and watched me do the same. For a split second, I was positive he was going to suggest we quit before we got in over our heads—*too late*—but instead, he grinned. "That sounds like a good idea to me."

We separated and got out of the car, and I couldn't help laughing when I caught him adjusting the front of his uniform as I was doing the same. God help me if any of my neighbors saw, but . . . hell, I didn't care.

We hurried up the walk, and I fumbled with my keys for a moment before finally getting the door unlocked. I managed to shut the door, and then Travis grabbed a handful of my shirt, pulled me in, and kissed me again.

Jesus. Fuck. *Yes.*

I hadn't realized until now how much the car had hindered us. In here, without its close confines or that stupid console between us, we were right up against each other—chest to chest, hands all over, even his knee sliding past mine and my boot between his.

We stumbled from the entryway to the kitchen. Bumped the counter. The stove. The fridge. Something fell, but it didn't sound important and I didn't hear any glass break, so it could wait.

At some point we came up for air, and we both needed it—I couldn't remember being this out of breath with someone. Funny how oxygen lost its importance with a skilled kisser like Travis.

"My God." He touched his forehead to mine. "This, uh, wasn't what I had in mind when I suggested giving you a lift home."

"Ditto. And I've, um . . ." I gulped. "Can't say I've ever done anything with someone I work with."

Travis's smile was gentle and playful at the same time. "I have." He combed his fingers through my hair. "It does have one unfortunate drawback."

My stomach somersaulted. "What's that?"

His smile turned to a grin, and his fingers curled against my scalp, drawing me in. "It'll make the work days go by *so much* slower." Then he kissed me again.

I could live with longer workdays, especially since we worked in the same building. I already spent a good portion of my time fantasizing about him—how much worse could it get if I knew those fantasies were real?

I gripped his belt, holding his hips against me so he could feel how hard I was. I loved aggressive kissing. *Loved* it. The way his hands were constantly on the move—running through my hair, sliding up and down my sides, curving over my ass—drove me wild.

"If it's not too forward," he said, lips barely leaving mine, "I would kill to see you naked right now."

Holy fuck. He was direct, and dirty, and . . . *dressed*. Why were we dressed?

"Well," I panted, "we could kick off these clothes and fuck right here in the kitchen, but I think a bed might be better."

"Like that idea. You do keep a bed somewhere here, don't you?"

"Last I checked, yeah." I lifted my head and brushed my lips across his. "Unless someone stole it while I was out."

"We should go check, then. You know . . . peace of mind and all."

"Screw peace of mind. I want a piece of *you*."

"Which means going to the same place you keep your bed, so . . ."

"Good point."

I led him down the hall. Halfway to the bedroom, though, he stopped and pinned me to the wall, and the way he kissed wound me up and made the bed seem that much farther away.

I pushed him back a step, took his hand, and led him the rest of the way to the bedroom. We stepped through the door, I flicked the light on, and immediately, Travis's arms were around me again.

"Look at that," I said against his lips. "Bed's still here."

"Good." When we kissed, his soft moan almost knocked my knees out from under me. "Bed can wait. I just . . . I can't . . ."

I kissed him, silencing him, and neither of us made any attempt to pull apart and continue on our way. Just needed to get to the bed, get these clothes off, and we could finally fuck each other, and—

I froze.

"Oh damn it."

He met my eyes. "What? What's wrong?"

"I just realized I'm out of condoms."

"Oh." He glanced toward the bed. A flicker of uneasiness crossed his expression, but then he looked at me again and shrugged. "Don't worry about it." He slid his hand over the front of my pants. "Plenty we can do without them." In fact, as he kissed me again, he seemed even more excited and less hesitant about what we were doing. No condoms, no problem.

Any disappointment I might've had evaporated then and there.

Our clothes, however, steadfastly refused to do the same. Fine. I started on his belt buckle, and he went for the buttons on my camo blouse. The buckle came open easily enough, but goddamn the Navy and their insistence on button fly pants instead of zippers. Normally I could have them open in a heartbeat, but when I was turned on, dizzy, out of breath, desperate to have Travis's hands on me? Christ, someone might as well have sewn in cipher locks and retina scanners.

"Fucking . . ." he growled softly, and a button on my shirt let go. Snapped off, maybe, but it could be sewn back on. Just . . . not now.

A second later, the last button on his trousers gave too. That one might've also snapped off. Whatever. I was one button closer to his skin. That was all I cared about.

Finally, we'd pushed enough clothes out of the way, and I closed my fingers around his thick erection. He groaned as he did the same to mine. Kissing. Panting. Stroking. Hadn't we just been coworkers earlier? Didn't matter—he was in my bedroom now, and he probably had no idea how many of my fantasies were all coming true at once.

I pressed him up against the wall, leaving barely enough room between our hips for our hands to move, and kissed him so hard I caught my lip between our teeth. It smarted, making my eyes water, and I broke the kiss, but Travis didn't miss a beat. He went right for my neck again. Shit. Soft lips and coarse five-o'clock shadow brushing my throat—so worth that momentary sting.

While he kissed from my jaw to my collarbone and back, I ran my hands all over him. His body was . . . *fuck*, he was hot. I hadn't even seen him naked—yet—but feeling his narrow waist and powerful shoulders while I stroked him with the other was driving me insane.

Abruptly, he turned me around, and now I was the one backed up against the wall. He kissed me, nudged my hand away from his cock, and then murmured, "Don't move."

"Don't—"

Just like that, he was on his knees, and my dick was between his lips, and moving wasn't an option anymore.

I blinked my tear-blurred eyes into focus, and . . . God in heaven. The sight of Travis like that—kneeling in a half-removed blue digicam uniform with a hand on my hip and the other steadying my cock as he took me into his mouth again and again—was insane. There was hot, there was sexy, and there was *this*.

He'd told me not to move, but I assumed that meant not to move *away*. Which meant rocking my hips was still fair game. And, hell, even if he hadn't meant it that way, I wasn't sure I could've stayed still if I'd tried. All I wanted was to fuck his talented mouth, and oh yes, he was complementing my motions perfectly. Complementing me and urging me on until I must've been pushing his gag reflex, and he egged me on anyway.

"*Shit.*" I clawed at the walls as if I might find something to hold on to. He didn't let up. His tongue teased every nerve ending from the base of my cock to the tip, and then he moaned like he was as turned on as I was, and the mere thought of reciprocating—the thought of him fucking my mouth like I was fucking his—sent a shudder right through me, curling my toes inside my boots.

A flash of panic surged through me as I remembered people before him saying, "Warn me before you come," and I had just enough presence of mind to groan, "Gonna come," and then there was no *gonna* about it.

My whole body jolted with the force of my orgasm. My knees forgot what they were doing, and only the wall kept me from collapsing. I distantly heard myself moaning and cursing. As I came back down, I was dizzy and delirious, the whole room spinning around me as the floor shifted under my feet. My throat was vaguely raw, like I'd cried out a lot louder than I'd realized.

Should probably slip apology notes into my neighbors' mailboxes tomorrow.

My own dumb thought made me laugh like I was drunk.

Travis rose, wincing slightly. "What's so funny?"

"Nothing. I . . ." I shook my head as I grabbed his belt and pulled him to me. "Nothing."

He must've accepted that, because he didn't resist when I kissed him.

His erection pressed against my hip. Oh, that needed some attention, didn't it? Which meant it was my turn to get on my knees, and once my legs stopped trembling enough that I could trust them, I gently pushed him back and knelt at his feet.

Before I'd even taken his cock between my lips, his fingers were in my hair, sending goose bumps from my scalp down the length of my spine. He didn't use any force, didn't try to choke me, so I didn't mind the contact. And when I did start going to town on him, the way his fingers twitched whenever he moaned or shivered was incredibly hot.

We couldn't fuck tonight? No problem. I was more than content to listen to him swear and gasp while I sucked his cock.

"*Jesus*, you're good at that," he ground out, kneading my scalp. "Oh fuck, that's so good." His fingernails dug in, and he pulled enough to sting. If he did that while he was being blown, I could only imagine how much he'd do it while he was fucking or being fucked, and thinking about *that* damn near got me hard again. I stroked him faster and teased him relentlessly with my tongue, and he rewarded every motion—sometimes with a moan, sometimes a catch of his breath, sometimes a tighter grip on my hair.

"Oh shit," he breathed. He rocked his hips like I'd done earlier, pushing himself into my mouth. "You're gonna . . . Oh God, don't stop, don't . . ."

Stop? Not a chance. I gave him everything I had, ignoring the ache in my jaw and my elbow.

Then his breath caught.

His whole body tensed.

And, holy shit, if my orgasm hadn't disturbed the neighbors, his definitely did. I kept right on licking and stroking him so he'd be even louder—I loved, loved, *loved* the sounds he made as he came in my mouth.

I cannot wait *to hear what you sound like when we fuck.*

He shuddered one last time and gently nudged my forehead. I stopped, rocking back on my heels, and he looked down at me with the sexiest, most blissed-out grin I'd ever seen.

"I think . . ." He licked his lips and shivered again. "I think we might have to make a habit of this."

I rose. "I am completely on board with that."

"Good." He tugged me in by the belt loops. "Because you're fucking addictive." His kiss cut off any response I might've had, but hopefully the message came through loud and clear—*so are you.*

Eventually, we pulled apart, and finally, we unlaced our boots, kicked them off, and dropped the rest of our clothes on the floor. On our sides, facing each other in the middle of the bed, we kissed lazily. I ran my hands all over his skin, and for the longest time, we lay there, kissing occasionally while we enjoyed the afterglow. All the while, two orgasms and a million kisses into this, and I was still marveling that

Travis was naked beside me. He was even hotter in reality than he'd been in my fantasies too. He wasn't perfect—who was?—but he was gorgeous. The other night, I'd had a sneak peek at his narrow waist and broad shoulders thanks to the cut of his dress uniform, and they were not a disappointment on their own.

There were some scars on his chest and abs, and I was pretty sure I'd felt a few on his back. Hard to say where they'd come from—I guessed either from surgery or some nasty gashes that had been stitched—but the most surprising thing about seeing him naked was his lack of ink. It was rare to find someone, even an officer, who'd been in the military this long and didn't have at least one tattoo. One that usually came with a story that started with "Me and my buddies were in port and got shitfaced . . ."

I suspected the scars had some stories attached to them, but with someone in the military, things like that could be an emotional minefield. I'd leave it to him to open up about those.

After a while, Travis sat up, rolling his shoulders stiffly. "Damn. It's definitely getting late now." He turned to me with an apologetic grimace. "I should probably go."

"Okay." I sat up beside him. "I'll, um, see you at the office tomorrow?"

He smiled a little, nodded, and kissed me softly.

He was leaving? No, no, no. With his body against mine like this, I wasn't ready for him to get out of my bed. I met his gaze and licked my lips. "You don't have to leave *quite* yet, do you?"

"Well—"

I slid my hand over his naked thigh. He sucked in a sharp breath, closing his eyes as a shiver went through him. Mission accomplished.

"I could . . ." He swallowed, then looked at me. "I could probably stay awhile longer."

I grinned, moving my hand higher. "I'll make it worth your time."

Travis wrapped his arms around me, and just before he kissed me, murmured, "I don't doubt that in the slightest."

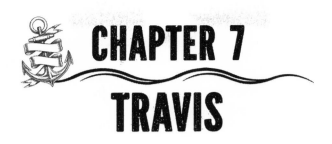

CHAPTER 7
TRAVIS

The next morning, I sent off some emails to my subordinates and long-winded, tedious reports to my upper chain of command. Same shit, different day.

The whole time, though, I was grinning like a fool. Normally, I'd be cursing under my breath and mentally putting hexes on the micromanaging assholes above me, but I let their stupidity slide today.

I hadn't seen Clint around the office yet, but that wasn't too surprising. It was only ten o'clock, and according to the whiteboard in the hall, he was teaching some early classes downstairs, so he wouldn't be around the office much before eleven or so. That was pretty normal, and probably not a bad thing if I had any hope of accomplishing anything today. We had lunch plans anyway, so I'd see him soon enough.

There was no such thing as soon enough, though. Now that I'd been in his bed, I couldn't get him out of my head. Okay, so I hadn't been able to get him out of my head anyway, but now he'd taken over completely.

Had all that really happened? I'd imagined the whole thing, right? It'd just been a dream—a good one, for once—that was so vivid and hot, I'd convinced myself it was real.

Except I could still feel enough to know it had been very, very real. My chin and throat were a little raw from some stubble burn. My lips were faintly tender after getting some long overdue attention, and giving some to Clint's cock. There was also some tightness between my shoulders that had started in the car outside his apartment. Twisting around in the seat so I could make out with him had been worth it in the moment—was still worth it in hindsight—but I was paying for it now.

I regret nothing.

That thought made me chuckle to myself. Like I was a teenager who should've felt guilty for sneaking off and parking with someone. No, nothing but a horny old dude who'd need a few extra Motrin today and had fortunately not forgotten his TENS unit.

As I adjusted the TENS unit's intensity for the hundredth time, my good spirits faded. Last night had been hot, but there was no mistaking that I'd gotten damn lucky. The planets had aligned, and when I'd gone to bed with Clint, my pain had been relatively mild. I'd also dodged a bullet—he'd been out of condoms, and I hadn't brought any. Anything beyond handjobs and blowjobs had been off the table. I was perfectly content with that much anyway, but it was always a gamble with a new guy.

A lot of guys could take or leave anal, and I'd been with a few of them. But even those who were indifferent about it—or outright hated it—didn't usually stick around after the "I can't do it" conversation. That always seemed to be the moment they realized sex with me meant a whole lot of limitations. No getting rough. No throwing each other around. No swinging from the chandeliers or trying out crazy sixty-nine positions.

Anal, they could do without. Realizing we'd be fooling around on eggshells because of my back?

"I need more than this."

"I'm always afraid I'll hurt you, so it's not fun for me."

"Man, I'm sorry—it's boring!"

I sighed, absently thumbing the dial on the TENS controller. Last night, Clint had shrugged things off and seemed satisfied with what we'd done. Question was, how long could the novelty of someone new gloss over anything that was lacking? How many nights could I stretch that novelty before Clint decided I was more trouble than I was worth? What would he think when he realized that one-time restriction was actually this time, every time, and any time we touched in the future?

I shook my head and shifted my attention to some of the work I'd been ignoring all morning. Tried to, anyway. I just couldn't shake the worry—the certainty—that Clint was in for a disappointment when we made it into the bedroom a second time.

At least we'd had some of that painfully sexy kissing and frantic dick-sucking. Even if that was as far as things ever went, I could live with it. And if we continued hooking up . . . well, I hoped his expectations weren't too high.

Guess I'll find out, won't I?

Classes must've ended, because the activity outside my door was steadily ramping up. Boots on the floor. People talking. I could always tell when the instructors had come back from teaching because even the most soft-spoken among them couldn't seem to shut off the "teacher voice." Normally, that annoyed the shit out of me. Nothing made me feel like I was running a daycare more than having to remind grown-ass adults to use their inside voices.

Today, it didn't bother me.

Because Clint was one of them.

And every time I heard him outside my office, I forgot what I was doing. Which also should have annoyed me, but I couldn't help grinning whenever I broke out in goose bumps at the sound of his voice. If anything, I wanted to call him into my office, shut the door, and make him do something about this hard-on that he was completely responsible for.

Someone knocked at my door.

"Come in."

When it opened . . .

Ah, speak of the Devil.

"Hey." His eyes met mine, and no, I had not imagined last night any more than I was imagining that playful, mischievous gleam. "You busy?"

Busy doing absolutely nothing except thinking about what you look like naked.

I cleared my throat. "No, come on in."

As he closed my office door behind him, I got up and came around my desk. "You do know that being in here behind closed doors is tempting as all hell, right?"

"I do." He stepped closer and grinned as he reached for my waist. "Why do you think I closed the door?"

"You devious bastard."

"Mm-hmm." And with that, he kissed me. We both stumbled a bit, but he pushed me up against my desk and held me there. In the short time that I'd known him, Clint had struck me as being on the shy side, so this boldness was amazingly sexy. Yesterday he'd gone from barely being able to look me in the eye to pulling me into a kiss in the car. Today he'd come into my office, and now he was kissing me like there was absolutely no reason not to.

And as I ran my fingers through his hair and cupped his ass with my other hand, I couldn't think of one.

Outside, some voices and footsteps went by, and we both glanced toward the door. When he looked at me again, Clint asked, "Think anyone's caught on?"

I laughed and squeezed his ass. "Well, we did leave the O Club together, but no one's said a word to me."

"Me neither."

"What they don't know . . ."

"Mm-hmm." He kissed me again, rubbing his hard-on against my hip. Abruptly, though, he tensed up. Didn't stop, but definitely tensed up. "I should go," he murmured between kisses. "Got . . . some more classes . . ."

"Me too." I tugged his hair back and kissed his neck. "We still on for lunch?"

"Are you kidding? Of course we are."

"I would hope so." I nipped his neck, then lifted my head. "You have any plans for tonight?"

"I think I just made some."

"Good."

"My place?"

"Hell yeah."

"Perfect." He paused. "Jesus, this is all I've been able to think about since last night."

My knees wobbled. "Me too." I met his gaze and struggled to catch my breath.

He licked his lips. "In fact, forget lunch."

My heart stopped. "Huh?"

"If we both work through lunch, we can bust out of here early." His filthy grin fucked with my equilibrium. "Then we've got the whole evening."

"Oh, I like the way you think." I ran my hands along his belt. "But . . . right now . . ."

"You've got classes . . ."

"They can wait." He hesitated. "Except I should still . . ."

"We should . . ."

I kissed him, and *should* didn't really matter anymore. He kept me pinned against the desk, and I held on to his blouse to keep him from going anywhere. This was too hot to stop, so . . . to hell with it. And as a bonus, my back was still behaving. With a little luck, that wouldn't change. I did not need that bucket of cold water when I had my hands all over Clint.

I pulled Clint closer and ran my boot up the inside of his leg.

"Keep that up," he growled, "and we're not going to get out of here."

"That right?"

"Mm-hmm." He put his hands on my thighs and leaned down until his lips almost met mine. "Not that I mind. I *am* kind of curious to see what happens if we get stuck here."

"You dirty bastard." Still holding the front of his uniform, I pulled him down and myself up, and my lips grazed his as I murmured, "We should definitely get out of here."

"I agree." And he kissed me.

I sat up, tilting my head and parting my lips as I slid my hand around the back of his neck.

Back—stay happy.

Coworkers—stay out.

Or at least knock. Please, for the love of God, don't let this be the day they forget to knock.

I drew him down so I could kiss his neck.

"Let's go," he whispered breathlessly. "We should . . . somewhere . . ."

"Why not here?" Gripping his blouse tighter, I nibbled his earlobe. "No one else is here."

"No, but . . ." He moaned softly and curved a hand over my hip. "Beds are a lot more comfortable."

"Hmm. Good point. And there aren't any beds *here*."

"Exactly. So maybe we should get out of here, then. Go someplace private." His erection rubbed against mine. "Go where I can see you." He turned his head, and our lips brushed as he murmured "naked" just before he claimed a deep kiss.

I shivered and held him tighter. It was so tempting to blow off work and go somewhere I could blow *him*. Not that we were getting anywhere with the whole "getting out of here" thing anyway. Or the "not doing this at work" thing. With fingers that weren't as dexterous as they normally were, I opened the first two buttons of his uniform, but then forgot what I was doing and shifted all my attention to making out with him instead. "For the record, I don't usually do shit like this at work."

"Usually?" He eyed me. "So it's not the first time?"

A memory flashed through my mind that threatened to kill the mood in a hurry, but I tamped it down and grinned. "You could say that." I skated my lips down his neck.

He shivered. "God, I want you." That hungry, hoarse whisper made my whole body break out in goose bumps. "Tonight? It's fucking *on*."

"Gonna hold you to that."

"Please do." Somehow, as we kept kissing and groping each other, he made it past my button fly, and his hand on my cock took my breath away. He exhaled sharply through his nose, as if touching me turned him on as much as it did me, and the way he stroked me said this was going to be *very* fast and *very* hot. Not that I was objecting.

"Gonna . . . make me come on my uniform." I gasped for breath. "And yours."

The gleam in his eyes told me that was definitely an option right then. All we had to do was lock the door and go for it.

And fifteen or even ten years ago, I would have gone for it, never mind the consequences. But . . . if a subordinate knocked. If someone heard.

The same concerns seemed to cross Clint's mind. He drew back, and the wild eagerness seemed to wane in favor of self-control. Maybe

RAPs and fighter pilots had more in common than we'd realized. "Maybe not now," I said.

"Yeah." He glanced back at the door. "Probably . . . not a good idea."

"But a hot one." I kissed him lightly, and we both fixed our uniforms. "This what you had in mind when you came back to the ball the other night?"

"It . . ." He blushed. "It crossed my mind, yes."

"Good. Then we're on the same page."

He threw another glance toward the door. "As long as, uh, nobody catches on."

"I don't think they will. The old training supervisor came into my office all the time, so no one would be surprised if you do."

"That's true." He paused, chewing his lip. "Think we should keep this on the down-low at work, though?"

I shrugged. "I don't think we should necessarily advertise it, but I don't really care if anyone knows. Unless you do."

"Not really. We're not in the same chain of command, so it won't affect anything."

"Wouldn't be the first time people in our building dated, either." I smiled. "And hey, we're both out, so it won't be a big shock."

Clint laughed uneasily. "That's true." He cringed. "God, I still feel like an idiot for showing up the other night with Logan."

"But it's done." I brought his hand up and kissed the backs of his fingers. "And hey, if you hadn't . . ."

Our eyes met. After a moment, he relaxed and finally smiled. "Guess it was worth it, wasn't it?"

"Well." I wrapped my arms around him. "I happen to think so."

"Yeah, I'm leaning that way myself." He kissed me. "And I really had better get back to work before we end up leaning over your desk."

"Good point." One more kiss, and I gently nudged him back. "All right. Back to work." With a wink, I added, "I'll see you tonight."

"Looking forward to it."

We exchanged grins, and then he was gone. Oh yes. Tonight was going to be amazing.

And while I was thinking about it, I texted Kimber to let her know I wouldn't be home tonight. Even if I didn't stay over at Clint's—and

I likely wouldn't—it was better to let her assume she wouldn't see me until tomorrow. And as much as she probably didn't need to think about her dad dating, or what "not coming home tonight" meant, she'd assured me a long time ago that some TMI was better than the alternative.

She texted back, *K. See you tomorrow.*

Will you be ok tonight?

Dad, I'm 22. And I have the Netflix password.

I chuckled and started to relax. She was an adult, and she'd been in a pretty good state of mind recently. I fully intended to keep it that way.

With her evening taken care of, my own mind shifted toward my own. Behind closed doors with Clint? Knowing he wanted this as much as I did?

Oh yes.

I am so ready for tonight.

Bring it on, Clint.

CHAPTER 8
CLINT

Thanks to skipping lunch, I was able to slip out of the office around four thirty. Travis was held up for a while because he had a meeting with the CO, but about ten minutes before I got home, he texted me to let me know he was on his way.

While I waited for him, I couldn't sit still. I'd showered and changed into a pair of jeans and a T-shirt, and now all there was to do was wait. And wait. And try to keep myself calm and cool.

Why isn't he here yet? He should've been here five minutes ago.

Did he remember how to get here? Wait, I'd given him my address, and his car had GPS. He'd find the place. Right? Did I need to text him with my apartment number?

What the hell is wrong with me?

And then . . .

Footsteps on the walkway.

The distinct sound of boots.

Fuck yes.

I opened the door right as he stepped onto the porch. Neither of us said a word. He hooked his fingers in my waistband and pulled me in close, and we were back in each other's arms. We kissed. Stumbled. Somehow made it off the porch and into the apartment without falling on our asses, and I was so tangled up in him, I couldn't even remember for sure if we'd closed the door.

I opened my eyes briefly. Glanced past him.

Yep. Door was closed.

Where were we?

I cradled the back of his head and kissed him even harder.

"Sorry I took so long," he panted against my lips. "Fucking traffic through the gate."

"'S'okay. You made it."

"Finally."

"Mm-hmm."

His hands slid across my bare skin, emphasizing how dressed he still was. That wouldn't do. This uniform needed to be on the floor right now.

He must've had the same idea, because we both started fumbling with buttons. One by one, they gave. I pushed the blouse off his shoulders.

"By the way," I said as I ran my hands up the front of his snug T-shirt, "one more hour at work, and I would've run out of military bearing."

"You and me both," he said between kisses, and slid his hands down over my ass. "Today was killing me. Even before you showed up in my office."

"Tell me about it." I started kissing my way down his neck. "You didn't have to stand up in front of a class and try not to get a hard-on."

He laughed, tilting his head to the side as I inched toward his collarbone. "Maybe I should've teased you a bit more."

"That wouldn't have been a good idea." I bit his shoulder through his clothes, and he responded with the most delicious groan.

"Not a good idea?" He pressed against my dick. "Why not? What would've happened?"

"All kinds of . . . court-martial-worthy . . . offenses." I groaned softly. "On government property."

"More than what we already did?"

"So much more."

"Hmm. Scandalous." He dipped his head and kissed my neck. "Might have to step up my game at work. See what happens when you lose all your—"

"Don't you dare," I growled.

"Or what?"

"I'll tell the CO." I curved my hands over his ass. "Tell her you seduced me in my office." I kissed beneath his jaw and murmured, "Tell her I was . . . helpless to resist . . . your charm."

We both broke out laughing.

"Go ahead and tell her," he said. "I won't deny it."

"Shameless bastard."

"You better believe it." He gripped the back of my neck and kissed me even harder, and I melted against him. Fuck, I hadn't wanted a man this bad in a long time. And why the hell did the Navy insist on so many buttons?

Whatever. I managed to get them open, and finally—after fantasizing about him all damned day—I had his very hard cock in my hand.

As he nibbled my neck and I stroked his dick, he whimpered softly. "Jesus . . ."

"Been thinking about this all day," I said.

"M-me too." He nipped above my collar. "Now you're gonna make me . . . gonna . . . fuck, I'm gonna come on your clothes."

We weren't at work anymore, so I pumped his dick faster and grinned. "Damn right you are."

He moaned, fucking into my fist.

"One of these days," I panted as he fell apart in my arms, "I'm gonna get you naked before I start getting you off."

His fingers tightened on my shoulders. "Fuck . . ."

"But every time I get near you, I just can't stop."

A low groan turned to a helpless whimper, and he shuddered in the same moment his nails bit in through my shirt, and a second later, his whole body jerked, and suddenly my hand was slick and hot, and I stroked him even faster as he swore and gasped and trembled between me and the wall.

"Jesus Christ," he breathed, sagging against the wall. "I've been needing that all damn day."

"You and me both." I leaned in and kissed under his jaw. "I hope you're not done yet."

He laughed. "Done? We're not even naked yet."

"Hmm, you're right. We should do something about that."

"Yes, we should." Still out of breath, he unbuckled my belt. I tugged his shirt free and started to push it up and off, but as I did, my finger snagged briefly on one of the wires he had on that box he always carried.

"Shit." I froze. "Am I— Did I—"

"It's fine. It's fine." He peeled his shirt the rest of the way off, then disconnected the wires from the pads, and put the box and wires in his pocket. "There. Now it's out of the way."

"But is—"

He cut me off with a deep, desperate kiss that could only mean stopping was absolutely out of the question, so I took his word for it and wrapped my arms around him. Jesus—his skin was hot under my hands, and his body heat radiated through my shirt.

I broke the kiss with a breathless "Need to get this off."

Travis didn't miss a beat. Between us, we pulled off my T-shirt, and then we were skin to skin all the way down to my belt and the still-clothed bulge beneath it. We'd get to that. For now, I just fucking loved touching him like this.

Abruptly, though, he pulled away and dropped his gaze. "Fuck."

"What? You okay?"

"Yeah, I . . ." He let his head fall back against the wall and swore again. "Listen, before we go too much further . . ."

My heart sped up. I swept my tongue across my lips. "Something wrong?"

"I should . . . now that you know I have that thing on . . ." He exhaled and looked in my eyes. "I'm kind of, uh, limited on what I can do."

"Oh." I froze. I was suddenly afraid to touch him. It was like he might break right there in my arms if I did anything wrong. "*How* limited?"

"Well, on a bad day, I can't do much of anything." He sighed. "And even on a good day, anal is pretty much a no go. Like . . . giving *or* receiving." He cringed, as if bracing for my response.

"Oh. Really?"

"Yeah. I mean, I love it. Loved it. But I . . ." His eyes lost focus for a second before meeting mine again. "You know how they say pilots are an inch shorter after an ejection, right?"

I nodded, suppressing a shudder.

"It's no exaggeration. And that kind of compression injury makes sex really . . . Basically it's not something I can do without aggravating my back. Even if I just lie there. I've tried a million different positions, but it's—"

"Okay." I shrugged. "You can still get head, right?"

He nodded. "You know I can. And I can give it too."

I grinned, relieved as hell that I could still touch him, and slid my hands up his chest. "Then we'll be fine." Before he could speak, I kissed him, and I held on to the back of his neck so he knew I wanted him to stay right there. He didn't protest—he wrapped his arms around me again and moaned softly as I slipped my tongue past his lips.

Aroused as I was, my heartbeat was coming down. When he'd said he needed to tell me something, I'd wound myself up, expecting him to drop some huge bomb. What, I couldn't imagine, but as nervous as he'd obviously been, it had seemed like something more earth-shattering. I was curious about when and why he'd had to eject, but that story could wait until he was ready to tell it.

No anal? Dude, keep kissing me like that, and I couldn't care less what we don't *do.*

In my bedroom, he lay on his back, and I carefully got on top of him. I kept my weight off him as much as I could, and holy shit, I was in heaven. Neither of us was in any hurry now. We were in private. We were in bed. We were naked. His body was hot against mine and his breath was cool on my skin, and we had hours and hours at our disposal to touch and explore each other if we wanted to. Before long, Travis was recovering from getting stroked off, his cock hardening against my thigh.

In the back of my mind, I was constantly aware of what he'd said about being limited by his pain. With every move I made, I worried I'd hurt him, but if I'd given him so much as a twinge, he hadn't let on. He kissed me as hungrily as he had in his office, and I decided then and there I would never get tired of his hands running all over my body.

"You know what I've been wanting to do all day?" he asked breathlessly.

"Hmm?"

He squeezed my cock and whispered, "I want to suck you off *so* bad."

There wasn't an inch of skin that didn't suddenly have goose bumps on it. "What a coincidence—because I've been wanting to do the same to you."

"Then what are we waiting for?"

We shifted around so we were lying in opposite directions, and I closed my lips around his dick in the same moment he closed his around mine.

Holding back was one hell of a struggle. I wanted to come in his mouth, but . . . not yet. I loved this way too much. I loved the way he responded to everything I did—when he moaned, the vibration thrummed against my own cock, and when he shivered, his lips and hand tightened.

I lifted myself up on my elbow and used that hand to stroke him, freeing my other to roam all over his thigh, his hip, and his side. I couldn't get enough of touching him, and as if I wasn't already in heaven, *he* was still working his magic on *my* cock.

His hips rocked faster. A moment later, I realized mine had started doing the same without any conscious effort on my part. I didn't make any effort to stop them, either. Not when the result was my cock sliding between his lips like that. Jesus. I was fucking his mouth, he was fucking mine, and every time he moaned around my cock or his own cock seemed to get even thicker, I went a little further out of my mind.

Oh God. Oh God, yeah. How do you do that?

A shiver ran down my spine and curled my toes. I didn't bother holding back anymore. He was stroking faster and licking and sucking with the kind of intensity that meant only one thing—*I want you to come.*

Ask and ye shall receive.

And . . . fuck . . . yes.

My whole body shook with the force of my orgasm, and somehow—God only knew how—I kept pleasuring him, moaning as he pushed his dick deeper into my mouth, and then he was coming too, and his throaty groan made my climax even more intense, even longer, until we both stopped and sank onto the bed.

Holy shit.

As soon as my head had cleared enough that I could get up without passing out, I lifted myself up on rubbery limbs and shifted around again to join him. The second he could reach me, he grabbed the back of my neck and pulled me down to kiss him.

"In case it wasn't clear," I said in between kissing him and catching my breath, "I definitely don't regret coming out at the Navy Ball anymore."

"Good. Because I'm really glad you did."

And he kissed me again.

"Lieutenant Commander Fraser," Major Carter said frostily, "I need to see you in my office. Now."

That tone. She *never* took that tone with me.

Everyone was looking. No one spoke, and no one moved, but they watched. Under their glares, guilt swelled in my gut. Shame, even though I had no idea why.

Without a word, I got up and followed her, and the scrutiny of my peers made me feel smaller and smaller and guiltier and guiltier.

Major Carter stopped outside her office and waved me in. "I need you to explain a few things to me."

I hesitated, then stepped through the door.

In her office, the recon images weren't in a folder. They weren't even spread out on the desk. They were on the walls. Floor to ceiling. In HD. Every contorted, obliterated, charred body. Every lifeless stare. Every piece of burned flesh. They kept changing too, getting more graphic, more horrifying.

I tried to back out of the office, but got tangled up in something. Couldn't get away. Couldn't—

Sheets.

I opened my eyes.

Heart pounding, breath coming in too fast, way too shallow gasps, I kicked off the sweaty sheets and sat up in my bed.

My bed. In my apartment. In Anchor Point.

That office back at Nellis was a distant memory. The meeting with the major. The fallout. The cancerous secret I'd had to carry, that I couldn't even tell my wife or the chaplain or a goddamned therapist, even as my entire life crumbled at my feet.

It was all behind me. Three years and hundreds of miles behind me.

I was okay. As okay as I'd ever be, but that moment in the major's office . . . it was behind me.

Shivering, I grabbed the bottle of water beside my bed and took a swig to wet my parched mouth. I could have some variation of that nightmare every night for the rest of my life—in fact, I probably would—and I'd still wake up sweaty and shaking like it was the first time. Like it was the real thing. I wondered if the nausea would get better over time, or if I'd be seventy and still have to get up and hurl my guts out once or twice a week. Better than every single night, so that was promising.

And I wasn't out of the woods yet tonight. Still queasy, I got out of bed and stretched my arms as I walked back and forth across the floor. My body was still too jittery with too much nervous energy to even think about going back to sleep—walking it off helped sometimes. If I could walk off the jitteriness, that usually took care of the nausea too.

As I paced, I glanced at the other side of the bed, which was empty. Travis had left shortly before midnight, and though I'd hated to see him go, I hadn't tried to make him stay. It didn't matter how much I missed sleeping beside someone. He didn't need to be there when my past showed up.

Sooner or later, the subject was going to come up. It always did. Eventually, it would be really late, and we'd both be exhausted from getting each other off a few times. After all, neither of us was twenty anymore—a couple of fortysomething guys were bound to fall asleep after sex. What happened if we drifted off, and Travis woke up to *this*?

Logan had usually been passed-out drunk beside me, so if I'd woken up freaking out, he'd slept right through it. If he'd been sober, he'd firmly believed he knew exactly what would put me back to sleep. It should've been a clue about our relationship that in this case, I'd preferred the nights when he'd been drinking.

I ran a hand through my sweat-dampened hair. I would have sold my soul for something that would at least help with all this bullshit, but so far, nothing had worked. I was forbidden from talking about what had happened, so therapy was out of the question. Even the most basic details of the incident were strictly need-to-know, and the reams of nondisclosure agreements I'd signed before and after had warned me that it wasn't my decision who needed to know. I could get help with the PTSD, but my pursuit of help ended where the need for national security began. Not even a therapist or a chaplain with my clearance or higher qualified.

I sighed. And people wondered why RAPs drank.

One doctor had recommended a sleep aid, but that had turned out to be a disaster. The only thing worse than having a nightmare-flashback was having one when I was sleeping too deeply to wake up.

The only thing that had ever "helped" was alcohol. I usually woke up hungover and terrified, but couldn't remember the dreams, so it was . . . better. Sort of. And alcohol wasn't an option anymore anyway, so it didn't matter.

I went into the bathroom and ran a towel over my face and neck to dry off some of the sweat. Though the nightmare's claws were slowly releasing their grip, I was worried now about Travis. If things continued with him, we'd have to cross this bridge sooner or later.

I closed my eyes and took a deep breath.

I told myself over and over that Travis was a good guy, and he was familiar with PTSD. He'd squashed the situation of showing combat videos in the office without making a big deal out of it. If there was a man in this town I could sleep beside without being scared it would end in disaster, that man was Travis.

And that was exactly why I was terrified to spend a night beside him.

Because what if I was wrong?

CHAPTER 9
TRAVIS

Though sleeping with someone in the office made the days crawl by, it did add some excitement to the nine-to-five monotony. Clint quickly became a normal part of my life. It was hard to believe it had taken only a couple of weeks to fall into such an effortless routine.

Morning hellos at the office. Subtle flirting and less subtle texting throughout the day. And, when we were absolutely certain we could get away with it, a breathless quickie in his office or mine.

Of course, there were also the evenings, which gave me something to look forward to most days. Hot sex followed by long kisses good-bye. Neither of us had spent a full night at the other's place. I kept wondering when he'd suggest it, but he hadn't so far, and I sure as hell wasn't volunteering. He'd already been subjected to more of my chronic pain than I would have liked. I wasn't ready to show my PTSD card quite yet. Before I knew it, October was nearly over. Our coworkers were plastering the office with jack-o'-lanterns and black cats, not to mention a zombie that looked suspiciously like the XO.

Unfortunately, with an inspection coming up the first week of November, our easy, comfortable schedules were suddenly crammed full of bullshit meetings and pre-inspection inspections. Office quickies ceased altogether. We exchanged grins when we passed in the halls, and exchanged texts whenever we had the chance, but time and privacy? Not exactly in great supply. If we hadn't worked together, we probably wouldn't have seen each other outside of the one or two nights a week we could muster up the energy to spend some time between the sheets.

It would be over soon, though, and I kept myself sane by counting down the minutes until Friday night. We'd made plans to watch a movie on his couch, and I couldn't wait to fail miserably and wind up making out again. All I had to do was get through the rest of the week and the inspection.

Finally, on Thursday, the inspection was over. The whole office could breathe again. Clint and I didn't hook up that night because we both needed some sleep, but tomorrow ... tomorrow, he was all mine.

And surprise, surprise—I woke up on Friday morning feeling like someone had used my spine as a landing strip.

Go figure. We'd had damn good luck so far, so my body was bound to act up at some point and torpedo our plans.

There was still time, though. From the moment I gingerly rolled out of bed, I did everything I could to lessen the pain. I tried a hot shower. An ice pack. The TENS. The TENS along with an ice pack. Before I headed out the door, I took as much Motrin as I could handle without getting sick.

They each took the edge off in their own way, but it was like taking the very sharpest edge off an ax-head buried in my back. That little bit of relief was not enough.

Hope springs eternal, though, and on my way to work, I crossed my fingers that this would be a rough morning followed by a more comfortable afternoon. I might've slept weird, and the knots would gradually work themselves out as I moved around. Yeah. I'd be all right. Just needed to knuckle through it until the worst was over, and I'd be fine by the time Clint and I were in bed again.

Come on, body. Get it together.

Like we usually did, Clint and I arrived in the office parking lot at the same time. As we got out of our cars, he took one look at me, and I knew he knew. The pinch of his brow gave it away almost immediately.

Embarrassment gnawed at me. As always, the tightness in my back was worse on one side. It pulled at my hip, and no matter how much I tried, I couldn't *not* favor my left leg. Anyone who saw me take more than two or three steps could see clear as day that I was hurting, and I fucking hated that.

As we walked inside, he said, "Not moving very fast today?"

"Not if I can help it, no." I sighed. "Tonight's probably going to be a bust." I should've known by now he wouldn't huff and bitch, not even when it was clear this would throw a monkey wrench into our plans for the night.

He had to be disappointed to some extent, but he just shrugged. "Doesn't mean we can't still meet up."

"Seriously?"

"Sure. Why not?"

"Because I won't be able to move, so I won't be a lot of fun?"

Clint smiled. "Nights like that are why the good lord gave us movies and Motrin."

I laughed humorlessly. *Oh, if Motrin could even touch the kind of pain I was in . . .* "Sorry about tonight."

"Don't be." He glanced at me. "Are you going to be okay today, though?"

"Don't really have much choice."

At the base of the stairs, I paused. Oh fuck my life. I hated these goddamned stairs. There was an elevator at the other end of the building, but it was too close to the office that handled our physical readiness scores. Rational or not, I didn't want them noticing me limping into the elevator. I continued using the stairs for the same reason I would continue to properly run the Physical Readiness Test until I absolutely *had* to resort to an elliptical—because I didn't want to raise questions. Questions that had a funny way of—officially or unofficially, right or wrong—influencing whether or not I got promoted.

So . . . stairs.

Clint had stopped beside me, and I could hear the question before he even said it.

"I'm good," I said through my teeth, and started up. Funny how most of my pain was in my middle and upper back, but even the simple task of climbing the stairs was enough to aggravate it. Anatomy and physiology could seriously eat a dick.

At the top of the stairs, a cold drop of perspiration rolled down the back of my neck. I couldn't ignore Clint's worried expression. He wasn't stupid. He knew I wasn't good.

I swallowed my pride as I rolled my shoulders. "Okay, I'm sore now. But I'll be good by tonight."

His eyebrows climbed his creased forehead. "You sure? We can always take it easy. If you're—"

"No. No. Give me a few hours to move around and stretch a bit, and I'll be fine."

He studied me for a second, then shrugged. "It's your call. Either way, I'm all yours tonight."

I smiled despite the nerves and embarrassment. "I will definitely take you up on that."

"Good." He grinned, but it faded quickly. "Just take it easy today, okay?"

I bit my tongue before snapping back that no shit, I was going to take it easy. The fact that people had been telling me that for years didn't change the fact that he meant well.

So I nodded. "I will. See you at lunch?"

"Definitely. See you then."

He headed toward his office, and I hobbled toward mine.

And before I'd even reached my door, I turned the TENS up to max.

This was going to be a long day.

By noon, it was clear that "a few hours to move around and stretch a bit" was not going to cut it. The simple act of getting in and out of my desk chair made my eyes water.

With every hour, my enthusiasm about tonight waned even more. So far, I hadn't been in too much pain to function in the bedroom, but I'd known all along that trend wouldn't last forever. After a solid week of extra stress and no sleep, which had aggravated all my muscles as well as my brain—and waking up shaking from nightmares never helped with the pain—I was lucky to be walking. Who was I kidding if I thought I was having sex tonight?

There was no point in fighting it. I could knuckle through a lot of things. I could even run the damn PRT because my career—and who was I kidding, my ego—depended on it, but I definitely didn't enjoy it. Something that was meant to be enjoyed but caused too much pain? Not really an option when I felt like this.

No two ways about it—it was time for Clint to experience one of those nights that my last few partners had grown tired of *really* quickly.

Well, better now than after I'd had a chance to get attached to him.

More attached to him.

You're an idiot. This is going to be a disaster. You know that, right?

Of course it was, and I was one hundred percent convinced we were a time bomb that was down to T-minus the rest of the day . . .

Until Clint walked into my office.

One look at him, and despite the ax in my back and the knot in my stomach, my heart fluttered.

Oh God. Does this disaster have to crash and burn today?

Probably.

"Hey." He smiled uncertainly. "How are you feeling?"

Like I don't want you to leave but I also don't want you to see me like this.

"Eh." I shrugged as much as my cable-tight muscles allowed. "Like forty-five is the new eighty-five?"

"Ouch. Any better since this morning? Worse?"

He couldn't possibly imagine how much I wanted to fake it and tell him I was well on my way to normal, and that tonight, it was so on. I wasn't that good of an actor, though.

I exhaled. "Not great. Tonight's definitely still going to be . . ."

"I'm fine with that. Your place or mine?"

I chewed the inside of my cheek. As much as I hated giving up on our hotter plans for the night, there were worse ways to spend an evening than just hanging out with someone. "Your choice."

He quirked his lips. "You know, if it's not too weird for you and Kimber, your place might be better. That way you don't have to drive home at the end of the night."

It was all I could do not to sigh with relief. He got it. He . . . he fucking got it?

I nodded. "That would work, yeah. You don't mind?"

"Of course not." He ran his thumb back and forth along my arm. "I know PRT is coming up, and we should both probably be watching what we eat, but I could go for something unhealthy tonight."

"Hmm. Unhealthy sounds good."

"You like chicken?"

"What the fuck kind of question is that?" I laughed, though my voice hitched slightly when a spasm reminded me that laughing was *not* permitted. I muffled a cough—which also hurt, damn it—and grinned through the pain. "Of course I like chicken."

He laughed with enough enthusiasm for both of us. "All right. I'll pick something up. See you around six?"

"Six works. I'm looking forward to it."

The instant Clint walked into my house, the whole place smelled like the most deliciously fragrant fried chicken.

"Oh my God." I took in a deep breath of it. "That smells amazing."

"I know, right?" He held up a paper bag with a few grease spots on the bottom half. "This place is unhealthy as hell, but I've been hooked on it since the first week I lived here."

"Well, I'll probably be hooked on it after tonight. Open that shit up."

As we pulled cartons and cups out of the bags, Kimber walked into the kitchen in her work clothes and sniffed a few times. "Someone went to Larry's."

Clint made a mock toast with a box of boneless wings. "Guilty."

"Oh, you bastards." She groaned. "Now I want some." She narrowed her eyes at me. "Hey, isn't PRT coming up for you guys?"

I glared back at her. "Isn't there a time clock you need to be punching into?"

She huffed. "All right, *fine*. I've gotta go. I'll see you guys later." With a wistful sigh, she added, "Enjoy the chicken."

"Oh, we will. Get to work."

Rolling her eyes, Kimber turned to collect her wallet and keys. A moment later, she headed out.

"I guess I should've asked if she'd be here," Clint said after she'd gone. "I didn't even think about it, but I could've picked up some for her."

"That wouldn't be weird? Having her join us?"

"For junk food and movies?" He shook his head. "Of course it wouldn't be weird. I mean, not for me."

"Not for me either." I pulled a couple of plates down from the cabinet, ignoring the fresh spasm below my shoulder. "Maybe the next time we do this."

He smiled. "Perfect. She works nights, though, doesn't she?"

"Sometimes. Her department has been short-staffed lately, so she's been taking extra shifts." I put the plates and a stack of napkins on the table. "I'm worried she's working herself into the ground, but she's happy. Especially since she's doing over-the-phone tech support now, which is much more her speed than retail. And the overtime is putting a huge dent in her car loan."

"Can't complain about that, right?"

"Nope." I set a box of wings beside the plates. "She was miserable working in retail. Forty hours of that shit took more out of her than seventy hours of tech support. Long as it makes her happy . . ."

"Good for her." He smiled as we took our seats. "Glad she's found a solid job. And tech support—she must be making pretty good money even without the overtime."

"More than I made at her age," I muttered. "I mean, granted that was right after I'd graduated from the Academy, but still."

He laughed as he put a couple of wings on his plate. "Is that adjusted for inflation? I mean, I'm pretty sure you graduated from the Academy a few years ago."

"Just a few." I chuckled and tore open a packet of Buffalo sauce.

"Like, when Jesus was a cadet, right?"

"Hey! Come on. I'm not that old." I shot him a sidelong glance. "And I'm pretty sure you're not that far behind me."

"Not really, no." He shifted a little. "I turned forty right before I transferred here, and God, some days I feel every minute of it."

"I know the feeling."

He grimaced. "Sorry. I probably shouldn't be bitching about . . . I mean . . ."

"Relax." I waved a hand, then reached for the Styrofoam bowl of mashed potatoes. "Believe me, there are days when it's not old injuries coming back to haunt me. Sometimes it's just being forty-fucking-five."

"Aging is a bitch, isn't it?"

"The worst."

We ate in silence for a minute or so. Then Clint turned to me. "I'm curious about something."

"Sure."

He hesitated, searching my eyes as if he could somehow find the answer before he'd even asked. "When we're in bed, does it . . . I mean, is the pain always there?"

You better believe it.

This was the part I hated. When reality showed up and wouldn't be ignored, and there was no avoiding the conversations.

"It comes and goes. Sometimes it just aches. Sometimes there's spasms. That's where I'm at today." I paused. "I have to be really careful not to move too suddenly or contort myself too much."

He held my gaze for a moment. "Does it hurt when you come?"

Every time, but it's still worth it.

"Sometimes." I took a drink. "It's okay, though." With a grin that was hopefully reassuring, I added, "Not enough to stop me from wanting to."

Clint's forehead creased.

I touched his arm. "If it was a problem, we'd have stopped by now."

"Just . . ." He swallowed. "When we're in the bedroom, tell me if you're in too much pain. I don't want to hurt you."

"Of course." I bit back a comment that he would know before I had a chance to tell him. He'd been great about not handling me with kid gloves, and I didn't want that to change. Sometimes the pain was worth it just to have someone touch me like they meant it.

"Well, I'll always follow your lead. So if it's too much, say so. I don't mind backing off. And I don't mind this, either." He gestured at the array of food. "Kicking back with dinner and a movie is fine too."

"Good to know."

And I pretended my brain wasn't prodding me with that ever-present question: *This is fine . . . but for how long?*

After dinner, clearing the table was as complicated as rinsing two plates and tossing everything else. I didn't usually like meals that resulted in quite so much trash, but there was no way in hell I was loading the dishwasher tonight, so clearing away the remnants of takeout was fine by me.

Once we'd done what little cleaning was necessary, I pulled an ice pack from the freezer, and we moved into the living room.

On the couch, I leaned back against the ice pack. The cold was uncomfortable as fuck even through the towel and my shirt, but hopefully—please God—it would soothe some of the relentless tension in the muscles.

It took longer than I cared to think about to get myself situated on the couch. Motrin within arm's reach. TENS unit and spare batteries in case the damn thing crapped out on me again.

Clint looked me over and chewed his lip. "If I sit next to you, it's going to move the cushions you're sitting on."

"I can cope." I smiled. "I don't want to sit across the room from you."

He hesitated, but then carefully sat beside me. "Is the ice helping?"

"Not yet, but it will be. Maybe. I hope."

"That's a start. Right?"

"Yeah."

"How long does this usually last?" His eyes and his voice were filled with genuine concern, not impatience. "Are you going to be able to sleep tonight?"

"I'll be fine. It . . ." I paused. Sooner or later, he was going to figure this all out, so maybe I should be straight with him. "Okay, remember how I said earlier that the old injury comes back to haunt me sometimes?"

Clint nodded.

"The truth is it never goes away. It always hurts. Sometimes it's bearable. Like a low-grade ache. Sometimes I can't move. But it always hurts."

"Wow," he said softly. "I can't imagine."

"I couldn't either, but here I am. And . . . when you asked if it hurts when I come? I said sometimes."

"It hurts every time, doesn't it?"

I nodded.

"I know." He squeezed my hand. "To be honest, I can tell."

I winced, weirdly ashamed that I couldn't hide it from him, not even during sex. "I'm sorry."

"Don't be." His thumb ran back and forth along mine. "I'd rather you tell me. I mean, I'm as careful as I can be not to hurt you, and I figure if you didn't enjoy it, you wouldn't do it at all. But if I *do* hurt you—"

"You don't. You never have. And . . . I really appreciate it. That you're careful. It can be kind of a mood killer sometimes, having to—"

"Not at all." He leaned in and kissed my cheek. "I want you to feel good, so just tell me."

"Okay. I will." Easier said than done, but okay. "And really—thank you."

"Don't mention it." He laced his fingers between mine. "I'm surprised the Navy hasn't medically retired you."

"Not yet, thank God. Not as long as I can do my job and pass a PRT."

His eyes widened. "How do you pass a PRT when you're hurting all the time?"

"I take as much Motrin as my liver can handle, grit my teeth through the test, and spend the rest of the day wishing I was dead." I paused to gingerly stretch out some tension, grimacing when something popped. Fortunately, no pain followed. "You know how a lot of guys finish the run and then puke? I do the same thing."

"Except it's from the pain, isn't it?"

I nodded.

"Haven't you tried the elliptical? Or the swim?"

"Swimming is . . ." I shuddered. "The elliptical is like putting a big red sign on your forehead that even though you can kinda fake it, your physical readiness is unsat." I sighed. "I know, I know—it's allowed, and it's valid. But let's face it. When promotions are based on what boards decide, we all know they factor in things they technically shouldn't."

Twin creases deepened between his eyebrows. "But why do you stay in? Doing the PRT twice a year has to be hell."

"The PRT is awful. Honestly, though?" I released a long breath. "I'm scared to get out."

"Why?"

I hated this topic. *Hated* it. "Because as long as I'm in, I've got a paycheck and access to medical. What happens when I'm retired and I have to rely on the VA for medical?" I shifted, and couldn't help wincing. "And let's face it—on paper, I'm set for any post-Navy career I want. My résumé can get me in the door for all kinds of DOD contracts, upper management, you name it. Right up until I walk into a job interview and they see that I can barely walk."

Clint shifted uncomfortably. "They can't reject you for a disability, though."

I flinched at the word. My pilot ego would take a lifetime to accept that label. "Again, on paper. A buddy of mine had a Skype interview that went really well, but when he went for the in-person, they took one look at his cane and the tremor in his arm, and suddenly didn't have any enthusiasm." I laughed bitterly. "It's only illegal if they say they're not hiring you because of a disability. Doesn't stop them from *doing* it."

"But aren't there places that make a point of hiring disabled veterans?"

"I think so. I mean, my RIO is paraplegic and works for one of the shipyards down in San Diego. Obviously it's not universal." I struggled to hold his gaze. "But from what I've heard from vets trying to make it in the civilian world, for every one employer hiring disabled vets, there's ten more who are decidedly not, and I'm not sure I'm ready to face that yet."

"Jesus. So what's your plan?"

"I'm trying to make captain and stick it out until thirty years. At least then I'll retire at three-quarter pay instead of half."

"And at thirty, you'll be making more anyway, so it'll be three-quarters of more money."

"Exactly." I forced a smile. "So, fingers crossed I hold out that long."

"Fingers crossed." His smile seemed equally genuine.

I cleared my throat and gestured at the TV. "So, movie?"

"Movie sounds good."

We pulled up some Oscar bait movie I hadn't heard of, but as it started playing, neither of us could quite get comfortable. I was about to suggest pushing apart, but Clint shifted around and lay across the couch with his head on my lap.

And it was perfect. With his weight distributed, the cushions didn't bend in weird ways. Since he wasn't next to my arm or shoulder, there was little chance of jarring my back.

For the first time since we sat down, I relaxed. The movie continued, and I barely paid attention to it. Aside from the relentless spasm in my back, it was hard to think about anything besides Clint and . . . this. Everything about this evening was a first. I was still hurting and would be until at least tomorrow, but I was as comfortable as I could expect to be, and Clint had found a way to still be close to me without putting extra strain on my back. Even when he needed to shift or fidget, he was extra careful, and somehow managed to adjust his position without jostling me.

What sorcery was this? Someone who was willing to accommodate me without acting like I'd asked him to move mountains. He was the most attractive man I'd encountered in a long time, but he was also exactly the kind of person I'd been needing for ages. He was well aware of the pain that ruled my life, and so far he'd treated it as something to be taken in stride, not an annoyance or inconvenience. Even when I'd admitted how *much* it ruled my life, and how often it interfered, he'd nodded and said he'd picked up on it since the start. And yet . . . he was still here. And going out of his way to make sure I was comfortable.

Again and again I reminded myself that most people could sustain this for a while. I'd been guilty of that temporary consideration myself. When my ex-wife had needed surgery on her ankle, I'd bent over backwards to make sure her crutches were always within reach and she had her foot elevated properly and on enough cushions to keep her comfortable. If she'd needed anything—food, ice, the remote, pain pills—I'd never hesitated to jump up and get it.

For about three weeks.

Looking back, I hated myself for every time I'd muttered "Jesus Christ" on my way to get her another goddamned ice pack—out of earshot, of course—or when I'd been quietly annoyed after her doctor had said she needed to stay off her foot for another week. Really? Seven more *days* of our entire world revolving around her damn foot? Such bullshit.

Now that I knew what it was like to be limited when it came to movement and basic daily tasks, I felt like the world's biggest jerk for being impatient and irritated, even if I'd—hopefully—kept it out of her sight.

Clint had been a saint so far, but he hadn't been a part of the chronic-back-pain shit show for very long. It was still easy for him because it hadn't worn him down yet.

And because he only knew about the physical limitations right now. He didn't know about Dion. Not many people did. They also didn't know how much losing him had hurt my ability to love even more than the crash had hurt my ability to fly.

I watched my fingers running through Clint's graying blond hair. I was probably putting the cart before the horse. We were friends, and we fucked, but that didn't mean it had to, well, mean something. It probably wouldn't last. It never did. But, damn, it was hard not to feel like we would've had a chance if my body hadn't been quite so jacked up.

The movie wound down, and before I knew it, the credits were rolling.

Clint shifted onto his back and looked up at me. "Still comfortable?"

I smoothed his hair. "Yeah. You?"

He smiled. "Very."

I smiled down at him, still running my fingers through his hair and ignoring the sharp pain across the middle of my back. What I wouldn't have given for the flexibility to lean down—even meet him halfway—for a kiss. But that smile alone was enough to make my whole body tingle.

He gestured at the TV. "Game for another one?"

"If you are."

"Definitely."

Good. I want you to stay awhile. "I could probably use another ice pack, though."

He sat up, and I started to stand, but he stopped me. "Don't. I know where the freezer is. You want me to put that one in while I'm up?"

As much as I hated someone waiting on me, I nodded and handed him the ice pack. He returned with a fresh one, and oh God yes, I needed that. The cold felt great against my still-annoyed muscles.

While I got situated again, we went through the movies available for streaming until we settled on a comic book adaptation we'd both practically memorized.

Clint took his place on the couch again, lying across it with his head in my lap. The movie started playing. And considering how much trouble my back had been giving me all day, I felt pretty damn good.

This is fine, my brain reminded me for the thousandth time tonight, *but for how long?*

CHAPTER 10
CLINT

Before I left for work one morning, I logged on to my laptop, turned on Skype, and waited. My stomach was so knotted up, I couldn't even drink any coffee yet. Not like I needed it—despite the lack of sleep last night, I was wide-awake. Funny how that always happened the night before my scheduled Skype chats.

My ex-wife's avatar popped up—a little daisy with *Mandy* underneath—and the call request came through.

With my heart in my throat, I accepted.

At the camera was my seven-year-old, Crystal, and I smiled.

"Hey, kiddo. How are you?"

"Good." She grinned, revealing a gap where her front teeth used to be. Damn, they were growing up without me.

"How's school?"

She was the chattiest of my three kids, and told me all about her current teacher, the new girl in her class who had a pet iguana named Ringo, and a field trip they were taking next week to an old mine. I would've been thrilled to chaperone that one—the old mines and ghost towns were some of my favorite parts of living in Nevada.

After she'd finished, she glanced at her mom, who was always just off camera when we chatted. She looked at me again. "When are you going to come see us, Dad?"

Her question made my chest hurt. "I'm—"

"We're working on that, sweetie," Mandy said. "Now hurry up so your brothers can talk to him."

I clenched my teeth. They had to get to school and I had to get to work, but it still grated on me when she rushed them.

"But we'll see you soon, right?" my daughter asked.

"I sure hope so." I prayed to God she couldn't see how much this hurt. "I miss you guys."

"We miss you too." She glanced offscreen. "Okay. I have to go. Love you, Dad."

"Love you too, kiddo."

She moved out of the chair, and my twelve-year-old, Danny, took her place.

Not surprisingly, he didn't look nearly as thrilled to see me. "Hey, Dad."

"Hey. Um, how's school going?"

He shrugged. "Fine."

"What about football? How's that going?"

Another shrug. "Fine."

I forced myself not to let any impatience slip into my voice or my posture. These kids had every right to keep their distance from me. I was lucky he was talking to me at all—that had been a hard-won victory.

"You going out for wrestling in January?" I asked.

"Maybe." That seemed like all I was going to get, but then he added, "I don't know if I want to play this year. Everyone's so serious about it now, and it's not really fun anymore."

"Well, if you don't want to, you definitely don't have to."

"Oh."

"I don't want you playing it to the point you hate it. And you can always play again next year if you decide to."

"Oh." He relaxed slightly. "Okay. I'll think about it."

"All right. Whatever you want to do."

"Cool. Thanks, Dad." He even gave me a hint of a smile. It was a start.

After he and I talked for a few more minutes, and I'd chatted with my eight-year-old, Allen, their mother sent them off to get ready for school. Then she took their place in front of the camera.

"So, how are things?" she asked.

"Good. Good."

She squinted, leaning in. "Your eyes look red. You okay?"

"Yeah." I waved a hand. "Just didn't sleep very well last night."

Her eyes narrowed. "Same as last time we talked?"

Why do you think I didn't sleep?

I knew what she was looking for, though, and sighed. "Mandy, I'm serious. It's lack of sleep. I haven't had a drink in ages."

She avoided my gaze. "Are you getting help? For everything else?"

"I can't. What good is a therapist if I can't talk to them about what happened?"

"Then you should've talked to someone at Nellis," she snapped.

"They couldn't discuss it either. I couldn't even go to the damn chaplain." I exhaled sharply. "I've said it a million times—I would gladly talk to someone if—"

"Jesus Christ." Scowling, she rolled her eyes. "I'm not buying it, Clint. I've asked around. The military has *got* to have someone you can talk to about—"

"We've been through this. I'd show you the nondisclosures I had to sign if those weren't classified too. My hands are tied, but I'm doing the best I can."

There were people with the proper clearance to help counsel traumatized troops who'd been involved in classified and secret incidents, and in theory, I should've been able to talk to one. But I'd been warned time and again to keep my mouth shut. To this day I didn't even know if it was an official thing, or even a legal one, but I couldn't ask for the same reasons I couldn't get help.

"I'm sorry," I said. "If I could . . ." Why did I bother? This conversation wouldn't end any differently than it had the previous five hundred times.

Mandy didn't speak for a moment. Then, "They're having a hard time, you know."

Eyes down, I nodded. "I can't imagine they wouldn't be. Are they . . ." I hesitated, then looked at the screen. "Have they gotten any better?"

She let out a long breath, shoulders sinking as she did. "Sometimes I think they are. Sometimes I don't know."

I forced back the lump that always rose when we got on this subject.

"I remind them constantly that you love them," she said softly. "But it's harder and harder to explain how that works when you're gone."

My stomach dropped. Our eyes locked, and I swore her unspoken thoughts came through as clearly as if she'd typed them on the screen.

Don't say it, Mandy. Please don't say it.

It had come up a few times in the beginning, back before the ink had even dried on the divorce papers, but neither of us had mentioned it in a long time. Still, every time we spoke, every time the subject came up of the kids struggling with the divorce and my absence, I braced for it.

"Maybe it would be better if they didn't see you at all."

She'd said it out of anger the first time. Desperation the second time. An ultimatum the third time. Now that things were more or less civil, neither of us said it, but it was there. Part of me was terrified she'd get exhausted and throw it out there with more force than before. The other part wondered how long I'd last before I played it myself like a desperate Hail Mary because I couldn't keep hurting my kids like this anymore. Of course giving up my rights and bowing out of their lives would hurt them too, but would it be worse than slowly eroding their trust by stringing them along with sporadic weekend visits in between long, long absences?

"I'm getting better," I whispered, wondering if that sounded as useless as it had the previous thousand times. "I haven't had a drink in—"

"The drinking's only part of it, Clint. You know that."

I sighed, raking a hand through my hair. "It's a start. It's behind me. I promise."

"But what about the rest? The . . ." she hesitated, swallowing, "the nightmares and . . ."

Wincing, I looked away again. "It's better, but . . ."

"How much better will this ever get?"

"I wish I knew."

She huffed sharply. "And yet you still want me to send the kids to stay with you."

"I don't know what you want me to tell you. PTSD, it . . ." I shook my head. "There's only so much I can do."

"I know, but . . . this is tough on all of us. You're not the same person anymore."

I couldn't even argue. "I'm still their dad."

"You'll always be their dad. But they need more than a face on a screen."

"So do I."

Mandy flinched. "This isn't for spite. I'm trying to protect them and so are the courts. They need a father who's stable and on an even keel."

I exhaled. "I don't know what else I can do. I haven't had a drink in a year and a half. I'm keeping my career and my life on the rails. I can't make the PTSD magically go away."

"But can you get some help with *some* of this? Even if you can't disclose it all, there *has* to be someone—"

"If there was, don't you think I'd be talking to them?" I snapped. Instantly, I regretted my tone, and softened it. "Mandy, this is hell for me too. I don't like living with it. If there was someone I could talk to—I mean *really* talk to—I'd be in their office in a heartbeat."

Her lips pulled tight, and she looked away again.

As per usual, we were going through the same shit we'd fought over before and during the divorce. We'd do it again next time I called. The only differences now were that I was sober and neither of us had the energy to raise our voices anymore.

"Just tell me what I can do," I said. "I'm not asking for custody. All I want is to see my kids."

"I know," she whispered. "I want you to see them. I really do. But I'm not ready to let them come stay with you alone."

In the beginning, that confession would've had me frothing with anger, but now, I could only nod. "What will it take to work up to that?" It wasn't her decision, really, but I'd vowed not to drag her or the kids through a custody battle. I wouldn't petition for joint custody or even increased visitation until I knew she wouldn't fight me.

"I . . ." She released another long breath. "I don't know." She glanced offscreen. "But I need to get them ready for school. We'll . . . we'll talk about it. Okay?"

"Okay," I said. "I'll talk to you—"

The video shut off.

I swore into the silence and rubbed my eyes with my thumb and forefinger. This cold, bitter divide and the custody arrangement stung more and more as time went on. Just over three years ago, Mandy and

I were somewhat happily married. In a rut after sixteen years together, maybe, but content.

Then there was that catastrophic incident involving my drone, and everything had gone to shit. Three years, a messy divorce, and a hard-won recovery later, I briefly saw my kids on Skype and during short, supervised visits. I was a stranger to them now, and I couldn't even be alone with them because her attorney had somehow convinced the judge that drinking myself into oblivion over a combat-related mishap meant I was a danger to myself and others. Never mind that I didn't drink anymore.

I'd self-destructed after the mishap, and no one would take it seriously because I'd been in an air-conditioned room in Nevada while the incident occurred in an undisclosed location in the Middle East. And I couldn't provide details because the mission—including every way it had gone awry—was classified. As far as the lawyer, judge, and my ex-wife were apparently concerned, I had as much of a leg to stand on as if I'd told them I'd been traumatized while playing a bootlegged video game that I didn't even have anymore, so I couldn't show them the part that had fucked me up.

I ran a trembling hand through my hair, and wondered when the hell my hair had gotten wet. Was I sweating? And was I really shaking that bad?

Shit. This wasn't good.

I got up and took a few deep breaths as I paced across the living room floor. I'd gotten the hang of talking myself down if an episode didn't come on too fast. This one had crept up on me, but I hadn't passed the point of no return yet, so I walked and breathed and concentrated on not letting my mini freak-out turn into something worse. If there was one thing I hadn't expected when I'd been diagnosed with PTSD, it was that *any* significant stress could trigger a flashback, even if it wasn't related to what had happened. Because that was something I really needed.

Slowly, my blood pressure came down. The shaking stilled. I went into the kitchen for some water—coffee was a bad idea at this point— and took a few gulps while I continued to talk myself down.

As I came back to earth and the panic stopped, I cautiously let my mind return to my conversation with Mandy. What would happen if I finally had to tell her I was dating a man? Maybe Travis, maybe whoever came along after him. She didn't know I was bisexual. She sure as hell didn't know about the dozen or so men or all the women I'd slept with in the wake of our divorce. She had no idea how much of that had been self-destruction versus long overdue exploration. Hell, *I* didn't know that part. I'd needed sex and distraction, and took it from anyone willing to give it.

But I'd settled into being single. I'd sobered up. I'd come to grips with the side of my sexuality that I'd repressed my whole life. These days, I was comfortable in my own skin, and it felt right to share my bed with a man.

And wasn't that the problem now? I'd shared my bed with men, women, and on occasion, both. These days, there was only one person I wanted like that, and if things progressed beyond sex, I'd have to be open about him—about us—to my ex-wife. Eventually, to my kids. As if they hadn't already been through enough. Where was the line between "I'm dropping yet another bomb on you" and "This is part of the newer, healthier, more honest me"? And what if it was like with Logan—I worked up the courage to say "Hey, y'all, I'm with him," only to realize we needed to split up?

I took another swallow of water.

I didn't have to figure it all out today. For now, I needed to get to work. I'd figure things out . . . eventually.

Even after I'd been working for a couple of hours, the jittery, semipanicked feeling remained. Tonight was going to be rough, no doubt about that, but hell, I wasn't even sure if I was going to make it through the day. My concentration was shot. All I could think about was how I couldn't tell my kids when I'd see them again, and how the hell I would eventually tell my family that I wasn't straight, and why the fuck did I have to have PTSD on top of all this shit?

I put down the training module I was supposed to be revising. Sooner or later, I had to figure out a way to deal with stress in general. I'd debated seeing a therapist on base, but it was pointless if I couldn't tell them the hard details about the core cause of my problems.

Making vague allusions to "something bad" and "a mission gone wrong" didn't get me very far, so why fucking bother? Man, if that mission were ever declassified, my life would become a *whole* lot easier.

Until that time, though, I had to get my shit together. I had work to do. And maybe if I stared at it long enough, I'd either remember how to do it, or it would magically do itself.

One can hope . . .

A while later, Travis appeared in my office doorway and tapped his knuckle on the frame. "Hey. Busy?"

I should be, but I'm not getting anything done.

I pushed the training module away. "Not really. What's up?"

He cocked his head. "You want to go grab lunch?"

It was early yet. Not even eleven o'clock. But . . .

"Yeah." I pushed my chair back and got up. "That sounds like a good idea." Wasn't like I was getting anything done here.

Most days, I'd walk over to the Navy Exchange and pick up something unhealthy from the food court. The thought of all the noise, though—people talking, kids crying, wrappers crinkling, TVs blaring—made my skin crawl.

Instead, we went over to the O club, which was considerably quieter. Travis didn't object, thank God. I really didn't want him to see me getting agitated from everyday noise. Wouldn't that be fun—explaining to a former fighter pilot that I was so traumatized by my time as a remote aircraft pilot that I couldn't even handle the damn food court.

We sat down at a booth, and Travis didn't even open his menu. Instead, he folded his hands on top of it and looked right at me. "What's going on?"

I gulped, which probably didn't help. "What do you mean?"

"I mean you've been on edge all morning. You're either ready to jump out of your skin, or off in your own world."

That about summed it up, didn't it? "I haven't even seen you all day. How do you—"

"Clint." He inclined his head. "We talked at the coffeepot an hour ago."

I blinked a few times. Had we talked? Shit, I didn't even remember getting coffee.

"And," he went on, "I said hi to you in the hallway—twice—and you didn't respond." His brow creased. "Look, I know that thousand-yard stare. You don't have to give me details, but I want to make sure you're okay."

I ran my thumb back and forth along the edge of the menu, almost hoping for a papercut to distract me from that jitteriness that was rising again.

He leaned closer. "Just tell me if you're okay. I've seen guys with PTSD before, and . . ." He let his raised eyebrows finish the thought.

Oh fuck. Did that mean the rest of the office had caught on? That was just what I needed. A building full of ex-pilots figuring out the guy who used to fly drones allegedly had PTSD. It was well-documented on paper, but I hadn't met a lot of non-RAPs who took it seriously.

But if there was anyone in that office I could trust, he was sitting across from me.

"Okay." I scratched the back of my neck. "Yeah, I do have it. Stress triggers it, and I was Skyping with my ex-wife this morning, so . . ."

"So that triggered it."

"Yeah." Suddenly self-conscious, I squirmed under his scrutiny. "I know it probably sounds insane to a 'real' pilot, but RAPs get PTSD too."

Travis nodded. "That's what I've heard."

I studied him. "But do you believe it?"

"Yes." He didn't miss a beat. No hesitation whatsoever.

"Really?"

"Of course. Admittedly, I know nothing about what you guys do or how it affects you, but I mean . . . I know how fighter pilots can be affected by dropping bombs on targets. We're miles away before the impact, and we see everything from a distance, but it still gets to you."

I sat back. "Yeah. Yeah, that's true. I guess not many people think we're susceptible to it, you know?"

"I've heard. Believe me."

"And I guess I get it." I blew out a breath. "It's not the same as being at the front lines. We're not in any physical danger. No one's shooting at us. We don't jump when doors slam or cars backfire. Not like the guys who've been boots on the ground." I thumbed the edge of the table, watching that instead of looking at him. "And we can't talk about it. It's like this shit happens, and there's nowhere for it to go. Even if we could talk about it, people don't take us seriously. I mean, yeah, we're in a cushy-ass room on the other side of the world from the actual war zone we fight in. But we're . . . I mean, we're . . ."

"You're still in a war." Travis's voice was smooth and calming. "You still have to kill people, just like the rest of us."

I couldn't hide the full-body shudder. "Yeah." I lifted my gaze. "We do."

He nodded slowly, and folded his arms tightly on the edge of the table. I wondered if he was tempted to put a hand on mine. Damn shame we were in public, because I could have used that contact right then.

"Look," he said after a moment. "War is hell for everyone involved. I was dropping bombs on targets I couldn't see, going so fast I was out of there before anyone knew what hit them. No one can tell you you're right or wrong for being affected by the part you played in the ops."

"I wish I could tell you that was enough to stop them."

"I know." Travis paused. "You want to know what fucked me up and keeps me awake at night? And why I can't fly anymore?"

I nodded, even though I wasn't so sure I did want to know. "You said something about landing in stormy seas, right?"

"Yeah. Thing is, I flew missions on three separate combat tours." Travis swallowed. "And I lost my wings and my ability to sleep because of a training exercise."

"A training—" I blinked. "Really?"

"Mm-hmm. The carrier landing that fucked up my back? It wasn't during combat ops. I wasn't even carrying ordnance."

"Wow. So . . . what happened?"

He shifted uncomfortably. "A wave hit the ship when I was coming in to land in the dark during a bad storm. Flight deck jumped, and I almost hit the stern, but pulled up just enough. I mean, we still hit it, but not dead-on, thank God. I lost control, slid across the flight deck, and we ejected right before the bird went in the drink." It was his turn to shudder, which made his breath catch. He grimaced, shifted again, and slowly exhaled. "I don't remember anything after that, but my RIO and I both barely pulled through. He's in a wheelchair now. Paraplegic. One of the SAR swimmers got fucked up too." He exhaled slowly and met my gaze. "It's been eight years, and I still get flashbacks from the parts I remember and even the parts I don't."

"Jesus," I breathed.

"Yeah." He moistened his lips. "I have chronic pain from it. Nightmares. I'd rather cut my wrists than watch *that* scene in *Top Gun*."

I didn't have to ask which one.

"My best friend was in a similar crash. They didn't eject or go off the deck, and he more or less walked away from it, but you won't hear me tell him he shouldn't be traumatized from his crash just because mine was"—he made air quotes—"'worse.'"

"I hadn't thought of that."

"Most people don't," he went on. "Thing is, a lot of people are traumatized by different things. It's not like front line combat vets have the monopoly on PTSD. Hell, my *daughter's* got it."

I sat up. "What? Kimber has PTSD?"

"It's . . . well, it's a long story. Something that happened when she was a teenager, and something else from a party she went to a couple of years ago that rattled her pretty hard." He paused. "In fact, it's one of the reasons she still lives with me. She's got a good job and could go out on her own, but she stays with me because we both get each other's PTSD. Her mom has a hard time handling it, and they stress each other out. But me and Kimber, we get it. We're both messed up from completely different things, but we still get it." He met my gaze. "So I'm not going to judge yours."

"Wow," I said. "I can't imagine what it's like when your kid has it."

His lips tightened and he nodded. "Seeing it in her is worse than having it myself. Especially since I can trigger it."

"You . . . how?"

He avoided my eyes for a second. "Mostly if she can't reach me. If I say I'll be home at a certain time, or that I'll call or text, but I don't? She panics. Even when she knows I probably got tied up in a meeting or something, she can get into a downward spiral pretty fast."

I hesitated, then asked, "What caused that?"

Travis took a deep breath. "When she was fifteen, I went on deployment. We had a designated day and time every week when I'd call her. And one night I didn't call. Her mom told her that sometimes the phones on the ships don't work, or I might have been working, and she was fine with that . . . right up until her mom shook her out of bed the next morning to get on a plane to Germany because no one knew if I was going to make it."

"Wow. Poor kid."

He nodded. "So if there's one thing I regret about my career, it's how much it's affected my kid. But the point is, I know PTSD is very, very real. And you don't have to be at ground zero of a war zone to be affected by the war. So you'd better believe I'm the last person who will question if yours is real, or if you've got a good reason for it."

He couldn't have known what a relief that was to hear. Or, hell, maybe he did. Just talking to him brought my blood pressure down a few notches. As much as I wouldn't wish PTSD on my worst enemy, there was something to be said for being in the company of someone who had it. If he had it, he understood it, and that had an almost paradoxical effect.

You get it, so if I freak out, you'll understand. So now I'm not going to freak out.

And after keeping my cards close to my vest because I didn't imagine any pilots would understand, it was liberating and validating to hear him say he did. At least someone did, and the fact that it was someone I was this intimate with . . . well, I'd count that as one hell of a blessing.

Clearing my throat, I looked at the time. "I guess we should eat something and get back before they send a search party after us."

Travis didn't pick up his menu. "You're good, though?"

"I think so, yeah."

"Okay. When we go back, if you're still having a hard time and need to escape, you know where my office is." Our eyes locked. Any other day, there would've been some suggestive subtext there, but not this time. He was offering refuge, not a clandestine quickie.

"Thanks." I paused. "And thanks again for the talk. I . . . really needed that."

"Don't mention it." Finally, he opened his menu. "Now let's see what we can scare up to eat."

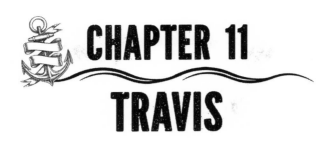

CHAPTER 11
TRAVIS

Now that my good friend Paul was retired, it was a hell of a lot easier for us to meet up. Of course, he was busy with volunteer work and a fiancé, and I was spending most of my non-working hours with Clint these days, but we still managed to carve out time for leisurely Saturday lunches on a somewhat regular basis.

This weekend, while Clint was running errands, I met Paul at the officers' club. He'd been golfing today—my God, when *wasn't* the man golfing?—so he beat me there and got us a table.

He stood as I came in, and I gave him a half handshake, half hug.

"Hey, how are you?" I asked.

"Not bad." As we took our seats, he added, "I could do without some of this wedding-planning shit, but otherwise . . ." He shrugged.

"Wedding planning? I thought you guys were keeping it simple. Doing the whole beach thing or whatever."

"We were." Paul sighed dramatically as he flipped open his menu. "But the future mother-in-law thinks her only son should have a big wedding with everyone they've ever met."

I grimaced. "Who's winning that argument?"

"Don't know. I'm staying out of it." He scowled. "I swear, the first year we were together, he talked to her maybe twice a month. The minute we set a date, she's on the phone with him every other day and constantly bombarding him with emails. Much more of this, he'll be grayer than I am."

"Would he even notice?"

"Well, if he ever lets his natural hair color come back, yeah."

"Is he planning to do that for the wedding?"

Paul grimaced. "With as much as his mom is haranguing him about it, I'm not even going to ask."

"Ouch." I laughed. "So knowing him, he'll show up to the wedding in an electric blue Mohawk."

"At this point, I wouldn't put it past him." Shaking his head, he chuckled. "He's not the spiteful type, but my God, I think he's reached his limit."

"I can only imagine. Smart move on your part to stay out of it."

"Hey, I've been married before. I know better than to argue with a future mother-in-law about anything, *especially* a wedding."

"Yeah, I hear that."

We both laughed again, then picked up our menus. We'd been here enough times we both had the menu memorized, but once in a while, the powers that be mixed things up. Today, it was the usual fare, so I ordered a salmon wrap while Paul—ever a creature of habit—got the steak salad with an extra side of balsamic vinaigrette. As long as I'd known him, he'd done that—when he found something he liked at a restaurant, he'd order it over and over until the end of time.

After the waiter had brought our drinks and taken our orders and menus, Paul folded his hands on the table and gave me an odd look. "So. Who is she?"

I blinked. "Who's who?"

He rolled his eyes. "Oh come on. I'm not as dumb as I look. Spill it."

"But I—"

"For fuck's sake, Travis." He chuckled and ticked off the points on his fingers. "You've been busy as hell lately. You've been grinning like a fool ever since you walked in today. The floating hearts around your head are practically visible from space. And if I'm not mistaken"—he gestured at my neck—"*that's* a bite."

"What? Where?" I tugged self-consciously at my collar.

He snickered. "There isn't one, but you're blushing, so . . ."

"Asshole."

"Come on. Tell me."

It wasn't like he would let it go until I told him, and I'd been guilty of prying Sean's existence out of him when they'd first started dating. Fair was fair.

"Well . . ." I scratched the back of my neck. "First of all, he's not a she."

Paul's eyes widened. "Really?"

I snorted. "Oh, like you're surprised." We'd slept together enough times in our younger days, he was the last person on the planet who could claim surprise that I was with a man.

"I'm just . . . I can't remember the last time you actually *dated* a man." He grimaced apologetically. "I mean, besides . . . um . . ."

"Well." I shifted in my chair, heart sinking because I could read too easily between the lines. "Dion and I never really dated anyway." More to myself, I added, "That was part of the problem."

Paul chewed his lip. "I'm sorry. I shouldn't have . . ."

"It's all right." I rolled my stiff shoulders. "And I mean, you're right. He's the reason I've never had a relationship with a man." I pushed out a breath. "Which is stupid. It's been ten years, for God's sake."

"It's not stupid," Paul said quietly. "I can't imagine anyone could go through that and not be affected by it for a long, long time."

I winced, but didn't speak.

Paul went on, his tone soft and cautious. "Things are going well with this guy, though?"

"Yeah." I managed to smile. "They're going really well. My limitations haven't scared him off." I laughed. "Guess that's promising, right?"

"Sounds like it. So when do I get to meet this guy?"

"Well . . ." My humor faded. I absently tapped my knuckle on the table. "I don't know. I mean, he can deal with my back. But that's one mine in a very large minefield. The novelty of navigating that bullshit might wear off before I have a chance to introduce him to my friends."

"Travis." Paul sighed. "You're not the basket case you think you are."

I arched an eyebrow. "Uh, yes. Yes, I am, and he knows it. And he knows the how and why of the physical stuff." I traced a finger through the condensation on my glass. "But . . . I haven't told him about Dion." Fuck. All these years later, and just saying that man's name still hit me in the chest.

Paul held my gaze. "You think you're going to?"

"Eventually. Maybe?" I sighed. "I don't know. That's kind of a heavy thing to put on someone I haven't been seeing for very long."

"It is." He lifted a shoulder in a half shrug. "But it's a big piece of who you are. At least when it comes to . . . um . . ."

"To getting involved with men?"

Paul nodded.

I couldn't argue with that. No one had ever left an imprint on my life as indelible as Dion. I'd never fallen in love with any other man quite as hard as I had with him, and ever since, every sexual and nearly romantic interaction I'd had with a man had been colored by Dion's death. Losing him had left me terrified of getting that close to someone else, because I could *not* go through that kind of loss twice. It was ridiculously irrational, especially since I hadn't had as much trouble getting close to women, but there it was. The day I'd watched them put Dion in the ground, a wall had gone up around me that no man had ever stood a chance of getting past.

My mind went down this road every time I had more than a one-night stand with a man. The fact that he and I were colleagues and passed in the halls a million times a day didn't help. When things inevitably went to shit, there'd be no avoiding each other.

Or if he were suddenly gone, there'd be no avoiding his absence.

I shuddered.

"You all right?" he asked.

"Yeah." I took a deep swallow of ice water and held on to the glass for something cold to center myself. One of those PTSD coping methods I'd learned years ago. As my pulse slowly came down, I said, "You know, maybe having you meet him wouldn't be a bad idea. At least then you can smack me upside the head if there's some huge red flag I'm not seeing."

Paul shot me a look. "And you really expect me to believe that you'd listen to me if I pointed one out?"

I laughed. "Fair, fair."

"I'll do my best though," he said. "Tell me when and where, and Sean and I will be there."

"Okay. If we're going to do dinner or something . . ." I hesitated. "PRT's a week from Wednesday, so we're both going to be eating like birds until after weigh-ins."

"Put that on the list of things Paul does not miss about the Navy."

"Asshole," I muttered. "Anyway, after Wednesday, we'll both be ready to eat."

Paul grimaced. "You gonna be *walking* after?"

I shifted, ignoring the spasm in the middle of my back. The Physical Readiness Test was the bane of my existence, and I'd be living on Motrin, ice packs, and prayers for a day or two after, but it was a necessary evil. "Okay, maybe we should plan for the day *after* PRT."

"Good plan." He tapped his fingers beside his glass. "You think you'll be okay for the PRT this year?"

"Don't have much choice, do I?"

Our eyes locked. Yeah, I had a choice, but we'd talked about this before. He'd even tried to persuade me onto an elliptical when he was my CO, but . . . no. Even if the elliptical was, on paper, the same as a run, everyone knew it didn't look that way to the boards who determined our promotions.

I'd given in and had a few PRTs waived entirely in the past, but waiving three in a row for the same reason would put me in front of a medical board and my career on the chopping block. If I waived this one, it'd be my luck the next would fall on a day when I could barely get out of bed. So I didn't dare waive a PRT or half-ass it on the elliptical unless I absolutely couldn't run it. As long as I could stand up unassisted on Wednesday, I'd get through it.

Just thinking about it made my stomach turn. Even though I wasn't drinking at the moment, I was tempted to have a cigarette, but not around Paul. For one, he still struggled with his own cravings from time to time. For another, he'd give me endless crap about it and probably threaten to call my mom and tell her I was smoking again. He was kind of a dick like that.

So I held off on the cigarette and shifted the conversation into a direction that wasn't so bumpy. As we talked, though, my stomach was still in knots. I was more nervous about the prospect of a double date than I should've been, but sometimes it was weird to be with Paul and whoever I was dating. We'd never dated, but we'd slept together a few times. Our friendship was intimate to say the least.

Now that I thought about it, I wondered if he approached sex as gingerly as I did these days. Back then, we'd been rough and unbreakable. A couple of aircraft carrier landing mishaps later, we'd both been given a literal crash course in our own mortality. Ever since, the thought of rough sex made my breath catch for very different reasons than it had in my twenties. I hoped it wasn't the same for Paul.

Oh hell, of course it wasn't. He wouldn't be marrying someone twenty years younger than him if he couldn't at least hold his own in the bedroom. I wanted to believe sex wasn't that crucial, but I was too cynical—and had been dumped too many times for being a disappointment in bed—to believe it.

So, I was thankful that age and injuries hadn't stopped Paul from finding the love he'd always deserved.

And I wished I wasn't too damned cynical to believe I'd ever have the same thing.

Even with Clint.

It was that time of year again. Time for everyone in the Navy to prove to the powers that be that we were in shape. Time for the physical readiness test. The PRT. The Periodic Required Torture.

The push-ups I could cope with. Sit-ups made me want to throw myself headlong into a jet intake. Or curl-ups, as they were cruelly called—the last thing a man with back problems wanted to think about was anything that involved his spine and "curling." But I could get through them.

The run, though. God . . . the run.

I reminded myself it was a necessary evil. Alternatives existed, but I was angling for captain, and the boards side-eyed the shit out of anyone who took the so-called easy route.

By the time we eventually went down to the track for the mile and a half run, I'd already be sore as fuck from the first part of the test. Even now I was sick to my stomach just thinking about how sick to my stomach I was *going* to be after the run.

At least it was normal for quite a few people to finish the run and promptly lose their breakfast onto the sidelines. No one would look askance when I joined them. They just didn't need to know I wasn't puking from exertion. I'd pass the test, hopefully with excellent ratings, and nobody would realize it was the pain making me sick. Or that the very mechanism of getting sick made the pain even worse. I shuddered at the thought.

There was no way in hell I would run voluntarily, but when that mile and a half was what kept me from getting booted out of the military, I'd run it like my life depended on it. Sometimes I thought it did. Give up active duty medical care and start relying on the VA after retirement? No, thanks. I preferred to force myself through a run so painful it made me vomit.

In the gym with everyone else from my department, I started the test. I couldn't wear my TENS unit during the sit-ups unless I wanted to grind the leads into my skin. As soon as that segment was finished, though, I put the pads on, connected the wires, and cranked that fucker up to try to calm down the spasms currently spiderwebbing across the middle of my back. During the push-ups, I kept the box in the pocket of my shorts, and prayed it didn't fall out. Which gave me something to concentrate on besides the pain, so it was its own weird silver lining. I'd take it.

With a satisfactory on the sit-ups and a hard-earned excellent on the push-ups, I headed outside with everyone else for the really fun part. As expected, nausea was already churning in my gut. On the way down stairs to the track, muscles were twisting and knotting in my back. How much of that was from the sit-ups and push-ups, and how much was from my anxiety about the run, I had no idea, but it hurt either way.

Clint's eyes widened. "You're really running?"

I laughed. "Until the Navy lets me do the PRT on a Segway, I don't see how I have much choice."

His expression didn't change. "What about the bike?"

"No way." I shook my head. "That's worse on my back than running."

"Really?"

I nodded. "Learned that one the hard way a few years ago."

"Damn." He paused. "You know you can get a medical waiver, right?"

I set my jaw, trying not to be irritated. He did mean well. "Not if I want to get promoted. Same reason I don't fuck with the elliptical."

Though my scores probably didn't help my prospects of getting promoted anyway. *Satisfactory* kept people in the Navy. It didn't move them up the ranks. On the other hand, being over forty put me in a much gentler set of standards—what was *excellent* for me would barely be *satisfactory* for the younger officers. Age had its advantages.

"Well," Clint said. "Good luck."

"You too."

The group stopped on the track to wait for the last few stragglers. As they caught up, I took advantage of the pause to stretch a little and loosen up the muscles in my back. I also turned the TENS up again.

And then, along with everyone else in my department, I ran.

Every step sent pain rocketing up my spine, but I gritted my teeth and kept going. It was only three laps, and it always played out the same way. After the first lap, I was invincible. If I could run with a mile and a half in front of me, I could run with a mile in front of me. And then, after the second lap, there was only half a mile left. I was sure bones were breaking, that ribs and vertebrae were carving their way through my skin and my T-shirt, but the finish line was in sight. All I had to do was cross that line, and I could still make captain. Once I crossed it, I could puke, scream, collapse . . . didn't matter as long as I'd secured my place in the Navy for another six months and still had a vague shot at a promotion.

Halfway through the last lap, I was coming up on a group of younger guys who were jogging leisurely as they carried on a conversation. Oh hell no. Not when Big Navy would have a fit if our base's collective scores weren't up to snuff.

"Come on, kids!" I called out. "You really gonna let an old man pass you?"

They glanced over their shoulders, and as a group, picked up the pace. I stayed hot on their heels—nothing motivated lazy youngsters like trying to stay ahead of the old guy who limped around the office.

I focused on keeping up with them, subtly urging them forward like an aggressive driver on the freeway, tailgating them to encourage a few seconds off their run times. This was yet another reason I insisted on running—I was supposed to be leading these guys, which meant pushing them. I was a lot more effective on the track than on the sidelines.

The pain was excruciating, shooting up and down my spine and even into my hips, but I was almost there. Almost to the end. I'd make it.

Three of the guys in front of me broke from the pack and burst into a sprint. A second later, two more followed. The last two picked up some speed, though they were struggling as it was—they stayed ahead of me, but there was no catching their peers.

The first three crossed the line.

Then the other two.

Then the last two.

And finally . . .

I crossed the line.

It was over. I'd made it.

Vision darkening and head spinning, I slowed down.

Staggered to the sidelines.

Took a knee.

And heaved.

CHAPTER 12

CLINT

I couldn't believe Travis had made it through the run. He'd obviously been in pain, especially toward the end, but I had to give him credit—the son of a bitch made it.

He spat in the grass one more time and took a few breaths, as if making sure that was really it. Then, slowly, he stood, and even more slowly, straightened. When he was just shy of his full height, his breath caught and his eyes flew open. For a second, I thought he was going to get sick again. Somehow, though, he didn't. He exhaled, stood all the way up, and gingerly rubbed his back. Then he took the electronic box out of his pocket, made an adjustment, and put it away again.

My muscles hurt just watching him. His back must've been in agony right then, especially after he'd thrown up.

"Hey," I said. "You doing all right?"

He turned to me and offered a tight smile. "It's over. Can't ask for much more than that."

"Yeah, but are you hanging in there *now*?"

Travis nodded. "I might bust out of the office early today, but once I've had some ice and some sleep, I'll be fine." He gestured at the steps. "We should get back to the locker room."

I didn't argue. I fell into step beside him, and as we walked, couldn't help but notice that his limp was slightly more pronounced. I'd expected it to be significantly worse, but it wasn't. His gait was tight and deliberate, though, like every motion hurt like hell. Maybe that was why he wasn't limping as badly—that kind of faintly jerky movement probably hurt more than a normal, if cautious, step.

I shuddered. I could only imagine navigating through that kind of pain on a daily basis, never mind after something like the PRT.

We followed the rest of the group toward the stairs. As they started up toward the locker rooms, I smothered a laugh. It was easy to tell the guys who worked out on a regular basis from those who pulled it together enough to pass the PRT by the skin of their teeth. For the latter, the long staircase was a killer. While the regular runners headed up like it was nothing, the others took those steps like they were on the last leg of a Mount Everest ascent.

I chuckled to myself. I wanted to rib some of them and ask if they'd learned anything, but that was a no-brainer. They'd all been in long enough, if they were going to learn, they would have before today.

At the bottom of the steps, Travis stopped. He took a deep breath, pushed his shoulders back, and started up. As he walked, he gripped the railing so tight the muscles stood out on his forearm.

His struggle with the ascent wasn't amusing in the slightest. He'd already been sweating from the run, and by the time we reached the top, his hair was dripping.

I fought the urge to put a hand on his elbow as the ground leveled out. "How's your back?"

"It'll be better once I have my date with Lady Percocet tonight." He turned to me and grimaced. "I probably won't be much fun to hang out with."

"It's all right. Just, you know, text me if you need anything."

Travis smiled. "Thanks. Kimber will be home, but I appreciate the offer." His smile faltered a bit. "You, uh, don't mind, do you? If I call it a night tonight?"

"Do I mind? Are you kidding? Go take care of yourself. I'll be okay on my own for an evening." I winked. "Promise."

He studied me uncertainly. "Okay. I guess I, uh . . . I'm sorry. This drives me insane, so it's probably annoying as hell for you."

"Annoying?" My jaw dropped. "Are you kidding? You're the one in pain. What do I have to be annoyed about?"

"Give it time," he said through his teeth as we continued up the path. "You'll figure it out."

"What do you mean?"

He sighed, avoiding my eyes. "My back pain kind of runs my life. I get nervous when it starts interfering with other people's lives, because they don't tend to stick around at that point. And I can't say I blame them."

"Travis." I stopped, and he did too. "You're talking to someone whose life is ruled by something that happened three years ago and won't leave here." I tapped my temple. "I've been told to ignore it, or get over it, or that I'm faking it, because it's literally all in my head." I paused. "Do you really think I'd give up someone who takes me seriously because you've got something from the past fucking with you too?"

His lips parted, and he slowly released a breath. "I hadn't thought of it that way."

I smiled. "Seriously, don't worry about it. You'll have to do a lot worse than have a bad back to get rid of me."

At that, he actually laughed, lowering his gaze.

"Take care of yourself tonight," I said. "See how you feel tomorrow, and then maybe we can do something easy this weekend. I've been meaning to check out the pier in town, so if you want to, we could go walk down there. I mean, if you can move."

"That sounds like fun." Travis paused. "Actually, I have a friend who'd like to meet up with us for dinner if you're interested."

"Sure, I'm in. Let me know when and where."

The smile broadened a little. "Okay. Let me recuperate a bit, and I'll let you know."

"Great. Looking forward to it."

It was a little over a week before Travis had fully recovered and his friends were available. They all knew the town better than I did, so I deferred to them to pick a place. They settled on a bistro a few blocks from the waterfront. I hadn't even heard of it, but apparently Sean and Paul swore by it, and Travis had been impressed the few times he'd been here. That was a good enough endorsement for me.

So, on Saturday afternoon, we sat down at a table by the window.

While we waited for Sean and Paul, I opened the menu and was greeted with all manner of entrées involving sauces and cheeses I'd never even heard of. Everything looked utterly decadent. "Wow. This all sounds amazing."

"Doesn't it?"

"Yep. Thank God PRT is over."

Travis laughed. "This is the best part about post-PRT." He flashed a toothy but somehow uneasy grin. "Eating."

"Damn right." I touched his leg. "You okay today? You seem kind of nervous."

"What? No." He held my gaze, but the tightness of his lips gave him away.

"What's going on? I'm the one who's supposed to be nervous, remember?"

He laughed softly, shifting his eyes toward the menu. "I . . ."

"Talk to me. Is there something I should know before I meet them?"

"Actually . . ." He gnawed his lip.

My stomach clenched. "Travis?"

He inhaled deeply and turned to me. "Okay, it's probably not even a little bit relevant, but I'd feel kind of weird going into this if I didn't tell you."

"All right . . ."

"Paul and I have known each other a long time. Most of my career. When we were younger, we . . . uh . . ."

"He's an ex?"

"Well, not exactly." Some color rose in Travis's cheeks, and he laughed shyly as he lowered his gaze. "I wouldn't say we had a relationship."

"But you slept together."

He nodded. After a second, he looked at me, brow pinched with what seemed like uncertainty. "So I guess I just wanted it out in the open. So there's no—"

"Relax." I patted his leg. "It's not a big deal to me." I paused and faced him again. "Uh, one question."

Travis tensed. "Hmm?"

"Am I allowed to ask him for pointers, or is that—"

He burst out laughing. "Shut up."

"What? It's a valid question, don't you think?"

"If you do, I swear I will—" He glanced at the door and did a double take. "There they are." He turned to me. "Don't you dare."

I smothered a laugh. We both stood as a couple approached, and Travis introduced us.

"This is Paul and his fiancé, Sean," he said. "And this is Clint."

"We've been hearing a lot about you." Paul extended his hand. "It's great to finally meet you."

"Likewise," I said.

We shook hands all around, and they took their seats opposite us. As we all perused the menus, I stole a few looks at them.

They were not a couple I would have expected to see together. At the same time, they were perfect together. There was at least twenty years between them. Even if Sean's hair hadn't been dyed—mostly black with some blue highlights—I was pretty sure he wasn't hiding as much gray as his fiancé had.

And as they discussed dishes and appetizers, all it took was one glance and a quick smile between them, and it was obvious they were madly in love. They were affectionate too. Subtly, but considering they were a same-sex couple out in the open, any little touch could attract unwanted attention. Maybe they felt safe enough here and with us, or maybe they were like this all the time, but I admired how casually and comfortably they touched each other. Sean had his arm slung across the back of Paul's chair for a few minutes. Whenever Paul wasn't flipping through the menu or buttering a piece of bread, he had his hand resting on Sean's leg beneath the table. Once in a while, one would playfully nudge the other, and get an elbow back. They'd go back and forth a few times before erupting into laughter like a couple of kids.

After we'd ordered, gone through a shared plate of brie quesadillas, and were waiting for our entrées, Travis asked, "So how goes the wedding planning?"

Groaning, Sean buried his face in his hands.

Paul laughed, patting Sean's shoulder. "That answer your question?"

"Wedding planning is a nightmare," I said. "I don't envy either of you."

"Ugh." Sean dropped his hands and leaned against Paul. "I really should've put my foot down about keeping it small and simple. My mom wants to invite everyone she's ever known, and . . ." He rolled his eyes. "Every time we talk, the whole thing gets bigger."

"We could always elope," Paul said.

Sean grumbled something I didn't understand. More clearly, "You think she won't leave me alone *now*?"

"Fair point," Paul said into his drink.

Travis and I exchanged glances, and chuckled.

"Anyway." Sean sat up, shaking himself. "Enough about that bullshit." He reached for his drink, and as he did, looked at me. "So you just moved here?"

"Yeah. End of the summer."

"What do you do?" he asked.

"Well, I work in training now, but before I came here, I was a . . ." I hesitated, glancing at Travis. He gave me a slight nod, and I hoped he understood I'd been looking for encouragement before admitting my job to an ex-pilot. "I was an RAP."

"A what?" Sean asked.

"Remote aircraft pilot," Paul said before I could. "He flew drones."

Sean's eyes lit up. "Really? That sounds like a really cool job."

I laughed uncomfortably. "The novelty wears off pretty fast, believe me."

He scowled. "Happens with any kind of work, doesn't it?"

"Well . . ." Travis looked at Paul, and they both grinned.

"Hey, that's not fair." I elbowed Travis. "I wouldn't call screaming around the sky at Mach 1 'work.'"

Paul shrugged. "I got paid for it."

"I had to get out of bed at ass thirty to do it," Travis said.

"There was paperwork involved," Paul said.

"Ah." Travis pointed at him and looked at me. "Paperwork. That makes it work."

Laughing, I put up my hands. "All right, all right. You guys win."

Sean chuckled and patted Paul's shoulder. "No wonder you're bored with retirement."

"Of course I am." Paul sighed dramatically. "What is a guy supposed to do with himself when he doesn't have to be out of bed until whenever-he-wants o'clock?"

"Oh, shut up," Travis muttered. "And besides, what about that volunteer gig you had? At the animal shelter?"

Paul sobered and shook his head. "I had to quit. Too depressing. We're still going to send them donations when we can, but I just . . . I couldn't keep doing it."

Sean turned to him and raised an eyebrow. "And the other reason?"

Paul laughed sheepishly, resting a hand on Sean's leg. "Because I kept coming home and asking you if we could adopt one more critter?"

"Uh-huh."

I laughed. "So how many did you collect before you quit?"

Sean released an exasperated sigh and held up seven fingers. "Four dogs. Three cats. And we fostered a parrot for two very, very long months."

"How did that go?"

Sean facepalmed. Paul groaned.

"That good, eh?" Travis chuckled. "I thought you liked birds."

"I did," Paul said. "Right up until I had to keep chasing one around the house and pulling him down from the crown molding, which he was trying to chew. And I had to use a damn oven mitt so he didn't take my hand off."

"We tried to have his wings clipped," Sean said. "But neither of us could do it, everyone at the shelter was afraid of him, and then a lady came along who knows how to handle parrots. So he's her problem now."

"And he's probably still talking trash about us," Paul grumbled.

"Well." Travis shrugged. "Can you blame him?"

"Fuck you, Travis."

Sean and I both snickered. To me, he said, "See why these two get along?"

"Mm-hmm." I glanced at Travis. "Two batshit peas in the same batshit pod."

"Hey!" Travis wagged a finger at me. "Show some respect."

"Respect my elders?" I shot back.

Sean and Paul both laughed.

"He's got you there, Travis," Paul said.

"And you'll always be older than me," Travis said. "So bite me, Gramps."

Yeah, I thought as the banter went on, *I could* definitely *get along with this group.*

A few hours, an amazing meal, and a lot of shit-talking later, we said goodbye to Paul and Sean, and walked back toward Travis's car.

"So," he said as he took his keys out of his pocket. "What'd you think?"

"They're a lot of fun." I paused. "What do you think they thought of me?"

Travis shrugged. "Well, I can usually tell if Paul's giving my date the side-eye, and I didn't see him do it once today. So . . . I'd say he likes you."

"Phew." I made a theatrical gesture of wiping my brow. "Then we can keep fucking."

He laughed, elbowing me gently. "It would take a lot more than Paul's disapproval to chase me out of your bed."

"Really?"

"Mm-hmm." He stopped, and when I faced him, he grinned. "In fact, you could probably chase me into it right about now."

"Is that right?" Never in my life had I wished more for the confidence to touch a man in public.

"Yep." He nodded toward the car. "What do you say we get the hell out of here?"

"I say, 'Why are we still standing here?'"

"Good point."

We hurried to the car, got in, and headed back to my place.

And even if I couldn't touch him in public, I had no reservations whatsoever about touching him in the privacy of my apartment.

Faster, Travis, faster . . .

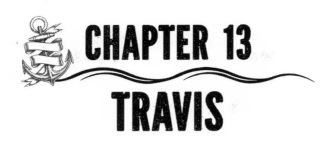

CHAPTER 13

TRAVIS

Since Clint hadn't been to Anchor Point's infamous pier, I took him down there on Sunday afternoon. Of course, being November, it wasn't exactly packed with people or vendors like it would be in the summer. I preferred it this way anyway.

So I parked in the mostly empty lot, and we strolled out onto the wooden pier.

There was a sparse crowd today. I suspected the whole place would've been empty if the weather hadn't been unusually nice for this time of year. The Oregon coast could be sunny and gorgeous, or shitty and gray, and the last few days had been beautiful. This morning had been chilly—almost enough to turn the dew on my lawn into frost—but the afternoon was just cool enough to require a light jacket to fend off the wind coming in from the ocean.

During the summer, the smell of funnel cakes and popcorn would overpower the diesel fumes from the booths' generators, not to mention the saltwater. Today, though, the only places selling food aside from the restaurants along the waterfront were a permanent ice cream shop that apparently never closed, and a row of vending machines next to the restrooms.

Along the south edge of the pier, a few of the game booths were up and running. Most of them were deserted. A young dad was coaching his kids—they couldn't have been more than four or five—on how to pop balloons with darts, and some teenagers were earnestly debating whether to cough up another five dollars to try knocking over milk bottles with a softball. Otherwise, the operators alternated between checking their phones and trying not to look *too* bored.

"Man, my kids love these games." Clint's smile was equally sad and nostalgic as we slowed down. "My older son is like a wizard at some of them."

"Yeah? I thought they were all rigged."

"They are. But I think he googled how to beat them or something." He stopped in front of the milk-bottle game, gaze fixed on the pyramid of bottles. "We practically needed a garbage bag to get all of his prizes out of Circus Circus."

I laughed. "That's impressive. How old is he?"

"He just turned twelve." He picked up one of the softballs, tossed it up in the air, and caught it. "He was eight when he relieved Circus Circus of most of their stuffed animals."

"Wow." I whistled. "Smart kid."

His smile broadened, and he nodded. Motioning toward the milk bottles, he said, "This is the only game I've ever been good at. Once you figure out how the bottles are weighted, it's not that hard."

"Yeah?" I took out my wallet and put a ten on the counter beside the softballs. "Prove it."

Clint chuckled. "Seriously?"

"Yep." I waved for the girl running the game to collect the money. "Seriously."

She picked up the ten, handed me a dollar in change, and stepped out of the way. "Each throw is three bucks. You have to knock all three bottles down in one throw to win."

"Fair enough." Clint took off his leather jacket and handed it to me. Then he tossed the ball in the air and caught it again. He did that a couple of times while he eyed the bottles. "All right. Here we go."

He didn't just throw the ball. He wound up like a major league pitcher and *slammed* that fucker into the stack of milk bottles. For a second, I didn't even notice if the bottles had fallen. I was much too busy replaying the image of him throwing it. *Holy . . .*

I turned my head. He'd knocked the top bottle over, but the other two were still standing. As the kid behind the counter reset them, Clint picked up another ball.

"So." I cleared my throat. "You figure out how they're weighted yet?"

"Not yet. Might take a couple of tries."

Fine by me.

The second throw fucked with my pulse as much as the first one had. Maybe even more this time because I'd known it was coming, and I was already drooling just thinking about it. I swore the whole thing happened in slow motion—Clint drawing back, T-shirt pulling snug over his shoulders, lips tightening across his teeth—before he launched that softball across the counter.

This shouldn't be that hot. He's throwing a ball, for God's sake.

"Damn." He laughed, shaking his head. "Let's hope the third time's the charm."

My mouth had gone dry, so I just nodded. While he sized up the pyramid of bottles, I glanced around, wondering if there was an ATM nearby. At three dollars per throw, I might need some more cash to keep this particular bit of entertainment going for a while. I didn't even care if he won—I was perfectly content to watch him throw.

I shook myself. It had been a long time since a man had made my pulse race quite like he did. The fact that I already knew what he was like in bed was almost surreal.

"Finally!" He pumped his fist and grinned, and when I turned, all the milk bottles had been toppled over. One of them even rolled, teetered on the edge, and dropped onto the concrete with a satisfying *clank*.

"Nice!" I laughed. "So I guess I can't bust your chops at work, can I?"

"Nope." Under his breath, he muttered, "Asshole."

The kid running the game handed over his prize, which turned out to be a steering wheel-sized plush . . . doughnut. It even had pink frosting and multicolored sprinkles.

We both stared at it.

To the kid, Clint asked, "When did you guys start doing stuffed pastries instead of stuffed animals?"

She shrugged. "That's what the company sends."

"Oh. Okay." He eyed it, and then his face lit up with a wicked grin. "I think I know what we can do with this! We should give it to one of the sentries on base."

I snorted. "Oh, I'm sure they'd love that. I mean, cops and doughnuts . . ."

"Exactly."

The kid rolled her eyes and laughed. Clint tucked the doughnut under his arm, and we stepped away from the booth.

"So, um." I looked around. "You want to keep going?" I pointed toward the far end of the pier. "Check out what's down that way?"

"How's your back doing?"

"Not bad."

"You're okay to keep walking around?"

"Yeah, yeah." I waved a hand. "I've got some Motrin with me if it acts up."

"Sure, we can keep going, then."

So, we did. Strolling along, talking about nothing, we kept going toward the middle of the long pier where several people were fishing over the edge next to the No Fishing signs. A couple were hoisting up a crab pot, and a dozen seagulls patrolled the area in search of handouts or unattended catches.

Clint stopped. "Do I hear seals?"

I craned my neck. It was hard to hear much over the squawking seagulls and the country music blasting from someone's radio, but then I heard the distinctive barking. "Yeah, I think you do. Or sea lions. I think that's all they have here."

We moved toward the sound and looked over the railing into the water.

Sure enough, four sea lions were bobbing below us, heads poking through the surface as if waiting for the fishermen above to toss them something.

"Looks like there's a couple more." Clint pointed at the water a few feet away from them. Either it was a trick of the light, or there were others swimming underneath. A second later, another whiskered head popped up.

While Clint leaned over the railing and watched the sea lions, I surreptitiously adjusted the intensity on my TENS. The pain was mild today, but there was a hint of tension in the middle of my back that *could* turn into a vicious spasm if I didn't stay on top of it. Walking around on the slightly uneven pier probably wasn't helping, but I wasn't ready for this day to be over, so I prayed for the TENS to work its magic along with the ibuprofen I'd dry-swallowed earlier while

Clint wasn't looking. Not that he'd have judged—I just hated people seeing how much I relied on pain control.

The sea lions kept on playing below us, and we watched for a while. After they lost interest and swam away, we kept walking out to the far end of the pier, which was completely deserted.

There, Clint folded his arms on the weathered railing, and took in a deep breath through his nose. "Man, I didn't even realize it until I came to Anchor Point, but I fucking missed being close to the ocean."

"Yeah, every time I've had to be away from it for any length of time, I started going crazy."

Clint nodded. "Seriously. Told you before—I did *not* join the Navy so I could go live in the desert."

I laughed. "Well, I didn't join it so I could work behind a desk, but . . ."

"God, isn't that the truth." He turned toward me. "Could be worse, right? I mean, the whole Monday-through-Friday, nine-to-five stuff has its perks."

"Oh, no kidding. I do not miss duty weekends or night ops."

He grunted softly and nodded. "Double-digit shifts are the worst. And months-long deployments."

"Hear, hear." I paused. "But, hell, they can stick me on a ship if they have to. As long as they don't move me away from the water."

"Yep. I don't even know what it is." He shook his head, gaze fixed on the water. "I spent my first eighteen years in Colorado. Didn't even see the ocean until I was fifteen. Now I can't stand to be away from it."

I just nodded. The ocean was a funny thing. It had nearly killed me, and to this day, the thought of swimming in saltwater made my heart race, but after twenty-three years on ships and coasts, I didn't like being far from it. Being landlocked for any length of time was disconcerting for reasons I couldn't quite explain. It was . . . suffocating somehow. Lakes and rivers didn't cut it, either. I needed to be close to water that reached a horizon.

"You would think we'd be tired of the ocean," I said quietly. "After six months on a goddamned boat, I couldn't imagine wanting to see water again as long as I lived. But two weeks after we came home . . ."

"Yeah," Clint breathed. "After my first deployment, I went home to Denver for a while. Hadn't been on the ground three days, and I was already itching to get back."

"Amen to that. My ex-wife and I went to see her family in Oklahoma after I came home." Shaking my head, I muttered, "I couldn't tell if it was the dry land or my in-laws, but I was ready to go AWOL and haul ass back to Norfolk."

He laughed. "In-laws were that bad?"

"Eh, they were a mixed bag. Brother-in-law was a hard-core pacifist who liked to regale me with statistics about civilian casualties—"

Clint shuddered hard, humor vanishing.

"But for the most part they were all right," I said quickly. "Just . . . you spend six months on a boat with your squadron, and suddenly you're surrounded by a completely different crowd. Like the whole world's got a completely different rhythm, and nobody gets why you're not used to it. It's weird."

"It is, yeah." He shifted his weight and nodded, and slowly, he started to relax again. Tilting his head to one side, then the other, he said, "I guess I was lucky. My ex-wife was a Navy brat, so her family knew what it was like. They knew—and she knew—that it was an adjustment coming back to shore. They followed my lead with everything."

"Wow. I would've sold my soul for an adjustment period when I came back." I paused. "I mean, like I said, they were great people. My ex-wife too. But they had no idea. It took two deployments before she realized that when I came back, the last thing I wanted to do was go out and do everything I hadn't been able to do at sea. Mostly I wanted to sleep, be around people I'd missed, and have some downtime." I laughed softly. "Ironically, about the time we'd figured it out, and we knew how to handle me coming back from a deployment, we split up."

Clint grimaced. "Damn."

"Yeah. I kind of knew it was coming, though. We were going through a bad patch, and I had to go to sea again."

"Ah, yeah. Nothing like a deployment to make an actual separation seem like a better idea."

Nodding, I said, "Uh-huh. So I'd basically call home once a week, talk to my daughter, and fight with my wife. Halfway through the deployment, we decided we'd had enough. So . . ." I paused, then shook my head. "Anyway. That's a downer of a conversation, so forget I brought it up."

Clint shrugged, facing the water again. "I don't think it's possible to talk about the Navy life without divorces coming into it."

"No, but . . ." I glanced around, making sure we were absolutely alone. Then I turned toward him and slid a hand over the small of his back. "We came out here to enjoy an afternoon together. Not talk about all of that shit. Why wallow in our pasts when the present is pretty damn good?"

He straightened a little, muscles moving subtly under my hand and his jacket, and the corners of his mouth rose. He faced me, and as he moved, my hand wound up on his waist. He snaked his own hand under my jacket, and I inched closer to him.

"You're right." A grin played at his lips. "This is a much better topic."

And then, right there, out in the open in a public place, Clint kissed me.

Everything else disappeared. The pier, the past, the people who might or might not see us and notice there were two men getting close like this—they were just gone.

Wrapping my arms around him, I took in a deep breath through my nose. God. Clint's kiss and the smell of the ocean. What more could a man want?

Through my shirt, his fingers grazed the TENS wires and one of the pads, but if he noticed, he didn't let on. And I couldn't bring myself to care. The pain was bearable at the moment, and anyway, I was much more interested in how his lips felt against mine.

I loved this. I loved it so much. Maybe I'd just been on my own too long, but I was completely overwhelmed by the feeling of someone being so brazenly affectionate. He knew I could barely walk sometimes. He knew our sex life would always be limited.

He knew, and here we were—kissing in the sun with his fingers on my back and my arm around his waist.

One part of my mind wanted to slam shut and push him away. I'd never let myself get close to a man before because the inevitable end scared the hell out of me. Either he'd get tired of the reality of my situation—a reality where TENS units, ice packs, and pain pills were part of every-single-day life—or the universe would throw us some horrendous curve ball.

I was fucking terrified, but I also wanted to see where this thing went. Maybe the inevitable disastrous end wasn't as inevitable as I'd convinced myself it was. These things worked out for people all the time. Why not me? Why not us?

I drew back and looked in his eyes, and when he smiled, I thought my knees and the pier were going to collapse right out from under me.

Yeah. Why not *us?*

He gulped. So did I. How long had we been standing here looking at each other like this?

Oh hell, I didn't care. I touched his face and kissed him softly. When our eyes met again, his smile seemed shy. He glanced back toward the shore, and some color bloomed in his cheeks. Or maybe that was from the nippy sea breeze, and I just hadn't noticed till he turned his head.

"We should, um . . ." He cleared his throat and looked at me through his lashes. "Should we head back?"

"Sure. Guess we can't stay out here all day, can we?"

He laughed. "Probably not. Unfortunately."

"Might start getting weird looks."

"Might?" He leaned in and kissed me again. "We stay out here like this, we'll end up doing something that'll get us nailed for public indecency."

Dear sweet Jesus, Mary, and Joseph . . . "That . . . that's not really going to convince me we should leave."

"Right?" He nodded toward the land end. "Come on. Let's go grab something to eat, and then maybe we can indulge in some private indecency later."

"Have I mentioned how much I love the way you think?"

"A time or two, yes."

"Seemed like a good time to remind you, I guess."

We both laughed, and as we started back, he said, "So since you know your way around Anchor Point better than I do, I assume you know a few decent places to eat?"

"Absolutely. Kimber and I have grazed our way through every inch of this town."

He chuckled. "Perfect. By the way, dinner's on me tonight." With a sheepish smile, he added, "Since you paid for, uh . . ." He held up the doughnut.

"My pleasure." An image of him pitching that ball flashed through my mind. *No, really. My pleasure.* "You know, you could probably throw a few more and see if you can upgrade that thing."

"To what? A giant Bundt cake?"

"Or a dozen doughnuts?"

"Just what I need." He eyed it. "Though I have been meaning to get some throw pillows . . ."

"I'd pay to see that."

"Of course you would."

Wandering back toward the game booths, Clint glanced around, and that sad, nostalgic smile came back. "I'll have to bring my kids here one of these days."

"They might have more fun during the summer. There's a lot more going on."

Clint nodded. When he turned to me, his smile was a touch more guarded. "Hopefully they'll be able to come out then. I think they'd have a good time."

I wasn't sure what to say, but fortunately, he picked that moment to ask, "So . . . dinner?" He nodded toward the shore end of the pier again. "Looks like there's a couple of places down that way."

"Sure. Yeah. Let's see what's there."

We fell back into amiable conversation, avoiding the subject of his kids and why they weren't with him, and he seemed to relax a bit. My curiosity ate at me, but I figured that, as with everything, the information would come out in due time. When he was ready to open up, he would, so I let it go.

The first restaurant didn't seem all that appealing—too crowded and with a weird smell wafting out the door—but the next one was quieter and didn't smell like bilge water. The menu was posted outside the door, so we stopped and gave it a look.

"Anything sound good?" I asked.

"Hmm." His lips quirked. "The soup of the day sounds interesting."

I skimmed the menu until I found it. "'A classic recipe with a local touch.'"

"What does that even mean?"

I glanced out at the ocean, then scowled at the menu. "I'll bet it means they put some kind of seafood in it."

Clint laughed. "What's wrong? You don't like seafood?"

"I don't mind seafood. What I don't like is *surprise* seafood."

His eyebrow arched. "Surprise seafood?"

"Yeah. Like when I ordered pasta in Guam, and after a few bites, I realized the little dots of parmesan cheese were actually suction cups that had fallen off the tentacle that was buried in the noodles."

He made a gagging noise. "Oh. God. Gross."

"Exactly. So I'm fine with seafood—I just want to know in advance if it's in there, you know?"

Shuddering, he nodded. "I think that would put me off pasta forever."

"Eh." I shrugged. "It wasn't *that* bad. No worse than the things they serve on ships."

"Ugh. Seriously. I could tell you some stories about things I've eaten underway, but you've probably eaten variations."

"I'll bet," I said. "And I've probably heard or told variations of most sea stories anyway, food-related or otherwise."

"Probably, yeah."

I schooled my expression. "You know the difference between a sea story and a fairy tale, right?"

He raised an eyebrow. "No . . ."

"A fairy tale starts with 'Once upon a time,'" I deadpanned. "And a sea story starts with 'Y'all ain't gonna believe this shit!'"

He threw his head back and laughed, and my stomach fluttered. God, I loved the way he smiled. "That one I hadn't heard."

I just chuckled, pretending he hadn't made me weak in the knees by laughing. Then I gestured at the restaurant. "So, uh. Think we should give it a try?"

Clint smiled and motioned for me to go inside. "After you."

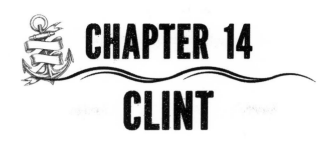

CHAPTER 14

CLINT

This was my new normal, and I loved it—lying in bed with Travis, naked and satisfied. Sometimes we'd watch TV. Sometimes we'd just talk about whatever. The nights when we couldn't be together like this were weird. I'd spent my whole life not lying in bed with him, and now when I wasn't doing that, I wasn't sure what to do with myself.

There was one part I hated about nights like this, though—the inevitable end.

Tonight, we were kicked back in bed where we'd been watching some dumb cop drama, and the episode was winding down. They'd figured out who the perp was, and were exchanging wisecracks to kill time before the credits rolled. In a minute or so, we'd have to decide if we'd watch another, or if we'd give in to the clock above the screen that said it was quarter to eleven.

As if on cue, a cop made one last snarky comment, everyone laughed, and the credits came on.

Beside me, Travis sat up. He arched and twisted his back, which popped audibly a couple of times.

I ran the backs of my fingers up his arm. "You all right?"

"Yeah." He put his hand on my thigh. "Just a little tight from staying in one place too long." He glanced up at the clock, and I barely kept myself from sighing with preemptive disappointment before he said, "I should probably call it a night." He kissed me softly. "Early meetings and all that."

"Yeah. I've got a few myself."

We both rose, and between us, found the various pieces of clothing we'd tossed on the floor. I pulled on a pair of boxers while he got dressed. As we headed for the front door, I was tempted as always to ask him to stay the night, but that wasn't a good idea quite yet. We were fine in bed when we were both still awake. When it came time to go to sleep, that had the potential to get . . . complicated.

So like we did every time, we paused at the door for a long kiss good night, and then he was gone.

Alone in my bedroom, I lay back on the pillows, hands laced behind my head, and grinned up at the ceiling. A year ago, all I'd been hoping for was some light after two solid years of darkness. Six months ago, I'd been content to make it through the day without losing my mind. No amount of encouragement from my few remaining supporters had helped. It was always darkest before dawn? Fuck you. This won't last forever? Kiss my ass. You'll get through this? Fucking prove it.

In all that time, I had never once imagined feeling like this again. Genuine happiness? Affection? Excitement about anything?

Holy shit. There really was some light at the end of all this. Maybe I was finally coming out on the other side.

Nothing would ever be the way it was before, but for the first time in a long time, I could believe that the future had a shot at being a good one.

The next night, after we'd found ourselves in the usual tangle of sheets, it was getting close to that time again. When one of us would have to broach the subject, and another amazing evening would come to an end.

But throughout the night—when I wasn't balls-deep in his mouth, anyway—a thought had been nagging at me. We'd been doing this for over a month now. Maybe it was time to test the waters.

I pushed myself up on my elbow. "Do you, um . . ." I pretended my heart wasn't pounding. "Do you want to stay here tonight?"

Travis tensed, avoiding my eyes. "I . . ."

We were in my bed, naked and comfortable, and though I was nervous about the prospect of sleeping beside him, I wasn't ready for him to leave. Except if he stayed, then there was a good chance he'd see me at my worst.

I cleared my throat. "You can say no."

"It's not that I don't want to."

"But . . .?"

"I guess it's just something new." He laughed halfheartedly. "Something we haven't done before."

"True."

He ran his hand up my bare chest. "I would like to, though. If you're sure."

"I am. I . . ." I hesitated. "Listen, in the interest of full disclosure, my PTSD is no joke. I, uh, have the occasional night terror." *Occasional?* "They can be kind of . . . um . . ."

"Violent?"

Swallowing hard, I nodded. "Yeah."

"Me too."

My heart skipped. "Really?"

"Yeah."

We held each other's gaze. Just like when he'd first told me about his PTSD, as much as I would never wish this kind of trauma on anyone, I had to admit I found a hell of a lot of relief in the realization that he knew what it was like to dread going to sleep at night.

"So we both know what can happen," I said.

Travis nodded. "We do. I'm still in if you are."

My nerves were slowly subsiding, so I grinned. "I'm in."

Before long, we were settled in to go to sleep together. It was strange, not watching the clock or trying to force myself to stay awake so I wouldn't accidentally drift off next to him.

"On the bright side," he murmured, brushing his lips beneath my ear, "you've worn me out enough tonight I'll probably sleep like the dead."

"Me too." I wanted to believe that so badly.

Please, God, don't let my past fuck it up. Give us a few good nights first.

Travis draped his arm over me, and we lay like that for a while. Eventually, though, it got a bit hot with both our body heat and the covers. I was on my side. He was on his back. We weren't touching anymore, but I still loved having him here. I'd hated sleeping alone ever since my ex had kicked me out of the house.

Now if we could get to sleep, we'd be in good shape.

From his breathing, he was still awake. Maybe he was staring into the darkness like I was, or maybe he'd closed his eyes and was patiently waiting for sleep to take over. And it could show up and take over any time. Any minute. Any fucking time now. Tonight, preferably. Please?

Maybe this was a bad idea. It had seemed like an okay idea, but putting it into practice was . . . not so much.

It had been fine with Logan. Most of the time, he'd slept right through any episodes that rattled me awake. Slept? More like stayed passed-out drunk. When he'd been sober enough to wake up with me, he didn't mind. As far as he was concerned, if both of us were awake, that was an opportunity for some more sex. I went with it every time because that was easier and less embarrassing than focusing on the nightmare that had woken us both up. And as much as I hated to admit it, the sex did help me slip back off to sleep afterward.

I wasn't in the mood for sex with Travis. I was too nervous. Too freaked out about freaking out. About him seeing me freak out. Every time I came close to drifting off, I imagined myself thrashing out of a dream and startling the hell out of him. Or, worse, smacking him with a hand or an elbow. That was what had driven my ex-wife into the guest room a few weeks before she'd kicked me out. Even she had understood it had been a dream, that I'd been completely unconscious when it had happened, but could I blame her for not wanting to sleep next to someone who'd flailed hard enough to bruise her arm?

He was still awake too. Every move I made, he'd hear it. If I breathed, snored, murmured—he'd hear it. Which would've been fine, except a few exes had mentioned that I muttered in my sleep sometimes. Usually right before I freaked out and woke up panicking and convinced I was somewhere other than here. As long as I stayed awake, I wouldn't freak out.

It occurred to me that Travis had PTSD too. He'd mentioned he had night terrors like mine. So what if he had one, and I was sound asleep and couldn't try to rouse him from the nightmare? Or what if we had one at the same time? Would we make each other's worse?

And what difference did it make if we were both so goddamned worried that we couldn't sleep?

This was a mistake. We should've stuck with going back to our respective houses after we'd fooled around. What were we thinking?

That night was one of the longest I'd had in recent memory. I drifted in and out of sleep. Never far enough to dream, and definitely never far enough to get any rest. When the birds started chirping and the morning light knifed its way through the edges of the downturned blinds, I was both frustrated and relieved. I hadn't had nearly enough sleep, but there hadn't been any night terror disasters. So . . . kind of a win? Not a complete loss?

Travis must've finally fallen asleep, and he was still out, so I quietly got out of bed and went downstairs to put on the coffee.

He wasn't far behind, shuffling into the kitchen in his boxers as I was taking my first desperately needed sip.

"Morning," I said.

"Morning." He rubbed his hand over his unshaven jaw. "I smell coffee, right? I'm not hallucinating?"

"Nope. Not hallucinating." I pushed a mug toward him on the counter. "Help yourself."

"Thanks."

As he poured his coffee, I asked, "You get any sleep?"

Travis yawned, shaking his head. "I'd be lying if I said I did."

Awkward silence elbowed its way in between us. We sipped our coffee, but didn't look at each other and didn't speak until I finally couldn't take any more.

"Listen." I set my coffee cup down. "Maybe we should get this out in the open."

Travis swallowed. "Okay?"

"We know we both have PTSD. And that it apparently comes out when we sleep."

He nodded, suppressing a shudder. "Yeah. It does. Do you get flashbacks during the day? Anything like that?"

Avoiding his eyes, I fidgeted. "Sometimes. Nightmares more than anything." I paused. "The nightmares are almost constant, but it takes a lot—like some really bad stress—to set off a flashback."

"Almost constant?" He shifted his weight. "Like, every night?"

I nodded, face burning as if it were something to be ashamed of. "Sometimes more than once."

"Jesus. That must be hard to live with."

"That's why I usually don't ask anyone else to live with it."

Travis came closer and put his forearms on my shoulders. "I meant it must be hard for *you* to live with. You're the one who has the nightmares."

"I know." I dropped my gaze again. "But you have them too."

"And does that make you any less inclined to stay the night with me?"

"No."

He smiled. "Same here. So, I think we'll be all right."

I rested my hands on his waist. "Nightmares are kind of a regular thing for me, though. But sometimes they're . . ."

"Really bad?"

"*Really* bad."

He grimaced. "Yeah. Mine too. Doesn't happen often, but it does happen." He reached up and touched my face. "So it's out in the open. We know it's bound to happen sooner or later. Eventually, one of us is going to have a really bad episode and the other's going to be there for it."

I shuddered. "Can't wait."

"Yeah. I know. Me too. But I mean, if and when it does happen, we both know what it is. It's nothing to be embarrassed about."

I chewed my lip. "True."

"We can ease into it if you want. Maybe start on the weekends. Couple of nights here and there. See how it goes."

I mulled it over for a moment. "Or we can start with tonight and go from there."

Travis smiled. "I'm good with that."

"Okay. We can try."

"For what it's worth," he said, "it's nothing to worry about. I promise. You're not going to scare me off by having the same damn thing I've lived with for eight years."

"Thanks. I'll, um, keep that in mind." I finally managed to return the smile. "For next time."

CHAPTER 15

TRAVIS

One of us and *eventually* turned out to be *me* and *less than a week later.*

Once we'd had our conversation about PTSD episodes, Clint and I had relaxed enough to actually sleep next to each other, so most nights, we did. We both had the odd nightmare that jostled the other, but nothing severe. At least, not severe by our standards. If he started thrashing, I'd put a hand on his arm to keep him from smacking me, and talk to him gently until he woke up. Then I'd wrap my arm around him and we'd both fall back to sleep. He'd do the same for me. Every time it happened and wasn't a big deal, I swore we both slept better afterward.

Thursday, though. Thursday, I was fucked, and I knew it. The deck was stacked against me as soon as I walked in that morning.

At nine o'clock, I accompanied the CO and XO to the base pool to watch a demonstration by the newly minted class of search-and-rescue swimmers. At first, I didn't think anything of it. I'd swum in that pool myself, and overseen swim tests from time to time. That chlorine-scented building with its cavernous echo was as familiar as my own office.

Sitting with the other officers in the bleachers, though, I started to get a creepy feeling at the base of my spine when the team of swimmers walked in carrying their fins, masks, and snorkels. Even then, I didn't expect the demonstration to trigger anything. After all, I had no memory of when the SAR swimmers had pulled me out of the Atlantic. The last thing I remembered was hitting the back of the ship. I didn't remember skidding across the flight deck. I didn't remember the split-second decision to eject just before the jet careened off the side. I sure as fuck didn't remember landing in the storm-tossed ocean or being pulled—bleeding and unconscious—from the same.

Maybe that was the problem. I couldn't remember how everything had gone down, so it was a giant question mark in my head. A series of events that had meant the difference between me living or dying—whether by drowning or bleeding out—and it had been completely out of my control. One wrong move could have paralyzed me like my RIO. A line could have snapped. A machine could have failed. One of the violent waves could have pulled us under or slammed us into the ship's hull or smacked someone with a piece of debris from the aircraft. A goddamned shark could have followed the scent of all that blood in the water, especially after one of the swimmers got a little too well acquainted with a jagged piece of metal and had to be rescued herself.

I never did find out how many swimmers were in the water to save Charlie and me. How many more could have been injured like the one who'd torn her leg open? By the grace of God, though, everyone—the wounded swimmer, Charlie, the rest of the SAR swimmers, and myself—had made it out of those storm-tossed seas and onto the ship. Ultimately, we'd all survived.

And today, in the safety of a calm indoor swimming pool on the other side of the world, I couldn't breathe. I had no memory of ever believing I was going to drown, but right then, my lungs were filling up with saltwater. My eyes and sinuses burned. Did I smell jet fuel? I couldn't—

"Commander?" Captain Rodriguez's voice jarred me back into the present. When I turned to her, she cocked her head. "You all right?"

I nodded, absently wiping the sweat off my forehead and trying not to appear too relieved that the cold saltwater had vanished. "Yeah. Sorry." I cleared my throat, which didn't taste like the ocean or blood or fear. "The chlorine gets to me sometimes."

Her eyes narrowed a bit, skepticism etched across her features.

And suddenly I realized everyone was staring. At us. At me. Christ—how obvious had I been?

The master chief putting on the demonstration muffled a cough, drawing everyone's attention back to him, and continued his introduction. Cool relief and hot embarrassment both rushed over me. I didn't hear a word the man said, but at least I was back in the here and now. I concentrated on staying here. Breathing slowly. Being consciously aware of the chlorine instead of salt and jet fuel.

After the demonstration, I left as soon as I could do so without drawing attention to myself. I calmed down in my office and shifted my focus to my work, but I was still rattled. It blew my mind that something as simple as a SAR demonstration could bring so much shit bubbling up from my subconscious from *years* ago. For the rest of the day, my skin was crawling.

So I knew damn well that if I stayed at Clint's tonight, I was asking for it. His place was familiar, but not familiar enough to calm down my fucked-up psyche if—when—I woke up in the middle of an episode.

But I also didn't want to sleep alone. Which was weird. I slept alone more often than not, and having an episode with someone else beside me had always been embarrassing as hell.

For some reason, though, I wanted Clint there tonight. Maybe because I wanted to see if he knew what he was getting into when we'd agreed that something like this would happen eventually. If I was going to scare him off, I might as well do it sooner than later.

Around noon, he poked his head into my office and gently knocked on my open door. "You busy?"

I smiled as I pushed a binder aside. "Not really, no."

"Want to go grab lunch?"

Lunch. Food. My stomach lurched just thinking about it.

And my response must not have been all that subtle, because Clint's eyebrows rose. Then he stepped in and shut the door behind him. "You all right?"

"Yeah, I . . ." I rubbed a hand over my face. Then I got up and came around the desk, mostly because I was suddenly full of nervous energy and needed to *move*. I leaned against the desk and drummed my nails rapidly on its edge. "Listen, um . . ." I shrugged away a shudder. "This morning was . . . sketchy." I tapped my temple. "Some triggery shit that's still kind of under my skin."

Clint nodded. "Understood."

"Tonight's going to be rough. If you don't want—"

"Travis." He put a hand on my waist and kissed me lightly. "It's fine."

"I'm serious. Nightmares are one thing. When something has me this rattled during the day, the night is going to suck."

He nodded again. "Believe me, I know how it goes."

"I know you do." I wrapped my arms around him. "But it's not pleasant. So if you don't want to be there for it, I'll understand."

"I want to be there for you." His cheeks colored. "Okay, that sounded a lot cheesier than it did in my head, but seriously—it sucks to go through, and it's worse to go through it alone."

"True." I released a breath. "All right. We can give it a shot, I guess." Funny how it was so much easier to assure him it'd be no big deal when *his* PTSD took over than it was to stomach the idea of him being there when mine did.

"Maybe it would be better at your place tonight." He paused. "I mean, if it's not too weird, me staying there while your daughter is home. Just, you know, being in a familiar setting might be better for you."

"That's probably not a bad idea. And I've had people over before. She knows about you. So, it wouldn't bother her." I blew out a breath. "All right. If you're sure you're up for it."

"I am. I'd be a hell of a hypocrite not to be." He cupped my face and kissed me. "We'll get dinner, maybe watch some TV. Whatever you need to relax." He ran the pad of his thumb along my cheekbone. "And after that, we'll take the night as it comes."

"Thank you," I whispered.

"Don't mention it." He kissed me again. "So, for now, do you want to go grab some lunch?"

My stomach turned. "I think I'm going to hold off on lunch for a while. Why don't you go on without me?"

His brow pinched. "Do you want me to bring you anything from the food court?"

That made me want to gag even more, so I shook my head. "No, thanks. I'll figure something out later."

"Okay. If you change your mind, shoot me a text."

"I will. Go. You've got classes this afternoon. Eat."

"Okay, okay, I'm going." He kissed me gently, and then left.

After he was gone, I still pressed my hip against my desk. I let my head fall forward. Rubbing the back of my neck with both hands, I sighed.

Tonight was going to be rough.

If we were going to do this, though, if we were going to make a relationship of some kind work, then sooner or later we had to cross this bridge. Might as well do it now, see if we could handle it, and move on if we couldn't.

And I tried not to think about the fact that relationships were dangerous territory for me anyway. What if things were okay when we slept in the same bed? What if we could handle each other's PTSD? What if . . .

I exhaled.

What if I let myself get as close to him as I had to Dion?

I rubbed my eyes and tried to force that thought out of my mind. It was irrational. Dion and Clint had nothing to do with each other, and there was no reason to believe things would turn out the same way. Right?

Well, we'd see how it went.

All I knew was this was the first time I dreaded going to bed with Clint.

Between the PTSD flare-up and my back pain, I felt like I'd been run over by a truck by the time we were calling it a night. My mind was still going a million miles an hour, but I was too exhausted *not* to sleep.

In my bedroom that night, I started to take off my shirt, but winced.

"Need a hand?" Clint asked.

"I got it." Holding my breath, I peeled my shirt all the way off. "See?"

His lips quirked. "Well, don't say I didn't offer."

We finished undressing—him more easily than me—and I got into bed. He joined me, but didn't settle in quite yet. "Go ahead and arrange the pillows however you need for your neck. I don't want you making it worse."

"I think you're the first guy who's ever waited for me to organize all this shit."

He laughed. "Eh, I've had stiff necks before. Not the same thing, but I know what it's like trying to sleep when my neck hurts."

"Much appreciated."

"Don't mention it."

We both left on our boxers and climbed into bed. Though we hadn't broached the subject of whether sex was on the table tonight, the clothes seemed to telegraph that we both knew it wasn't. Sex would have been a welcome distraction too, but naturally, my back was killing me. The tension in my neck and shoulders had spread down my spine, and well, that was all she wrote. My night would be made of TENS, Motrin, and attempts at relaxation.

If Clint was annoyed or frustrated, he didn't let it show. Instead, he lay beside me with his arm over me and kissed behind my ear. "How's your back?"

"Good as it ever is."

"That bad?"

"Mm-hmm."

"Sorry to hear it." He kissed me again. "You took some Motrin, right?"

"Always." Tonight, Motrin was about as effective as using paper airplanes for an airstrike, but it was better than nothing.

And even though I was supposed to use ice rather than heat, I had to admit Clint's body heat felt really nice against those painfully tight muscles.

I closed my eyes. Just being beside him was enough for me to start getting hard. Judging by the way he drew his hips back slightly, it might've been the same for him.

I was way too tired and sore, though. And Clint didn't push.

Before too long, my dick gave up. Not much longer after that, Clint was asleep.

So I closed my eyes and followed suit.

Every time I tried to swim to the surface, the pain in my back paralyzed my arms and shoulders. Every time I stopped swimming, I sank deeper into the cold, dark water. My lungs screamed for air. My muscles screamed for rest.

A shadow hovered in the water nearby, barely illuminated by . . . the moon? Searchlights?

It was Charlie. I knew it was. I couldn't see him, but it was him. He didn't move. Didn't try to swim. Just sank deeper.

Lungs burning and body on fire, I tried to get to him. Couldn't.

Swimmers. Their masks and insignia were vivid. The only thing I could really see.

But they couldn't get to me.

Sinking too fast.

My motionless RIO floated away.

Swim harder. Swim. Harder.

"Travis, can you hear me?"

The question jolted my surroundings. Scrambled them like a glitch in a computer program. The water wasn't quite right anymore. Different somehow. Why was there a ship in a swimming pool?

I choked and coughed. Salt. Fucking salt.

A wave crashed over my head. I thought I'd go under, but something solid kept me in place. Why was I lying down?

"Travis?" Calm. Firm. Soothing. "Travis, do you know where you are?"

I held on to his voice like a lifeline.

"Travis?"

Warm, dry fingers touched my face, and suddenly everything around me was warm and dry too. I wasn't submerged in cold saltwater. My lungs were clear.

"Hey. Can you hear me?" More soft, calm touches.

My eyes are closed.

I forced them open, and the nightmare vanished.

I sucked in a breath of air. Slowly, the world around me came into focus. It was dark, but some light came in through the window, and the blue numbers on my alarm clock glowed beside the bed.

The bed. Where I was lying next to Clint. Safe and sound on dry land.

The warmth of Clint's body as reassuring as it was alien. Normally, partners kept me at arm's length after an episode like that, as if they were afraid to touch me, or they wrapped me in a suffocating bear hug until I nearly collapsed into a fresh panic.

Even as I caught my breath and my heartbeat slowly came down, he stayed close. He didn't hold me—he just stayed here, his hip against mine and his arm loosely over my waist.

I looked at the clock again: 11:26. Shit. Still a lot of night left between now and daylight.

"You okay?" he asked after a while.

"Yeah." I started to get up, and he lifted his arm off me. I swung my legs over the side of the bed and rested my elbows on my knees as I rubbed my neck with both hands.

He put his hand on my shoulder. "Need anything?"

"One of those mind-eraser things from *Men in Black* would be nice."

"God, wouldn't it?" He kneaded my shoulder, and I closed my eyes and exhaled. For a long, long time, we were silent, and I focused on his gentle touch while I waited for the room to stop rocking like a ship on rough seas.

Eventually, I lay back on the pillows. Clint was on his side next to me, barely illuminated by the streetlights coming in through the window. He ran a hand up and down my arm.

"Doing better?" he asked.

"Yeah." I paused. "You ever dream you're drowning? Not as a flashback, I mean. Just in general."

Clint nodded. "Sometimes, yeah."

"That's what it is. Every time. Drowning." I licked my lips, and was genuinely surprised when I didn't taste salt. I ran a hand through my damp hair. *Sweat. Not seawater. Sweat.* "The fucked-up thing is, I don't actually remember it. I don't remember anything. So when I dream about it, I don't know if that's what really happened, or if my subconscious is filling in the blanks. And to be honest, I'm not sure which option is worse."

"Wow. I don't think either option would be pleasant."

"Seriously." I glanced at the clock. It was after midnight now. "Shit. We should get some sleep. The workday comes early."

"You going to be able to sleep?"

"I hope so." I paused. "I'm going to end up keeping you awake, though. I can take the couch if—"

"Jesus, Travis." He slid closer and draped his arm over me. "I'm not going to kick you out of your own bed. Especially not over something like this. We'll take the night as it comes." He kissed my shoulder. "Both of us."

I closed my eyes and sighed. I was too tired to argue with him, and admittedly, I was grateful for his company even if I was keeping him from getting a decent night's sleep.

So I didn't argue. We lay in silence, and before long, he'd drifted off.

After that, I would've liked to say the rest of the night was quiet and uneventful.

But it wasn't.

CHAPTER 16

CLINT

We didn't talk about it the next morning.

Over showers and shaving and shuffling out the door with coffee cups in hand, we didn't say much of anything. I was exhausted, so I could only imagine how he felt, especially with the heavy shadows under his eyes, and the way his limp was more pronounced.

At work, we both clung to our coffee, and I cringed as we walked up the stairs together. As sore as he obviously was, that elevator down the hall had to be tempting as hell today. Still, whether out of pride or God knew what, he insisted on taking the stairs. This time. Every time.

Then we went our separate ways down the hall to our respective offices.

Now that he was out of sight, I couldn't stop worrying about him, not to mention reliving last night. I'd known exactly what was happening, but I also knew all too well what it was like to be in his position. Afterward, it was obvious that it had been a nightmare or a flashback. In the moment, though, the only obvious thing was the bone-rattling panic. I didn't envy him in the slightest.

On the bright side, I hadn't had to deal with any of my own nightmares last night because I hadn't been able to sleep long enough. And at least I worked in a mostly admin position these days. I didn't need to be piloting a zillion-dollar remote aircraft while my brain kept wandering off and my eyelids kept sliding shut.

After I'd returned a few urgent emails and put out a couple of fires, I had a cup of coffee chased by a Red Bull, left my desk, and headed down the hall toward Travis's office. The door was shut, so as always, I knocked.

"It's open," came the response.

I glanced over my shoulder, then slipped into his office and closed the door behind me. "Hey. I wanted to see how you were doing after last night."

Travis's face colored. "Uh . . . better now that it's daylight. Definitely better." He pushed himself up out of his chair and came around to me. As he put his arms around me, he said, "What about you? Did you get any sleep?"

"Enough to get me through the day. I'll be all right."

He winced. "I'm sorry. I really—"

"Don't apologize." I kissed his forehead. "Honestly. And weren't you telling me it's nothing to apologize over?"

"Yeah. I did. And it's . . ." He lowered his gaze. "It's actually kind of ironic. I'm constantly telling Kimber it's nothing to be embarrassed about, but . . ." He looked at me. "Guess it's different when it's you, you know?"

"Yeah." I tilted my head. "Out of curiosity, what happened to her? If it's something you can talk about."

Travis scowled. "Well, my crash shook her up pretty bad. But more recently . . ." He pulled in a breath. "The reason she came to the Navy Ball with me is that she wants to be able to go to parties, have a few drinks, and dance, but she's scared to go alone or even with friends. She goes to things like the ball with me because she feels safer."

I blinked. "Safer?"

He nodded. "She and some friends used to go to parties when she was in college. Then some guys got drunk, and . . ." He gulped, shook himself, and quietly added, "Things got out of hand."

My stomach flipped. "Jesus."

"Someone intervened before anything got *too* far out of control. Shook her up pretty bad, though. Especially when she realizes all the things that could have happened if someone hadn't stepped in."

I shuddered. "I can imagine."

Travis sighed. "She's tough. Always has been. But that whole incident left enough of an impression that even if she can work up the nerve to go to a party or a club, she's too anxious and wound up to have a good time. And I know it bothers her that she can only relax if her dad's there. What woman wants to have Daddy babysitting her, you know?"

"There's a difference between babysitting her and giving her a place where she can actually have a good time without being nervous."

"That's what I tell her. And it's why I go to the Navy Ball with her even though I hate it—she can dress up, have a few drinks, maybe dance, and she knows no one's going to mess with her because of me."

"It's still a damn shame she has to be that worried."

"It's a damn shame I never got my hands on the guys who fucked with her." The murderous tone left little to the imagination about what would've happened if he had. "And last year, some dick-bag thought it was creepy that I brought my daughter as my 'date.' I straightened his ass out, believe me."

"Good," I said. "What an idiot."

"Yep. So yeah. My kid's got some things that trigger her. I've got some things that trigger me. It sucks that past traumas kind of dictate our current normal, but it is what it is."

"At least you've got support. You can talk to each other."

He nodded. Then he offered a tired smile. "I can talk to you."

"Absolutely."

He rolled his shoulders and tilted his head to one side, then the other, as if trying to relieve some of the visible stiffness. "Thank God mine doesn't trigger very often anymore. It's been years since—" He cleared his throat. "Since the crash that caused it."

I nodded. "Yeah, they say it gets better with time. I'm holding on to that, believe me."

"It does," he said softly. "But, I mean, as you saw last night . . . it doesn't necessarily go away."

"No, it doesn't." I grimaced. "Man, that must be hard, having it yourself and knowing your kid's going through it too."

"Yeah. Hers has always been fairly mild, thank God, but if she's expecting me to come home or call, and I don't, she . . ." He pursed his lips, and his eyes lost focus, as if he couldn't find the right word. "She struggles, let's put it that way. She won't quite have a panic attack or a flashback or anything—it's never been that severe—but she'll get really anxious. Can't sleep. Can't concentrate. One thing I absolutely do not do with her is text her or leave her a message saying she needs to call me right away. She'd rather I just tell her whatever it is in the message."

"So she doesn't amp herself up with all the worst-case scenarios?"

"Exactly."

"Does she see a therapist?"

Travis shook his head. "She did for a while, but hasn't really felt the need since we moved to Anchor Point. It doesn't really impede her ability to function from day to day. If she changes her mind, she knows how to reach Fleet and Family, or she can see a civilian doc in town. It's up to her."

"Makes sense. What about you?"

He waved a hand. "Nah. I did for a while, but I don't anymore. It's mostly nightmares and the occasional bad night if something sets me off. Which . . . it's weird what can trigger it, you know? I mean, I don't even remember anything after my plane hit the flight deck. I sure as fuck don't remember being in the water. And even if I did, it was saltwater, for God's sake. But five minutes into a SAR demonstration in a goddamned pool, and . . ." he tapped his forehead, "something goes haywire."

"Oh man, I know exactly what you mean," I said. "It's the weirdest thing. I had a buddy who was hurt in a mortar attack in Afghanistan. After he came home, he could handle fireworks shows, the gun range, violent movies—you name it." I exhaled. "Then we were at a restaurant one day, and a certain song started playing in the background. He just . . . he lost it. Full-on flashback."

Travis's eyes widened. "From a song?"

I nodded. "Turned out that song was playing when the mortar came in."

"Jesus." Travis whistled. "Amazing what can set that shit off."

"No kidding. Fortunately, he was with a group of guys who knew a flashback when they saw one. I can only imagine what would've happened if he'd been out with his family. Or driving!"

Travis grimaced. "Shit. Yeah."

"So he absolutely could not have the radio on when he was driving after that."

"Oh wow. I hadn't even thought of that. Amazing how this stuff permeates every part of your life."

"It is. And people wonder why I drank myself stupid the first year."

"I feel that. I did my fair share of self-medicating, believe me."

"Really?"

"Oh yeah. But things are better now. I mean, aside from nights like last night."

I wasn't sure what to say. If he still had nights like that eight years on from his crash, how long would it be before mine were less of a problem? Fuck. One of those mind erasers would've been really, *really* nice.

"You know . . ." Travis put his arms around my waist. "In a weird way, I feel better after last night. Like, it's out of the way now." He laughed. "No surprises."

I chuckled and kissed him softly. "It's kind of a relief for me too. I guess having it out in the open like that, whether it happened to you or me, does make it easier."

"It really does."

"So, um. Now that that's out of the way . . ." I hesitated. "Do you want to come by my place tonight?"

Travis held my gaze, and I had two seconds to be preemptively disappointed before he smiled and pulled me a little closer. "I'd love to." He started to say something further, but of course the phone on his desk picked that exact moment to ring. "Damn it."

"Figures."

He gave me a quick kiss, and leaned across to pick up the phone, not quite hiding the wince as he moved. With his hand resting on the receiver, he said, "It's the CO. Come by when you're heading to lunch?"

"Will do."

I stepped out of his office, leaving him to his call, and released a long breath. So that was out of the way. We'd been through a PTSD-induced shitty night. Neither of us had had a lot of sleep, but we were a step closer to really knowing what it was like to function together with the not-so-great cards we'd each been dealt.

On my way down the hall to my own office, I couldn't help smiling. It had been a rough night, and it wouldn't be the last one like that, but now I wasn't quite so worried about what could happen when one of us slept over. It was progress in its own fucked-up way.

Tonight, we'd see what happened.

And for right now, I needed another goddamned Red Bull.

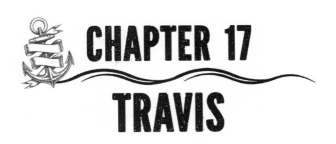

CHAPTER 17
TRAVIS

The night I'd woken us both up with a nightmare quickly became a distant memory. Now that I'd broken the ice in a way, we relaxed with each other. We could both sleep as much as our fragged brains would let us. There was no more fear of the other seeing us in that vulnerable, disoriented state.

It wasn't all smooth sailing. Clint's trauma was much more recent than mine, and the psychological wounds were much more raw. I hadn't even realized how little he'd been sleeping when he was beside me until after my bad night. Now that he wasn't afraid of me seeing him like that, he slept. Which meant he dreamed. Which meant there were some *rough* nights. We both had to drag ourselves to the coffeepot in the morning, and there were occasional mysterious bruises thanks to one or the other of us thrashing in our sleep.

I didn't mind, and he didn't seem to mind my back interfering with our sex life at every turn. Not that I had any illusions of that lasting forever, but hey, I'd enjoy it for the moment.

Today, the pain had been a constant irritating ache. Not a spasm yet, so I was doing everything I could to keep it that way. Motrin, ice, TENS, Motrin, ice, TENS.

Clint, being the saint that he was, hadn't just caught on that I was barely moving today, he hadn't missed a beat in coming up with something else to do for the evening.

"Why don't I cook something?" he'd asked. "In fact, if Kimber's not working, she's welcome to join us. Then we can all watch a movie or whatever."

Fine by me, so at six thirty, he came into my kitchen and set a handful of plastic commissary bags on the counter. "So, I need a couple of pots and a casserole dish."

"Um." I looked around. "They're . . ."

Kimber pointed at the drawer below the oven and the cabinet next to it.

"Got it," Clint said.

"Good thing someone knows their way around in here," I said.

"Mm-hmm." Kimber shot me an earnest look, forehead creased as she put a hand to her lips. "Has that stove even been used since we moved in? Do you think it'll work?"

"Really?" I rolled my eyes. "We've used it."

"Like twice. Maybe."

Clint snickered. "Not the culinary type, are we?"

Before I could respond, she burst out laughing.

"Oh my God—he is *so* not."

"Hey." I wagged a finger at her. "You're not helping."

She shrugged. "Wasn't trying to."

"Like father, like daughter." He snickered as he took out the pots and casserole dish. "Tell me you at least have a decent set of knives."

"Right behind you."

He turned around and looked over the knife block. I barely used it, but at least it wasn't a cheap, dull set.

"You need help with anything?" I asked.

"Nope." He took three knives out and laid them next to the cutting board. "I've got this."

"I feel like we should have a camera out," Kimber said in a stage whisper. "To prove that actual cooking has happened in here."

I glared at her, but as Clint started making dinner, I wondered if she was right. He definitely put my cooking skills to shame. I thought I was doing all right when I managed to follow the directions on a box and didn't set off the smoke detector in the process. This guy . . . holy shit. He chopped and sliced without seeming concerned that the blade might land on a finger. And weren't you supposed to measure things before tossing them in?

I was almost afraid to talk to him while he worked. He was spinning so many plates, I didn't want to distract him and cause the whole thing to fall apart.

He looked up from dicing some green peppers and said to Kimber, "So your dad says you work in tech support?"

"Yep. In between going to school."

"What are you studying?"

"I'm finishing a bachelor's in computer science. I took a year off to—" She tensed, eyes flicking toward me. Then she cleared her throat. "Anyway. I'll graduate in June, and then I'll start working on a master's."

"Wow." He glanced up again. "All that while you're working as many hours as you do?"

"Eh. I can do computers in my sleep." She snatched a piece of bell pepper off the cutting board and tossed it in her mouth. "I just hope graduating means I can get a decent job someplace else, or move up to supervising my department instead of doing what I do now. Seems like most of my friends graduate, only to turn around and rack up more hours at the job they've had all along."

Clint scowled. "Yeah, that's the market these days." He paused to drop a few crushed garlic cloves into one of the pots. "My ex-wife has an MBA, and she had such a hard time getting a job, she finally threw up her hands and became a blackjack dealer."

"Really?" Kimber's eyes widened. "Does that pay decently?"

"Better than unemployment."

She turned to me. "Maybe I should learn to deal cards."

I shrugged. "You already know how to count 'em."

Clint arched an eyebrow, peering at both of us through the steam rising above the pots. "You know how to count cards?"

"I, uh . . ." my cheeks burned, "might've taught her."

He chuckled, shaking his head. "You know, most dads teach their kids how to change tires and barbecue. Counting cards?"

Kimber laughed. "It's a survival skill!"

"What?" Clint scoffed. "How the hell is that a survival skill?"

"Come to a Wilson family reunion and play a few hands," she said. "*Then* tell me it isn't."

"Yep," I said. "None of us spend much time in casinos, but my family is cutthroat at blackjack and poker. So I taught her how to count cards so she'd have half a chance when she played against them."

"Yeah?" Clint stirred something into one of the pots. "So how do you do against them?"

Kimber snorted.

I beamed, patting her shoulder. "I think I taught her a bit *too* well. My brothers are almost afraid to deal her in now."

Clint chuckled. "That's impressive."

"And let me tell you." I whistled. "Do *not* play poker with this one."

"What? Counting cards doesn't really help in poker, does it?"

"No, but you can sure benefit from having a rock-solid poker face and a killer bluff."

"Really?" Clint glanced at her, then me, then her again. "You?"

Her lips quirked. "Yeah. Why not?"

"Well, you know." He shrugged. "I can't imagine a child of his having a poker face or—"

I laughed. "Shut up and cook, asshole."

After an amazing meal of baked pasta with steamed vegetables, we all hunkered down in the living room to watch a couple of movies. Kimber had been after me for a year to give some Bollywood films a try, and over dinner, she'd gotten Clint on her side. And after the two movies were over, I had to admit they were pretty fun.

"Drag him over again next time I have a night off," she said. "I've got a ton more where those came from."

"You won't have to drag me over to watch those." Clint sighed and looked at his watch. "For tonight, though, I should probably bail. I've got a meeting at 0700 tomorrow."

I grimaced. "At 0700? Who the hell scheduled that?"

"The CO. Obviously."

"She's a sadist, isn't she?"

"Very much so." He motioned toward the kitchen. "Let me clean all that up before—"

"No, no, no." Kimber jumped to her feet and shooed him toward the door. "You cooked. We'll clean."

"But I—"

"Don't argue with me."

He turned to me.

"You heard her," I said. "Don't argue with her."

"Fair enough."

We both stood, and I winced at a few fresh twinges in my back. As I kneaded them gingerly, I turned to Kimber. "Let me show him out, and then I'll give you a hand."

"Okay." She went into the kitchen, and Clint and I went to the front door.

"Thanks for cooking," I said. "Dinner was amazing."

"Anytime." He wrapped his arms around my waist. "It was nice hanging out with you and Kimber."

"It was. So are you free tomorrow night?"

His grin made my knees weak. "If I wasn't before, I am now."

"Perfect." I slid my hands up his chest and around the back of his neck. "I have no idea what we'll do with it, but I'm already looking forward to it."

"Me too. When I get home, I'll see if there's anything good to queue up on Netflix. Anything in particular you want to see?"

Nothing you'll find on Netflix, no.

"Surprise me." I glanced back toward the living room. "More Bollywood, I'm guessing?"

"Maybe." He kissed me lightly. "We'll see." Another kiss, longer this time.

As much as I wanted to stand there in the doorway and make out, or maybe go up to the bedroom and do even more, I put a hand on his chest and gently separated us. "You've got an early meeting. I don't want to be the reason you're nodding off in front of the CO."

"Yeah." He scowled. "Being an adult sucks, doesn't it?"

"So much."

He smirked. "Though, you have more experience being—"

"Fuck you," I laughed and drew him back to me so I could kiss him.

He grinned against my lips, and then he cradled the back of my neck and let the kiss linger. As he pulled back, he ran his tongue across his lips. "You know, I just realized the command Christmas party is coming up." He blushed. "Do you want to go?"

"Is that a roundabout way of saying you want us to come out to the command?"

He laughed, lowering his gaze, and the color in his cheeks deepened. "I guess that's what would happen if we showed up together, but I . . ." He met my eyes. "I want to go with you."

I smiled. He was so cute, being all shy like a teenager trying to ask someone to the prom, and who the hell was I kidding? Forty-five years old and I was getting all fluttery inside at the thought of being asked. I hated command Christmas parties almost as much as I hated the Navy Ball. But going with Clint?

"Sure," I said. "Guess I'd better get my uniform ready."

"Me too." He gestured over his shoulder with his thumb. "Anyway, I'd better go. I'll see you tomorrow."

"Yeah. See you tomorrow."

One last kiss—a long, gentle one that made it really tempting to ask him to stay—and he was gone. Still smiling like an utter tool, I turned the dead bolt and went back into the kitchen.

As I came in, Kimber looked up from rinsing a plate. "Can you have him over more often? His cooking is amazing."

I laughed. "So you want me to use him for the meals?"

"Well, it's either that or one of us takes a cooking class."

"Good point." I picked up a dish towel. "And we both know that's not happening."

"Not without the paramedics or fire department getting involved."

"Oh come on. I'm not that bad."

She shot me a side-eye as she put another plate in the drying rack.

"Hey now." As I dried one of the pots, I said, "What do you think of him? Besides his cooking, I mean?"

"He's a nice guy." She glanced at me. "What do *you* think of him?"

My hand stopped. "I like him."

"You don't say." She started scrubbing out the casserole dish. "So is it serious?"

I shrugged. "I don't know. We'll see where things go."

"I'll keep my fingers crossed." She held up her soap-covered hand, index finger crossed under the middle. "It's about time you were happy, you know?"

I forced myself not to visibly wince, and managed to return her smile. "Thanks." I wanted to believe being happy was a possibility now. Things with Clint had been smooth sailing so far, but seas could change on a dime and so could a relationship.

We finished cleaning up the kitchen, and she went to her room to study while I went to mine to get some sleep.

It had been an awesome evening. My pain had been manageable enough that I hadn't even needed to wear the TENS unit. Clint had cooked me and Kimber the best meal either of us had had in a long time.

And for that matter, it had been cool to be with both Clint and Kimber at the same time. They'd met before, but this was the first time we'd all really sat down and talked. I'd admittedly been nervous—she hadn't always been thrilled with people I'd dated—but they'd gotten along great.

One more point in his favor, as if there'd been any shortage of those lately. All the signs were there that this wanted to turn into something bigger. If we let it, God only knew how high it could go.

That thought sent fear and dread surging through my veins. The higher we went, the harder we'd crash when it was over. Relationships that started out this perfect were disasters in the end. So much more so than the false starts—the ones that barely lasted beyond a week or two and had all the emotional investment of a conversation with a seatmate on a long flight. I'd had more of those than I could count. Then there were the flings that kind of leaned toward becoming relationships and didn't. Those weren't fun, but they weren't catastrophic either, because they were pretty much over before they started.

This thing with Clint, though . . .

It was terrifying because a failure to launch was a hell of a lot less painful than crashing and burning.

And even though I was almost certain the crash was inevitable—every relationship I'd ever had eventually wound up a smoldering wreckage—I couldn't make myself back away. I was even willing to go with him to the Christmas party and practically announce to the command that the rumors going around were true.

Yes, everyone, Lieutenant Commander Fraser is my boyfriend.

Shit. I was being an idiot, wasn't I? There was no doubt in my mind I'd regret this later.

But for now, on the microscopic chance we got it right, I wanted to see where we could go.

The Christmas party was the first week of December, and it didn't require dinner dress uniforms. No, it required standard dress uniforms, which meant yet another frantic round of cleaning, ironing, trying on, and arranging insignia. I swore if the Navy required any more uniforms, I'd need a bigger closet than my daughter's.

At least this uniform fit better since I wore it more often. The jacket fit much more comfortably than the other one, and also managed to hide any extra pounds I might've put on. Winter weight and all that.

Dressed and ready to go, I went downstairs to the kitchen. Kimber was in her pajamas and making herself some dinner, and since the table was covered in notes, pens, books, and her laptop, it looked like she had her night planned out.

"You going to be all right tonight?" I asked.

"Of course." She put a plate of Hot Pockets in the microwave. "I need to catch up on some homework anyway before things get busy at work."

I fussed with my sleeve. "So you really don't mind if I take Clint to—"

"Dad." She smiled. "You don't have to take me along to everything."

"I know, but I can still get a ticket for you too if—"

"*Dad.*" Kimber rolled her eyes. "I'm not going with you on a *date*, for God's sake."

"Not even as a chaperone?"

She groaned. "Especially not as a chaperone. And besides, things are about to get crazy at work because the new software releases on Monday." She pointed with her fork at the pile of homework. "I need to finish that."

"All right. But if you do want to go to the next event, all you have to do is say so."

"I will." She hesitated, but then smiled and hugged me gently. "And thank you again for taking me to the ball. It was nice to be able to party without looking over my shoulder."

I held her tighter. "Anytime, kiddo. And you can always come to stuff *with* us."

"Maybe." She pulled back. "But you guys are still in that gross googly-eyed stage, and I don't want to be there for that."

"Really? Gross googly-eyed stage?"

"Just saying."

"You're full of it."

"Whatever. I saw you two at dinner the other night." She made circles with her thumbs and forefingers and put them over her eyes like mock glasses. "Googly eyes, Dad. I saw them."

I huffed and was about to fire off a comeback, but the doorbell rang. "Since you're so bored, would you mind getting that?"

"Sure." She disappeared down the hall.

"Gross googly-eyed stage," I muttered to myself as I tugged my sleeve again. "Please."

Down the hall, the door opened, changing the air pressure in the house.

"Hey!" Kimber said. "Look at you!"

My heart skipped. I hadn't seen him in *this* uniform yet.

Clint laughed shyly. Even from down the hall, I could hear the sharp click of his dress shoes on the hardwood.

And when he appeared in the kitchen doorway . . .

Oh. Wow.

Like me, he wore dress blues. Basically a dark-blue suit and tie with gold stripes on the sleeves and his ribbons on the left side. He must've had a hell of a rapport with the base tailor—the jacket and trousers fit him just right to make my mouth water. His cover was tucked under his arm, and his dress shoes gleamed enough he could've signaled an aircraft with them.

Holy—

"See, Dad?" Kimber patted my arm. "Gross googly eyes."

"Shut up." I gently shoved her away as my cheeks burned.

She snickered. "Aww, come on. You guys are cute. Oh! Let me get a picture!"

"Really?" I eyed her. "Shouldn't you wait until we put on the corsages?"

Clint chuckled. "Well, I didn't bring one, so I guess that's prom-date fail."

"It really is." Kimber clicked her tongue. "Shame on you. He's been looking forward to that corsage all day."

"And on *that* note," I said. "Let's go." But I paused, and turned more serious. "You're good for the night, right? You don't need—"

"Dad. Relax. I'm going to finish a paper, and then catch up on *House of Cards*."

My jaw dropped. "What? You're watching it without me?"

"I won't erase them."

"But . . . that's our show!"

"And you're going to a party." She made a shooing motion. "Go."

"She's obviously your kid," Clint said. "I can see where she gets her smart-ass genes."

"Hey! I resemble that." I grabbed my wallet and keys off the counter. "All right, let's get out of here before you two completely gang up on me."

They both laughed, of course.

"Come on, you." I nudged him toward the door. "Let's go."

"Have fun, you kids!" she called after us.

"Apple doesn't fall far from the tree, does it?" Clint asked under his breath.

"Remind me why I let you two meet?"

He just laughed again.

CHAPTER 18

CLINT

This was going to be a long, long night, and not only because military functions could be tedious as hell or because there was a lot of liquor flowing. No, it was because the man walking in with me was insanely gorgeous, and he was in his dress uniform.

On the right physique, these uniforms were utterly hot. And Travis . . . well, Travis had the right physique for damn near anything. He was hot in PT gear, for God's sake. I doubted there was anything he could put on that wouldn't make my mouth water.

In his dress blues, though? Sexy. As. *Hell.*

On the way in, after he'd tucked his cover under his arm, Travis slipped his hand into mine. We exchanged glances, and both grinned. I wondered if it gave him as much of a thrill as it did me, being able to walk into an official military function with a boyfriend. I wasn't even nervous this time, because it didn't feel like a huge mistake. On my way into the Navy Ball with Logan, I'd nearly turned back three times because my gut had said no. Nothing felt wrong this time.

I had a flicker of panic that a picture or a rumor might make it back to my ex-wife, but I pushed the thought away. We didn't have any mutual friends at this base, and the photographer's mates were pretty good about asking before posting photos on social media. It would be fine.

We grabbed drinks—a Coke for me, a beer for him—mingled with coworkers and the odd acquaintance from another department. Slowly, we made our way around the ballroom, which had been decorated to the gills with fake holly, red bows on evergreen boughs, and a huge Christmas tree lit up with white lights.

And, of course, there was the pile of presents at the front of the room.

"Good lord." Travis gaped at the enormous mountain of gifts. "Did MWR rob a fucking bank this year?"

"Kind of looks like it, doesn't it?" Morale, Welfare, and Recreation always managed to pull together an impressive cache of giveaways for the Christmas party, but even some of my larger commands hadn't come up with this much.

In between several gaming consoles, there must have been half a dozen laptops, and they didn't look like the cheap-ass ones I'd seen down at the Navy Exchange. Some good-sized flat-screen TVs. An enormous display of gift cards. High-end electric shaving kits. A few gift baskets.

The grand prize was, as always, a gigantic television. In this case, a sixty-inch HD plasma screen.

"Wow." I shook my head. "A few more years and they're going to be giving away IMAX screens at these things."

Travis chuckled. "Now I feel old as fuck because I was about to say back when I first started coming to these things, the grand prize was one of those giant CRTs that took twelve people to move."

I burst out laughing. "Oh my God. I remember those. I had to help move a few of them too."

He nodded. "Yeah, same here. Never did win one, though."

"Nah, me neither. Those are a pain in the ass. Wouldn't have minded getting picked for something like *that*, though." I tilted my Coke toward the plasma screen. "Hell, I'd still like one of those."

"Same here."

"Maybe I'll buy one eventually. Especially since they don't cost more than my car anymore."

Travis laughed, which still, even after weeks of sleeping with him, made my heart skip.

We mingled some more, and at one point, stopped at the bar so Travis could get a glass of wine and I could get another Coke. It didn't bother me at all that he drank, especially since I'd never seen him have more than one or two in the course of an evening. A couple of beers if we were out with the guys from work. A glass of wine with dinner.

Nothing more. It never showed, either. I'd never once heard him so much as slur, and he always walked as steadily as he ever did.

As for me, I wasn't even all that tempted to drink anymore. Definitely not socially—a few bouts of alcohol poisoning in rapid succession had killed any taste I had for the stuff. The only reason I'd kept drinking after that—or was still sometimes tempted now—was in the name of sweet, sweet oblivion.

And I didn't need that tonight. No, I was pretty content to be absolutely aware of what was going on, because what was going on was I was walking amongst my coworkers with my hand in Travis's.

A few people did double takes, but didn't seem hostile. Just surprised. Others talked to us like nothing was out of the ordinary—especially people from our own offices who had been reading between the lines for a while now.

There were a couple of dirty looks, and I thought I saw some people whispering behind their hands and shaking their heads. No one said a word to us, though.

Eventually, the cocktail hour ended and everyone took their seats. Like we had at the Navy Ball, we sat with some people from work. Someone's wife wrinkled her nose and gave us some side-eye over her wineglass, but didn't say anything. No one else even looked twice at us. A few years ago, it would have been scandalous. Apparently same-office relationships had lost their novelty after Chiefs Hanson and McKinley in security had gotten married last year, and same-sex ones weren't exactly a shock since they all knew Travis and I weren't straight. So when we started seeing each other, it had warranted about as much gossip as someone losing their change in a vending machine.

Fine by me. I could get used to this progressive Navy.

The Christmas party didn't have anywhere near the pomp and circumstance of the Navy Ball. The chaplain did the invocation as always. The color guard presented the colors. The CO said a few mercifully brief words. After that it was booze, food, and more booze.

A couple of guys from the office below ours were having an animated and possibly heated discussion about . . . something. They were both gesturing wildly and speaking loudly, but hell if I could make out anything they were saying.

I glanced at Travis, and he was watching them too. His expression was half-amusement, half-horror—eyes wide, but lips quirked.

Shaking his head, he laughed. "I don't miss those days. Do you?"

"Not at all." I rested my hand on his leg. "And it's kind of refreshing, being here with someone who isn't drunk out of his skull."

Travis turned to me. "Not a fan?"

"No. Not at all."

"Then, if you don't mind my asking . . ." He searched my eyes. "Why the hell were you with that guy you brought to the ball? Was the sex really that good?"

Warmth rushed into my cheeks. "Not really. To be honest . . ."

He put his hand over mine.

I stared into my drink. "I don't know. When he was sober, he was great. We had a good thing . . . sometimes. And . . ." I sighed, pinching the bridge of my nose. "But it was a disaster waiting to happen, and I . . . God, I guess it was just so good to be with someone again, I didn't want to let it go. So I held on, and realized the reality of the situation when we were at the fucking Navy Ball."

Running his thumb alongside my hand, he said, "At least you didn't hang on after that."

"Oh yeah. I'm glad it's over."

"At the risk of sounding like an opportunist—" he kissed my cheek "—me too."

I met his gaze, and we both laughed, and it took a second to realize he'd kissed me—even if it was only a peck on the cheek—in public. Not just in public like the day I'd kissed him on the pier, but around people from our command. And no one was freaking out. Not even me.

He smiled and leaned in. He stopped, though, hovering in that safe zone between being close and being *close*.

My heart sped up. I resisted the urge to self-consciously glance around. No one had given us any shit so far, so why the hell not?

I closed the remaining distance and pressed my lips to his.

It was quick and light, followed by a long look and a smile from him that turned my bones to liquid, but it felt great. A chaste kiss with my boyfriend at the command Christmas party? Jesus. Times had really changed, hadn't they?

Some commotion turned our heads. Captain Rodriguez and Commander Johnson had taken center stage with the microphone and the box of tickets for the gifts. The CO was almost too shitfaced to stand without her husband's help, and the XO was slurring so bad I doubted even *he* understood what he was saying. Somehow, they were supposed to draw the tickets for the gifts, but I suspected they'd need some help before they were halfway through the box.

Travis and I exchanged glances as the top of our chain of command slurred their way through . . . whatever it was they were trying to say.

"She always get that drunk at these things?" I asked.

"Not usually," he replied. "But everyone seems to let their hair down at the Christmas party, so . . ."

"Yeah, seriously." I picked up my Coke and took a sip. "I went to one of these a few years back where a junior enlisted guy managed to knock a glass of red wine down the front of the CO's uniform and get away with it."

Travis laughed. "You're kidding."

I shook my head. "Nope. And we're all pretty sure it wasn't an accident."

"Why's that?"

"Call it a hunch. He was"—I made air quotes—"'trying to take a picture of the ice sculpture' and 'accidentally' backed into the CO. And that might've been true, but man, something about the way he told the story . . ."

"Sounded a little premeditated?"

"You think?"

"What'd the CO do?"

I shrugged. "Had another glass of wine. He was so wasted by that point, he probably didn't even remember the next day. Probably woke up with a stained uniform and figured he'd dumped it on himself."

"Sounds about right."

"Fucker deserved it anyway," I muttered.

"That kind of CO, huh?"

"So much." I rolled my eyes and reached for my Coke. "He was a fucking dick, and I defy you to find anyone on that boat who disagreed."

"Pretty sure we've all worked for someone like that."

"Mm-hmm. We just usually don't get the chance to knock wine all over the bastards. And even if we do, none of us have the balls to go through with it."

"I hope that kid realizes he's a goddamned legend now."

"If he doesn't, the rest of us sure do."

"Amen to that."

We watched for a while as the CO and XO stumbled their way through drawing some gifts. Half the people who'd won them were equally drunk, and with the amount of glass being given out—bottles of wine and liquor, mostly—I was amazed nothing had shattered yet.

Beside me, Travis sighed. "I think these were more fun when I was younger." He looked at me. "Does that mean we're getting old?"

"I'm pretty sure we're already there."

"Fair point." He slid his hand over my thigh. "You want to stick around, or get the hell out of here?"

I glanced down at his hand, then at him, and the mischievous gleam in his eyes told me he didn't mean *let's go home and watch TV*.

"Hell yeah," I breathed. "Let's go."

We both stood, but I paused and picked up our tickets. "What should we do with these?"

Travis shrugged. "Give 'em away?"

"Sounds good to me."

So we handed off our tickets to a nearby ensign and her husband, and got the hell out of there.

Our uniforms would need some serious ironing later, but for now, they could stay in their rumpled heaps on my bedroom floor.

Tangled up in a kiss, we sank onto the mattress, Travis guiding me down with a hand behind my head.

Oh yes. *This*. This was what I wanted. Being out in public with him, openly letting the world know that Travis was my boyfriend, had been fun. Sharing a kiss where I wouldn't have dared a few years ago had been amazing.

But now I didn't want the public. I wanted him. Alone.

I slid my hands up his sides, and he tensed, sucking in a sharp breath.

I froze. "You okay?"

"Yeah." He laughed, his lips grazing mine. "Just, uh, kind of ticklish right there."

"Oh. Okay." I hesitated. "Is your back all right, though?"

"Mm-hmm." He kissed under my jaw. "It's good. Maybe we should take advantage of it while it's not throwing a fit."

I shivered, arching under him, and ran my nails down his waist. "Anything you want. I'm all yours."

"Good," he moaned against my throat. "Because I want you so bad right now." He pushed himself up and looked in my eyes. "Seriously, anything you want tonight." He swept his tongue across his lips. "We can even fuck. If . . . if you want—"

"All I want is you."

"But if—"

I kissed him. "I want you," I whispered. "No way in hell are we doing something that'll hurt you." And before he could protest, I claimed another long kiss, and his body relaxed against mine.

I pushed him onto his side, and he grunted softly when I wrapped my fingers around his cock. He did the same to me, blanking my brain and sending goose bumps up my spine.

It didn't matter that we couldn't fuck. I enjoyed some wild, headboard-pounding fucking as much as the next man, but this was amazing. Lying here, stroking each other and kissing, in no hurry at all but already out of breath—it didn't get any better than this.

And what kind of man would I have been if I'd taken him up on his offer, knowing how much pain he could very well be in afterward? No way was I making him spend a night in more pain because of me. I couldn't imagine hurting him.

So we stayed like that—legs intertwined under the sheet, hands moving in unison, lips moving lazily together. Little by little, the intensity grew. Grips tightened. Strokes picked up speed. Kisses were more frantic, more breathless. His skin was hot against mine, his breath cool as it rushed across my skin. He hooked a leg over mine. I held on to his shoulder with my free hand.

I wasn't in any hurry, but I sure as hell wasn't putting on the brakes either. If we came too fast, well, we'd have to catch our breath and start over again. And if we did this all night, keeping each other on the brink while the room spun around us, that was perfectly fine by me too.

It blew my mind that he'd thought for even a second I might not be satisfied with the kind of sex we had just because anal was off the table. I could take that or leave it anyway, but nothing we did was lacking at all. His kiss alone was mind-blowing—I'd have happily made out with him for hours on end even if we never took it further. And my God, his hands and mouth were magic. I had never once come away from a night with him and wondered how much better it could be if one of us fucked the other.

Travis whimpered and broke the kiss. Tilting his head back, he closed his eyes and bit his lip. His dick seemed to get even harder, even thicker in my hand, so I pumped it faster. He did the same, and my vision blurred as I rocked my hips to fuck his fist.

It was impossible to say who came first. We both tensed. Both trembled. Both shuddered. Our strokes were suddenly slick, and he didn't stop, and I didn't stop, and the leg he'd hooked over mine pulled me in tighter, and he breathed "Oh my *God*" as if he'd felt the shudder that was curling my toes and straightening my spine.

In unison, we exhaled and relaxed. I grabbed the box of tissues off the nightstand, and once those had served their purpose, Travis moved them out of the way and moved himself closer to me. I lay on my back so he could rest his head on my chest, and I wrapped my arm around his shoulders and kissed the top of his head. Oh, this was perfect. His body always fit just right against mine. The fact that he was still warm—still feverishly hot—was utterly perfect.

He trailed his fingers up and down my chest. "Your heart's going crazy."

"Of course it is." I laughed. "You just made me come."

He lifted his head, grinned wickedly, and kissed me. Then he rested his head on my chest again and draped his arm over me.

He didn't need to know right now that it was more than my orgasm making my heart race like that.

It was . . . this. Being with him. I suspected my pulse would've been going crazy even if we'd been lying here fully clothed and hadn't laid a hand below each other's belts. Though there was definitely some of that postcoital euphoria, and my body felt fucking fantastic now that he'd worked his magic, this excited nervousness was becoming my natural state when he was in the same room. Even if we were in a meeting, or passing in the halls, or sitting across from each other and talking about nothing over lunch.

And in bed? Wow. Only one other person had ever narrowed my entire focus, my entire universe, to simply being overwhelmed by their presence.

That other person was the mother of my children, and I'd never imagined feeling like this for someone again. But damn, holding Travis close, with my mind replaying the look on his face as we'd stroked each other, there was no denying how I felt about him.

I cuddled closer to him. It was too soon to say for sure if this was love or infatuation, but infatuation had never burrowed so far beneath my skin. Not that it had ever had much opportunity—I'd been with my ex-wife for most of my adult life, and since the divorce, hadn't actually *dated* anyone besides Logan. But even in my younger days, when I'd had the occasional girlfriend or the odd fling, I'd never been dizzy, giddy, speechless, delirious—except with Mandy.

Until now.

I kissed his forehead. This was still a young, nebulous thing. It was entirely possible we were still riding the novelty of being with someone new. Maybe I was just enjoying the thrill of an actual functional relationship with a sober man.

I didn't know if I was in love with him.

I just knew I wanted to be.

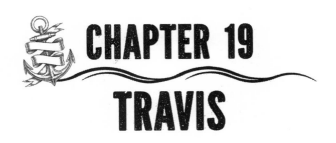

CHAPTER 19
TRAVIS

We put on gym shorts and T-shirts—Clint kept a few at my house now—and went downstairs to get some water. I wouldn't have minded if he went around without a shirt, especially since Kimber was at work, but I wasn't a fan of going shirtless because of the various scars on my torso. They had a tendency to become conversation pieces—especially when we weren't in bed with something more interesting to keep us occupied—and I was enjoying the evening too much for that conversation.

As he sipped his drink, I said, "Well, if anyone at work didn't know we're dating . . ."

He nearly choked, but caught himself. "Uh-huh. I'd say the secret is out."

I shrugged. "Eh. I can't imagine anyone's all that surprised."

"Not if they've been paying attention." He took a deep breath and released it. "It's so weird. Two months ago, I was sweating like crazy about the command knowing I was with a man."

"It's a tough move to make. Been there."

"Seriously." He paused. "Would you believe I've only been out at all for the last two years or so?"

"Really?"

He nodded. "Never touched a man in my life until after my divorce."

"So are you . . ." I tilted my head. "Gay? Bi?"

He blew out a breath and looked up at the ceiling. "Honestly? I'm not a hundred percent sure. I know I'm into men. But women . . ."

I watched him, letting him find the words.

He leaned against the counter. "The thing is, I never once questioned that I was attracted to my wife, and we were married for sixteen years. Aside from a few one-night stands while I was drunk and falling apart right after our divorce, I haven't even been able to look at a woman since she and I split up."

"Really?"

"Yeah. Partly I feel guilty for destroying our marriage. And, I mean . . ." He sighed. "What can I say? It still hurts."

"I know that feeling."

"Yeah?"

"Oh yeah. I . . ." I swallowed. "That stuff can follow you for years, believe me."

"It can." He drummed his fingers on the edge of the counter beside him, studying me like he wanted me to elaborate. When I didn't, he went on. "So sometimes I think I'm not attracted to women at all anymore, or that I was lying to myself through my entire marriage. And sometimes I think I've sort of shut that off because I feel so terrible for doing her wrong like I did." He paused, then took my hand and laced our fingers together. "Make no mistake, though—I am definitely attracted to men."

I laughed cautiously. "You don't say."

He chuckled and kissed the backs of my fingers.

And looking in his eyes, feeling this close to him, I debated opening up to him. Showing him a piece of my past that very, very few people knew about. Because hadn't I been in his shoes? Wondering how much my sexuality was fluid and how much of it was affected—muted or amplified—by grief?

"So, um." I cleared my throat. "What you said about not knowing if you're still attracted to women—I can relate."

"So you said." His brow pinched.

"I mean, I'm bisexual. I'm definitely bisexual. But after I lost someone, I pretty much shut off one side for a long, long time."

"After Kimber's mom?"

"No. I mean, it hurt when we split up, but not like . . ." My chest tightened. "I was madly in love with this guy. Dion." As always, even saying his name fucked with me. "We were in the same squadron.

Long time ago. Ten years now. He was a buddy's RIO, and . . . God, I was crazy about him."

"Oh. Bad breakup?"

"Worse," I whispered. "We never even really had a relationship. We fucked a few times, but this was back when DADT was still in effect. We both had kids to take care of, and careers to think about. I was still afraid if my ex-wife found out I was sleeping with men, she'd use that as leverage to take my daughter away. His divorce had been nastier, so . . . I mean, what could we do?"

"Shit. Man, I remember those days."

"Yeah. So we backed off. And that only made it worse. I couldn't stop thinking about him. It was probably just as well he transferred out of the squadron."

"Did you guys lose touch after that?"

"Yes and no. I, um . . . We didn't talk much. Not for a while. Then we kind of got back in touch, but things were tense. Then . . ." I closed my eyes for a moment, trying to summon up the energy to say the words. Finally, I met his gaze. "These days, I just try to visit his grave at least once a year."

Clint's lips parted. "Oh my God. What—" He hesitated. "If you don't mind my asking, what happened?"

"Officially? He was on his way home from work, fell asleep at the wheel, and hit an eighteen-wheeler head-on in the oncoming lanes." I sighed. "Unofficially, the consensus is he killed himself, but wanted to make sure it looked like an accident so his kids were taken care of."

"Jesus."

I suppressed a shudder, mostly because I could feel a small spasm looming and didn't want to give it an excuse to get worse. "It was horrible. Took me years before I could even look at a man, and even when I could start getting physical with them again, connecting with one took a *long* time."

"How long?"

I looked in his eyes.

Up until more recently than I'm comfortable admitting right now.

"Years." I exhaled. Then I muffled a cough. "Anyway. Sorry to be such a downer."

"No, no. It's okay. I brought up my ex and being confused about my sexuality, so . . ."

"Don't worry about it." I drew him in for a kiss. "For the record, heavy subject matter notwithstanding, I really did have a good time tonight." I paused, and added with a grin, "Especially the after-party."

Clint laughed. "Much better after-party than the Navy Ball."

"You're telling me." I touched his face. "But I guess that worked out too. Gave me an excuse to give you a ride home after work."

"So was that your devious plan all along?"

"Totally."

"Well, it worked." He pressed a gentle kiss to my lips. "And now I keep coming home with you."

"To be fair, I go home with you too."

"Hmm. Yeah. Seems pretty fair and balanced to me."

Our eyes met, and we laughed.

"To be serious," I said, "I like how things have worked out. It's been . . . it's been really nice."

"Yeah, it has."

And how long can I realistically expect it to last?

I shoved that thought away. "Listen, um . . . You have plans for the holidays?"

"Not at the moment, no."

"Well." I hesitated again. Oh, to hell with it. "I'm going down to San Diego for a few days. Spending Christmas with my old RIO and his wife. Do you want to come along?"

"Really?"

"Yeah." I shrugged as if it were no big thing. "Could be fun, you know?"

"Are you sure your friends wouldn't mind?"

"Oh hell. I could bring the entire command to their place, and they'd just put more leaves in the table." Truth was, I'd texted them earlier to be absolutely sure. And of course, because that was their way, they'd responded with *We'll put another leaf in the table.*

Clint pursed his lips. "Are you flying or driving?"

"Flying. No way in hell is my back tolerating a drive that long."

He grimaced. "Oh yeah. I can imagine."

"Is that okay?"

"Yeah. Yeah." He exhaled. "Just, um, *really* don't like flying." He laughed self-consciously. "And I'm saying this to a pilot . . ."

I touched his face. "It's understandable. I'm not a real big fan of it myself. So, bad experience? Or a phobia?"

"Phobia."

"Damn. And I'd be happy to drive down, but . . . my back . . ."

"No, no. I get that. Flying is fine. Just, uh, don't be surprised if I'm not real chatty." He avoided my gaze. "It's not a long flight. I'll be all right."

"Are you sure? You can say no if it's—"

"No." He lifted his head. "I'd love to go. I can handle the flight . . ."

"You sure?"

"Yeah." He put his hands on my waist. "I'll buy a ticket tomorrow. And thanks. For the invite, I mean."

"Don't mention it." I smiled. "All right. Great. I'm looking forward to it."

"Me too."

I wrapped my arms around him. "Well, with that taken care of, we're already here." I gestured toward the stairs. "Want to call it a night?"

Normally, one of us hesitated, but this time, he nodded. "Sounds good. I am beat."

"God, me too."

He must've been exhausted, because he faded fast. In minutes, he was back to slow, steady breathing—probably out cold.

I smiled and kissed his shoulder, wincing as that motion strained my neck. The pain lessened, though, and I closed my eyes.

This wasn't the first night we'd spent together, but it felt different. Less temporary, in a strange way. More *normal*.

It was like we could relax into this now because we'd passed a bunch of tests. We'd been out publicly as a couple in front of our coworkers. My best friend thought Clint was great. We'd seen each other in the throes of PTSD nightmares. He'd had more than one good hard look at the chronic pain I tried like hell to keep hidden, and it hadn't scared him off or reminded him that things weren't going to get any better. In fact, he was the first to ever let me get comfortable so he could adapt to me.

There was no such thing as *comfortable* when my injuries were flaring up, but this was as close to it as I could get. Having Clint's warm skin against mine, and his arm slung across my stomach, was nice. Kind of addictive, but that was no surprise—everything about him was addictive.

Okay, so we'd see how things went, and for the time being, I had this. And hell, as long as my back was keeping me awake tonight, I'd damn sure spend the time enjoying the crap out of lying here next to him.

Smiling to myself, I kissed the top of his head.

Yeah, there were definitely worse ways to spend a night.

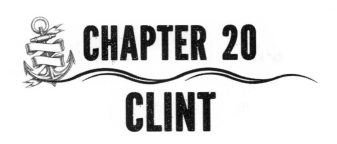

CHAPTER 20

CLINT

It was cheaper to fly out of Portland than anywhere else, so we drove up the night before and stayed in a hotel. Early the next morning, we left my car in the airport's long-term parking, grabbed our bags, and headed inside.

Being Christmas, the lines were obscene even at our airline, which had automated check-in kiosks. Of course we'd arrived here way early, but as I scanned the thick crowd waiting to check in, I wondered if we'd given ourselves enough time. I could only imagine what the security lines would be like.

"Think we'll make it?" I asked.

Travis scowled. "I hope so."

The line crawled forward. The people around us grew progressively bitchier and less patient, probably for the same reasons Travis and I kept checking our watches and phones. Over and over, I told myself we'd be fine. We still had almost three and a half hours between now and when our flight would start boarding.

I glanced at Travis, and my stomach tightened. If we were down to the wire, I had no problem sprinting across the airport. The thought of that would probably make Travis turn green. And for God's sake, his back wasn't bothering him today, so I prayed to the gods of air travel that everything went smoothly so it stayed that way.

And while I was at it, I added a couple of prayers for the plane to take off, stay in the air, and land gently at the other end without reducing all of us to a smoldering wreckage of metal and Christmas gifts.

I shuddered.

"You okay?" Travis asked.

"Yeah." I fussed with the strap of my carry-on bag just for something to do. "I'm good."

He eyed me uncertainly, but didn't push. I'd briefed him already on my fear of flying, and for a man who used to rocket around the sky in a fighter jet, he was remarkably sympathetic.

Of course he's sympathetic. He's survived a crash before.

My heart stopped.

How many crashes do people get to survive in one lifetime?

Is he tempting fate by pushing his luck and flying again?

Is he insane?

No. No, I was pretty sure he wasn't the insane one in this line.

I pulled out my phone and perused my email, social media, sports scores . . . anything that didn't involve air travel and plane crashes. I'd already resigned myself to getting on this plane, and assuming the line moved in the near future, I'd get on it, I'd get to San Diego, and I'd be fine. People flew every single day without incident. The odds were completely in our favor. We'd be *fine.*

Hopefully.

The line started moving faster—it looked like the airline had opened up a few more kiosks—and before long, we were at the front. We printed our boarding passes, and since we had no bags to check, headed for security.

Naturally, the line was three miles long. People who'd probably quietly stewed in their check-in lines had given up all pretense of going with the flow. In the back, there were loud comments about missing flights for sure. Closer to the middle, those comments were laced with increasing amounts of profanity. Near the front, we had apparently hit the jackpot, and were surrounded by at least a hundred people who were mystified by the notion of shoe removal, liquid restrictions, or body scanners.

Travis and I got separated in the shuffle. One minute, we were right next to each other, and the next, we were directed to different conveyor belts.

"Meet you on the other side," I called over my shoulder.

He offered a two-fingered salute, and we moved to our respective lines to dump everything we owned into trays.

My line was short, and I got lucky—I wound up behind the only people in this airport who seemed to know what they were doing. Shoes, belts, phones, change, wallets, laptops—everything went into the trays and onto the belts, and each person went through the body scanner in no time flat.

On the other side, after I'd collected my things, I sat down to put my shoes back on. I looked around for Travis, but he hadn't come through yet. By the time I'd finished putting myself back together, he still hadn't appeared. What the hell?

I glanced at my watch. We had less than half an hour to get to our gate. Hopefully they hadn't decided to strip search him or something. Maybe I'd give him some hell later about looking like a suspicious shady bastard, but that could wait until we were out of the airport. We didn't need to wind up in a TSA office getting questioned about exactly what *suspicious shady bastard* meant.

Where the hell are you?

Then I caught sight of him. He was standing on the other side of the body scanner, arms folded and features hardened like they were when he was chewing someone out at work. And in front of him, keeping him from getting through the damn scanner, was a well-dressed man arguing with the TSA agent. Travis couldn't go around him, especially since his bag had already gone through the X-ray machine.

He looked my way and rolled his eyes. Just what he needed.

I got up and collected his things for him. A moment later, the obnoxious passenger finally moved, and Travis stepped into the scanner.

As he joined me, he grumbled, "About fucking time."

"What was his problem?"

"Oh hell, I don't know." He started putting his belt back on. "I was too busy trying to kill him with my mind to actually listen to what he was saying."

I laughed. "You and all the people behind you. What a dick."

"One in every airport."

"Joy. Well, we should get to the gate, so—"

"Wait. One more thing I need to do now that we're through security . . ." He pulled the TENS unit out of his carry-on. "Time to put this back on."

"Oh. I thought your back was doing okay today."

"It is." He tugged the back of his shirt free from his pants. "But I want to keep it that way, and planes tend to aggravate things, so . . ." He reached back to attach one of the wires. "I would've had it on already, but I wore it through security *once*. Won't make that mistake again."

"Oh shit. I can imagine. You need help putting it on?"

"Nah." He paused, making some adjustment I couldn't see, then slipped the controller into his pocket. "If I can't move enough to put it on, I'm putting it on too late."

Now that his TENS was on, he slung his bag on his shoulder, and we hurried down the concourse to our gate.

And before I knew it—more like before I was ready—it was time. As our flight started boarding, my heart started pounding. I could do this. It was a short flight. No big deal. All the way onto the plane and to our row, I talked myself down as best I could. I'd flown before and survived. I'd be all right. Nothing was going to happen.

We settled into our seats. Travis had the window, and before we'd even put on our seat belts, he closed the shade. He didn't have to, but I appreciated the gesture.

"I'll be fine," I said. "I just won't look out the window."

"Okay." Travis squeezed my hand and ran his thumb alongside mine. "You sure you're all right?"

I'm on a sardine can that's about to be hurtled up into the sky. Yeah, I am groovy.

But I nodded. "I'm good."

The flight attendants shut the door. As they went through their safety briefing, my blood pressure climbed and climbed. No amount of oxygen mask demos or seat belt instruction could distract me from the motion of the plane and the knowledge that we were moving toward the runway. The parts about knowing where the exit was—*ten steps ahead of you, lady*—and seat cushions being used as flotation devices and how to go down goddamned slides . . .

Oh, fuck my life. I hate this.

It didn't last long, though. No, they were finished, and now it was time for the really fun part.

Once the flight attendants took their seats, I closed my eyes and tried to breathe.

Travis, being the saint he was, didn't try to pry my death grip off the armrest. Instead, he stroked the back of my hand with his fingers, and that was a much better distraction than the flight attendants' demonstration. I focused on that. On his gentle touch and the circles he drew with his fingertips. On—

Oh shit. Here we go.

God, I hated that feeling. And the plane always seemed to race down the runway a little too long. Just long enough for my heart to stop because I was absolutely certain something had gone wrong and we weren't lifting off and the pilots were probably panicking now and—

The front end tilted up.

Then the road noise ceased as the ass end lifted off.

And we were airborne.

So now, instead of careening into the end of the runway, we could crash from higher up. Perfect.

Pity I can't drink . . .

A couple of hours later, the plane touched down in San Diego.

As we taxied toward the gate, Travis took my hand. "You doing all right?"

"Much better now that we're on the ground."

He smiled and squeezed gently. "Good."

God bless the man for not giving me crap. Whenever I had to fly, I dreaded the comments almost as much as the flight itself, and sweating bullets next to an ex-pilot seemed like an invitation for some ribbing.

Travis had been nothing but kind the whole flight, though. Even now that we were on the ground, he didn't smirk and say, *See? There was nothing to be scared of.* It was like he just went with it. I was afraid of flying, and no amount of talking me down would change that, and he'd been calm and understanding about it. That was more refreshing than he probably could have imagined.

We finally got off the plane and walked out into the crowded concourse. Since we'd only brought carry-ons—Travis had shipped a box of gifts a week ago so we wouldn't have to haul them with us—we went right past the baggage carousels.

Travis paused to look around for his friend. "Ah, there he is." He gestured up ahead at a guy in a Yankees cap waving at us from a wheelchair. We made our way through the crowd, and Travis leaned down for a hug. As he stood, he said, "Charlie, this is my boyfriend, Clint. Clint, this is my old RIO, Charlie."

"Old?" Charlie sputtered. "Who you calling old?"

"Shut up and shake hands."

I laughed as I shook hands with him. "It's good to meet you."

"You too," Charlie said. "Your man's been telling us all about you. Maxine is looking forward to meeting you."

"Where is she, anyway?" Travis asked.

"She had to work, or she'd have come with me."

Travis huffed sharply. "Does this mean *you're* driving?"

"Well you're sure as hell not driving my car, hotrod."

"Ugh." Travis looked at me. "Don't forget your seat belt."

"Never do." I grinned. "Mostly because I've been in the car while you're—"

"Hey, that's enough out of you."

Charlie wagged a finger at me. "We're gonna get along, aren't we?"

"Probably."

"Oh great," Travis muttered. "And I thought introducing you to Kimber was a bad idea."

Charlie chuckled as we followed him out to the car. After we'd put our bags in the trunk, he said, "Do either of you mind sitting behind me?" He pointed at the backseat. "The chair's easier to reach if it's behind the passenger seat."

"Yeah, sure," I said. "Travis, why don't you ride shotgun? Probably more comfortable than the back."

He nodded. "Thanks."

Charlie eyed him. "Your back still giving you shit?"

"Will be till the day I die." Travis laughed dryly. "That's why the good Lord gave us painkillers." With slightly less humor, he added, "Now if He'd just give us the good ones over the counter . . ."

"I hear ya." Charlie shook his head. "Motrin works about as well as throwing water balloons at a house fire."

"So true." Travis groaned. "Well, maybe I'll get lucky and wind up with another kidney stone. That should be good for a refill."

Charlie and I both shuddered. I could only imagine the level of pain someone had to experience to use *get lucky* and *another kidney stone* in the same sentence.

Charlie lifted himself into the driver's side, folded the wheelchair, and twisted around. "Here, don't want to hit you with this." I leaned out of the way, and he put the chair behind the passenger seat.

As he drove us away from the airport, he and Travis caught up—mostly about how the base in San Diego had and hadn't changed in recent years—and I looked outside and took in the scenery. I didn't mind. They didn't see each other often, and I was still just enjoying the fact that I wasn't at thirty thousand feet anymore. Plus I hadn't been to San Diego in a while, so it was cool to see it again.

An hour or so later, Charlie pulled up in front of a small rambler with a rock-and-cactus garden and an American flag on the porch. Inside, a small Christmas tree sat on an end table, and a few Santa-themed decorations hung on the walls.

"Welcome to Casa Benson," Charlie said. "The guest room is down the hall." He pointed to the right. "Second door on the left. Everything is all set up, but let me know if you need anything."

"Perfect. I'll take everything in." I held out my hand for Travis's bag.

Travis handed me the bag. "Thanks."

"Either of you want a beer or anything?" Charlie asked.

"None for me," I said.

Travis glanced at me. To his friend, he said, "Same here. A couple of Cokes will probably do us."

"Two Cokes, coming right up."

"Great." I gestured at the hallway. "Second door on the left, you said?"

Charlie nodded.

They went into the kitchen while I went into the bedroom. There, I set our bags down and paused for a moment to roll my shoulders and exhale. I tried not to think about the fact that I'd be flying again in a few days. For now, I was going to enjoy being here with Travis and his friends, and I was going to enjoy Christmas. If I was lucky, I'd even get to have a nice conversation with my kids on Christmas Day. The flight home ... well. Fuck. Maybe I'd bail and hitchhike home. I'd see how I felt when the time came.

When I joined them in the living room, the guys had settled in. Charlie had taken the end of the sofa, and Travis sat in one of two armchairs. Probably easier on his back, especially after being shoehorned into coach this morning.

I took a seat on the end of the sofa closer to him, and also where my Coke was waiting.

Charlie gestured at both of us. "So how long has this been going on?"

Travis blushed. "Couple of months. We ... well, we didn't *meet* at the Navy Ball." His eyes flicked toward me, and his subtle smile brought my body temperature up. "But I think that's kind of when it started." His eyebrows rose. *Right?*

"Yeah," I said. "Close enough."

He nodded, then turned to Charlie. "And what about you? You been staying out of trouble?"

"Eh." Charlie shrugged. "Maxine might say no, but I think I've been behaving well enough."

More serious now, Travis asked, "How's work going?"

"Well, the graphics work has taken off, especially since I picked up some new contracts last year. Don't think I've worked this many hours in my life."

"Wait." Travis cocked his head. "Aren't you still working down at the shipyard?"

"Nah. I was pulling in enough on my own, so I quit."

Travis's eyes widened. "Oh, I didn't realize you'd gone full-time. That's great."

"Beats the hell out of commuting." Charlie stuck out his tongue. "The traffic in this town is bullshit."

"Well yeah," I said. "It's California. What do you expect?"

"You ain't lying."

"So you do graphics work, you said? What kind?"

"Oh, you know," he said. "Commercial work. Logos, websites, advertisements."

Travis looked at me. "You've got to see some of his work. It's amazing."

"Cool," I said. "I'd definitely love to see some of it."

Charlie gestured dismissively. "Maybe after we've all had a couple of beers. So Travis says you're Navy too, right?"

"Yeah. Transferred to NAS Adams recently. We actually work in the same office."

"And they let you two date?" Charlie's eyebrows jumped. "Really?"

"Well, we're not in the same department," Travis said. "Just the same office. I'm running admin and he oversees the training department."

"Ah, that makes sense." To me, Charlie said, "So where were you before?"

"I was at Nellis Air Force Base before. I, uh, flew remote aircraft."

Charlie's eyes lit up. "Oh, you flew drones?"

I nodded, ignoring the imaginary spiders crawling up my spine. "For a few years, yeah." I cringed inwardly, fully expecting the usual barrage of comments from people who flew real aircraft.

"Which one did you fly?"

"Mostly the MQ-9 Reaper. I trained on the Predator too, but they needed pilots for the Reaper, so . . ."

"Man, I would've loved to get into that." Charlie grinned. "When the drone program started up, I actually made a few calls to see if I could get in. But . . ." He gestured at his legs. "Even drone pilots have to pass physical readiness, so . . ."

"Well, it's not quite as exciting as you might think. The biggest problem we all had was fucking *boredom*."

Charlie laughed. "Yeah, I guess it wouldn't be quite as exciting as Mach 1."

I shuddered. "I'll take your word for that part."

"Not a flier?" he asked.

"Not when I can help it, no."

"Yeah, flying isn't for everyone. I *hate* flying commercially."

Travis wrinkled his nose. "Who doesn't? Just getting to our gate this morning was miserable as fuck."

"I know the feeling." Charlie pointed toward his wheelchair. "And believe me, that thing does not simplify things."

"I can imagine." Travis scowled. "Almost makes me want to get my private pilot's license, but I doubt I'll be buying a plane anytime soon."

"On Navy pay?" Charlie threw his head back and laughed. "Good luck with that."

Right then, the front door opened and closed. Footsteps came down the hall, and a second later, a woman with a graying black ponytail stepped into the living room.

"Hey, trouble!" She hugged Travis. As he sat back down, she extended her hand to me. "So you're the infamous Clint we've been hearing all about."

I chuckled as I shook her hand. "Great. My reputation precedes me." I turned to Travis. "You'd better not have been talking shit."

"Doesn't really matter what he said." Maxine gestured dismissively. "Just the fact that you're here with him tells us all we need to know."

"What's that supposed to mean?" Travis and I asked in unison.

She rolled her eyes. "Idiots. Okay, let me grab some coffee, and I'll join you." She headed for the kitchen, and Charlie swatted her on the butt as she walked past.

"Hey!" She wagged a finger at him before continuing into the kitchen.

"Still as feisty as ever," Charlie said, beaming.

"She has to be." Travis shrugged. "She's married to you."

"Hey!"

"Just saying."

A moment later, Maxine came back and sat between her husband and me. "Travis, honey, don't let me forget—we've got a couple of gifts for you to take back to Kimber."

"Oh, cool." Travis smiled. "She also sent something for you guys."

"What? She didn't have to do that."

"If you want to tell her not to, you go right ahead and give her a call."

Charlie and his wife both put up their hands and shook their heads.

"No, I don't think I want to challenge her," she said. To me, she added, "That girl is as stubborn as her father."

"So I've noticed," I said.

"Hey!" Travis shot me a glare.

"What?" I batted my eyes. "Just saying."

"My God." Maxine clicked her tongue. "I see why you two get along."

Oh, if you only knew . . .

"So," Charlie said. "You still liking that base?"

Travis nodded, absently twisting and stretching—his back was probably not thrilled about this morning's flight. "The base is nice. Kind of a small town, but after living here and in Norfolk, I'll take it."

"Yeah," I said. "It's one of the nicer bases I've been stationed at. I thought the weather would be gray and horrible all the time, but it's really not."

"The weather is gorgeous most of the time." Travis put his hand over the top of mine. "I mean, there's gray, shitty days, but when it's not raining, it's amazing."

"We'll have to come up and visit you one of these days," Charlie said. "I've been hearing nothing but good things about that whole area."

Travis nodded. "You should! The guys I work with say the fishing is great."

Charlie's eyes lit up. "Well, looks like we're coming to visit."

Maxine playfully smacked at her husband. "As if you don't do enough fishing here."

He scoffed. "There's no such thing as enough fishing."

"Great." She shook her head. "Well, no one's fishing today. What do you boys say we put together something for dinner?"

"Sounds good to me," we all said.

"Typical military boys." She laughed. "Quickest way to your heart is through your stomach."

We chuckled and followed her into the kitchen.

On the way, Travis took my hand. We exchanged smiles, and he paused to kiss my cheek.

And despite the way the day had started—God, I hated flying—I was glad I'd come along. Travis's friends were great, and hell . . . who was I kidding?

Air travel or not, I just loved being with him.

.

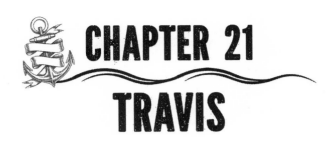

CHAPTER 21
TRAVIS

"My God, Charlie." I sat back in my chair at the dining room table. "I forgot you could cook."

He laughed, spearing a piece of steak with his fork. "Apparently you need to visit more often, then."

"If it means getting steaks like this, you're not going to be able to get rid of me." I turned to Clint. "Wait until you try his salmon."

"Oh." Clint put a hand to his chest. "Yes, please."

"Well, no salmon on this trip unless you guys want to go fishing." Charlie wrinkled his nose. "I don't cook that store bought shit."

Clint's eyes lit up. "Oh, I'm with you. Fresh caught is the only way to go."

"Hell yeah, it is." Charlie grinned. "You been fishing up there in Oregon? Or even up into Washington?"

"Not yet, but I definitely want to."

"Oh lord." Maxine shook her head and rose. "While you two talk fishing, I'm going out for a smoke. You coming, Travis?"

Even though I wasn't drinking, a cigarette did sound good right then, so I got up too. "Sure." I looked at Clint. "You don't mind if I—"

"Nah, go for it." He smiled. "I'm not going anywhere. Pretty sure I won't be able to move after eating that much."

"Get used to it." I patted his shoulder. "These two will not let guests go hungry."

"So I noticed."

I leaned down and kissed him, then followed Maxine outside. On the back porch, we both lit our cigarettes. We smoked for a moment before she finally broke the silence.

"Well, now you've done it, Wilson." She put her smoke between her lips. "You let them start talking about fishing."

I laughed. "Eh, that'll keep 'em busy for a while." I held up my own cigarette. "Maybe we can even sneak two."

"Sneak, hell." She winked. "Unless he's after you to quit?"

"Nah. I usually only smoke when I drink anyway, and I don't drink very often." I shrugged. "He hasn't said anything about it." I scowled. "Now if Paul would get off my back . . ."

Maxine snickered around her cigarette. "Good luck with that."

"Right?"

She'd only met Paul a few times over the years, but she'd witnessed us giving each other shit about our respective smoking habits. During one of my virtuous smoke-free periods, I'd harangued him every time he'd so much as glanced at a pack of Marlboros. After I relapsed and started chain-smoking, he'd threatened to call my mom again every time I lit up.

I took a drag and tapped some ashes into the tray. "So how are you doing these days?"

She looked out at the backyard, and pushed her shoulders back. "I'm doing all right."

"Are you?"

Her eyes flicked toward me, and she offered a tight shrug before putting her cigarette between her lips again. "The VA's been jerking us around to no end. Between that and my bosses throwing around the idea of layoffs . . ." She blew out some smoke, her posture deflating a little. "Hopefully we won't have to move, but if I lose my job, there's no way we can afford to live here."

"Damn. Sorry to hear it." I studied her. "If you guys need anything, you know—"

"We'll be fine, Travis." Her expression hardened just enough to warn me against pressing the issue, so I let it go. She was a proud woman, and I knew she'd never ask unless they were in absolute dire straits, but I at least wanted her to know the option was there. It always was.

Facing the yard again, she took in and blew out some more smoke. "It's stressful, but we'll be okay. Charlie's making enough now that we won't be on the streets or anything, and I'm getting us some health insurance that's . . . well, expensive, but better than some of the other options out there. We just won't be able to afford to live *here*."

"I'm surprised anyone can live here."

"No kidding." She rolled her eyes. "Southern California is highway robbery with beaches."

I laughed dryly. "Sums it up, yeah."

She laughed too, though she sounded tired. Then she faced me. "So how are *you* doing?"

I shrugged as much as my tight muscles would allow. "I can't complain."

"Yes you can, sweetheart."

I turned to her.

Her eyebrows pulled together. "You're still having a lot of pain, aren't you?"

I looked out at the yard again. Yeah, I was in pain, especially after my flight, but I couldn't justify bitching about it to the woman whose husband had been paralyzed—and nearly died—after the plane I'd been flying had hit the ship. Sure, the weather had been to blame more than anything. Sure, I'd corrected enough to keep us from getting killed. There'd been a million factors, most of them way beyond my control, but I'd obsess over those I could control until the day I died. What if I'd pulled up a second or two sooner? What if I'd—

"Travis." She touched my arm, startling me. "We've been through this. The fact that you can still walk after the crash doesn't mean it didn't mess you up. I know you're in pain. I can see it." She smiled faintly. "It's okay to acknowledge it."

I slowly released my breath. Somehow we never made it through a visit without having this discussion, so might as well get it out of the way now. "I'm doing okay. Just . . . a lot of pain."

"I'm sorry to hear it. I'm surprised the Navy hasn't tried to force you into retirement."

"Long as I keep passing my PRT, and the pain isn't interfering with my job . . ." I shrugged.

"It's interfering with your life."

"That won't go away when I retire."

"Maybe not." She crushed her cigarette and rested her elbow on the railing. "But doing the PRT twice a year probably isn't helping your back."

"Probably not." I cringed, expecting another lecture about killing myself for the Navy. We'd beaten this dead horse into the ground, but that didn't mean we wouldn't beat it again. She'd been on me for ages to at least stop *running* the PRT, and probably knew by now I'd run it until I had to crawl.

Thank God, though, she let it go for now.

She glanced in through the sliding glass door. "You and Clint seem to be pretty close."

I laughed softly, thankful for the subject change. "Yeah. He's a good guy. And, um, thanks for letting him come along. I don't usually try to bring strangers around, so—"

"Travis, if you're dating someone seriously enough to bring him along for the holidays, then he's not a stranger."

That gave me pause. How serious was this?

I shook myself and banished the thought. "Well, and he's on his own. New to town, no way to go visit family for the holidays—couldn't let him spend Christmas by himself."

She raised her eyebrow and gave me that lopsided grin that meant she saw right through me. "Uh-huh. And that's the only reason, right?"

"Well. I mean. I didn't say it was the *only* reason."

"Of course it isn't." She winked and elbowed me playfully. "Seriously, though, he seems really sweet. And to tell you the truth, I was kind of surprised to hear you were actually dating someone."

"Yeah, tell me about it." I blew out some smoke and crushed my cigarette in the ashtray. "Feels weird to actually date a man. After . . . I mean . . ."

"Travis. Honey." She put a hand on my arm. "You've grieved for Dion long enough. No one's going to fault you for letting yourself move on."

I winced.

"Especially after all this time." Squeezing my arm, she added, "He'd want you to be happy. We all do."

"I know." I focused on pulling another cigarette from the pack. "And it's not . . . I mean, I know it's been long enough. I guess part of me is afraid of . . ." The thought tightened my throat. My hand shook as I lit my smoke.

"You're afraid of the same thing happening with Clint?"

Heart pounding faster, I nodded. "It's completely irrational, I know. Especially since I can date women without worrying. But every time I think about getting close to a man . . ."

"Just because the fear's irrational doesn't mean it isn't real."

"It's . . ." I paused for a deep drag. After I'd released some smoke, I tapped the ashes. "It's not just everything with Dion. I guess I'm . . ." My cheeks burned, and I sighed. "To be honest, I'm terrified he's going to get tired of me being limited at every turn."

"He will."

I turned so fast I was surprised I didn't snap my neck, and blinked. "What?"

"He will." She shrugged, waving a hand toward the house. "It's exhausting. It is what it is. The difference is that when you love someone, you stay around."

My throat tightened, and I swallowed hard.

She touched my arm again. "I'm not going to blow smoke up your ass and tell you it's easy or that it's for the faint of heart. Chronic health problems are hard for everyone involved." She glanced in the general direction of where we'd left Clint and Charlie. "You think I don't have days where I scream into a pillow, or I cry about the things we can't do and the places we can't go? I saw a travel blog post about Machu Picchu last year, and bawled for an hour because I know Charlie and I will never be able to go there."

I absently tapped my cigarette, not sure what to say or how to take her candor.

"It's okay to be pissed about the shitty cards you're dealt," she went on. "But don't let that stop you from enjoying the good cards." She gestured over her shoulder. "Especially the aces." I didn't know if she meant Clint or Charlie, but the message came through just the same.

Barely whispering, I asked, "How do you do it?"

"It's not easy sometimes. What keeps me going is realizing how lucky I am that Charlie is alive, and how much would be missing from my life if he were gone. I can have my moments of being sad that there are things we can't do, and I can be depressed sometimes, but then I think about when I was at the hospital in Germany, waiting to find out if he'd even survived that first surgery. I remember how I felt when I was absolutely certain Charlie was dead." She shrugged tightly. "And it puts things in perspective. We might never make it to Machu Picchu, but he's still here."

I blew out a breath. "And thank God for that."

"Right?" She paused. "Look, I know it's different for me and Charlie because I was sticking with him after his injuries. Clint's coming onboard when your pain is already part of the package. So no, it's not the same."

"Okay, that's fair."

She nodded. "And the thing is, if Clint is the kind of guy who can't deal with you being in pain, then he isn't someone you want in your life anyway. Let him go." She waved her hand dismissively, as if it were that simple. "But if he's as good a man as he seems to be, *and* he's strong enough to be there when you're hurting . . . hold on to him, sweetie."

I stared at the cigarette smoldering between my fingers.

She absently tapped her cigarette pack on the railing. "I just don't want to see you jump ship and miss out on something amazing. Being with someone means there's always a chance you could lose them. And the more you love them, the more it'll hurt if you do lose them. But some people are worth that risk."

If it were anyone else on the planet, I'd have mentioned that was easy to say. But Maxine knew exactly what she was talking about, and exactly what a person could lose by taking that risk.

I tapped my cigarette over the ashtray. "You're right. And I guess . . . I mean, I guess I'll see where things go."

She smiled. "That's all you can do. And for what it's worth, I hope things work out with him."

I returned the smile but said nothing.

"Well." She nodded toward the house. "Should we go see how those two are doing without responsible adults present?"

That broke the tension enough for me to laugh. "Good idea." I finished my cigarette, put it out, and followed her inside.

Clint and Charlie had moved into the kitchen and were cleaning up from dinner. Charlie was loading the dishwasher while Clint was scrubbing out a pan. They both glanced at us, nodded in acknowledgment, and went right back to their conversation.

I stopped in my tracks. One look at the two of them took my breath away. It was like seeing my past life and my current one colliding right there in Charlie's kitchen. The man I'd torn up the skies with until that all went down in flames, and the man who I . . .

The man I was quickly . . .

Oh my God. You fit right into this world. It's like you belong here.

I looked at Maxine. She met my eyes with that knowing look on her face, and as warmth rushed into my cheeks, she smothered a chuckle.

I started to mutter something snide about her smugness when Clint went to take a step, and his foot caught on a wheel.

He stumbled. The wheelchair jerked to one side.

Charlie grabbed the counter, and so did Clint, and they both froze for a second.

"Shit." Clint stared at Charlie in horror. "My God. I'm sorry. Are you okay?"

"Relax." Charlie waved a hand. "I trip over it all the time."

"You . . ." Clint blinked. "Wait, what?"

Charlie snorted and clapped Clint's arm. "I'm fucking with you. Don't worry about it." He paused and must have seen the horror still on Clint's face. "Seriously, it's no big deal."

"Oh. Okay." Clint exhaled.

"Relax, honey," Maxine said. "We've all done it. In fact, it's pretty much a rite of passage."

"Yep, she's right." Charlie paused to pour detergent in the dishwasher. "So I guess your initiation is complete."

Clint shook his head. To me, he said, "I'm starting to see why you get along with them."

Charlie, Maxine, and I all nodded, murmuring in agreement. Wasn't like any of us could argue—we were some smart-assed little peas in a pod.

And you fit right in, Clint, so don't judge.

I gulped.

He did, didn't he?

So what? Just means we're all going to get along while we're in town. Quit reading so much into it.

I cleared my throat. "Can I help with anything?"

"Nope." Charlie shut the dishwasher and turned it on. "We're almost done in here. If you two want to have a seat in the living room, we can get some coffee."

"Sounds good to me," I said.

"I'll get the coffee." Maxine shooed the three of us out of the kitchen. "You boys go sit down."

While she prepared the coffee, Charlie hoisted himself onto the couch, and Clint and I took the same places where we'd been sitting earlier. A moment later, she joined us, and over coffee, they continued effortlessly chatting like we'd been doing all day.

I sat this one out, though. As the three of them talked, I let my gaze shift from Clint to Charlie to Maxine and back.

I still remembered when Charlie had first met Maxine. We'd been dumb kids, and even then I'd envied their relationship from the start. I'd only ever fallen in love like that once—with Dion.

Then Maxine had nearly lost Charlie. And even though Dion and I hadn't been together, I'd still loved him so much it hurt, and losing him had been a type of hell I wouldn't have wished on my worst enemy.

The first couple of years after the crash, none of us had been sure if Charlie and Maxine's marriage would survive. It had been such an enormous upheaval, and the adjustment had taken its toll on both of them. With some time and the help of a counselor who specialized in disabled veterans, though, they'd pulled together and come out stronger on the other side. The crash and its aftermath had tested them at every turn, that was for sure, but they'd made it through the worst. Almost twenty years together, with more hell behind them than most couples ever faced, and they still looked at each other like newlyweds.

I'd eventually gotten back on my feet after losing Dion, but I'd been alone ever since. But it didn't mean I didn't want to fall in love. I did. Very much. I wanted what Maxine and Charlie had. I *envied* them. I wanted that. I wanted to know what it was like to be that much in love with someone, but I'd been terrified to go there because my one taste of it had nearly destroyed me.

Even now, all these years later, the prospect of being that much in love scared the shit out of me.

So did the fact that every time I looked at Clint, my heart sped up. *Oh shit . . .*

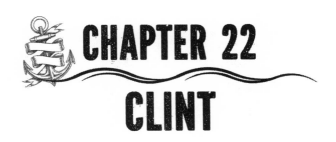

CHAPTER 22

CLINT

I barely touched dinner on Christmas Day. I told them I was still stuffed from the enormous breakfast they'd cooked in the morning, and everyone seemed to buy that. Well, maybe not Travis—he'd eyed me from across the table, but he didn't say anything.

When the clock said seven, I excused myself to the guest room, and while they all relaxed in the living room, I fired up my laptop.

As it always did, my gut wound itself into knots as the Skype call initiated. The screen came to life, and I couldn't help smiling.

"Hey guys," I said to my three kids, who were crowded in front of the camera.

"Hey, Dad," they said in unison. "Merry Christmas."

"Merry Christmas." *Oh God, don't get emotional. Keep it together.* "You guys having a good Christmas?"

They regaled me with everything they'd been doing since we last talked. My ex-in-laws had been to visit recently, and the kids were going down to Phoenix next week to see my mom and stepdad. It was hard to hear about some of our family Christmas traditions— the chocolate oranges in their stockings, the annual addition to the Disney DVD collection, spending Christmas Eve in pajamas while watching the original *Grinch*—but the kids were all smiles. That was the important part. The first Christmas after the divorce had been rough. The one before that had apparently been a disaster too, but I didn't remember any of it. Last year was better. This year . . . well, I couldn't ask for much more than this.

They thanked me for the gifts I'd sent, which had apparently arrived on time. That was an improvement over last year. While they watched, I opened the package their mother had sent on their behalf.

"Oh wow." My throat tightened as I pulled out the framed photo of the three of them grinning in goofy sunglasses. They'd each written their names on the frame, and it was a recent photo, since Crystal had lost both her front teeth. I forced my emotions to stay solid, and smiled at my kids. "This is great. I'm going to put it on my desk when I get back to work."

After they took off to go play with their new toys, their mother took their place in front of the camera.

"Hey," she said.

"Hey." I took a breath. "Merry Christmas, Mandy."

"Merry Christmas." She leaned closer to the camera and squinted. "Where are you? That doesn't look like your apartment."

"No, I'm, uh . . ." I glanced around as if I'd never seen this place myself. "I'm in San Diego. A friend invited me along for the holiday."

Her lips tightened, and she sat up again. "So that's why you aren't coming to see us."

It took all the self-control I had not to roll my eyes. "You told me—repeatedly—you didn't think the kids were ready for that. Where was I supposed to go?"

"I . . ." She chewed her lip. "I guess I didn't . . ."

"Was I supposed to stay home alone?" I asked coolly. "I can't at least *try* to enjoy Christmas?"

She opened her mouth to speak, but hesitated. Slowly, she deflated, and then she shook her head. "You're right. I'm sorry. I guess sometimes I forget you're . . ."

Our eyes locked.

Alone? Not allowed to come near my family outside of scheduled visits? Exiled?

I muffled a cough. "It's all right."

"No, it's not." She sighed. "I'm sorry. That was out of line. You're . . . I hope you're having a good time."

"I am." It was all I could do not to tell her exactly why I was having a good time. Now that I was seeing Travis, I desperately wanted to tell her, but . . . not now. Not on Christmas. Things were tense enough, and this wasn't the time to drop a bomb on her.

I couldn't even put my finger on why I thought she wouldn't take it well. She wasn't a homophobe by any means. Her older brother was gay, and he'd come out after being married to a woman for quite a few years, so she'd seen this kind of thing play out before. She hadn't rejected him or been angry with him. On the other hand, she *had* made some comments about not being able to imagine being her brother's now-ex-wife.

"That must've been a kick in the teeth," she'd said when we'd been alone after hearing the news.

"Clint?"

I shook myself, and wondered how long I'd fallen quiet. "Sorry. Sorry. I . . ." I blew out a breath. "Sorry."

She tilted her head. "You're not—"

"I'm sober. I promise."

She studied me, and I didn't have to ask if she believed me. The fact that I could calmly string together a coherent sentence was a huge point in my favor. My eyes probably weren't as red as they'd been during my drinking days either.

She sat back and glanced off-camera. "I should go make sure they aren't destroying the tree."

I forced a quiet laugh. "Okay. Send me some pictures, will you?"

"Sure." She nodded. "Take it easy, Clint. Maybe next year, we can . . ." She dropped her gaze.

"We'll cross that bridge when we get there. This year's an improvement. I'll take it."

"Me too. Anyway. Um. Good night. Merry Christmas."

"Merry Christmas."

We hung up, and I closed my laptop. For a good hour or so, I sat there. Sometimes staring at the photo they'd sent. Sometimes staring into space. The whole time, replaying the conversation. Things *were* getting better. It was a slow process, but we were getting there. The kids were talking to me. I had a new picture of them for my desk at work.

And maybe next year . . .

We'll cross that bridge when we get there.

I sighed, not sure if I was drained, relieved, or both.

A knock at the door pulled my attention from the picture. "It's open."

Travis stepped in. "Hey. I didn't want to interrupt, but . . ."

"No, no." I set the frame on top of my bag. "We hung up a few minutes ago."

He sat on the bed beside me and squeezed my shoulder. "So how'd it go?"

"It went all right. I'm fucking exhausted now, though."

"I don't doubt that at all."

I chewed my lip. Then I reached for the photo. "They sent me this."

He took the picture from me and smiled. "Wow. They look just like you."

"Trust me—the boys look a lot more like their mom."

He glanced at me, then at the photo, and shrugged. "Well, I've never seen her, but I can sure see the resemblance to you."

Setting the frame aside again, I couldn't help but smile. "Let's hope for their mother's sake that they haven't inherited *all* of my traits."

Travis patted my leg. "You don't give yourself enough credit." He kissed my cheek. "But I can imagine you were a handful as a kid, so yeah, let's hope."

"Ass." I elbowed him, and we both laughed. Then I sighed. "Man. I'm beat."

"Me too. I might be about ready to call it a night." He waved toward the door. "Charlie and Maxine have already gone to bed."

"This early?"

"They're not night owls like us."

"And yet we're the ones who have to be up at ridiculous hours to go to work."

"The gods favor no one, apparently." He stood and toed off his shoes, but otherwise, left everything on as he lay back on the bed. "Ahh. That feels nice."

I joined him on the bed, propping myself up on my elbow and resting a hand on his chest. "How's your back?"

"Still attached." He slid his hand around the back of my neck and drew me down. He kissed me lightly, then met my gaze. A devilish little grin formed on his lips. "Actually, before we hit the hay, I have one more present for you."

My stomach curled inward with dread. If this was a holiday-themed come-on, it was going to take a hell of a lot of effort to pretend I was into it right now.

I smiled, though. "You already gave me too much. You didn't have to get me anything."

"I know. But..." He got up, dug through his bag, and then handed me a wrapped package slightly larger than a shoebox. "I thought you'd like this."

It had some heft to it, and it was soft. I was definitely curious, and prayed like hell it wasn't some sort of sex toy he expected to use tonight.

Please, not tonight.

As he lay back on the bed again, I tore off the paper, and no, it was not a sex toy. No, it was the brightest, most hideous blanket I'd ever seen. Soft as hell, yes, but the pattern was a bunch of frosted, sprinkle-covered pastries.

I arched an eyebrow at Travis.

He didn't even try to hide his smirk. "I thought it would go with your throw pillow."

I burst out laughing. "You dork."

"What?" He snickered. "It seemed like your style."

"Of course it is." I leaned over him and kissed him. "Thank you."

"You're welcome."

"And, um..." I touched his face. "Thank you for bringing me here with you. This beat the hell out of spending Christmas alone."

"Even if you had to get on a plane?"

I suppressed a shudder and smiled. "Yeah. It was worth it."

"Glad to hear it." He slid a hand around the back of my neck and pressed a light kiss to my lips. When we parted again, his brow furrowed. "You okay? You've been kind of distant all evening. Stressed about talking to the kids?"

"Just a bit. And I should feel better now that it's over, but I..." I lay back on the pillows. "I'm exhausted."

"I believe it." He took my hand and squeezed gently.

I stared at the ceiling. "Looking back, I don't think the divorce could have been avoided. She was right—I'm a different person now. And I have no idea if she could have coped with my PTSD or not. I still don't know sometimes if *I* can." I closed my eyes. "But of all the ways things could have gone down, I could have handled things so much better. Without hurting her and the kids like that."

"You were traumatized and you couldn't talk about it," he said. "In hindsight, I can't imagine many people would blame you for not choosing the healthiest means of coping."

"Maybe not. But I sure as fuck do. You're right about one thing though—I'd have been so much better off if I could have talked about it."

He said nothing. Just squeezed my hand.

"This must sound crazy to you." I avoided his eyes. "An RAP being so fucked up by something that happened in a safe, comfortable office."

"We've talked about this," he said. "It's not a competition. And even if you're not in the line of fire, you're still part of the war. You're going to be affected by it."

"Yeah. That's for damn sure." I raked a hand through my hair, then turned to him. "That job killed my marriage, and it almost drowned me in a bottle. And I . . ." My face burned. "Listen, I'm not proud of this. Any of it. But I . . . The thing is, I couldn't cope with my job. With what happened three years ago. So I dove into a bottle, and . . ." Shame twisted in the pit of my stomach. I couldn't keep holding his gaze as I whispered, "When I get drunk, I get crazy."

"Crazy, how?"

I forced back the bile in my throat. "Crazy violent."

Travis stiffened.

I quickly added, "I never laid a hand on my wife or kids. I swear. Never did. But I, uh, I had to patch a few walls in the house. I never touched them, but I scared the shit out of them, and I will *never* forgive myself for that."

I fully expected Travis to recoil away from me and give me the same horrified expression the judge and my in-laws and the cops had. The last thing I expected was a gentle hand over the top of mine, or a reassuring squeeze.

Without looking at him, I took a deep breath and went on. "The thing is, everything RAPs do is classified. The missions. The recon. The outcomes. No matter what happened, I couldn't go home and tell my wife about my day. Which was stressful enough. But then when . . ." My skin crawled. "When things got really bad, I couldn't tell anyone." Stomach somersaulting and heart pounding, I turned to him and whispered, "All I could do was drink."

The understanding in Travis's eyes almost broke me. No judgment, no disgust—he just nodded, his expression full of genuine empathy. "This job fucks people up. No two ways about it."

A lump rose in my throat, and I nodded. "Yeah. But Jesus—they didn't deserve that."

"Neither did you."

My shoulders dropped. "You don't even know what happened."

"No, but I know you." He squeezed my hand again. "War is brutal."

"Yeah. I just . . . I wish I could talk about it. But the details are . . ."

"Classified?"

"Very." I paused. "And . . ." I released a long, heavy breath and sat up. "You know what? Fuck this. I shouldn't . . . but, I mean, you have secret clearance, right?"

He straightened. "Of course I do, but this shit's on a need-to-know basis."

Heart thumping, I laced our fingers together. "I think this qualifies, to be honest."

His eyebrows jumped. "Why's that?"

"Because one of the reasons I drank myself stupid and fucked up my marriage was that I couldn't tell anyone what happened. I . . ." I gulped. "I'm completely fucked up, Travis. And if we're going to do this—or hell, if I'm going to stay fucking sane—I *need* you to know what happened."

Travis's eyes widened. He brought our hands up and softly kissed the backs of my fingers. For a moment, I was sure he was going to tell me he wished he could help, but that was a line he couldn't cross. And if he'd said that, I wouldn't have blamed him.

Instead, he whispered, "Nothing leaves this room. I promise."

I held his gaze. My heart was going even faster now—after keeping this all bottled up for so long, under strict orders to never breathe a word of it, I wasn't even sure I had the vocabulary to talk about it.

Acid burned my throat. "It was . . ." I closed my eyes and pushed out a ragged breath. "It was about three years ago now. We'd been monitoring this target for months. By the time we got the green light to strike, we knew every inch of that building and who was occupying it. When they came and went, when and where they shit, what they ate, what websites they were using . . ." I looked at Travis. "There was nothing about those guys we didn't know."

He nodded slowly, a silent *go on.*

"So we got the order—take out the building and everyone in it. Everything went smoothly. The ground crew over there turned the drone's controls over to me. We flew in, we bombed the shit out of it, and flew it back. Handed the controls back, and we were done." The acid in my throat burned hotter. I swallowed, trying to tamp down some of the queasiness.

Travis put a hand over my forearm, but he didn't speak.

I tamped down the nausea. "It wasn't until the next day that we knew something had gone wrong." I leaned against the headboard. Staring up at the ceiling, I went on. "I don't know how the enemy knew, or if they did, or if it was just horrible luck. All I know is, when I took out that building I had every reason to believe it was full of high-ranking enemy combatants . . ." My mouth went dry. I combed a shaky hand through my damp hair. "The only bodies they found afterward were civilians."

Travis's breath hitched.

"Fifty-seven civilians. Mostly women and kids." I forced back a fresh wave of nausea. "They didn't recover a single combatant, but even if they had, I mean . . . *fifty-seven civilians.*"

"Jesus." He gripped my hand even tighter.

I coughed to get my breath moving. "My command tried to hem up everyone involved, but after the investigation, it was obvious we had no way of knowing. They combed through every shred of intel, and agreed we had every reason to believe beyond a shadow of a doubt that our targets were in that building." I rolled my stiffening shoulders. "So, after that, we went back to work. And the next time I tried to fly a mission, I choked. I couldn't do it."

"Is that why you came to Adams?"

"Not . . ." I closed my eyes. "Not right away. They moved me into an admin position. Kind of like what I'm doing now. It was supposed to be temporary. Something to keep me working—first while they investigated me for wrongdoing, and then while I recovered from the trauma." Even queasier than before, I met Travis's gaze. "But recovering . . . I mean, how the fuck was I supposed to recover from something like that?"

He traced his thumb alongside my hand. "I don't guess you had a lot of people you could talk to."

"There was no one. Absolutely no one." I moistened my lips. "The crew involved in the incident didn't want to talk about it." Rubbing my eyes, I sighed. "During the debrief, we had to sign even more nondisclosure forms than we'd already signed, and our chain of command reminded us a hundred times that even chaplains and therapists were off-limits, no matter their clearance."

"Is that . . . is that *legal*?"

"I don't even know anymore. Anyone I asked just told me to keep my mouth shut." I dropped my hand and met Travis's gaze. "I couldn't tell a shrink. I couldn't tell my wife. I couldn't tell *anyone*. And it was eating at me. One of the guys I worked with, he said it was like an invisible cancer. It's there, and it's killing you, but you can't tell anyone about it. Not even a doctor. You just have to sit there and pretend it doesn't exist until it finally finishes you off."

"Shit," he said. "That's unreal."

"And I shouldn't have even told you." I made myself meet his gaze, and damn my voice for shaking as I whispered, "But I can't carry this by myself anymore."

"You shouldn't have to."

"Not that I have much choice." I pushed back some fresh nausea. "I'm telling you, I never knew there could be such a fine line between collateral damage and a war crime. And when you're the guy pulling the trigger . . ." I shook my head. "I don't think that line really exists. Or if it does, it doesn't matter."

Travis ran his thumb back and forth along mine again, but said nothing.

When the silence started getting unbearable, I went on. "It was like a switch was flipped. One day I had this job that was stressful and taxing, but it was doable. And the next . . . the next I was all kinds of fucked up. After that, I hid in a bottle. I'd walk in the door after work, and I wouldn't even change out of my uniform before I was pouring something." I rubbed the back of my sweaty neck. "And things went downhill from there."

"I can't even imagine," he breathed.

Except he could. After what he'd gone through, crashing into the carrier and being pulled from the water, I didn't think anyone would begrudge him if he spent some time in a bottle. That was a level of danger RAPs never had to worry about.

"And yes, people think . . ." I paused. "They can't see how this job fucks people up. They don't get it. Being thousands of miles away from the war zone doesn't make it less traumatic to fire the weapon."

He tipped up my chin and kissed me softly. "War is our job. It's going to affect all of us, even if we're not right there at the front lines."

"I know. But it . . ." I stared at my wringing hands. "We're working with people who are close to the front lines. Drone warfare keeps our guys out of harm's way, but not all of them. There's a ground crew over there. They're not right in the middle of the shit that's going down, but they're a hell of a lot closer than the RAPs." I turned to Travis. "How do you tell one of those guys you're as fucked up as he is when he had to sleep in a tent or a shipping container in hundred-degree heat, knowing he could get bombed during the night?"

"Clint." He covered my hands with his and stilled them. "Even if somebody is more affected than you, like to the point they can't even function, it doesn't negate what happened to *you*."

I exhaled hard. "Thank you. And it's . . . it's a load off my mind just to be able to talk about it."

"I believe it. You shouldn't have to hold on to that by yourself."

"It's hell," I whispered.

He pulled me in for another kiss. "I don't doubt that at all. I'm sorry you have to deal with it."

I didn't speak. Just talking about the incident and its fallout had left me numb, but looking in Travis's eyes woke up some feelings. It was this bizarre sensation, like talking about it for the first time had been a way of reliving it, and when I was done, I was still alive. My life wasn't in the chaos and shambles it had been after the real thing had gone down.

I was alive. I was here. I was sober.

And Travis was still looking at me the way he always did.

"You know, to be honest . . ." I moistened my parched lips. "Now that it's off my chest, I don't really want to think about it anymore tonight."

"What do you want to think about?"

I didn't answer right away. I wasn't exactly sure how. What *did* I want to think about tonight?

Then, heart thumping, I touched his face. "You."

Travis said nothing. He wrapped his arm around me, tilted his head, and pressed his lips to mine.

And all I thought about after that was him.

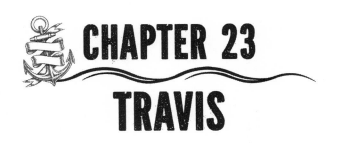

CHAPTER 23
TRAVIS

I hadn't been in the mood all day, but now that he was pressed up against me, heat radiating through our clothes while our lips frantically moved together, my whole body responded. If Clint wanted something else to think about, that was one thing I could definitely do for him. I couldn't erase what had happened to him, or the way it had all but destroyed his life, but I could make damn sure he felt good tonight.

I kissed him like it was the first time—hungrily, breathlessly, pushing him down into the mattress as he held on to handfuls of my hair and my shirt. An annoying spasm knifed its way along my spine, but Clint was panting and shaking, so I ignored the pain and kissed him some more. Despite my stupid back and everything that had been churning inside my skull since last night, losing myself in his kiss relaxed me. All the apprehension about what this was and what we were doing and what I might do to fuck it up—none of that mattered right now.

He tugged my shirt free from my waistband. Once it was loose, he slid his hands under it, and we both sighed as his palms ran across my bare skin. Jesus, I needed to feel more of him. I came down a little, so my chest touched his, and kissed his neck. He tilted his head back. His fingers curled against my sides, almost enough for his nails to bite in, and goddamn, even through our clothes, I loved the way his hard-on felt when it rubbed mine.

In fact, I loved how his skin felt against mine, and right now, there was too much in the way. Carefully, so I wouldn't jar my stupid back, I sat up, still straddling him. I peeled off my shirt, tossed it aside, and reached back to disconnect the TENS wires, but Clint caught my arm.

"Wait. What are you doing?"

"I'm . . ." I swallowed. "Just taking off the wires. So they don't get in the way."

"But doesn't that keep the pain down?"

"It helps, yeah."

"My God—don't take it off, then!"

"But . . ." I glanced at the box in my hand. "The wires. I don't want you getting tangled up in—"

"Relax." He kissed me and grinned. "I'm pretty sure I can navigate around some wires. If it's helping the pain, leave it on."

I hesitated.

"I'm serious," he said. "Let's get these clothes off, though."

With our clothes on the floor, we lay on our sides, facing each other, and set the TENS unit on the narrow sliver of sheets between us. The wires were draped over my waist, a vague reminder that I wasn't as naked as I wanted to be right then.

"This all right?" he asked.

"You tell me."

He cupped my ass and kissed me softly. "It's perfect."

I shivered. "Even with—"

"*Perfect*." He brushed his lips across mine. "Just let me know if I bump it or something."

"Don't worry about it." I combed my fingers through his hair. "It takes a beating every day."

"Good to know." He slid closer, and his fingers closed around my cock, and to hell with talking. We made out, and we stroked each other, and I didn't know if this had gotten his mind off anything, but it had sure as hell pulled my focus to him and nothing else.

Anything you want right now, I wanted to tell him. *As long as you feel good. Anything.*

But talking meant breathing and it meant not kissing, and his kiss was too good to pass up. There was something different about him tonight too. Something . . . unrestrained. Like he wasn't in any rush, but he was more relaxed than he'd been before.

I knew the feeling well. He'd been keeping a card tightly against his vest for too long, and tonight he'd shown it, and now that he knew that card hadn't chased me off, his relief needed to go somewhere.

One of his recent comments echoed through my mind:

"It'll take more than back pain to get rid of me."

I grinned into his kiss. *Likewise. You're not getting rid of me that easily.*

We stroked each other faster until I was breathing too hard to keep kissing him, so I pressed my forehead to his and concentrated on what I was doing with my hand.

"That feels so good," he breathed.

"Mm-hmm. Always does when we're in bed."

"So does." Then he pushed me onto my back and climbed on top. Though his chest was against mine, he held himself up enough to keep from putting his weight on me.

As soon as his lips started down my jaw toward my neck, I damn near came unglued.

Yes, please. Yes, lower. Lower. Oh fuck, lower . . .

I could barely breathe as I watched him trail soft kisses down my chest and midsection. Anticipation wound me up like nothing else, especially since I knew how good he was, and he didn't disappoint—he took my cock between his lips, and I was in heaven.

No one sucked dick like Clint. He'd get me off, there was no doubt about that, but he was in no rush. There wasn't an inch of my cock or balls that his lips and tongue didn't tease. Little kisses, soft licks, squeezing with his lips, swirling with his tongue—he was relentless and patient at the same time. Like he could've done this all night. And the sounds he made were unreal. He moaned like he was the one getting sucked off, and that would've been a turn-on all by itself. Coupled with the magic he did with his mouth? I was a goner. Completely his slave right then.

Just . . . please . . . keep . . .

"Oh my God, Clint." I bit my lip as I combed my fingers through his hair, and he bobbed his head over my cock. "You're fucking amazing."

He moaned, driving me wild with that vibration against my insanely sensitive skin.

And then he wasn't fooling around anymore. His lips focused on the head. His tight grip slid up and down the shaft. Faster, harder—he wanted me to come now, and I didn't fight him. I gave in completely, letting him take me higher, higher, higher, until I must've been levitating off the bed and halfway to the stratosphere, and then—

Oh. Fuck. Yes.

It didn't even matter that my friend and his wife were right down the hall—I doubted I could've made a sound if I'd wanted to. Sheets bunched in my hands, and air stayed just beyond my lips, spinning, spinning, spinning, and Clint didn't let up, and spinning, spinning, spinning . . .

My hands relaxed. The air came back. My body sank back to the mattress. Before I could even be sure which way was up again, Clint was over me. I dragged him down into a deep kiss. His mouth was vaguely salty from getting me off, and I wanted nothing more than to do the same for him. I closed my fingers around his hard dick, and he rewarded me with a soft, helpless groan.

He started rocking back and forth, pushing his cock into my hand. It was almost like he was riding me, fucking me.

"We've got some lube," I said. "I can put—"

"N-no. This—" He released a ragged breath. "No, this is perfect."

In that case . . .

I tightened my grip and pumped him in time with his thrusts, adding the slightest twist to my strokes. "Like that?"

"Uh-huh." He screwed his eyes shut and bit his lip. Holy shit, he was sexy like this—moaning, trembling, the cords standing out on his flushed neck. I'd never been so overwhelmed with the need to make someone feel good. Hell, with him, I was drunk off that need. Just the thought of making him come—feeling, hearing, seeing him come— made me dizzy.

He kissed me, but then broke away with a gasp. "Oh God." His head fell beside mine, and his shoulders rose each time he thrust into my hand.

And then he whimpered.

And threw his head back.

And shot semen all over my hand and stomach.

And nothing—*nothing*—had ever been as sexy as watching him come right then. The way his eyes flew open and lost their focus. The way his lips parted and no sound came out. Muscles tensing beneath his skin. I was so caught up in his orgasm, I forgot for a couple of seconds that I wasn't coming right along with him.

Then he exhaled and sank down on top of me. He kept his weight on his forearms, but his hot skin pressed against mine. He buried his face against my neck, and his breath came in sharp, cool huffs across my sweaty skin.

With my clean hand, I stroked his hair.

"I feel a hell of a lot better now," he murmured.

"Good." I kissed the top of his head.

After a moment, he pressed his lips to my neck. Then the underside of my jaw. And finally, my lips. I wrapped my arm around him, and our lips moved lazily together. His body was still feverish and trembling, and I secretly hoped my back would hold out for another round. I was exhausted, and I wasn't twenty anymore, but damn, this was amazing.

One more round? Even if we don't come? That's not too much to ask, is it?

If we did, I'd pay for it tomorrow on our flight, but even that seemed like a small price. I'd already had him once, and I already wanted him again so much it hurt.

Even if we don't have sex again, I still have you in this bed tonight. That's all I need.

Clint pushed himself up on his arms.

Our eyes met.

Oh my God.

I touched his face.

I love you.

The clock said *3:31.*

Clint was out cold. We'd settled into bed with his head on my shoulder and his arm slung over me, but we'd separated once our combined body heat became too much. Now I was on my back, he was on his side facing away from me, and my stupid brain was going a million miles an hour. I couldn't make it shut up.

He'd woken up twice, both times shaking and sweating. The second time, he'd taken a few deep breaths, then gone into the bathroom and gotten sick. He'd apologized profusely, and I'd assured him it was nothing to be sorry for or ashamed of. And it wasn't like he'd woken me up, since I hadn't been sleeping anyway, but I kept that part to myself. He was rattled enough without catching on to my anxiety-fueled insomnia.

Now, fortunately, he was asleep. For his sake, I hoped that lasted the rest of the night. I listened for the slightest twitch or murmur that sometimes preceded one of those violent nightmares, but at least for now, he was still and silent except for his slow, steady breathing.

Beside him, I was wide-awake, staring at the ceiling and, in between listening for him to stir, sweating bullets over what was happening between us.

I was getting in way too deep. At the same time that I wanted to jump in headfirst and see where it went, I wanted to pull back and run like hell. I was utterly terrified of falling in love with him. And yet, I wanted to.

I didn't know what I should do. What I wanted to do.

Tonight, the only thing I knew for sure was how good it felt to fall asleep next to Clint. I wasn't nervous anymore about him being there when I had a nightmare, and I'd gotten used to him having them. We'd relaxed into something that had always been a massive challenge in relationships before this one.

I absently stroked his hair.

What the hell was happening? We'd started dating a couple of months back, and suddenly . . . this. We were talking about our haunted pasts.

I understood what he meant when he'd said what happened to him counted as need-to-know, and I couldn't imagine having to hold on to that kind of thing by myself. Bottling up an incident like that and keeping it out of a partner's sight was excruciating. I knew guys who'd done it because they didn't want their wives to know what they'd seen or done in a war zone. I knew others who'd had no choice because even hinting about what had happened meant talking about classified information.

I firmly believed Clint wouldn't have opened up to me about it if I hadn't had the proper clearance, but he knew as well as I did that now

I could destroy his career with one phone call. It was unnerving that he'd trusted me enough to tell me.

Which meant we were a lot closer than I'd realized. And I didn't know how I felt about that. I'd had plenty of sex with men over the years but never let myself get attached to one. Not since Dion had died. The minute feelings started to materialize, I was gone.

Except this time. Emotions had shown their faces, and I was still here. I'd been here long enough to be invested, which meant when Clint exited stage left, I was going to be in a world of hurt.

I refused to let myself cling to the hope that he wouldn't leave. I was as fucked up in the head as I was in the body, and one of those two things was usually enough to send someone packing before we'd gone too far. My last girlfriend had stayed around for a year or so, but being with a man like me got old fast.

Sighing into the stillness, I wiped a hand over my face.

Emotionally, we were disasters. Ten years later, I still didn't go a day without thinking about Dion. Clint's marriage had crashed and burned so recently, the wreckage was still smoking. Who were we kidding if we thought this thing could take off without going up in flames?

And physically? Shit. Most women I'd dated had gotten tired of "no, really, it hurts my neck," and the men got bored with gentle blowjobs and languid handjobs. One guy'd been perfectly happy without fucking, but had decided it'd been enough of a concession that he shouldn't have had to give up sex *entirely* on nights when I could barely move. I'd been with two people who'd decided without mentioning it to me that if I couldn't give them everything they wanted, they had carte blanche to get it elsewhere. Which had been fine—I rarely dated exclusively—right up until they each had decided that since their needs *were* getting met elsewhere, I was more trouble than I was worth.

"Just once," a former fling had complained, *"I want to have sex without being reminded that you've got all these injuries."*

Three years later, that one still hurt, and we hadn't even been that close. It was just the kick in the balls about being defective. Damaged. Broken.

I gazed at Clint in the near-darkness, and resisted the temptation to kiss his forehead. So far, he'd been a saint about everything. Limited sex life? No problem. PTSD dreams? Something to commiserate over. Nights where I was lucky to stand up, let alone get it up? Movie night. He took it all in stride as if this was how normal, functional relationships actually happened.

For now.

I was fine with people being temporary fixtures in my life and in my bed. Clint, though . . .

I closed my eyes and released a long breath. I was getting too invested. Hanging way too much hope on the stupid idea that this might be the one time falling in love didn't end in disaster for me. Or that he'd be that one person in a million who could cope with someone whose life was ruled by pain.

The last time I'd started getting close to someone, I'd gone off the deep end of stupid. Anything she'd wanted in bed was suddenly doable. Even if I was blinking back tears or praying I could stay hard despite how much it hurt to breathe, I'd given her anything she wanted because I was less afraid of the pain than I was of her leaving.

And ultimately, she'd left anyway.

Same as everyone before her.

And everyone after her.

And eventually . . .

Inevitably . . .

Clint.

If being in pain all the time and being fucked up in the head had one advantage, it was that a sleepless night was easy to excuse. If I had circles under my eyes and couldn't form a coherent sentence until my seventh or eighth cup of coffee, I could wave off any concern with a muttered "back was bugging me" or "you know . . . nightmares." As much as those things sucked, they were useful smoke screens when I didn't want to admit I'd been an emotional train wreck.

So, as we said our good-byes and Maxine dropped us at the airport, no one questioned me. Clint and I shuffled into the airport, made it through the lines, and after another debacle of getting through security—seriously, why did I always end up behind the assholes who wanted to argue with TSA?—we made it to our gate. By this point we were both out of patience, though neither of us turned it toward the other. His jaw was tight, and I was quietly stewing, but no sniping or snapping between us, so that was a plus.

Once we'd acquired some more coffee, we both started to relax a bit.

He sipped his and turned to me. "How's your back doing today?"

"Eh." I grimaced. Truth was, though it hadn't been what kept me up all night, it sure as fuck wasn't feeling great now. I couldn't say what had set it off—something during security? lack of sleep? moving wrong when I'd picked up my bag?—but it definitely hurt.

Clint nodded toward the podium, where a couple of airline employees were cheerfully handling a thin crowd of customers. "Why don't you see if they have upgrades? The last flight was almost empty in first class."

I pursed my lips. It did sound pretty tempting.

"Go for it." He offered a hand. "I can watch your bag."

I hesitated, but then gave him my bag and went up to the podium.

Fifteen minutes later, I returned to where we'd been sitting. "They had first-class upgrades, but only one seat."

"So did you take it?"

"What? No. Of course not."

"Are you kidding?" His eyes widened. "Those seats will be so much better for your back."

"Yeah, and you'll be sitting alone."

Clint scowled. "I'm going to be a nervous idiot no matter what." He motioned toward the counter. "Take the upgrade so you can be comfortable."

Oh, it was tempting.

But after spending the whole night wondering how long this thing would last? And knowing that taking the seat meant leaving Clint to endure the flight alone? When he'd come to San Diego because of me in the first place?

"I'll be fine," I said.

"But—"

"I'll be *fine*."

He held my gaze, but then shrugged, and God bless the man, he didn't bring it up again.

I wondered a few times if I'd made the right call, though. Especially when we started to board. On the way through first class, I stole a glance at one of those wide, plush seats that no doubt reclined until they were almost horizontal.

Should I have upgraded?

I should have upgraded.

Fuck. Why didn't I upgrade?

But . . . Clint. I wasn't leaving him alone for the flight.

We took our seats in row twenty-seven. After he'd put on his seat belt, Clint closed his eyes and released a breath. A hint of sweat gleamed at his hairline.

"You all right?" I asked.

Eyes still shut, he said, "I could ask you the same thing."

"I told you—I'll be fine."

"Are you sure?" He put his hand over mine and turned toward me. "You really didn't have to give up that seat."

"I know. But I don't think I'd be all that comfortable up there while I knew you were back here . . . you know . . ."

"Freaking out?"

I nodded.

His cheeks darkened. "I'm sorry. I—"

"Don't." I squeezed his hand. "I didn't invite you along on this trip so I could ditch you on the flight home."

"But your back—"

"Don't worry about it."

The plane started toward the runway, and Clint stopped arguing. He was probably focusing on not panicking, so I clasped his hand between both of mine and tried to keep his mind off the flight.

I told myself I'd only passed on the upgrade because it would be a dick move to ditch him back here when he was afraid of flying. It had nothing to do with that familiar insecurity creeping in like a sneaky muscle twinge, making my heart pound at the thought of letting Clint out of my sight. As if the minute he were alone, he'd start to realize how much simpler life was without someone who could do literally *nothing* without stopping to consider how it would affect his pain level. It had gotten old for me in a hurry—if *I* could've walked away from me and my bad back, I would've. So how could I hold it against him if he did the same?

And who was I kidding if I thought staying close to him would prevent the inevitable?

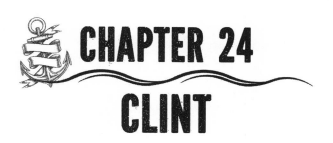

CHAPTER 24
CLINT

The airport had barely faded into the rearview before the painkiller knocked Travis out. He'd hemmed and hawed about taking it because he was down to his last two hard-core pain pills, but by the time we'd made it back to the car, he'd made up his mind.

As I drove, I still felt guilty that he'd given up a comfortable seat for me. Guilty, and a little stupid—there was something embarrassingly ironic about being more afraid to fly than a guy who had actually been in and narrowly survived a crash. If either of us had an excuse to break a sweat during takeoff, it sure as fuck wasn't me.

We'd made it back to terra firma, though, and now Travis was dozing beside me thanks to the painkiller. I had the radio on to keep me awake and fill the silence as I followed the winding highway toward Anchor Point, and of course kept the volume down so it wouldn't disturb him. Though with as quickly as that pill had put him on his ass, I probably could've blasted Judas Priest while badly singing along and he wouldn't have noticed.

While he slept and I drove, I thought back to our trip. I hadn't had that much fun in ages. Charlie and Maxine were awesome people, and even though they'd been strangers a few days ago, I'd left their house feeling like I'd known them my whole life.

And was it weird that Travis and I were only a couple of months into this and already spending holidays together in other states? We'd spent Christmas together. We were out at work. We'd seen each other in the throes of night terrors, and accepted the fact that flashbacks were always a possibility now. He knew my deepest, darkest secret. The one I couldn't tell my ex-wife and shouldn't have told him, but had finally been able to get off my chest.

And afterward, he hadn't looked at me any differently.

I glanced at him. This had the potential to get serious if it wasn't already.

On one hand, I was thrilled. Excited. Couldn't wait to see how things played out. On the other, my mind kept going back to my kids and ex-wife. If I was seriously involved with someone, then sooner or later I would need to explain that to them. And if that someone was a man . . .

I gripped the wheel tighter. I'd already put those kids through hell. They'd watched me devolve into a distant, drunken asshole who rarely came home. They'd watched their mother struggle to put on a happy face. When I had come home, they'd had front-row seats to our screaming matches, and they'd watched in uncomfortable silence while their hungover father patched yet another wall.

The memories made me squirm. Acid rose in my throat. Mandy and I had almost never raised our voices at each other until things had started spiraling downward. We'd always been that couple who would argue by way of calm discussions. Then almost overnight, I'd been regularly buying paint and drywall, and we'd gotten on a first-name basis with everyone in base security thanks to our twice-weekly domestic disturbances. That had nearly destroyed my ex-wife. I could only imagine what it had done to the kids.

So how much did I want to pile on top of that? Things had been a lot better lately, but we weren't out of the woods yet. At what point would Mandy decide enough was enough, throw up her hands, and petition the courts to revoke what little contact I still had with our kids? I wanted to believe the judges weren't so archaic that they'd see my non-heterosexuality as a sign that I was an unfit parent. After I'd self-destructed as badly as I had, though, I could see one particular judge—and my ex-wife's pit bull of an attorney—calling it evidence that I was still unstable.

But would Mandy see it that way? I told myself she would accept my sexuality and my relationship. She wasn't homophobic. She'd adored her brother before and after he'd come out. But how would she feel when her ex-husband, the father of her children, the man she'd slept next to for sixteen years, came out at forty? How was I supposed to explain, without hurting her more than I already had, that I'd always known I was attracted to both men and women? That yes, I had absolutely been attracted to men all the time we were together, but I'd been afraid to tell her? That one of the reasons I'd been afraid was that while she was fine with gay people, she'd always thought of bisexuality as some sort of fad or a pass to cheat?

Resting my elbow below the window, I chewed my thumbnail as I watched the white lines fly by in the headlight beams. Bisexual or otherwise, I never would have cheated on my wife. Never. I'd have happily gone my whole life without ever touching a man if we hadn't split up. After all, we'd been monogamous, and I'd had every intention of being married to her until the day I died. I'd never told her I was bisexual because what difference would it have made if I was interested in men? It would make about as much sense as mentioning to my redhead wife that I thought blondes were hot.

And now I wasn't even sure what I was. The wounds from my divorce had at least started to heal, but apparently not enough for me to feel anything for women. Sure, I'd fucked a few during my self-destructive period right after she'd kicked me out, but once I'd sobered up, calmed down, and started to pull myself together, I'd only been interested in men. Because they were new? Because I had sixteen years of pent-up curiosity? Because touching a woman made me feel guilty for what happened with—no, *what I did to*—my ex-wife?

That part was bothering me less, now, thank God. After Travis had told me his attraction to men had dropped off for a while after he'd lost the man he loved, I was more at ease. Maybe my numbness toward women right now was a coping mechanism. A lull while my brain sorted itself out.

I glanced at Travis. Whatever the case, my attraction to men—especially this man—was strong and solid.

I blew out a breath and scratched the back of my neck while I kept my other hand on top of the wheel. Whatever I was now, I had to tread lightly with Mandy. I wanted to be honest with her, but I didn't want to hurt her by making her believe the years we'd spent together were a lie. They weren't. That much I knew.

So did I come out to her, let the shock wear off, and then tell her I was seeing someone? Or cut right to the chase and tell her I had a boyfriend? If I'd introduced someone like Logan to her, I could've anticipated one hell of a side-eye. But someone like Travis? What wasn't to love about him? He was one of the kindest, sweetest men I'd ever met. If she didn't get hung up on the fact that he was my boyfriend, she would adore him. I just knew it.

I stole another glance at Travis, still sound asleep in the darkness, and something settled in my chest. I slipped my hand into his. Though he was out, he curled his fingers between mine, and I smiled to myself as my pulse slowly came down.

This would all work out. Coming out to Mandy wouldn't be easy, but if I was going to drop that bomb on her, I could do a lot worse than add "... and *this* is the guy I'm seeing."

It still wouldn't be easy. And how would the kids take it? Hard to say. They loved their uncle. They'd been pretty young when he and his wife had split, and he'd brought a few boyfriends to family gatherings since then. The kids had never seemed put off or confused. But would it be different when it was their dad?

I tried to put myself in their shoes. What if, on one of those weekends when I'd been staying at my dad's house, he'd told my sister and me that he was gay? How would I have felt? Would it have been any different than when he'd told me he had a girlfriend? Shit, what if my kids met Travis, and they liked him, and then we split up? How would they take that? How would *I* take that?

I shuddered. No point in following that train of thought. Things were going great right now. Better than I'd imagined anything in my life ever would after the divorce. The future was anyone's guess, but right now, I wasn't about to dwell on the bad things that might happen.

I ran my thumb back and forth along his, and as I faced the road, kept right on smiling like an idiot.

Everything would be all right. It would take some time, and there'd be some adjusting for everyone involved, but for once, I actually believed everything would work out. First things first, I needed to come out to Mandy, then to my kids. So, after I was back in Anchor Point, and I'd slept on it, I'd do it. I'd get her on Skype and tell her I was seeing a man.

And we'd see where things went from there.

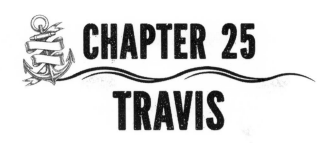

CHAPTER 25
TRAVIS

The day after we came back from California, Clint had some errands to run and another Skype chat with his kids, so he left my house after breakfast. He'd barely pulled out of the driveway before I was texting Paul.

You free for lunch?

In minutes, he replied, *When & where?*

I had never been so relieved to have someone take me up on a lunch invite. Thank God the man was retired now and, since he'd quit the volunteer gig, had a lot more time on his hands these days. That wouldn't last. He'd find some sort of part-time thing to give himself something to do—and so he wouldn't drive his fiancé crazy.

For today, though, he was free. And it was a shitty, rainy day out there, so he wasn't golfing. Sometimes things just worked out.

I picked the first restaurant that came to mind, suggested meeting around eleven, and stepped into the shower. When I got out, he'd confirmed both the time and place. Now if I could keep from losing my mind before I got there.

I'd been awake for way too long last night. Part of it had to do with the Percocet knocking me on my ass in the car. Though it was chemical sleep and not really "rest" per se, it'd been enough to throw off my ability to sleep for the rest of the night.

At least half a dozen times, I'd considered waking Clint in the middle of the night and hashing this out. All the *I can't do this* and *Do you have any idea what you're getting into with me?* and *Look at me— I'm a train wreck* had been on the tip of my tongue, but I'd stopped myself. I wasn't going to wake him when he was sleeping soundly for once. Good nights were rare for him. Plus he'd already had to deal with air travel, not to mention driving us back from the airport while I was in my Percocet coma.

Let the man sleep, for God's sake.

Even if it's really because you're a fucking coward.

So I'd just lain there awake, staring wide-eyed into the darkness while he'd snored softly beside me. All fucking night, I'd swung back and forth between wanting to call it quits before we got in too deep, and realizing we were already in *way* too deep and I'd be stupid to leave.

I'd never met someone like Clint before. And I'd never felt this way about anyone. Male or female. Not even my ex-wife. The one time I'd ever come close, a car crash and a funeral had left me in the emotional equivalent of a tornado's aftermath—nothing but shards, splinters, and disbelief.

By four in the morning, I'd made the decision to reach out to Paul as soon as the clock showed a civilized hour. He'd never been one to pull punches. Whatever I needed to do here, he'd set me straight.

Because heaven knows that's exactly what I need right now.

Like a lot of businesses here in Anchor Point, the restaurant was situated in an old Cape Cod–style house with a tiny gravel parking lot outside. It was pale gray—typical of seaside buildings. I would've bet money the paint they'd used had been called "driftwood" or some variation thereof. Against a backdrop of mist and clouds, the whole place could've passed for a black-and-white postcard if not for the bright-blue sign propped up on top of the roof's dark shingles.

At a table by the windows, I looked out at the ocean. The weather wasn't pretty, so the seas were predictably rough. Just the sight of the whitecaps made the floor rock beneath my feet. I'd long ago broken the habit of holding on to my drink if I was near stormy seas—my brain had finally accepted that the table wasn't going to move no matter how big the swells were—but I could still feel the motion of the ocean sometimes.

I shook myself and shifted my attention to the menu.

I'd arrived early, but not five minutes after I'd sat down, Paul strolled in too.

You have no idea how glad I am to see you.

I played it cool, though, and grinned as I laid down my menu. "You're early. Haven't broken out of that military indoctrination yet, have you?"

Paul chuckled as he took the seat opposite me. "Are you kidding? I'll never break out of that as long as the assholes down at the golf course cancel my tee time if I'm not there twenty minutes early."

"Oh, the suffering you endure." I clasped my hands over my heart. "How *do* retirees withstand such hardship?"

"It's a rough life, but someone's gotta live it."

"Uh-huh." I ran a finger around the rim of my water glass. "Your other half didn't mind me running off with you for a couple of hours?"

Paul laughed. "I don't think he minds getting rid of me every now and then."

"Must be why he doesn't mind you golfing every other day."

"Hey, it works out for both of us. I'm not going to complain." His amusement faded, and he tilted his head slightly and raised his eyebrows. "All right, I left my crystal ball at home, but the spirits are telling me there's something bothering you."

Okay, so we're diving right in, are we?

I gulped. "Is it that obvious?"

"I've known you for how many years?"

"Fair enough." I sighed and rubbed my neck. "So I took Clint to California with me. To spend Christmas with Charlie and Maxine."

"Okay. How are they doing, by the way?"

"Good. Good. And the trip was great. Clint's really . . . I mean, he's . . ." I folded my arms on the table. "We go pretty well together."

"So I've seen. And knowing you, the fact that you two go so well together is part of the problem."

"It *is* the problem." I blew out a breath. "Damn. Am I that predictable?"

Paul nodded, and the bastard didn't even bother offering a joke or a comment. No, he was giving me absolutely no diversion from the topic, and he was leaving it to me to fill the silence.

Well, this was why we were here.

"Now that we've been seeing each other for a while," I said, "I don't know how I ever thought things wouldn't get serious. It just makes sense to feel like this for him."

Paul's eyebrows climbed his forehead. "Whoa. I never thought I'd hear you say that about a man."

"Neither did I." I wrung my hands under the edge of the table. "It takes a lot for me to want to be in a relationship with someone. Always has, even before Dion died." I leaned back, subtly pressing against the hard-backed chair to stop the growing spasm beneath my shoulder blades. "The thing is, there are only a handful of things that have ever hurt like losing Jessica. And *nothing* that hurts more than losing Dion. I don't know if I could handle falling that hard for someone and losing them a third time."

Paul nodded. "Yeah, I can see that." He started to say something else, but the waiter showed up right then.

"Can I get you two started with anything?" he asked with cheeriness that seemed almost offensive at the moment. "Maybe an appetizer?"

My stomach turned. The thought of eating anything made me want to gag.

Paul glanced at me, then handed his menu to the waiter. "Just an iced tea for right now. We might get something else a bit later."

"Me too," I said.

"Okay, sounds good." The waiter left, and our conversation stayed on pause until he'd come back with our drinks.

"Anyway." Paul watched me as he poured a packet of sugar into his iced tea. "You were saying? About Clint?"

"Yeah." I rested my elbows on the table, but didn't touch my tea or my water. "I don't know. I guess . . . maybe this is just moving too fast, you know? I've known him, what? Three months? If I feel this way about him now, how is it going to be in six months? Or a year?"

"Better?"

I met Paul's eyes.

He leaned over his folded arms. "Look, I get why you're scared. I really do. And I can't imagine how hard it's been to move on after Jessica and Dion. But maybe this is your shot. Maybe the third time's the charm."

The air stopped in my throat, and a memory flashed through my mind of Clint using that phrase as he'd pitched softballs into a stack of milk bottles. I dropped my gaze. "A pessimist might interpret that to mean the third time is the one that'll—" The words *kill me* didn't make it past the tip of my tongue. Still avoiding his eyes, I muttered, "The one that'll finally do me in."

Paul studied me for a long moment. "Listen, I don't want to downplay how tough this is on you. I can't even imagine. But what was it some grizzled old ex-pilot told me once?" He inclined his head. "Something about even if it blows up in my face, nothing's worse than looking back and wondering what might have been?"

"I know. Except I'm kind of afraid of what could happen. Because I know what can happen. And I'm fucking terrified this time because to be honest . . ." I hesitated, a weird mix of shame, fear, and God knew what else churning in my stomach. "I haven't felt like this about someone since Dion."

Paul tensed. "Wow."

"Yeah. I guess . . ." I inhaled slowly. "Dion and I had a lot of valid reasons to stay apart." My own words made me wince. "I mean, I loved him. I always will. But what choice did we have? There was so much on the line . . ."

"I know," Paul said softly. "I can't imagine anyone blames you for the choice you made. The choice you both made."

"Except . . ." I winced.

"What?" He paused. "Talk to me. It's just us. Whatever you need to say, that's what I'm here for."

My throat tightened, but I finally managed to speak. "Even though Dion and I weren't together, God . . . I loved him. So much. And I think I'm scared to death to feel that way for someone else because I *know* how much it hurts to lose them. Maybe it would have been different if we'd been together, and things had gone bad, and by the time we broke up, we were done with each other. Kind of like when Jessica and I divorced. I mean, that one hurt like hell, and it took me a long, long time to get over her, but Dion . . ." I cringed. "I know, I'm harping on the past. And I'm probably a complete coward. But every time I look at Clint, and every time I realize how much I want to be with him, I'm fucking terrified of how much it's going to hurt when he's gone."

"When?" Paul shook his head. "Jesus. You're already completely resigned to him being gone?"

I moistened my parched lips. "Why wouldn't I be?"

He stared out at the ocean for a solid minute, and so did I. What was I supposed to say?

Paul turned toward me again. "Look at me, Travis." When I did, he held my gaze with unflinching eyes. "Let me ask you something."

I swallowed. "Okay . . ."

"If you had it to do over, and you knew from the start how things would turn out with Jessica and with Dion, would you have done anything differently?"

The question was a punch to the chest. I sat back again, slowly releasing a breath. "I don't know."

"Think about it for a minute. And ignoring the fact that without Jessica, you wouldn't have Kimber. I mean specifically your *relationship* with your ex-wife."

I ran my thumbnail along the edge of the faux-leather placemat. "With Jessica, I don't know. I really don't. But with Dion . . . yeah, I absolutely would have done things differently."

"Really?"

I nodded.

"In what way?" He studied me. "You would have pursued something with him?"

"I . . ." Chewing my lip, I stared at the table. "Probably not, no. I think it would have been better for him if we'd never made any kind of connection."

Paul didn't speak for a long moment. When he did, his tone was soft. "You still blame yourself, don't you?"

Every day of my life.

I looked in his eyes again. "Of course I do."

"Travis, Dion's feelings for you aren't what killed him." Ticking off points on his fingers, Paul went on, "A messed-up policy that kept him from dating men. Pressure to have a wife and a family so he could move through the ranks. Even more pressure to toe the line so he didn't lose his kids in the divorce. The complete and utter system failure that kept him, Charlie, *you*, and God knows how many other vets from getting treated properly after—"

"I get it." I pinched the bridge of my nose. "I do. I get it."

"So you get that Dion's death was not your fault."

"I . . ." I thumbed the edge of my placemat. "I guess I've never been able to stop wondering how much our . . . well, not relationship, but—"

"The relationship you *both* wanted?"

Ouch.

"Yeah. I guess I've always wondered how much of a factor that was. How much it pushed him toward the edge."

"And how many *more* years of your life are you going to spend questioning that?" He reached across the table and squeezed my forearm. "None of us will ever know what made him break. But I knew him, and you knew him, and you will *never* convince me that he would have wanted you to spend your life alone with a guilty conscience."

All the air rushed out of my lungs.

"Dion would have wanted you to be happy." He gave my arm another squeeze, then pulled his hand back. "Whatever drove him to end his own life, you know he never would have wished that on you or anyone else. He never got to be happy. Don't you think he would have wanted you to have what he didn't?"

My throat constricted, but damn him, he wasn't done.

"If he were sitting here now," Paul said gently, "don't even try to tell me he wouldn't be asking why the hell you're fighting so hard not to be in love with Clint."

"Pretty sure that ship's sailed." I rubbed a hand over my face. "I am definitely in love with him."

Paul smiled. "Then quit fighting it."

I should've been relieved. Smiling back at him. Nodding and thanking him for talking some sense into me.

But deep in the pit of my stomach, a knot of apprehension was turning into a ball of lead.

I drummed my fingers on the table as I let my mind wander back over the previous couple of months. Even though things had been challenging at times, Clint had never given me any reason to believe he was faking it. And hadn't he had the same worries when we'd spent the night together for the first time? I sure as hell wasn't put off by his nightmares any more than he seemed to be put off by mine.

I loved being in bed with him.

I loved being with him.

I loved him.

His past and his nightmares didn't make me love him any less, just like his phobia-level fear of flying didn't change anything.

"Maybe I'm overthinking this."

"Maybe?" Paul sniffed with subtle amusement. "Travis, take it from someone who's known you half your life—you're overthinking it."

"Good point. Well, um, thanks for the pep talk." I managed a quiet chuckle. "Next time we'll talk about football or cars or something."

"Golf?"

"Don't push your luck." I glanced around for our waiter. "Now that that's over, I think I could stand to eat something."

"Me too. Where the hell did he go?"

Thank God for Paul. He never hesitated to rip off bandages and dig in until he found what was keeping me awake at night, and he wasn't one to shy away from telling me like it was. It was never *fun* for me when he did that—probably not for him either—but in the end, I always had a clearer outlook. Even if that outlook wasn't terribly pleasant, like when he'd gently pointed me toward the realization that my divorce was inevitable, I wouldn't be lost and flailing so much anymore.

And this time, he'd brought me to the conclusion that seemed so obvious now—that regardless of how many times the past had thrown me against the rocks, I'd be a fucking idiot to let that steer me away from Clint. This was my shot at something that had eluded me for way too long.

All I had to do now was wait until I saw Clint again.

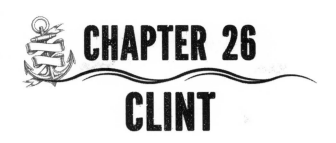

CHAPTER 26
CLINT

I was always nervous when Mandy and I Skyped, but today, I was Valium-level nervous. Not that I had any Valium, or would take any if I did, but I was pretty sure this was the kind of knee-shaking, stomach-churning, mouth-drying nervousness the stuff had been invented for.

And there was no turning back because she'd accepted my call.

Sitting back against the couch, laptop balanced on my knees, I forced a nervous smile for the camera a split second before she appeared on the screen.

"Hey," I said.

"Hey." She was at the kitchen table, elbows resting just off-camera and her hands loosely clasped under her chin. "I can't talk long. What's up?"

"Oh. Um." I cleared my throat. "Okay. I'll keep it short." *Here we go. I've got this.* "I need to be honest with you about something."

Her features hardened and her eyes narrowed slightly, the way they always did when I was on thin ice. "Okay."

"I'm, uh . . ."

"Did you relapse?"

"What? No!" I threw up my hands. "Mandy, I'm not drinking. I swear."

"All right." She folded her arms. "So, what's this about?"

I pulled in a ragged breath. "Well. Okay, when we talked on Christmas, and you asked where I was?"

She nodded slowly.

"I wasn't lying that I was spending the holidays with someone in San Diego."

An eyebrow rose, but she still didn't speak.

"I'm . . . Well, I . . ." *Here goes. No turning back.* "I was spending Christmas with my boyfriend."

The faintest catch of her breath seemed to echo from the computer speakers. Her hands tightened on her arms, and her shoulders lifted with fresh tension. "Come again?"

I swept my tongue across my lips. "I was there with my boyfriend. I . . . have a boyfriend."

She sat back hard against the chair. "You're—" Her eyes darted toward something off-camera. The kids must've been out in the yard or in the living room. Possibly within earshot, since she lowered her voice. "You're *gay*?"

My mouth had gone dry, and it took a moment to speak so I could clarify that I was actually bi, as if that somehow made a fucking difference, as if that wouldn't piss her off even more because of how she felt about bisexuality, but she spoke first anyway.

She pushed her shoulders back and lifted her chin. "I suppose you want me to tell the kids." A mix of defensiveness and anger *almost* hid the hurt in her voice.

"No. Not now. And I think it would be best if *we* tell them. Eventually. But for now, I wanted you to know."

"Oh." She squirmed, looking off-camera again. "How long has this been going on?"

"Couple of months." I paused. "Or did you mean me being interested in men?"

"Yeah. That part."

"That's . . . complicated."

"How so?" Her jaw clenched. "Have you been *gay* all along, or did you suddenly decide you like dick?" She jumped as if she hadn't expected the words to come out, and threw a horrified glance toward where the kids were probably playing. Then she looked at me again, and the irritation returned, tightening her lips. "I just don't get it."

I forced myself not to get defensive. "I knew for a long time that I was attracted to men. I knew . . . I knew I was bi. So when I was single, I acted on it."

"You mean during that period when you were drinking yourself stupid and fucking anything that moved?"

This time, I jumped. "I—"

"Yes, I knew about it," she hissed. "You never were very good at covering your tracks when you were drunk."

Well, shit.

I coughed to get my breath moving. "Okay. Yeah. You're right. And yes, to be perfectly blunt, when I was self-destructing after we split, I did a lot of stupid things. And somewhere in there, I decided it was as good a time as any to see if I really wanted to be involved with men."

Her lips looked like they were on the verge of twisting. "Apparently you did."

"Apparently. But after I cleaned myself up and started getting back on the rails, and I started dating again, I wanted to date men. So I did."

"So this one isn't the first that you've dated."

"Well . . ." I ran a hand through my hair. "He's the first one I can confidently call my boyfriend, if that means anything." Not entirely true, but she didn't need to know about Logan.

"Oh." She chewed her thumbnail and stared at her keyboard with unfocused eyes. After a long moment, she met my gaze through the cameras. "How long have you known?"

I hesitated, not sure how honest I wanted to be with her here. "I think I've always known. At least since I was a teenager. Just didn't really sort it out in my head until maybe ten years ago."

"While we were married?" she growled.

I patted the air with both hands. "I never acted on it. I *never* touched a man until after we'd split up for good. I didn't touch *anyone* while we were married."

Her eyes flicked away, but she said nothing.

"All I did was figure out who I was. I never, ever acted on it until after we'd divorced." I paused. "I know you think bisexuality is something people use as a license to cheat, but I would swear under a polygraph with my hand on a Bible that I never cheated on you." Another pause while I tried to pull my composure together. "I made a lot of huge mistakes, Mandy, but that wasn't one of them."

She looked at me again. "And yet in two years, you've gone from never touching a man to having a boyfriend?"

"Two years is longer than you think."

Mandy huffed sharply. "You don't have to tell me that."

The tension between us was palpable and swelling by the second, but goddamn it, I was not fighting with her today.

"Look, I just wanted you to know. I thought about telling you a while back, but things were still pretty rough between us. I wanted to wait until we were like this. More civil. And . . . when I had someone worth telling you about."

"I see." She pinched the bridge of her nose. "I'm just confused. This is so out of left field."

"I know." I moistened my lips. "Look, I've had to do a lot of thinking about myself and my identity. I went from being a husband and father to being a confused bachelor who misses his kids and is trying not to fall apart." I swallowed, startled by the sudden lump rising in my throat. "I don't know if I'm still attracted to women, or if I still feel too guilty after what I did to you to even look at one. All I—"

"If you're still hung up on our divorce enough that you can't look at women, do you really think this is a good time to be dating?"

I mulled that over for a moment, then released a breath. "Maybe? But the way I feel about him . . . To tell you the truth, I don't think anyone else could turn my head right now."

"Whoa." She blinked. "So it's getting serious. Quickly."

"Yeah, it kind of feels like that. We're not moving in together or anything, but it's . . ." I couldn't help smiling. "It's going really good."

"That's . . . that's good. Right?"

"It is. I mean, I'm still sort of figuring myself out. But damn, I know what I feel for him. At the moment, I'm not looking at men or women. Just him."

"Oh. Wow." A hint of a smile started to materialize, but it faded quickly. "I have a question."

I braced, not sure what was on her mind. "Okay. Sure?"

She tilted her head slightly. "Are you happy, Clint?"

The question brought a million emotions to life in my chest. Admitting to being happy with someone else—with a man—added some finality to my divorce from her. Of course it was over, and I'd made peace with it, but every now and then, the realization that that chapter of my life had ended took my breath away. After she'd kicked me out for good, I'd hated myself for destroying what we had, and that self-loathing surged to the surface now, along with the irrational resentment against her for not forgiving me. It was stupid, and rationally I understood exactly why she'd refused to take me back and why she was still standoffish now. In her shoes, I wasn't sure if I'd have been as civil as she had.

But feelings weren't rational, and that resentment existed whether it made sense or not. And the grief over losing her and alienating myself from the kids, and the anger, and the self-hatred . . . it all existed.

And at the same time, yes, I was happy. After three dark years and being convinced I'd never even feel human again, yes, I *was* happy. Now that someone had asked me point-blank, and I'd had to think about it, there was no way I could give another answer.

"Yes. I am."

"Good," she said quietly. "You deserve to be."

"I don't know about that. After—"

"Clint." She put up her hand. "Don't. We both know you've been beating yourself up for the last couple of years. And yes, I fueled that, and I'm sorry."

"You shouldn't be. I fucked everything up."

"No, the military fucked everything up."

The words knocked the breath out of my chest. Of all the things I'd needed to hear the most from her, I hadn't even realized how much I'd needed to hear that. Just an acknowledgment that it wasn't all on me.

She must've taken my silence as a need for clarification, and sighed. "I know you can't talk about it, but I can read between the lines. Whatever happened, happened. And whether you can tell me what happened or not, it affected you. Deeply. You're one of the strongest people I've ever known, so if it broke you, I don't even want to know the truth." She swallowed hard. "I had to protect myself and the kids. And yes, I was angry for a while, and I hated you for a while, but . . . you're a good guy. You always have been. And I'm really glad to see you're getting back on your feet and that you've found someone. We can't go back to what we were before, but please don't ever doubt that I *want* you to be happy."

"Thank you," I said. "And that's all I want for you too. Even with the military's bullshit, I made a mess of things for you and the kids. If I could go back and change it, I would."

Mandy avoided my gaze, glancing away and swiping at her eyes. "I know. And, um . . ." She cleared her throat and rolled her shoulders before looking at me again. "I really hope things work with this guy. If he's got you feeling like that, enough to tell me and the kids, he must be amazing."

"He is," I whispered.

"And we'll . . . we'll talk to the kids. Not right away. But we will."

Cool relief rushed through me. "Okay. I can live with that."

"I need to talk to my brother first. Get some advice from him."

"Sure. That's fine. Just let me know."

"I will."

"And, um . . . one more thing."

Her eyebrow arched, but she didn't speak.

I struggled not to visibly fidget, since it always made her nervous to see me agitated. Wringing my hands to work off some nervous energy, I said, "I know this hasn't been good for the kids. Maybe it wouldn't hurt to have them . . . talk to someone."

"Talk to someone? Like who?"

"Like a therapist. Someone who can help them sort things out."

She smiled subtly. "I didn't want to tell you because I wasn't sure how you'd react, but they've been going to a counselor for almost two years."

It was probably just as well she hadn't told me before. Back then, I'd still been seriously unstable. Finding out she'd sent the kids to a therapist behind my back would have set me off in ways I wouldn't have been proud to admit.

But now I was relieved. Anything to minimize the stress and trauma I had already caused them. "How is that going?"

"It's going good. Danny wasn't too sure about it in the beginning, but he's opening up. And Crystal and Allen have gotten better. They don't have so many nightmares anymore."

My stomach lurched. *What did I do to you, kids?* "Glad to hear it."

She shifted in her seat. "Maybe next time you come visit, you can go in with them. Talk to their counselor."

Nodding, I released a breath. "Okay. Sure. That doesn't sound like a bad idea."

Her smile seemed more relaxed and genuine than before. "We'll work it out. Anyway, I . . ." She glanced off-camera. "I should go. We're heading to Phoenix today."

"All right. Drive safe. Say hi to my folks for me."

"I will. Take care, Clint."

"You too."

After we'd hung up, I closed my laptop and sat back against the couch. What a bizarre mix of emotions. The kids were in counseling because of me. It was helping, but the fact that I'd caused them to need it . . . ouch. But they had what I'd needed all this time—an outlet for their feelings. A place to vent. Hopefully that was enough.

And now Travis and I were out to Mandy. We'd see how things went when it came time to tell the kids, but it was a start. A step in the right direction.

I smiled. There'd been a lot of steps in the right direction lately. My life finally felt like it was moving forward instead of circling the drain.

I just hoped it continued this way.

Travis arrived a few hours after I'd talked to Mandy. He was bleary-eyed, with heavy shadows under his eyes, and his limp was slightly more obvious than usual. I shuddered at the thought of what state he'd be in if he hadn't taken that Percocet last night.

He was in good spirits, though. His smile was sleepy but heartfelt, and his kiss promised a very, very good night for both of us. Hell, maybe a careful afternoon quickie if he felt up for it, but if not, that was fine too.

"Coffee?" I asked as we headed into the kitchen.

"Coffee sounds great." He leaned against the counter. "I'm wiped."

I could see that as soon as you came through the door.

I poured us both some coffee, and we drank in silence until we were halfway through our cups. I set mine aside and rested my hands on the counter's edge. "So I talked to my ex-wife earlier."

"Yeah, you mentioned you were going to." He put his own coffee down. "How'd it go?"

"It was all right. Better than the last few times. I, um . . . came out to her."

"Did you?"

I nodded. "She was upset at first, but I think once it sank in, she was okay."

Travis exhaled. "That's good. That's great! Does she know you're seeing someone, or just that you're, well, not straight?"

"She knows about you."

He gulped. "Oh."

"I called her specifically to *tell* her about you. And I think she's curious about you now." I laughed quietly. Man, I was tired—I hadn't realized how draining that conversation had been until now. "I guess I'll have to put you two on Skype one of these days."

"Yeah. Sure." He shifted his weight, wincing subtly.

"She's not ready for us to tell the kids *yet*, but she said we will."

Travis stiffened abruptly, almost like I'd smacked him. Eyes locked on me, he swallowed again. "She . . . really?"

I nodded.

"Oh." He shifted, and he was tense now. Really tense. "So your kids . . . When, uh . . . when do you think that'll be? That you'll tell them?"

"Don't know. She's going to talk to her brother and get his opinion." I smiled. "She said she hopes it works out with us, though."

He smiled too, but he seemed guarded. Not distant, necessarily, but something was off.

I pushed myself off the counter and crossed the kitchen. "Hey. You okay?"

"Yeah. Yeah. I . . ." He shook his head. "Just tired from last night."

"Oh." I touched his face. "You seem kind of . . ." Distracted? A million miles away?

"I'm good." His smile warmed up a bit, and he kissed me lightly. "And I spent most of the day thinking. About, um, us."

My heart fluttered. "Yeah?"

He nodded. "Yeah, I . . ."

Our eyes locked.

He held my gaze for a long moment.

And then his whole body tensed. Little by little, his expression changed. I couldn't put my finger on exactly how, but his warm, nervous smile was gone, and in its place . . .

I could've been imagining it, but I thought some color slipped out of his face. He was still looking right at me, and yet he had a thousand-yard stare too. Like he was looking at me and through me and somewhere else entirely, all at the same time.

"Travis." I squeezed his shoulder. "You okay?"

Abruptly, something shifted in him. He released a breath as he broke eye contact, and his shoulders sagged. Then he turned away and, hand trembling violently, ran his fingers through his hair. "Fuck."

"What's wrong?" My heart was in my throat. *What the hell?*

His back was to me. For what seemed like years, he didn't make a sound.

Cautiously, I took a step closer. "Travis?"

"I'm sorry." He turned back around, and when our eyes met, he whispered the four words I was dreading the most: "I can't do this."

Panic surged through me. "What? Why not? What's . . ." I blinked a few times. "What's going on?"

He wiped a hand over his face. "I'm sorry."

"Yeah, you said that. But what—"

"This has nothing to do with you. I promise." He swallowed hard, almost like he was trying to keep from getting sick. "But I . . . Look at me, Clint. I'm barely keeping myself together. I . . . I don't have it in me to be in a relationship. Not now."

"But, all along, we've been—"

"I know. But I—"

"You're dumping me out of the blue? For nothing?"

"Not for nothing," he snapped. "You didn't do anything wrong. You're . . ." He tightened his jaw, and his voice wavered. "You've been great. You're . . . God, you're perfect."

Oh, not even close. "Then what the hell—"

"I just can't." He put up a hand and shook his head. "This is too much, too fast, and I—"

"Then we can slow down. Just tell me what to do."

"No. There's no slowing it down. We're already too—" He snapped his teeth together, and his eyes widened like he'd almost said more than he should've. Breaking eye contact, he said, "I need to go."

"But—"

"Please." He met my eyes again, and he suddenly looked exhausted. As if we'd been standing here pounding our heads on this subject for hours and hours instead of barely a minute. "I need to go."

Before I could respond, he turned and headed for the door, walking fast enough to almost hide his limp as he left me staring slack-jawed at his back and wondering what the hell was going on. What did I do? What did—

The other night's conversation flashed through my mind.

He knew what had ended my career as an RAP. He knew what I had done to all those people.

Was that why he couldn't look at me?

And . . .

Oh shit. He knows!

I hurried after him. "Travis, wait."

Hand on the front door, he turned around.

I tried and failed to ignore the queasiness in my gut. "What I told you . . . about what happened to—what I did."

His eyebrows rose, an unspoken *Yeah?*

"That stays between us, right?"

Travis's lips parted. He stared at me like I'd just insulted his mother. "Of course it does. Why wouldn't it?"

"I . . ." My shoulders fell. "I don't know. I . . ." *Trusted you differently that night than I do now.* "I don't know."

He watched me for a moment. Then, without another word, he left.

I leaned against the wall, heart thumping and head spinning. All the air in my lungs was gone. Hell, all the air in the room seemed to be gone. Fuck—another minute in here and I was going to suffocate.

On shaking knees, I stepped outside into my tiny backyard. There, I dropped onto the concrete step and stared out at the postage stamp of lawn.

So that was it. Zero to sixty in under three months, and bam! Brick wall. I'd fallen hard for someone. Finally had some hope that

I really was worthy of being loved, that I was no longer the asshole who'd nuked my marriage, and . . . this.

I wasn't even angry. I was probably hurt, but I didn't feel it yet. I was just in shock. After the way things had been going, this was the last thing I'd anticipated, and I didn't know how to process it yet, never mind how to feel about it. All I could do was sit here and stare blankly into space and wonder why Travis wasn't here anymore.

I needed to get out of here and go think about something else. Maybe I needed to find *someone* else to get my mind off Travis. I could always go down to that other town. What was the name? Flatstick? Whatever it was called, there were apparently a lot of gay bars. Or I could reactivate my accounts on the latest find-me-some-dick app.

But even thinking about all that exhausted me. It didn't matter that usually the first thing I wanted after a breakup was to get between the sheets with someone else. Hell, less than twelve hours had elapsed between my ex-wife kicking me out for good and a Vegas streetwalker getting into my car. It wasn't my proudest moment, but it had happened.

Today, I didn't want to go anywhere with anyone. I didn't even think I had the energy to pursue—let alone engage in—sex.

The difference was obvious. When my ex-wife had dropped the divorce hammer, it was like yelling that we'd hit an iceberg after the ship was already ass-up and going down.

This breakup, though, had come out of nowhere. One minute, smooth sailing. The next . . .

The next . . .

This *was* the next minute.

And I still had no idea what had happened or where to go from here.

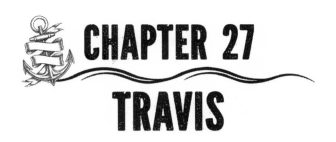

CHAPTER 27
TRAVIS

Did I do the right thing?
Of course I did.
What else could I do?

On the way home from Clint's, I wondered more than once if I should pull over and get my shit together. I couldn't concentrate. Not while I was still reeling from how things had gone. One moment, I'd been standing there ready to pour my heart out and tell him I loved him, and the next, he'd mentioned coming out to his kids, and suddenly my head had been full of Dion's long silent voice.

"If I could, I would. God, I would. But I can't lose my kids over this. They've—"

"I know." I could still feel myself choking back tears as I'd spoken. *"We can't. I know. I wish we could, but we can't."*

Then he'd kissed me. Then he'd left. Then he'd been gone for good, lowered in a box into a six-foot pit while the kids he'd sworn not to lose had bawled their eyes out—

And face-to-face with Clint, after psyching myself up to tell him that yes, we could . . . I couldn't. It had suddenly come down to either diving headlong into something that would end in painful disaster, or walking out and wondering if I'd fucked up.

So did I fuck up?

A truck roared past me, startling me, and I realized I'd dropped below forty in a fifty-five-mile-an-hour zone. Yeah. Time to pull over.

I slowed down a bit more, nosed off the highway, and came to a stop. With my hazards on and my engine idling, I scrubbed a hand over my face. I'd saved myself from going through the kind of heartbreak I'd had in the past. I had to do this if I didn't want to hurt like that again.

So why did it hurt so bad? Why was I shaking? *Shit,* did *I make a mistake?*

Fuck. Apparently I was too screwed up in the head to figure this out on my own.

Hands unsteady, I texted Paul. *You busy? Really need to talk again.*

Paul met me at my place half an hour later.

"Hey," he said as he came inside. "What's up?"

"Thanks for coming over. You don't mind me picking your brain twice?"

He shrugged off his jacket. "Sean and his mother are still arguing about wedding shit, so I'm happy to vacate for a while. So what's going on?"

"Let's go sit. You want any coffee or anything?" I didn't know why I bothered stalling. He was here now, and he was going to drag the truth out of me whether I liked it or not.

"No, I'm fine."

We walked into the living room.

"You're really wound up," Paul said. "Talk to me, Travis."

That was what I'd brought him here for, wasn't it? "I . . ." I rubbed both hands over my face, then turned and faced him. "I called things off with Clint."

"You did *what*?" Paul stared at me. "But I thought . . . Didn't you . . ." He shook himself. "*What?*"

I sank onto the sofa. "I had to. I—"

"Had to?" He sat beside me. "Travis, we *just* talked about this. How could . . . How did you get from being crazy in love with him to this?"

"I can't do it." I hated the pitiful sound of my own voice. "I went to see him, and I was going to tell him everything we talked about, and then I . . . I looked him in the eye, and I choked."

"Why? What happened?"

I swept my tongue across my lips. "I freaked out. One second we were talking. And the next, all I could think about was what happened with Dion."

"With—" Paul blinked. "But they're completely different people. And completely different situations."

"And feelings that are way, way too similar."

"Yeah, because you're in love with Clint." Paul shook his head. "But things are not even close to the same with Clint as they were with Dion. You two are out. You don't have the regs and custody battles to deal with."

"Except Clint does have a custody battle going. Well. Sort of. He wants joint custody at some point and . . . anyway." Nausea burned in my throat at the memory of that brief flashback while we'd talked. I could still hear Dion's voice sadly telling me he couldn't risk being with me, and my damn brain kept putting those words into Clint's mouth. I'd never ask anyone to choose me over their family—God knew I'd never have chosen anyone over my daughter—but that didn't mean someone would never be asked to choose their family over me. I didn't want anyone in that position again. Especially not Clint. No matter how much times had changed, or how many other factors had driven Dion to take his own life, that fear had drilled itself into my mind and refused to leave.

"Travis." He squeezed my arm. "Don't you think you deserve to be happy? And wasn't that exactly what you were with him? I mean, you were practically swooning over him this morning."

"I know. I . . ." I didn't know how to put it into words. All day long, I'd been equal parts excited and terrified to finally open up to Clint and tell him I loved him, but then . . . then he'd been there. In front of me. Looking in my eyes.

He'd mentioned coming out to his kids, meeting them—all steps toward making this real and making us something like a family, and panic had taken over. In an instant, everything Paul and I had talked about was gone, because losing two people I loved—one to a bitter divorce, one to suicide—had become too recent, too real, and I'd been overcome with the fear of a third. Excruciating memories had flooded my mind, but with Clint's name and Clint's face instead of Dion's. I'd remembered, more vividly than I had in years, the crushing pain of watching that casket sink into that deep hole. In the same instant, I'd remembered how all the pain of a crash and an ejection had instantly become nothing compared to the news that my RIO might not make it through the night.

I kneaded the back of my neck, wondering when I'd started sweating. "Look, I can't control what happens to people in my life. The only thing I can control is who I let in."

"So, that's it?" Paul blinked. "You're not going to let him in because you might have to let him go?"

I rubbed my eyes with my thumb and forefinger. "I know it's not rational. I sound insane even to myself. But I'm fucking scared."

"I know you are." He put his hand on my shoulder. "Don't you think everyone is?"

I dropped my hand and looked at him. "I don't think everyone has had to live with the kind of guilt I have." I shrugged out from under his grasp, got up, and raked my fingers through my hair as I paced across the floor. "The last time I fell this hard for someone, I had to watch them put him in the goddamned ground."

"Yes, exactly!"

I stared at him. "What?"

"Travis." Paul pushed out a breath and shook his head as he rose. "When you lost Dion, you almost went out of your mind, and the thing you kept saying was 'I shouldn't have let him go, I shouldn't have let him go.' Is that the kind of regret you want to have this time?"

"I—"

"No, listen to me." His captain voice shut me up. "You've also been beating yourself up over Charlie's injuries all this time, but have you ever stopped to think that if there'd been another pilot in that cockpit, Charlie might not have made it out at all? You both came out fucked up, but you came out alive. Maybe you didn't correct enough when the flight deck moved, but you had a fraction of a second to react without *any way* of knowing how much space you needed. Yet you still corrected enough to keep from slamming into the stern and killing you both."

My mouth went dry.

"You and Charlie are still alive. Some of that came down to luck, and some of it came down to you reacting the way you did. No one can blame you for misjudging how much you needed to correct when you were coming in to land on a moving target. I've been there, Travis. I've done the same damn thing. The only difference between what happened to you and what happened to me is how much the flight deck moved. So you know you can take it to the bank when I tell you that you did exactly what any pilot would have, and you did enough to save yourself and Charlie."

I kept my eyes down. Deep inside, I knew he was right, and he definitely knew what he was talking about. That wouldn't stop me from wondering for the rest of my life how different things would've been if I'd pulled up a *little bit* more.

"And Dion . . ." Paul sighed. "It was a tragedy, and no one will deny that. But it wasn't your fault."

"I should have stayed back from him. Not let him see how much I wanted to be with him. We both know that's what drove him over the edge."

"No," Paul said sharply. "You didn't put him over the edge. Being in a military that refused to let him openly acknowledge the man he loved—"

"That man was me, remember?" I struggled to keep my voice even. "He was in love with me and I was in love with him. And that fucking destroyed him."

"And if DADT hadn't been in place, it wouldn't have happened that way, would it? You didn't drive him to suicide, Travis. His depression did. And so did the bigoted bullshit regulations that made him choose between you and a career."

I said nothing.

"Look at me, Travis."

I hesitated, but met his eyes.

He looked right back into mine, almost like he was looking right *into* me. "Have you ever thought that maybe you're the reason Dion lasted as long as he did?"

My lips parted. I couldn't breathe, but managed to croak, "What?"

His hand tightened. "He had a lot of demons. You knew that even before he died. Who's to say he didn't hang on for a few more years because of you?"

My lungs turned to lead. A million memories flashed through my mind, mostly of those stolen interludes I'd had with Dion before we'd finally agreed it couldn't continue. His smile. How happy he'd always seemed when we were together.

And Paul, the bastard, wasn't finished. "You are *not* the reason Dion is dead. And I guaran-goddamn-tee that if he were here now, he would tell you the same thing I am, which is that you're making the biggest mistake of your life by letting Clint go."

I let my face fall into my hands, and focused on breathing and not throwing up. He didn't push now. He just kept his hand on me, rubbing gently as if to remind me he was there.

Was he right?

God. Maybe he was.

There was no way we'd ever know for sure. Dion hadn't left a note because, we all guessed, he hadn't wanted anyone to figure out he'd committed suicide. What had gone through his mind at the end—none of us he'd left behind would ever know. But what if Paul was right?

I straightened slowly, and that motion aggravated some muscles in the middle of my back. Because of course it did. As the twinge set in and chewed at my spine, my heart sank again. "It's not just my past with Dion that's keeping me away from Clint, though."

Paul raised his eyebrows.

I shifted a bit to try to stretch out the tightness. "Even if nothing happens to him, how long is he going to put up with a guy whose entire life revolves around how much his fucking back hurts on that particular day? Because I promise you, that novelty wears off *quick*."

"I understand." Paul nodded. "For God's sake, I might not be as banged up as you are, but I've got my share of old injuries, and I'm marrying a man in his twenties. You don't think I've been worried a time or two that he might get tired of my aches and pains getting in the way?"

"Do you still worry about it?"

"Every day." He squeezed my shoulder. "Every fucking day."

"But you guys have been together for . . . shit, you're engaged."

"Yeah. And let me tell you, after he's been arguing with his mother for an afternoon about the seating arrangements for our wedding, there's a part of me that still wonders if he'll suddenly decide it's not worth it."

"Jesus, Paul. That guy worships you."

"And I've seen the way Clint looks at you." He let go of my shoulder. "You said yourself the guy is terrified of flying, but got on a plane with you—*twice*—because you couldn't drive all the way to San Diego."

"Exactly. How many more times is he going to put up with that?"

"Long enough to fall for you."

The words were a punch to the gut, and I couldn't make eye contact with Paul.

"You asked me for advice," he said, striking an odd balance between his captain's voice and something more soothing and gentle. "So I'm giving it to you. If you wanted to walk away before you felt something for Clint, you missed your chance by a long shot. You've been swooning over him ever since the Navy Ball. You're setting yourself up to regret losing him just like you lost Dion. Except this time, you don't have a custody battle or DADT standing in the way. The only thing standing in the way of you being with Clint is . . . *you*."

My heart fell into my feet.

"You have to make a choice, Travis," he said. "Are you going to get out of your own way? Or are you going to realize a few months or years down the line that you let fear and pain push away the best thing you've ever had?"

I didn't have an answer for him.

CHAPTER 28
CLINT

The first day back at the office was going to be pure hell. Thank God our department was still on holiday stand-down until after the New Year. Travis and I wouldn't have to face each other again until January, but that was coming up faster than I was comfortable with. I didn't think I could get my head around *not* being with Travis before I had to be in the office with him.

For now, though, it was just me in this empty apartment.

The first night had already been awful. It wasn't like we'd spent every single night together, and I'd been all right—well, as all right as I ever was—on my own when he hadn't stayed over. But now that he was gone, I slept sporadically and restlessly. I didn't see that changing anytime soon.

On the other hand, I hadn't seen him dumping me anytime soon either, so what the fuck did I know?

I paced across my apartment, wringing my sweaty hands. I needed to do something besides moping around the house, but hell if I could figure out what.

One solution kept surfacing. There was a liquor store painfully close by, and they'd be open for a couple more hours yet. Wasn't Everclear legal in Oregon? Wouldn't take much to find out. A short drive, a swipe of the debit card, and I could get epically shitfaced enough to forget Travis ever existed.

I tamped that temptation down, though. This was a cycle I knew very, very well. Stress triggered my PTSD. Alcohol soothed the stress. I was tempted as hell to haul ass to that liquor store, but if my ex-wife even suspected I'd done that—if she called while I was drunk, or if

I drunk-texted her again—my attempts to gain some custody of my kids would be *done*.

I took a deep breath and let it out, and kept right on pacing. I wanted to hate Travis for putting me in this position. For pitting me against the bottle, giving me a reason to dive into something a hundred ninety proof when I had every reason to stay as far away from the booze as I could. I wouldn't give in, but damn him for making it more tempting than it had been in a long time. That he'd hurt me enough to make me want to drink myself numb—one time and one time only, right?—and quite possibly set back my efforts to see my kids.

And I wanted to hate him for leaving too, but every time I worked myself up to cursing his name, the sting of tears would take the wind out of my sails. I wanted to hate him, but goddamn it, all I could do was want him back.

I wanted to cry. I wanted to drink. I wanted to put a fist through the wall. Fuck my damage deposit. Fuck my career. Fuck my sobriety. Fuck—

No. Fuck my chances at joint custody? No man was worth losing them.

Well, one thing was obvious—I needed more time before I dipped my toes into relationships again. I hadn't been on my own for very long, and I was still dealing with all the mental bullshit that had led to the drinking that had led to the divorce. I'd fucked everyone I could get my hands on until I'd felt closer to sane, and I still wasn't sure if I was bi or gay or if it even mattered, and my two attempts at actually dating—first Logan, then Travis—had ended in disaster.

I stopped pacing and stared out the living room window at the park across the street. Comparing Logan and Travis in my brain was bizarre. They weren't anywhere near the same league. Logan had been cute and fun when he was sober, and the sex had been good. Sometimes he'd even seemed like an actual *friend* with benefits.

Travis, though. That man was something else. He'd been breathtaking back when I'd only stolen glances at him at work and fantasized about him on my own. And as we'd gotten closer and closer, tipping hands and showing cards that weren't for just anyone's eyes, he'd given me some hope that despite things I'd done and how badly I'd destroyed my marriage, someone might love me again. He'd made me believe the damage I'd done to my life was not irreparable.

And now . . .

Now this.

My chest tightened.

So much for not being able to feel angry. The hurt was still there, but now the fury was pushing it out of the way. The more I thought about what he'd said, and how he'd suddenly dropped that bomb not two days after I'd told him things I couldn't even tell a goddamned chaplain or therapist, the angrier I got. I paced on shaky legs, balling my fists and forcing curses through gritted teeth. My blood boiled as I played and replayed that conversation. Sour acid churned in my gut and climbed the back of my throat as I realized tomorrow was my regular Skype call with my kids, and I couldn't imagine I'd be in any state of mind to face them or my ex or anything, and all because of . . .

Because of Travis.

Because he'd been perfect, and then he'd been gone with no explanation that made any kind of sense. It was good right up until it wasn't, and now it was over, and I had no fucking idea *why.*

I stopped pacing. I clenched my jaw so hard it ached, and tightened my fists until my nails bit into my palms.

Fuck it. Fuck this. Fuck him.

Fuck letting this go and pretending I could move on like it was nothing.

I grabbed my wallet and keys.

Slammed the door behind me.

And headed out to my car.

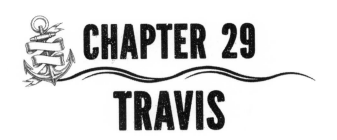

CHAPTER 29
TRAVIS

Kimber stared across the kitchen at me, her jaw slack. "Are you serious?"

"Yeah." I looked into my untouched cup of coffee. "I'm serious."

"But . . ." She exhaled sharply. "Dad, it doesn't make sense to leave someone because you're afraid they're going to leave you first."

I sighed. She was right. Paul was right. No, it didn't make sense. But neither did sticking around and waiting for the inevitable. Though I'd never breathe a word of it to her, there were times I wondered why *she* stuck around. She was an adult. She could afford to live on her own if she wanted to, and God knew she had better things to do with her life than make sure her dad didn't throw his back out unloading groceries. Especially when she'd been dealt some shitty cards of her own. How much less stress would she have if she only had her own PTSD to cope with instead of mine, not to mention the fact that it was *my* crash that had first traumatized her? Plus there were my pain issues and—

"Dad?" She touched my arm.

I jumped, wincing as that sudden movement jolted my spine. I hadn't even noticed she'd crossed the floor, but she was right in front of me now.

"Are you okay?" she asked.

I didn't know if she meant because of Clint or because I'd jarred my back just then, but the answer was still the same. And I lied anyway: "Yeah, I'm fine."

Kimber said nothing. I doubted there was much to say at that point that Paul hadn't already hammered into my head.

She was disappointed, of course. She and Clint had really gotten along, and she'd probably been hoping this would work out. Before she'd come home today—she'd flown into Portland last night and driven home this morning—I'd considered keeping it from her for a while. At least let her settle back in.

But no, her suitcase was still by the front door, and she was probably still jet-lagged out of her mind, and the first thing she'd said when she walked in had been, "Oh God. What happened?"

And now she knew.

I took a breath and was about to suggest we spend the afternoon at the pier, but right then, the doorbell rang. I jumped again—who the fuck was here?—and immediately regretted it. With as sore as my back was today, I really needed to fucking relax.

Yeah, right.

"I'll get it." Kimber left the kitchen.

I slumped against the counter, rubbing my eyes. The air pressure changed, and I was vaguely aware of Kimber saying something, but then another voice made my neck prickle.

"If he's here, I'd like to talk to him."

Oh shit.

Footsteps. Two sets of them.

"He's in here." She appeared first and gestured over her shoulder. "It's for you, Dad."

And right on cue, Clint walked in behind her.

My heart fell into my stomach. "Hey."

"Hey." He rocked back and forth from his heels to the balls of his feet. "Can we talk?"

Kimber glanced at each of us. Then, without a word, she took her purse and car keys off the hook, disappeared down the hall, and left the house. A moment later, her car turned on.

I cringed. She shouldn't have had to hightail it out of her own house because of her idiot father's post-breakup awkward confrontations. I owed her bigtime for putting up with this.

For the moment, though . . .

I met Clint's eyes. We were alone now. Nowhere to run. "Okay. Um. Let's talk."

"Yeah." He stared me down and folded his arms across his chest. "I need to know why."

Fuck. Of course he did. And after explaining it to Paul yesterday and Kimber today, I was drained. No fight left in me at all. Hell, I felt like I'd never had any fight in me to begin with.

But he deserved an explanation. If I couldn't pull myself together enough to be a halfway decent boyfriend, then I at least owed him that much.

I motioned for him to follow me into the living room. We sat on the couch, a cushion between us, and he watched me silently as I tried to summon up an explanation and the courage to say it.

Finally, I pulled in a deep breath and let the words come. "You know how when we went to California, you said it was odd that I'm not afraid to fly after my crash?"

Clint nodded.

"The thing is, I am. If I had to get into the cockpit of a Super Hornet again, I'd be scared shitless. I can one hundred percent promise you that I could never put a bird down on a carrier again because I know firsthand how badly it can go wrong."

"But you can get on a commercial jetliner."

"Yeah." I stared down at my hands as I folded and refolded them. "Because I'm not the one flying it."

"Oh."

"And with relationships, it's kind of the same." I turned to him. "I know how badly they can crash and burn. When I've been involved in them, people have been hurt—I've been hurt—so much, I can't—"

"So you avoid them now?"

I pursed my lips. "How many times does a guy have to get hurt before he can decide how to protect himself?"

Clint sighed. "We all want to protect ourselves. But there comes a point when you're protecting yourself to the point you stop living at all." His eyes lost focus for a moment, as if he were trying to figure out what to say next, so I let the silence linger. And sure enough, he wasn't done. "When we went to California, I was nervous as hell about getting on that plane. Probably even more than you realized." He paused, holding my gaze. "But do you know why I got on it anyway?"

I shook my head.

"Because no matter how scared I am of what can happen, the only thing that scares me more is what I might miss at the other end if I don't work up the courage to take the chance."

I focused on the coffee table. I wanted to know what was possible between us too, but couldn't shake the fear of what else could happen.

"I know it's a big risk," he said. "But I want to see where this could go. I've . . . Usually, if someone kicks me to the curb, I'm done. I'm gone. But with you . . ." He was quiet for a long moment. "You were the first person I ever told about what happened with the drone. You're the *only* person I've told. Shouldn't that tell you what you mean to me?"

"Yes." I made myself look him in the eye. "That's the part that scares me. I'm fucking terrified because whenever I get close to someone, it blows up in my face, and it's because of me."

"Which I completely get." He paused. Then he put a hand on my leg, and for several long seconds, we were both still, as if he were reeling as much as I was from that contact. "Remember, I torpedoed my own marriage with a bottle. Don't you think I know what it's like to be scared to death a relationship is going to fall apart because of me?" He shifted a little, like he couldn't get comfortable. I knew that feeling. "That incident that killed my career as an RAP? Even if that wasn't classified, I was still ashamed of it and hated the idea of telling anyone what happened. Either they'd think I was a horrible monster who'd murdered a bunch of people, or they'd roll their eyes at me for saying I'm traumatized when I was thousands of miles away from the combat zone." He rolled his shoulders like his skin was crawling from the thought of what had happened. "You weren't just the first person I could tell because of your clearance or because I knew you'd keep it to yourself. You were the only one I'd ever felt like I could tell and you'd *understand*."

I wasn't sure what to say.

"There are nights when I wake up in a cold sweat and have a fucking panic attack," he continued. "Normally, it's embarrassing to have someone else in my bed when that happens. With you . . ."

"What?"

"With you, it's a relief. Because I'm not alone."

I avoided his eyes. "It's . . . Yeah, it's nice to not be alone."

"And being with someone who *gets it* is even better." He paused. "Look at us, Travis. We're both fucked up. When I go to sleep at night, I never know if I'm going to make it through the night without coming apart. And that's probably never going to change." He touched my forearm. "But when I go to sleep next to you, at least I know I'm with someone who understands. I feel . . . I mean, maybe it sounds stupid, but when I'm with you, I feel safer going to bed with all my demons. Like I can come apart and freak out, and . . ." He chewed his lip. "It's like . . . well, you mentioned when we flew to California. Flying scares the fuck out of me, and I know damn well there's nothing you can do to keep the plane from crashing. There's a risk, and that's just how it is. But when you're there with me, I feel like I can face that risk." He sat back and blew out a breath. "I don't know. It sounded better in my head. I—"

"No, I hear what you're saying. And I understand. To tell you the truth, it's been a lot easier to try to sleep when you're here too." I pressed my elbows into my thighs and lifted my shoulders, hoping he couldn't tell I was stretching a new spasm out of my back. "We're good at keeping each other calm and coping through nightmares, but one thing that's never going to get any better is my back. The pain is always going to be there, and it—"

"I know it is. I've known that since the beginning."

"Yeah, well, the novelty wears off fast. Believe me. It might not happen in the first few months. Might not even happen the first year or two. But sooner or later, it wears thin when you're with someone who occasionally has to cut a trip to the commissary short because he's in too much pain to walk, let alone carry groceries."

He sighed. "It goes both ways, you know. What if we want to travel together? I mean, you've got enough to deal with when you fly. How long before you get tired of holding my hand and telling me we're not going to die when you're hurting bad enough to break a sweat?"

I wanted to tell him I couldn't imagine ever getting tired of holding his hand. "That's part of the problem, actually. That I'm always hurting bad enough to break a sweat." I swept my tongue across my lips. "You've got a lot to deal with. You don't need someone whose top priority, all the time, is minimizing pain."

"I could say the same to you." His tone was gentle, but invited no argument. "But it's not a matter of what I need. It's what I want. And what I want is to be with you."

"And what I want is for you to be happy, not having to . . . I mean, Jesus. You can't possible enjoy constantly having to accommodate me in the bedroom. That's going to get real boring, real fast. I promise."

He arched an eyebrow. "Have you ever heard me complain about the sex we have? I enjoy everything we do in the bedroom."

"For now. How long before that isn't enough?" I forced back the ache in my throat and tried to hold his gaze. "It's not that we can't fuck, you know? It's that every single time we're in bed, we're having a threesome with my pain. *Every* time. *I'm* sick of it, so why wouldn't you be?"

Clint sighed. "Do you think I'm an asshole?"

"What?" I sat up straighter, ignoring the jolt of pain. "Of course not."

He took my hand. "Then why are you so sure I'm only sticking around until the sex gets boring? I was married for sixteen years, for God's sake. I *know* people get into a rut, and the sex *does* get boring, and it takes work to keep it interesting. That's not going to be any different here."

"Aside from the part where our sex life is already—"

"Yes." There was a hint of exasperation in his voice, but also a sparkle in his eyes. The corner of his mouth rose a bit as he squeezed my hand. "What's it going to take for you to believe me?"

I tried to smile, but that crippling doubt and worry made it nearly impossible. "Time, I guess?"

"Then will you give me the time to convince you?"

"Would you think less of me if I said this scares the ever-loving fuck out of me?"

Clint's eyebrows climbed his forehead. "You think *you're* scared? Jesus, Travis. I lost my wife of *sixteen years* as a direct result of being fucked up in the head. I can't even see my kids without someone else there, all because my job traumatized me so bad, I fell apart." He brought my hand up and pressed his lips to the backs of my fingers. "So don't you think I understand what it's like to be afraid that something that happened to me in the past might destroy the best thing that's happening to me now?"

I . . . had no idea what to say. I stared at him, disbelieving. Of course I'd known about his trauma-fueled downward spiral and his divorce, but it had never occurred to me that he might be quietly afraid that I'd be the one to walk away. That he was afraid *he'd* send *me* packing.

"God, I'm sorry. I just . . . I freaked out." I released a long breath. "To tell you the truth, when I came over yesterday, it wasn't to call things off. It was . . . it was quite the opposite, actually."

"What do you mean?"

"I mean I wanted to tell you . . . I wanted to say that I . . ." I gently freed my hand, leaned forward, and rubbed my neck with both hands. "And then when you said you'd talked to your ex-wife, and that you might tell your kids, I panicked. It was like it was suddenly bigger than us, you know? There's family involved. There's kids involved. And my kid was already involved, and . . ." I looked in his eyes. "It just seemed too real all of a sudden, and all I could think of was how much I lost the last time I felt like this for someone."

Clint's Adam's apple jumped. "Felt like . . . how?"

"Do I have to spell it out?"

He held my gaze without flinching. "Couldn't hurt."

All the air rushed out of my lungs, and I pulled just enough back in to whisper, "I love you."

And there it was. Out in the open. No taking it back. Point of no return.

He laced our fingers together again. "I love you too. That's why I'm here. This isn't something I can give up on that easily."

"It isn't something I should have given up on." My shoulders sagged, provoking a fresh twinge in the middle of my back. "I'm sorry. I've been a fucking idiot."

"No, you haven't." He lowered our hands. "We've both been through hell. Different kinds, but it's still enough to make you wonder what the world's going to throw at you next." Laying his other hand over the top of ours, he added, "But we can do this."

"God, I hope so."

"We can," he said. "In fact, we've probably got a better shot because we understand each other. I never thought I'd find someone who I could sleep next to because they understood what might happen during the night. That gives us a pretty big edge, don't you think?"

"That's true."

"And there's also . . ." He chewed his lip.

My heart sped up. "What?"

He took a breath. "There's no shame in a little outside guidance."

"Outside—like a counselor?"

Clint nodded. "Something to keep us from going off the rails, you know?"

"That . . . that might not be a bad idea."

"I can go down to Fleet and Family after holiday stand-down. See what they have available."

I glanced down at our hands, then turned to him again. "You'd really do that?"

"Of course. Remember, I'm the one who would have sold his soul to be able to talk to a counselor over the last three years. I still can't talk to anyone about that, but there's nothing classified about us. So yeah. Absolutely."

I exhaled. "And, uh, for what it's worth—you can talk to me about what happened."

His fingers twitched ever so slightly, and he smiled. "Thank you." Sliding closer to me, he let go of my hand and reached for my face. "I love you, Travis. You and all your dings and dents."

This time I managed to laugh, and drew him in. "I love you too." Brushing my lips across his, I added, "Dings, dents, and all."

He held me tighter, and when we came up for air again, he touched his forehead to mine. "I don't know any more than you do if this will work. But I damn sure know I want to try."

The lump in my throat threatened to choke off my voice, but I whispered, "I do too."

He kissed me. Then again, and we pulled each other closer.

I let you go?

I can't believe you came back.

I really let you go?

Disbelieving he was here—and that he'd ever been gone—I met his gaze. Wow. He *was* here.

He touched my face. "You know, if we're going to start over and make this work, a good place to start might be in your bed."

I laughed, and God, it felt good to be laughing with him again. "I think you might be on to something."

"Only one way to find out." He rose and extended his hand. "Shall we?"

I took his hand. "Let's go."

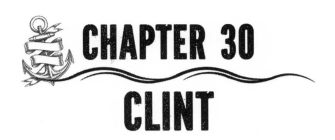

CHAPTER 30
CLINT

We couldn't get our clothes off fast enough. Why clothing had to have so many fasteners and bullshit, I had no idea. Pressed up against Travis's bedroom door, my shirt off and belt partially unbuckled, I was two seconds away from saying to hell with it and tearing everything apart at the seams.

Finally naked, we sank onto his bed on our sides. Travis hooked his leg around mine, pulling my hips closer to his, and he kissed me. Dear God, did he kiss me. Like he often did, he kept a hand on the back of my neck as if he thought I might suddenly pull away.

Not a chance, Travis.

As we made out and held each other and touched each other all over, I couldn't get over how relieved I was to be back in his arms.

"I know it hasn't really been that long," he murmured, "but it feels like you've been gone for months."

"Feels the same to me." I held him tighter, curving my hands over his ass and marveling that we'd made it back to this. "Just glad you're back."

"Me too." He leaned in to kiss my neck. "Don't know what I was thinking." He brushed his lips along the side of my throat. "I don't want to be without you."

I pulled him closer. "You don't have to. I don't want to be anywhere but here."

"Thank God for that," he growled, and sank his teeth into my shoulder.

I moaned, gripping his ass tighter and arching against him. "Fuck . . ."

He lifted his head and kissed me again. I couldn't get enough of him. Maybe because I'd had a solid twenty-four hours to believe this would never happen again, and now I needed as much as I could get to make sure it was real.

Panting hard, Travis broke away. Sort of.

"I want to suck you off so bad," he whispered. "But I just . . . can't stop . . . kissing you."

I cradled the back of his head. "Then don't."

He didn't. He draped his arm over me, pushed my lips apart with his tongue, and kissed me like he had in the car that very first night. Boldly, but not obnoxiously so, like he knew what he wanted and exactly how to get it.

Anything you want tonight. Anything.

He started to nudge me to roll over, but jumped, and the sudden intake of breath sounded more like a wince than a gasp.

"You okay?" I asked.

"Yeah. Just . . ." His cheeks colored.

"Maybe you'd be more comfortable on your back."

"Hmm. Maybe."

"Worth a try, right?" I rolled him over and climbed on top. Before I'd even situated myself, he had my cock in his hand, and . . . *Yes, please, just like that.*

"I think you're right," he breathed. "Being on my back works."

"Uh-huh."

"Frees up my hands." He slid his other hand between us, and I lifted my hips to give him some more room. He nudged me a little, encouraging me to move up toward the headboard.

When I did . . . wow. One hand stroked my cock, and the other teased my balls. Squeezing my eyes shut, I rocked my hips.

"Like that?" he asked.

"Oh yeah. A lot."

"Good."

Moaning, I buried my face against his neck and thrust into his hand. Each time I rocked back, his other hand gently stroked my balls. Holy hell. I didn't stand a chance—I was halfway to orgasm simply because I was against his naked body. With his hands on me like this—

"Oh, *God*!" I threw my head back and shuddered, and the friction of his strokes gave way to slick warmth, and he didn't stop pumping my dick until I begged him to.

"I love the way you sound when you come," he said.

"Feel free to hear it whenever you want." I lifted myself up and found his lips again. "And speaking of, I seem to recall you sound pretty hot when you come too."

"Yeah?" He grinned. "Just in case you're not remembering clearly, you're welcome to double-check."

"Hmm, such a giver." I kissed the tip of his nose. "And I have every intention of doing that."

He fidgeted under me. "Please do."

One more kiss, and then we paused to clean ourselves off. After he'd tossed the tissues away, I laid him on his back again.

"Now. Where was I? Oh, I remember . . ." I started down his neck. "I was going to turn you inside out."

He released a ragged breath. "You're already halfway there, believe me."

"Good to know." I planted a line of light kisses down his chest and his stomach. He squirmed, and his muscles quivered beneath my lips as I continued lower.

"Fuck," he breathed. "You're . . ." He trailed off into a shudder.

I looked up at him. "I haven't even touched your dick yet."

"I know. But you—"

I ran the tip of my tongue from his balls to the head of his cock.

"Fuck!" He stared down at me, lips apart and eyes wide. "Oh Jesus . . ."

"Already halfway there, huh?" I winked. "Better get you the rest of the way."

He swore softly and closed his eyes, and I took his cock between my lips . . . but I wasn't about to get him there quite yet. Outside of our office quickies, I was never in a hurry when I was with Travis. Orgasms would happen when they happened—in the meantime, I wanted him to feel so good he was losing his mind. Whenever I went down on him, I *lived* for the whimpers and profanity, the shivers and the hitches of his breath, and he didn't disappoint. As I teased his cock and balls all over with my lips, tongue, and fingers, he trembled like he was about to come unglued. He clawed at the sheets. His hips squirmed. Half the sounds he made were curses, and the rest were just helpless gasps.

I don't care if it was only a day and a night. I fucking missed you.

"Shit," he ground out. "You're gonna make me come if you keep going like that."

I moaned around his dick.

"Fuck yeah. Keep . . . keep going."

Game on.

I stroked the shaft and concentrated my mouth on the head, and his every sound told me I was very much on the right track. Trembling fingers ran through my hair, and the air was full of whispered profanity.

"D-don't stop." He shivered hard. "Gonna come. Oh God, gonna come. Oh my *God.*"

A shudder ran through his entire body. His cock thickened against my tongue, and then released, flooding my mouth with semen, and I kept right on stroking him and teasing him.

"S-stop," he stammered. "That's enough." He sank down into the mattress as I sat up. "Wow."

I wiped my lips with the back of my hand, then joined him on the pillows again, and he drew me into a kiss.

"Don't know if I've mentioned it before," he slurred, "but you have the most *amazing* mouth."

"Likewise." I dropped another light kiss on his lips. "And damn good hands too."

He chuckled. "You did seem to be enjoying them."

"No complaints at all." I grinned. "Five out of five stars. Would put my dick in your hands again."

We both burst out laughing, and God, it felt good to be laughing with him again. Somehow that made this seem even more real than being tangled up and turned on. Like we weren't just going through the motions, but had really come back to the way things should've been.

He pulled a sheet up over us, and we lay there for a long time, kissing lazily and enjoying the afterglow. I had absolutely missed his hands and his mouth, but mostly, I'd missed him. Now that I was beside him again, everything felt right in the world.

After a while, I said, "I missed you."

"It wasn't even all that long, but I missed you too. I'm sorry."

"We're here now. That's all I care about."

He lifted his head, and his eyes were full of uncertainty. Then he glanced over his shoulder. "I should probably give Kimber the all clear." He reached for his phone.

"I feel bad we scared her off."

"She'll be okay. She'd been trying to talk me into calling you, so I think she just wanted to give us some elbow room so we could talk." He quickly wrote out a text, sent it, and put the phone aside again. As he lay back down next to me, draping his arm over me, he smiled. "I'll talk to her about it later and make sure she's okay, but I'm pretty sure she'll be fine." With a quiet laugh, he added, "She'll be less inclined to kick my ass now that she knows we made up."

"Oh yeah?"

"Yeah. She and Paul both thought I was an idiot." He caressed my cheek. "They were right."

I took his hand and kissed it gently. "You weren't being an idiot."

"I'm sorry, though." He smoothed my hair. "I guess I freaked out."

"Don't worry about it."

"I'm going to worry about it. Trust me." Travis sighed. "It's par for the course with me, I'm afraid."

"I can live with that." I draped my arm over him. "We're both package deals, you know? And we both happen to come with a lot of preexisting shit. And none of it is going away. But if you can be patient with mine, I can be patient with yours, and I think we can make this work."

Travis searched my eyes. Then, slowly, he relaxed, and a smile came to life. "I can definitely be patient with yours."

"Me too."

His expression turned more serious. "I'm not going to pretend that it's going to be easy." He ran his fingers through my hair. "In fact, I'm pretty sure we're both going to have moments where we wonder what the hell we got ourselves into. But don't think for a second that's enough to make me want to leave." He cupped my face and added a barely whispered, "It won't be easy, but it'll be worth it."

"Absolutely." I kissed him gently, letting it linger for a moment, then touched my forehead to his. "I love you."

"I love you too."

The relief of being here with him, naked and satisfied and together, nearly drove me to tears. I didn't care if the future wouldn't be easy. I'd had a taste of being without him, and I didn't like it.

This was what I wanted, and somehow, it was what I had.

EPILOGUE
TRAVIS

The Following Spring

Sean and Paul's wedding couldn't have happened on a nicer day. Being the Pacific Northwest, there'd been plenty of rain lately—in fact, the sand was still damp from yesterday's downpour—but today was gorgeous. It was quite warm, actually, even with the cool breeze off the ocean, so thank God Paul and Sean had requested no uniforms. It didn't matter that Paul was one of my oldest and closest friends. I wasn't baking in a dress uniform just because he was tying the knot. I had my goddamned limits.

I had no idea what kinds of battles had ensued, but Sean and his mother had finally come to an agreement of some sort. The wedding was still happening out on the beach. With about sixty guests in folding chairs, it was probably small by her standards and huge by his, but he was smiling and relaxed, so he must've been okay with it.

Maybe it was the recent haircut, but I swore Paul was grayer than he'd been a few months ago. Which didn't surprise me, really—I'd planned a wedding before. No one made it through that particular gauntlet without a few gray hairs. Sean probably had a few too, but the black and cobalt-blue dye hid them.

While the grooms hurried around, making sure everything was running smoothly, Clint and I found seats in the rows of white folding chairs set up on the beach. The ceremony would be starting soon, so everyone was slowly making their way over here.

Beyond the white archway, Kimber and her boyfriend had strolled down toward the water. He was carrying her shoes in one hand, holding her hand with the other.

"They're pretty cute together, aren't they?" Clint asked.

I beamed. "Yeah, they are."

They'd been dating for a month or so, and I was still edgy about him, but that had less to do with him and more to do with the guys who'd rattled her in the past. He seemed nice. He was polite and respectful, and she was comfortable enough to be alone with him, which said a lot. As a nice switch from her previous boyfriend, he didn't get bitchy when she had to work long hours or focus on her classes, and he was almost as excited as she was about her graduation next week.

So, since he wasn't an asshole and she was happy with him, I was happy for them.

But if you break her heart, kid, I will break you in half.

Clint put his arm across the back of my chair and kissed my cheek. "You doing okay?"

"Yeah." My back was still as fucked up as ever, and the TENS hadn't even been helping all that much lately, but I'd loaded up on Motrin and taken it easy the last few days. So I felt as good as could be expected. I'd take it.

I turned to him. "What about you? How are you holding up?"

He nodded, smiling tightly. "I'm good."

I didn't press. I knew exactly where his mind was—on his kids.

It had been a long road, but his ex-wife had finally agreed to start taking steps toward an amended custody agreement that would allow unsupervised visits. There was even talk of letting them come stay with us for an entire summer. If not this year, definitely next year.

She'd dug her heels in at first, especially since she and I hadn't met face-to-face, but then Clint had persuaded her to fly up here for a weekend.

So, in a couple of weeks, she'd be here.

Ever since they'd made the travel arrangements, he'd been distracted almost constantly. If things went well while she was here, then she'd come back in July with the kids. He wanted so badly for the visit to go well. For her to like me. He was so stressed about it now, I suspected he'd sleep for a solid week after she left. He was guardedly optimistic, though, and seemed to be feeling better about it as time went on.

I was optimistic things would go well too. She and I had talked on Skype a few times, and we'd gotten along, but she wanted to come to Anchor Point by herself before she let the kids come up. That way she could see our house, see the town, and meet me in person.

Clint was frustrated, but he also understood. And his frustration had eased a bit because he'd gotten to spend some time with the kids this year. Since January, he'd been to see them four times, burning a hell of a lot of leave by driving to Vegas each time, not to mention worrying me when he had to go over the snowy passes. I would have been happy to go with him, but there was no way I could cope with the road trip. And really, the kids needed to see him a few times before they had to adapt to my existence.

He'd come out to them in February, and they'd all taken it well. Better than he or their mother had expected. It probably hadn't hurt that he'd done it while he was sitting with them and their counselor, who skillfully guided them all through questions and feelings.

When he'd told them he had a boyfriend, though, the walls had come up. With some time and patience, though, and with the counselor's help so the kids could vent and ask questions, everyone had gotten used to the idea. I hadn't talked to them yet—his ex-wife wanted to wait until she'd vetted me in person first—but they seemed excited to meet me.

I put my hand on his leg. "Stressing about everything?"

"Am I that transparent?"

"You think?" I kissed him softly. "It'll be fine. And I promise I'll behave."

Clint laughed, wrapping his arm around me. "I know. And things have been going really well, so I think it'll be great. I'm just nervous."

"I know you are."

And no amount of encouragement from me would change that, but I hoped he could at least relax enough to enjoy the wedding.

As the rest of the guests started filling up the chairs, and the grooms and chaplain headed toward the archway, I caught myself wondering if that would be Clint and me someday. More and more, it was seeming like a possibility. Hell, he'd moved in with me and Kimber a few weeks ago. He'd been there most nights anyway, so it made sense to only pay for one place instead of two.

It was so weird—a year ago, Kimber and I had both been single, all but swearing off dating after enough bad experiences. Now, my boyfriend was living with us, and hers was over at least once or twice a week to watch a movie or indulge in whatever Clint was cooking that evening.

The wedding started. In their tuxes—and probably sweating like crazy—Paul and Sean joined hands at the front. As the chaplain went into the ceremony, Clint took my hand. I glanced at him, and we both smiled.

We'd dipped our toes into the subject of marriage a time or two, but neither of us had pushed for anything more than vague suggestions and "maybe someday." I was fine with that. If the time came, I could absolutely picture myself standing up there with him like Paul and Sean. Or maybe we'd just take off and elope. Have a quick ceremony with the base chaplain. Something easy and stress-free with a couple of rings and some witnesses.

Or, as I watched the two of them smiling at each other with the ocean in the background, I wondered if we could pull off something like this.

Whatever we ultimately did, it didn't have to happen right away. As it was, Clint's mind was mostly on reconciling with his kids. Once this hurdle was behind him, and once we'd seen how we all got along as a family when his kids were in town, then maybe we could talk about rings and signatures.

It wouldn't be a fast process. Probably wouldn't be an easy one. But I had a funny feeling that we'd get there.

In the meantime, we were together.

And that was all I needed.

Explore more of the *Anchor Point* series:
www.riptidepublishing.com/titles/series/anchor-point

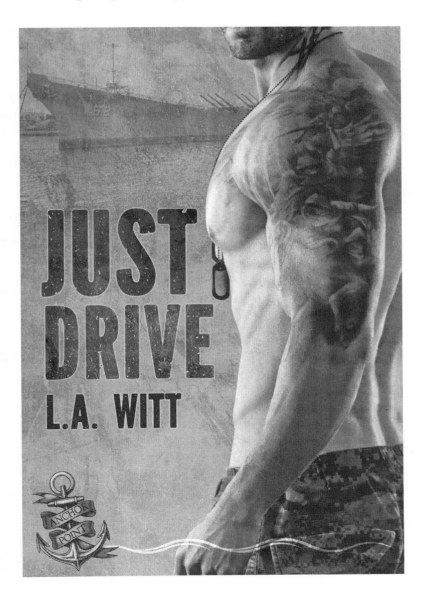

JUST
DRIVE

L.A. WITT

Dear Reader,

Thank you for reading L.A. Witt's *Afraid to Fly*!

We know your time is precious and you have many, many entertainment options, so it means a lot that you've chosen to spend your time reading. We really hope you enjoyed it.

We'd be honored if you'd consider posting a review—good or bad—on sites like **Amazon, Barnes & Noble, Kobo, Goodreads, Twitter, Facebook, Tumblr,** and your blog or website. We'd also be honored if you told your friends and family about this book. Word of mouth is a book's lifeblood!

For more information on upcoming releases, author interviews, blog tours, contests, giveaways, and more, please sign up for our weekly, spam-free newsletter and visit us around the web:

Newsletter: tinyurl.com/RiptideSignup
Twitter: twitter.com/RiptideBooks
Facebook: facebook.com/RiptidePublishing
Goodreads: tinyurl.com/RiptideOnGoodreads
Tumblr: riptidepublishing.tumblr.com

Thank you so much for Reading the Rainbow!

RiptidePublishing.com

ACKNOWLEDGMENTS

Thank you to J., who let me pick his brain for hours about flying drones.

ALSO BY
L.A. WITT

Anchor Point series
Just Drive

Kinky Sprinkles
Rain Shadow (a Bluewater Bay story)
Starstruck (a Bluewater Bay story)
Running With Scissors
Roped In, with Marie Sexton
Finding Master Right
Static
Covet Thy Neighbor
Where Nerves End
Hiatus
If the Seas Catch Fire

Writing as Lauren Gallagher
Stuck Landing (a Bluewater Bay story)
Razor Wire

Writing as Ann Gallagher
Lead Me Not
All the Wrong Places (a Bluewater Bay story)

Writing as Lori A. Witt
The Tide of War

See L.A. Witt's full booklist at: gallagherwitt.com

ABOUT THE AUTHOR

L.A. Witt is an abnormal M/M romance writer who has finally been released from the purgatorial corn maze of Omaha, Nebraska, and now spends her time on the southwestern coast of Spain. In between wondering how she didn't lose her mind in Omaha, she explores the country with her husband, several clairvoyant hamsters, and an ever-growing herd of rabid plot bunnies. She also has substantially more time on her hands these days, as she has recruited a small army of mercenaries to search South America for her nemesis, romance author Lauren Gallagher, but don't tell Lauren. And definitely don't tell Lori A. Witt or Ann Gallagher. Neither of those twits can keep their mouths shut...

Website: www.gallagherwitt.com
E-mail: gallagherwitt@gmail.com
Twitter: @GallagherWitt

Enjoy more stories like
Afraid to Fly
at RiptidePublishing.com!

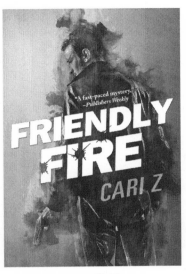

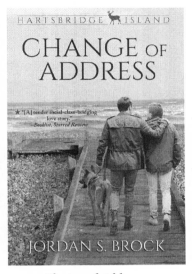

Friendly Fire
ISBN: 978-1-62649-482-4

Change of Address
ISBN: 978-1-62649-464-0

Earn Bonus Bucks!
Earn 1 Bonus Buck for each dollar you spend. Find out how at
RiptidePublishing.com/news/bonus-bucks.

Win Free Ebooks for a Year!
Pre-order coming soon titles directly through our site and you'll
receive one entry into a drawing for a chance to win free books for
a year! Get the details at RiptidePublishing.com/contests.

55573004R00178